Go
Luck
Yourself

Go
Luck
Yourself

Sara Raasch

BRAMBLE

tor publishing group
new york

GO LUCK YOURSELF

A Bramble Book
Published by Tom Doherty Associates / Tor Publishing Group
120 Broadway
New York, NY 10271

www.torpublishinggroup.com

Bramble™ is a trademark of Macmillan Publishing Group, LLC.

The Library of Congress Cataloging-in-Publication Data is available upon request.

ISBN 978-1-250-33321-6 (trade paperback)
ISBN 978-1-250-33322-3 (ebook)

Our books may be purchased in bulk for promotional, educational, or
business use. Please contact your local bookseller or the Macmillan Corporate and
Premium Sales Department at 1-800-221-7945, extension 5442, or by email at
MacmillanSpecialMarkets@macmillan.com.

First Edition: 2025

Printed in the United States of America

0 9 8 7 6 5 4 3 2 1

To you. Again.

Because we could all use a bit of luck.

Chapter One

Two Months after Christmas

I really was making a concerted effort not to be a prick today.

I took the time to work out because that always puts me in a better mood, but honestly, that was my first mistake, letting myself be in public. Home, classes, studying, that's it—I am not fit for community involvement yet.

So tripping off the treadmill and falling on my ass in the crowded gym when a text came through our group chat from Iris?

My fault. Entirely. I accept that. But I put on my big boy pants and attempted to reclaim said concerted effort by grabbing a ridiculously overindulgent mocha on my way to the library.

Which triggered mistake number two: I didn't see one of the café doors was locked and rammed right into it, mocha acting like a scalding, syrupy airbag.

So now, I don't have time to run back to my flat to change—I booked that study room and I'm going to *get it today*, goddamn it—which means the best I can do is towel off the caramel mocha mess in the washroom, zip my sweater over my ruined shirt, and cut over to the library, smelling faintly of espresso and cocoa.

Do not be a prick.

Do not be a prick.

It's been almost two months, and it isn't like I even broke up with her—so why does it *feel* like a breakup?

My phone buzzes in my pocket. I push into the Cambridge University Library, shower-damp hair falling in my face as I look at the screen like it's a bomb that might go off.

PEEP, MINI CANDY CANE, AND THE BEST CLAUS

IRIS
my sister delayed her wedding.
AGAIN.

COAL
what was it this time, she couldn't
book that metallica cover band she
wanted

IRIS
some bullshit about the center-
pieces

oh yeah coal you know my sister,
big into 80s heavy metal to go with
her Springtime Renewal theme

but my point is you can cancel
your travel plans, no wedding next
weekend

I exhale, loudly, and stop walking up the south wing staircase to collapse against the wall.

Some of my prick-ness does evaporate now.

I won't have to see Iris next weekend. I won't have to plaster on a smile like I didn't profess my love to her eight weeks ago, right after her engagement to my brother got called off, only to realize halfway through my drunken spewing of feelings that I was not, actually, in love with her. And she was not, in any way, in love with me.

Which should've deflated the awkwardness right out of the whole situation, but the singular moment my brain continues reliving, the thing that keeps me pinned to the wall in the staircase as another student sidles past me and down to the exit, is the bone-aching embarrassment of realizing that she *knew* I'd been at least *trying* to be in love with her *our whole friendship,* and she'd been dreading this proclamation all that while.

It made sense for us to be together. It'd made sense since we were twelve years old, and something about her walking into our Christmas Eve Ball like the personification of springtime, Persephone come to life in pastel purple and airy fuchsia, made all those stories I was obsessed with say *She's a Princess of Easter, you're a Prince of Christmas, that's happy ever after.*

But I'd realized at a younger age that being Santa's son isn't the storybook dream it should be. Not even my own father thought I should be the one to marry Iris when he wanted to forge an alliance with Easter; he'd foisted the situation on Coal. So why did I keep ahold of the *prince and princess, happy ever after* dream, when nothing else in my life was a fantasy?

Because marrying her would've made you useful, and you have nothing else to offer.

My eyes at least don't sting when I think that now. Two months of reeling in the vortex of realizing that I have nothing to contribute to Christmas has helped me progress past grieving to numbness.

Coal and Iris banter in our group chat some more, errant wedding stuff, and my thumb hovers over the *Settings* button. I could mute the chat. Why they continue to use it, to loop me in on their conversations, I don't know. Well, I know why Coal does—he's determined to keep our friend group from falling apart. He and Iris were never even remotely interested in getting married, so their relationship well survived any fallout of their almost-marriage. But is Iris going along with including me in the group chat because it's what Coal wants? Or does *she* want me in her life, even after I proved what an oblivious ass I am?

On paper, she and I worked. Oh my god, the *hours* of my life I wasted writing about that happy ending, bullshit poems and stories and letters, some love-struck sap. And I didn't realize until the very moment of telling Iris *I love you* that I only loved the idea of a happy ending, not her.

But the look on her face—she knew. And she gently said, "Kris . . ." in that delicate, trying-to-talk-down-a-crazy-person tone, and *that* was what clinched it for me.

Had I been that disgusting the whole time? Had I been using her for my own ends all along? We were *friends* once, right?

We have a whole separate text thread for the two of us, where she sends me the absurd, overly pompous words her professors use that she doesn't even believe are real; and I send her photos of objects that are particularly odd looking or interesting people around campus that she can use as studies for sketching or sculpting or whatever her art outlet of the day is.

That was real, wasn't it? That friendship?

I swipe over to that private thread. The last text was weeks ago, the morning classes started for this term:

IRIS

IRIS
this poli-sci professor just used the
word myrmecophilous
did i spell that right
even spell check is like wtf

She initiated it. She reached out. I was the one who chose not to respond.

I can't deal with this right now.

Ever the psychic, my brother sends me a private text.

COAL

COAL
you not responding to the group
chat is like if you were lurking
in the same room and creepily
watching us have fun without you

Then switch to a private
thread.

COAL
coward

Fuck off

COAL
asshole

Pissant

There's a long enough pause that I push off the wall and continue up to the third floor of the library. My shirt is stuck to my stomach now, the drying mocha making the fabric stiff and tacky. And I now connect that this means I haven't had coffee all morning, and it's, what, almost ten? I booked the study room for two hours, no time to make another coffee run before my reservation, so this session will have to be done sans caffeine and *this is still no reason to get fucking pissy*.

Deep breaths. I'm making an effort today. Shirking this fog.

My phone buzzes.

COAL
oh that's a new one. i had to
google it.

You're going to graduate from
Yale in three months and you
don't know what 'pissant'
means?

COAL
dude i love you but you text like a
boomer

That is quite possibly the
cruelest thing you've ever
said to me.

COAL
who else texts in full proper
punctuation

> Hex texts like an evolved
> human being too.

COAL
oh he does!

wait

oh ew is hex you

did i fall for someone who is
basically my brother but goth

> Better than someone who is
> Dad but goth.

In response, Coal sends about fifteen middle finger emojis.

One side of my mouth cocks. He'd be way too pleased with himself if he knew the only time I've smiled the past few weeks was at his bullshit.

> Got a paper on the French
> Revolution to finish, but I have
> time if there's anything you
> need me to do. I can work
> on more correspondence, or
> speeches? I sent a few things
> to Wren last week but haven't
> heard if you need more.

COAL
i'm good on all written requests.
i swear. besides, what have we
agreed on?

You agreed. I ignored you.

COAL
we agreed that i need to learn to
handle this stuff on my own. if
there's anything super important,
i'll loop you in. but for now, just
worry about making louis xvi your
bitch

Coal doesn't need to learn to stand on his own as Christmas's leader, though. He's already crushing it.

Which means he doesn't need me as much. He never really did.

I rub my chest as I mute my phone and push into the third floor.

Desks and tables sit in perfectly organized rows between shelves of reference books, but I weave through them all to reach the handful of private rooms. My third year at Cambridge, and just last term I found the *perfect* work setup: a study room that gets ideal air circulation because the vent actually opens, is far enough from the main stairwell so noise is minimal, and has whiteboard markers that always work. I'm not too proud to admit that I can be bought with office supplies.

But as I come up to the study room, I stop. Dead in my tracks.

The door is shut. The chalkboard on the front has a word scrawled across it in handwriting I know too well:

Occupied

That overly stylized cursive is mocking me. Flat out pretentious for pretentious's sake at this point. And the window to the right has the blinds drawn, but the light is clearly on inside.

I pull out my phone again—ignoring another stream of texts between Iris and Coal—and check the time. Five after my scheduled window started.

No fucking way.

I *booked* it this time. I fucking *booked it this time.*

It's a big university. I get that I'm not the only one here. Like, logically, I know that other people have discovered that this study room is excellent, and doesn't have that weird smell that the others do, but as I stand in the middle of the aisle between students typing away on papers like I should be doing, my vision goes red.

This is the *fifth time* in the past two weeks that I've come to use the room and found this same cursive OCCUPIED drawn across the chalkboard. The first two times, bad luck on my part, whatever; I'd try again later. C'est la fucking vie. But by the third time, I realized that something about this jackass's study schedule lines up exactly with mine, only they always get here before I'm able to no matter how early I shift things around, so today, I booked it in advance and *that study room is mine.*

There's something at Cambridge called the Week Five Blues: midway through a term, when the end isn't in sight yet, the drag of slogging through the first half catches up to students and everyone goes a little droopy. Only I'm not having Week Five Blues right now; I'm having Week Five *Blind Fury.*

I stomp the remaining space to the study room and bang my fist on the door. Which earns me a startled shush from a nearby guy who looks like he's on the my-blood-is-now-energy-drinks end of the Week Five Blues spectrum.

There's no response from the room thief.

I try the handle. Locked. Fucker.

Knock again. Louder. I get another shush and I concave my body around the door like that will muffle what is now full-on pounding.

Finally, there's the sound of a chair creaking inside.

Then a voice. Masculine, annoyed. "Yeah?"

"This room is mine," I say into the door's seam.

A pause.

The lock clicks. The door cracks open a sliver, and a guy peers out at me.

Pale skin. Red hair poking out from under a gray beanie. High, sharp cheekbones. Freckles scattered across his face, full lips twisted in derision through his short red facial hair. Chunky headphones hang around his neck with the faintest pulse of music vibrating out of them.

I have several immediate thoughts:

I should send Iris a picture of this guy. He'd make a great character study.

And: *fuck, he's hot.*

The latter one might as well be a mental ball gag for the way my throat closes over.

Aaaaaaand now there are two thoughts strangling me.

I legitimately cannot remember the last time I found anyone attractive outside of Iris. The people I dated as half-assed attempts to distract myself from her were more just . . . okay? And even the sight of Iris never choked me up like this.

I blink dumbly. I've been quiet for an unacceptably long time.

"The fuck you want?" the guy snaps in an Irish accent so thick my already teetering brain blacks out, resets, and barely registers what he said.

Stop thinking about ball gags.

I whip out my phone—Iris and Coal are still talking, now about how her sister almost had tiers of donuts instead of a wedding cake—and pull up the app to show him my reservation. "This study room is mine."

The guy squints at the screen. "I got no idea what you're showing me. Who the fuck is Lily and why does she hate—are those the words *cream filled*?"

I yank my phone back. The texts popped down over the app.

My cheeks burn. "Not that—"

"Cream filled. Ya pervert." Then he cocks his head and frowns. "Do I know you?"

I glower at him. "I don't make a habit out of associating with *thieves.*"

His eyes roll. "Christ—"

"*I booked this study room.*" I shove my phone into my pocket. "I got on the app. I booked this room. It's mine. You need to leave."

He sizes me up with renewed interest and leans one shoulder against the doorframe. "Ah. So you're the one."

"The one?"

"The bastard who's been stealing it from me."

I scoff. "Stealing it from *you*? You're the one illegally here now."

"Illegally? Get off it."

Someone shushes us.

I rip a hand through my hair as I drop my voice. "At the very least"—all right, let's not get carried away—"*negligently* here. I booked this room."

"I do na care if the King himself gifted this room to you. Is there some repercussion for not obeying that almighty app of yours?"

. . . is there?

My pause is answer, and he grins, victorious.

"I'll be getting back to my work, then."

He starts to shut the door.

I wedge my foot in it.

The look he gives is half disbelief, half disgust. "Oh, piss off—you canna be this high on the room?"

"*You're* the one high on it. Give it up. There are others you can use without breaching the agreed-upon social constructs of the Spacefinder app." Do I sound as batshit as I think I do?

The guy's brows twist in stifled repulsion.

Yeah. I do.

He leans towards me through the door. He's taller than I am, which isn't exactly a rarity, but he's using that height now to his advantage, so I hate him even more on principle.

A billow of spice hits me, too-rich cologne undercut with a bitter chemical scent that makes my nose itch. And I feel like a moron for *smelling* him, because he's definitely not *smelling* me, but I can't move back without relinquishing my hold on the door. He realizes that and presses closer, closer, and I bend back farther, farther, as mocking scorn rises on his face—

He stops. Sniffs.

"What kind of cologne is that, boyo?"

Boyo? "Eau de mind your own business."

He snorts. "Rather more of an eau de I dropped my coffee all over myself?"

I was really trying to break out of my gloom today.

And you know what? I am.

I'm going from wallowing in self-hatred to being actively irate.

Which is an ... unusual reaction for me. I can't remember the last time I got *angry*. Even my aforementioned prickish state manifests in me swallowing whatever irritable comments I want to make so I just end up depressed and sulky.

This is the first time I'm letting the anger *out*.

And I gotta admit. It feels good.

"Listen up, pal—I am two days from this paper on French political thought determining whether I pass this course on European politics," and that won't save me from having to do a fourth year at what is typically a three-year school, but fuck that. "Which means right now, my body is being held together by obscure facts about the French Revolution. I don't care how hot you are, if you don't get out of that room in the next ten seconds, I will grab you by that tank top you think makes you look effortlessly relaxed but really makes you look like you're trying too hard and go full Robespierre on your ass."

The guy peels back from me with a tawdry grin.

Then I hear what I said.

Ohhhhhh for fuck's sake.

"Hot, eh?" His eyes trail over me so very, very slowly, but his conceited smirk is an equalizer to any reaction that tries to prickle along my skin.

"Not ..." I stutter. "That isn't the point of what I said."

"Nah. Rather the bit where you wanted to grab me by my tank top and do what with me?"

Jesus fuck. "*Get out of my study room.*"

His jaw cocks to the side and he arches one thick brow. "Or what? You'll enact your fancy wee *death threat*?"

This situation.

Might be getting away from me.

I'm in too deep now. So I hold, seething, and the guy chuckles dryly.

"Christ, but this university will kill us all." He scratches his forehead and fixes me with a resolved glower. "I got my own overhanging schedule of misery to dance with, so bring it on, Coffee Shop."

He punts my foot out of the way and slams the door in my face.

I grab the knob, but he instantly locks it, and I rattle the handle futilely. I swear I hear him laugh inside.

Part of me wants to hammer on the door again, cause all kinds of pandemonium until he gives it up. But I don't want to risk being thrown out of the library or losing access to this study room entirely, so I force myself to breathe slowly through my nose.

What would I do if I wasn't mentally and emotionally drained from school and home shit, and overall stretched in like seventeen directions? What would I do. What would I . . .

No. Screw that.

I don't *want* to take the High Road.

I don't *want* to do the responsible thing because I *did* the responsible thing and this asshole is *in my study room.*

So what would my brother do? Or what would he have done before he reformed, back when he was a whirlwind of rashness and chaos?

I look down at my hand and flex my palm.

Christmas's magic lets me spread my Holiday's cheer far and wide. It also lets me create a lot of things spontaneously.

Like, for instance, for a totally innocent example, tinsel.

Enough to fill a whole study room?

This is a horrific use of magic. It breaks pretty much all the *don't use excessive displays of magic around normal people* rules, but Dad isn't really in charge of Christmas anymore, is he? Coal is. And Coal would absolutely be behind this use of Christmas's magic.

So fuck it.

There's a moment. Where I'm staring at the door. And I think to myself, *This is my rock bottom.*

But I might as well find out what the full depth of my rock bottom looks like. Maybe there's something interesting down here, like my dignity.

I lay my hand flat on the door and grab on to every connection I have to Christmas's magic and *pummel* that study room with tinsel. In Cambridge blue, school spirit and all.

A sharp cry pops from within the room.

"JESUS FUCKING SHITE—"

Time stretches in a weird pause as I nonchalantly walk a few feet back towards the desks. I get to a bookshelf and duck against it as the knob is twisting, and everyone seated is looking at the room. Someone is already shushing.

The door heaves inward, shoving against the tinsel, until he manages to get it open enough that he can stumble out—along with a waterfall, a deluge, a *whole ass bunch* of bright blue tinsel.

The study hub goes utterly still.

The guy stands there, arms out helplessly, looking like the Swamp Thing from the Cambridge lagoon. I can't even see his face, he's so covered.

I'm proud to say that I'm not the first one to laugh.

That honor goes to energy-drink-in-my-blood guy, who cackles and yanks out his phone and records, and soon the whole study hub is busting up and filming this guy getting pranked.

I pull out my phone and hit record as he removes a handful of tinsel from his face. His eyes snap around at the laughing students and he looks more irritated than embarrassed as he bobs his head in a *yeah, have a laugh at my expense* way.

His gaze locks on my phone.

I lower it and give him a cheesy grin.

He'll probably blame it on some kind of confetti bomb. I don't care. Let him know it was me though. I want this credit.

Don't mess with my study room, asshole.

His face dissolves into a withering glare and he flips me off.

If I'd known it was that easy to vanquish this squatter from my study room, I'd have tinseled him weeks ago.

The guy digs his stuff out of the piles of glittery mess and stomps off, leaving a trail of shimmering blue in his wake. I watch him go from where I'm leaning on a bookshelf, and as he gets to the stairs, he glances back, meets my eyes again, and grimaces.

I waggle my fingers at him, my princely upbringing channeled into that fuck-you cordiality.

He disappears down the stairs.

I do feel bad for whatever janitorial staff will have to deal with this mess, so after I magic away the tinsel from the room and finish my paper—in peace and quiet, the *luxury*—I follow that guy's path through the library and make the rest of the tinsel vanish when no one's looking. The trail takes me down into the main stacks, weaving among shelves dedicated to—art history? That makes sense. The beanie. The designer tank. That rancid expensive cologne. He'd definitely be in something as pompous as art history.

As I get rid of the final evidence of my first nefarious magic act, I can see why Coal got so into it; I feel a hell of a lot better than I did earlier.

At least until I do a calculation of how much magic I used to create all that tinsel and make it vanish.

Ordinarily, I wouldn't worry about magic use. We've always had enough, *more* than enough, and that was kind of our problem.

But now . . .

I honestly don't know how much magic we can spare for stupid shit.

My chest gets too hot, ribs tensing in a crush of shame.

See, this is why I *think things through.*

COAL

If one were to, say, fill a room with tinsel as retaliation in a totally justified study room war;

how much magic would that use and would that magic be within acceptable limits?

COAL
wait did you do something
interesting
study room war?
never mind, you did something
boring and cambridgey didn't you

I pull up the video and almost, *almost* send it to him.
The freeze frame is that guy peeking up through the blue tinsel. Gray eyes are pinched with annoyance. Mouth is agape in a breathy gasp.
A shiver walks down my spine and I close out the video.

Is everything all right? I didn't
drain the Merry Measure?

COAL
over creating tinsel? nah dude,
we're fine. go crazy with it
well not crazy crazy
but yeah use it to win a study room
war
like a fucking nerd
god you're dull

I don't know, you may have
some competition for future
tabloid grabbing.

COAL
oh no, my title shant be stolen
from me, take my eyes before you
take my disastrous reputation
you're coming home next weekend?

There's enough of a tone shift between Coal's last two texts that I can feel his anxiety twisted up in it.

He's back in Christmas, finishing out his final semester at Yale online; I came back to Cambridge after he damn near booted me out while claiming that *someone* needed to have a *normal collegiate experience* and it sure as hell wasn't going to be him, so I should go have fun.

Nothing says *fun* like intensive courses in a program I loathe with my whole being.

Coal had been so insistent, so hopeful about the idea of me *having fun* in a way that told me he felt guilty for letting me take care of him most of our lives, for being the rock while he was the wind. I'm not sure how much I like all the self-actualizing he did over Christmas; I'm happy he's gaining a better awareness of himself, but it also means he's gaining a better awareness of *me,* and I'll be damned if I can handle getting all introspective after . . .

After Coal discovered our dad had successfully overtaken half a dozen Holidays and was tapping their joy directly into ours.

After he confronted Dad with the backing of those Holidays and basically forced him out as reigning Santa in all but his control of our magic.

After Dad went from manipulative and angry to sitting quietly in meetings as Coal sets up a fair trade of joy with other winter Holidays, like he surrendered to Coal. But I don't trust it, and I shouldn't have come back to school. Coal's dealing with all this shit, and I left him to fuck around with term papers?

Of course I'm coming back.
Give me ten minutes and I
can be there today.

COAL
no, no, next weekend's fine
hex is coming tomorrow anyway
so i'll have a babysitter
i'm just all alone right now so who
knows what crazy shit i'll do left to
my own devices

Wren's there. And you have a
whole palace full of staff.

COAL
you know what i mean

You're sniffing Hex's pillow
right now, aren't you?

COAL
need i remind you that I am your
king
you dishonor me, i shall have you
excommunicated

That's the Pope, dumbass.
And dad's still the King of
Christmas, technically.

COAL
what the fuck do i mean then
exiled, that's what i mean
i'll have you exiled

I swipe to a new text thread as I make my way back out of the library.

HEX
Coal said you're going to visit
him tomorrow? How's he been
doing, really?

Hex is in a similar situation to mine—juggling school and his own Holiday duties, but at least his parents are actually doing their jobs and running Halloween. Like Iris, he's been into the online school thing for a while, so he's able to pop over to be with Coal more freely.

Which is . . . weird. Good. But weird. The prevailing theme that came out of Christmas: *good but weird.*

All these changes—Coal being in charge now, him having a stable relationship—are good.

It's only the shit I caused that's decidedly *not* good.

Nope. Not going to wallow.

HEX
I'm finishing up a few things to leave now, actually.

Now? Why? What happened?

HEX
Nothing happened. My schedule opened up. Really, he's been doing quite well. Understandably stressed. A few of the negotiation topics with the other winter Holidays have hit sticking points, and you know how he hates anything overtly political.

But I'm proud of him. He's happy.

Try not to worry.

I know, I know. It's my job to worry about him.

HEX
Mine as well.
Quite the career path we have, hm?

I stare at Hex's texts and feel the same lack of weight on my shoulders that I've noticed since Christmas. It's simultaneously freeing and staggering.

Thank you.

HEX
It's my pleasure, Kris. Truly.

The sun outside the library is bright and bursting through the almost constant British cloud cover, and I stand in its rays for a second, and breathe.

I'm still a Prince of Christmas, still part of Coal's restructuring to create a collective that pools joy between the winter Holidays. I've written a lot of official responses to other Holiday leaders and drafted speeches for Coal to use during meetings. I've been a sounding board for his ideas about how to interact with other leaders, what topics to bring up about resource divisions, how he's arranging to not only share magic among us all but also to pay back what Christmas stole over time—which makes pointless magic use like creating *tinsel* even dumber.

But is any of what I've been doing *necessary*?

I close Coal's text box. Close the one with Hex. The group chat remains, Iris and Coal's bantering filling my screen; and the private thread with Iris.

I almost text her about the cheekbones on that guy.

I almost join the group chat and tell them how Iris's comment on cream filling came at the worst possible time, join in their lightheartedness like nothing's wrong, like nothing changed.

But there *is* stuff wrong.

Things *did* change.

And I've never been good with change.

On autopilot, I swipe to a different text thread, one that's been silent since right after Christmas.

MOM

MOM

How could you not tell me what was going on? That Nicholas was getting MARRIED?? The mother of the groom should not have to stoop to asking about the wedding at all!

I've stopped hoping you could get any consideration for me from your brother, but I thought you at least were well past this childish behavior. Why don't you think I deserve to know what is happening with my own children?

Answer me!!

You're behaving like such a brat and now you've made me lose my temper. Stop being dramatic about this!!

I finally responded. Just once:

It wasn't a real engagement, that's why we didn't tell you. It was a weird political ploy and it's over now.

I almost said, *If it was real, you would've known.* But the thought of any *real* wedding, for me or Coal, being marred by our mother showing up had me ignoring the rest of her barrage of texts.

I scan them now, and even though they're the shit I expect from her—*how could you, get your brother to talk to me, why can't you do even simple things*—my hand shakes and I pocket my phone before I drop it.

A clamp squeezes around my chest.

I duck into the shadows between the wall of the library and an arching ornamental tree still winter-frozen. I dig my fingers into the mortar between the bricks and demand that I take a full, deep breath, in through my nose, in through my nose, in through my— *exhale* too, goddamn it—

A long, blown-out exhale finally comes, and I rock forward, all my weight on the wall, the coldness of the brick bleeding into my forehead. The rush and rumble of air entering and leaving my body drowns out my thoughts, and I focus on that noise. Nothing else.

And, in place of all other thoughts, I hear that guy say, in his thick accent, *cream filled.*

An unexpected laugh cuts through my chest, alleviates some of the lingering, relentless tension.

I breathe again, and this time, it goes in and out smoothly.

Three days later, my paper is submitted, it's almost the weekend, and I wake up feeling more like myself.

Until I turn on my phone and see two dozen missed texts and calls from Coal.

Shock freezes my veins, crackling and crawling up my body.

COAL

COAL
okay remember when i said i'd
only drag you home early for an
emergency

well

EMERGENCY

GET HOME NOW

ASAP

SOS

dad's ceding full control of
christmas to me

like the magic, the title, all of it

Chapter Two

I text Coal I'm coming and, ten minutes later, I bolt into the foyer of Claus Palace and nearly tackle Wren to the floor.

No other staff are around. It's our off-season, so most everyone is taking a much needed break, but the woodsy entrance to the palace is done out in our perpetual theme: draping greenery, lit candles that scent the air with cinnamon and cloves, jolly red ribbons hanging from the banisters of the two massive mahogany staircases that twist up either side of the room.

Wren rocks backwards, clutching her tablet to her chest. She's impeccably dressed in a sharp black pantsuit, her gray hair pulled into her usual severe bun. The only crack in her armor is the slight flush to her face from being startled. "Kristopher!"

"I'm sorry—I just—Coal—"

Wren nods, an irritatingly professional storm wall against my thrashing anxiety hurricane. "I was waiting for you. Follow me."

She heads off, and I fall in step alongside her.

"Where are they?" I ask, not needing to specify.

"The Merry Measure."

"And Dad's really . . ."

She shrugs one shoulder and her jaw twitches, but she's frustratingly locked down. "So it would seem."

Our father, the one who was so stubborn and prideful that he kept all kinds of disastrous secrets from us in an attempt to *secure our Holiday for you boys*—his words—is now . . . giving up entirely?

I want to ask if she talked him into it. She's been Dad's assistant longer than I've been alive, but she's always been exactly this, steady and competent and pulling the strings behind the scenes. She's never had much luck convincing Dad to do anything he didn't want to do, especially during the whole winter Holidays debacle. So it's unlikely she's the one who got him to give up his control of Christmas.

"He's really doing this?" I ask again, a quaking whisper.

Wren puts a hand on my forearm as we walk. She smiles at me, a break of reassurance through her formal mask.

"They're waiting." She squeezes my arm. "Come on."

We get to the massive gold and marble room that houses Christmas's joy meter. The Merry Measure is a monstrous steampunk machine of copper piping and brass fixtures that harvests the joy generated due to Christmas and transforms that joy into magic. And, until recently, more than half the joy stored here came from entirely separate Holidays, thanks to my dad.

Tubes lead out of the room, funneling to various departments— not so much used right now, but during the later parts of the year, this place is buzzing.

Dad stands in front of the Merry Measure, talking with Marta, the woman who oversees it. My gaze cuts around—and I clock Coal leaning against the inside of the door.

There's no greater representation of how much has changed these past few weeks than my brother. His whole bearing is different. More like . . . well, like our father, but not in a way that's bad, just commanding. His auburn curls are always neatly set now, and he relents to Wren's team of stylists so he's rarely ever a disheveled mess. Like now, at about eight thirty in the morning, he's in a suit, muted red with accents of green.

And I'm in sweats that smell faintly of caramel mocha because I accidentally put my coffee-doused shirt in a clean laundry pile.

Coal pushes away from the wall when he sees me. My insides twist, eyes darting back to Dad, then to Coal.

"Did he already . . . do it?" I try not to look uncomfortable. This is a good thing. Right?

Another good thing. Another good change.

One side of Coal's lips cocks up. "No—he wanted to do it last night, but I made him wait for you to get here. You text me all the time about aimless shit like study room wars, but when something *actually* happens, where are you to be found?"

Yeah, I don't offer daily to come home at all. "Us mere mortals call it sleeping."

But my chest warms with relief so potent I have trouble catching my breath. He waited for me to do this.

My hands flex. "Shouldn't this be a big event?" I eye Wren, still standing next to us.

She sighs, and I get the distinct impression that yes, if she had any say in it, this *would* be a big event. "Your father insisted it be done as quickly as possible."

I glance at the Merry Measure again, where Dad and Marta wait silently, Dad looking at the piping above.

"Why?" I ask.

Coal throws an arm around my shoulders. "I'm not questioning it."

But I don't move when he tries to pull me deeper into the room. "Wait, isn't Hex—"

"Hello, Kris."

I am not proud of the high-pitched shriek I make as the Halloween Prince manifests *right in front of me,* a swirl of shadowy Halloween magic dissipating around him.

He's as put together as Coal in his usual black on black, and maybe that's what's rubbing off on my brother, too—his very postured, very collected boyfriend.

Hex's big eyes do a good impression of innocence despite their demonic glimmer of amusement.

"You asshole." I smack his shoulder.

Coal pops me on the back of the head. "Don't hit my boyfriend."

"He gets off on torturing me! You're not going to defend your one and only brother?"

"No."

Hex steps over to take Coal's hand. But he gives me one more appraising look, and as my heart finally settles from that jump-scare, I roll my eyes at him to hide my smile.

Okay, it *was* a good distraction. Gave me a chance to reset.

My graceful shriek drew the attention of Dad and Marta. Dad faces us, and I stiffen, taking stock of his body language in one quick swoop. But he doesn't look upset—his shoulders are relaxed, hands in his pockets, and he smiles, a soft, wide smile I haven't seen in . . . fuck, years.

"Boys!" Dad flings his arms out like he always does, like we're going to run to him.

The three of us, Wren in tow, cross the huge room and stop a few paces back from him. If Dad barely acknowledges me, he's outright ignoring Hex, eyes fixed on Coal.

Dad drops his arms. "Are we ready now? I want to get this finished before I leave."

My head jerks.

"Leave?" Coal asks. "What? You're leaving?"

"Oh." Dad bats his hand idly. "I'm off to the island in a few hours. I just wanted to solidify this transfer before I go."

The Merry Measure moves. No—*it* doesn't move; *I* move. I take a step back, but I catch myself against a violent urge to run from the room.

Island.

He can't mean—

"You—what?" Coal asks Wren, like she'll have a better explanation than whatever's coming out of Dad's mouth.

But Wren is just as confused, her narrow eyes on our father.

The way he looks at Coal is, for once in our lives, candid. His eyes glisten with sorrow but he sniffs hard, breaking the emotion as soon as it congeals.

"It's high time I took charge of my family," he says. "Starting with this transfer of power, and continuing with my wife."

All the air sucks out of my lungs.

My fingers tingle, numbness that crawls up my arms, makes my vision go to black-and-white fuzz.

I was six. I'd gone to our parents' room. Dad was usually up already so I would climb into bed with her and cuddle until breakfast, only she wasn't there. The suite was empty. I looked and looked, the bathroom, the closet—her clothes were gone; that was weird, was she getting them cleaned?—then I sat on the bed, holding the edge of the comforter, until Wren found me.

No note. No word.

She was just . . . gone.

Until she texted Dad a few weeks later to let us know she was living in the Caribbean if we ever wanted to come visit. Like she was off on vacation and we should join her, not like she'd let us wake up with no clue where she was.

Coal laughs, fragile and frantic. Hex shifts closer to him.

"You're not serious," Coal says. "You're going to see Mom?"

Dad nods. "As I said, it's time I took charge of things. What's important is family. This family." He looks at me, and I realize that's the first time he has since we came into the room. "I let too much fall by the wayside, your mother most of all."

No.

She left *us.* She walked out on us when Coal and I were kids. Nothing *fell by the wayside;* she *chose* everything she did to us.

But none of those words come out, clogging my throat until the sounds of the room muffle behind my ragged exhales.

Coal glances at me, his expression shuttering as he grabs my forearm. "Kris. Breathe," he whispers.

I am. I'm fine. I *am* breathing, so why are my hands numb?

"Marta." Dad approaches the head of the Merry Measure as though nothing's wrong. "If you will."

Coal's worried gaze swings between them and me until I feel another touch on my arm—Hex.

"Go," he tells Coal, then positions himself right against my side, his long fingers wrapped around my hand. "Kris," is all he says, and he takes a deep breath in, slowly lets it out.

The oddity of him being this close has me echoing him unconsciously. In, deep; out, long.

"Fuck," Coal mutters but he turns to our dad. "Fine. Yeah. Let's do this."

Hex keeps taking deep breaths next to me, my body copying him.

Slowly, my fingers stop tingling, sensation inching over my limbs.

I hear Coal's words again. *Let's do this.*

Do this—?

Make him Santa. Give him full control of Christmas, no performative shit at meetings, no pretending to get Dad's approval for the changes he wants to make.

I straighten, but I don't try to pull out of Hex's grip and he doesn't move away.

Coal approaches Dad and Marta. "What do we need to do?"

Marta is messing with something on the Merry Measure. When she backs away, a flat panel of frosted white glass pops horizontally out of the wall of gauges.

"Both the current leader and the heir place their hands on this screen," Marta explains, her eyes averted—the tension in the room is sky-high, and I wouldn't blame her for racing away to less emotional ground. I almost did. "Magic is based in joy, so the transfer must be joyful. As long as the controlling leader is willing and eager, the transfer will be instant."

Coal walks up to the screen and plants his hand on one side. His eyes snap to Dad, ready to argue, ready for Dad to rescind this whole thing—

Dad is as fast as Coal. He crosses to the screen and places his hand on it.

Nothing outward happens.

But Coal wheezes like he stepped into the freezing tundra without a coat. He yanks his hand back, fingers curling into his palm, eyes flickering over our father. "You actually did it."

Dad grins. I've never seen him like this before, *giddy,* and it creeps agitation up and down my spine.

He claps once. "On that note, I'm off. You boys enjoy your New Year."

Like this is totally normal. Like we aren't—like I'm not—submerged in murky, inescapable anxiety.

He leaves, patting my shoulder as he goes. I flinch, bumping into Hex, who presses back to keep me from teetering too far.

We're left in the rubble of our shock, Coal flexing his fingers like it might help him wake up from this weird-ass dream.

"Well," he says, eyes going to me, down to Hex, "I guess I'm Santa now."

Hex squeezes my hand and releases me to cross to Coal, cupping my brother's face and pulling him down, forehead to forehead. It's such an abruptly tender moment that I shift away.

Wren is already working on her tablet again, but frantically now; this transfer of power no doubt shifted a *lot* of shit, and she's a woman on a mission, clicking and typing and scowling.

Marta is checking the Merry Measure, also scowling, studying a gauge like glaring at it will make it unleash an answer she's after.

Did that just happen?

Dad ceded our entire Holiday to Coal.

Last Christmas, he claimed he was blackmailing the winter Holidays to make Christmas more secure *for us.* Maybe . . . maybe he does care about us, on some level?

Doesn't explain how he can go see the woman who abandoned his children. I know he kept trying to reach out to Mom after she left, kept inviting her to Christmas functions and leaving that door open. But if he did care about us, he wouldn't want anything to do with her.

Then why do I keep responding to her messages?

Why does a little part of me whisper, *You should go with him, maybe the both of you can convince her to come back?*

Fuck. Fuck fuck *fuck.*

I rub the back of my neck and twist to the side of the room, wondering if I can slip away before Coal makes me talk about all this Dad-Mom crap—

Something green catches my eye at the base of the Merry Measure.

I cock my head. A tiny box is fixed to the bottom of the machine, blending in with the steampunk style, except for an indicator light that glows green. That's what caught my eye, something green. But it wasn't glowing—

I squat down, one hand on the floor for balance, and there—*that's* what I saw.

"What the hell?" I crawl forward and pluck the thing out of a crack between the Merry Measure and the marble floor.

Coal and Hex have noticed me now.

"Is that a—" Coal squints. "A clover?"

It is. Four perfect rounded leaves, bright, vivacious green.

"What the hell?" I ask again and look at the little box it was next to.

Marta follows my line of sight and whirls to Wren with a puzzled chirp.

"Did you authorize that?" she asks.

Wren drags her attention away from her tablet. When she sees what we're all gathered around, her frown deepens. "No. Nicholas?"

Coal shakes his head. "Absolutely not."

I stand up from my crouch, holding the clover. "What is going on?"

"That"—Coal points at the box—"looks like one of the devices that Dad sent to the other winter Holidays when he made them funnel some of their joy to us. It's what allowed him to drain their magic into our Merry Measure." He points higher, to a row of similar devices plugged in across the top. "We still have those connected to the other Holidays because we're working out who gets what joy, and we'll eventually use those devices to share a joy pool, but—*that* one? That's not one of *those*. Is it?"

Marta whirls back to the main screen with a horrified gasp, clicking on a few keys, shaking her head in tight, frantic jerks. "No, oh no—"

Coal, Hex, Wren, and I watch her through an invisible rising tide of warning.

"Our joy levels have been lowering." Marta feverishly works controls. "What with us sending joy back to the Holidays we took it from. My team has been tracking it all, and recently, there were discrepancies I couldn't account for. I attributed it to magic being used to wrap up Christmas, or to bringing the other winter Holiday leaders here, or a dozen other things—I was going to do a deeper trace once things slowed down, and I . . ."

Marta stops, reads the screen for a beat, and her face pales.

She turns shame-filled eyes on Coal.

"It's that device. It's been draining small bits of magic. I—I should have seen it. It wasn't there during my weekly check of the machine last Monday. But I should have investigated this as soon as the discrepancies emerged. I'm sorry, Prince Nicholas, I'm so—"

"Woah, woah." Coal holds up his hand. "Just—hang on. No one's blaming you, Marta."

She wilts.

"So . . . someone tapped our joy meter?" My eyebrows tug together. The peace we're working towards among the other winter Holidays is so new, so fragile—if one of them moved against us, we couldn't exactly *blame* them for it, but it wouldn't do anything to help us structure a fairer, more even spread of support.

Coal plants his hands on his hips and chuckles in a way that isn't at all funny. "Fuck me running. Someone's stealing Christmas's magic. Isn't *that* just karma?"

After some chaos, where Marta calls in the rest of her team to descend on the Merry Measure in a full top-to-bottom systems check, Coal, Hex, Wren, and I gather in the main office.

A fireplace and warm, dark wood accents make it cozy and atmospheric, but it's only *felt* like those things since Coal took over. Now, he crosses the room and drops to sit behind the desk with ease, not realizing the monumentality of this moment, how this is his first time being in *the* office as *the* Santa.

To be fair, we're all distracted.

And yes, it is terrible that someone's stealing our Holiday's magic, but I'm selfishly relieved that this incident is superseding Dad's *well, boys, I'm off to visit your mother* scheme.

"Ever since we figured out this whole mess last Christmas"—Coal scrolls over a report on a tablet—"Marta's team has been working to break down the joy we have. Obviously, we don't have *all* the joy we stole from other Holidays because we've been using it over the years, so we can't pay everyone back one big lump sum."

Which is one of the things Coal's been working on in negotiations, how much each Holiday is okay with being paid back and over how long.

I nod, but he's focused on the tablet, one hand dragging absently across his forehead.

"We're basing the joy distribution on the original percentages Dad required from everyone," Coal says. "So, the most recent tally was about sixty . . . three? Yeah, sixty-three percent of our total joy came from other Holidays, so we've been treating what we had in our Merry Measure after Christmas as if sixty-three percent was already spoken for, to be divided up and given back to other Holidays. The remaining thirty-seven percent is ours, and about twenty-five of that is needed for general Christmas functioning, so that leaves twelve percent extra. But we're planning a reimbursement system to pay back the amounts we've stolen in the past, and I was going to make the first payments from that full outstanding twelve percent as a goodwill gesture. Now, though, the amount that's been stolen from *us* this past week has taken up—"

He clicks through to a new screen.

And tosses the tablet onto his desk with a huff, fixing an exasperated glare on Hex.

"Math is evil," he grunts.

I don't take one of the chairs across from Coal, opting to stand, while Wren hisses into her phone off to the side.

"How much has been stolen?" I lay the clover on his desk. We left the device plugged in until we can figure out what's going on, so we don't arouse suspicion from whoever the guilty party is. But it means they can keep siphoning off our magic whenever they want.

"It hasn't been consistent. Marta's team has so far highlighted three instances that aren't attributed to our magic use: one big pull at the start of last week, then two smaller ones over the past few days. But rather than paying back the winter Holidays in a split from our outstanding twelve percent, now they'll get . . . eight."

Guilt over my errant use of magic to make tinsel rushes through me, and I almost apologize, but bigger picture: self-pity won't fix this theft.

"That is . . ." I scowl. "Not ideal."

"It's *insulting,* is what it is." Coal's jaw tightens. "I've already told the other Holiday leaders we'll set up a repayment schedule. I'm being open with what we have so they know there's no more funny business. When I come to them now, not only will we have less to repay them with, but we'll point fingers at another Holiday for stealing from *us* with one of the devices Dad forced on other Holidays in the first place? Yeah, that'll look good and trustworthy."

Hex goes around the desk and puts a hand on Coal's shoulder. "We will figure this out," he says, all calm confidence, and Coal relaxes under his touch. "Let's start with the *who.*"

Hex nudges the clover.

Coal sighs. "A by-product, you think?"

"By-product?" I ask.

"It happens occasionally," Hex explains, "with the way magic evolves based on the origins of our joy."

I squint. "Like magical traces?"

"It does not happen with every Holiday, I've found," Hex says. "Again, it is dependent on how the customs of a Holiday evolve."

Hex's eyes go to Coal.

Who grins.

It should be a jarring contrast, sudden joy against his obvious stress, but the shift in attitude is so welcome. All the chaos of our lives these past months, and he hasn't lost his ability to twist any situation into something happy.

"Do it. Do it." Coal bounces up and crowds in on Hex. "Kris needs a demonstration. Don't you, Kris?" He turns that grin on me.

"I'm not even sure what's being demonstrated."

"See?" Coal bumps Hex. "Do it. For science."

Hex fixes Coal with a look of bemused annoyance. "Only because I relish the rare opportunity to say you can be a delightful pain in my ass."

I rock backwards. "I don't think I've ever heard you *cuss*."

There's a sizzle in the air. The spark of magic.

Then a *black cat* appears on the desk.

Hex groans. "Oh. I hate when it's a creature."

"Oh my *god*! She's so cute!" Coal lunges for it.

The cat, justifiably, hisses, back arching, and bolts off the desk.

Wren leaps aside with an alarmed squawk as it bounds between her legs, but the door is shut, so it rockets back across the room and lodges itself under a bookcase.

I gape at Hex. "What. *The fuck?*"

"How the traditions of Holidays evolve throughout the world affects our magic. And cursing, in relation to Halloween, has come to do . . ." He waves at the cat. Beady eyes glint from under the shelf. "Similar, I suspect, to *this*." And he motions at the clover.

Not a clover.

A shamrock.

"So. Wait." I wave my hands, mind reeling. "You're saying someone from *St. Patrick's Day* is stealing our joy?"

Coal sits on the edge of his desk. His levity dips. "Quite possibly."

"Have we interacted with St. Patrick's Day? Like *ever*?"

"No," Coal says. "And I'd know. I've been eating, sleeping, and breathing Christmas's records for the past two months. We don't have anything to do with them."

"Do you think they know they left a shamrock?" I ask. "Or did they intentionally leave it, to taunt us?"

Hex nudges it with his finger. "I am not overly familiar with the attitudes prevalent in St. Patrick's Day, whether they would do such a thing with calculation—"

Someone knocks on the door.

Coal directs a cringe of apology at me before he spins to Wren. "My god, woman, you are *fast*."

Wren's still expertly juggling being in a heated phone conversation while typing on her tablet, but she breaks long enough to give my brother an absent smile.

"Fast?" I eye the door, then Coal. "What—"

"As we were finishing up with the Merry Measure, I asked Wren to invite . . . well. St. Patrick's Day is a spring Holiday—*Easter* is a spring Holiday—it's business. I thought it best not to tell you since you're still acting so *weird* around her."

"Around—? Oh my god. I hate you."

So not only did Coal covertly get Wren to bring Iris here ASAP, he figured out it was St. Patrick's Day the moment he saw this shamrock. In retrospect, *duh*; but to be fair, I didn't know magic by-products were a thing, and I'm unsettled from Dad's bombshells, and fuck, Coal's good at this.

Wren opens the door.

All that building strain pulling on my lungs drops into my stomach.

I take a breath, school my expression, and look back at Iris.

It really is no wonder I thought I was in love with her. She's stunning, inside and out, one of those rare people who glows with natural kindness. The first time I laid eyes on her, back when we were kids, she hit me with an awe that still lingers in the base of my chest. All the people I've been with have given me that same feeling, now that I think about it. Not that there's a wide assortment of people to take a sample from; I committed to my *I'm in love with Iris Lentora* identity to the point of only having two brief romantic encounters outside of her, and she wasn't even a full *romantic encounter*.

But all three people I could feasibly consider my exes gave me the same feeling of gentleness and comfort. Coal and Iris have never been shy about their bisexualities, but I've always been more fluid with any labels. It's a feeling I'm after rather than a type of person, the one Iris first ignited in me. *This is right. This is safe.*

Unprompted, the study room guy pops into my head. Nothing I felt towards him was *gentle*. So whatever that was had to have been base-ass lust.

. . . poor choice of words.

It was straight-up lust.

Still a bad descriptor.

It was lust, plain and simple. He was hot, emotions were heightened, and I haven't gotten laid in a long time.

This is not the train of thought I need to be riding right now.

Iris adds even more decorum to this room, wearing heels and a sleek purple dress that hangs to her knees, and I feel the grunge of my sweats all over again, made even worse by the fact that this is the first time I've seen her in person since everything imploded. And she, of course, looks *perfect,* while I look like I woke up, got a panicked text from my brother, and barely gave myself time to brush my teeth before I came here.

She stops next to me, across from Coal at his desk.

"Hi," I manage.

Iris's smile is tentative. "Hi. How are—"

The cat chooses that moment to launch itself out from under the bookcase and make a mad dash for the door Wren is closing.

Iris jumps about a foot in the air.

I spasm. "Fucking hell—"

Wren shrieks.

Coal cries out, "Catch her!"

And Hex snaps his fingers.

The cat vanishes mid-leap.

Coal whirls on him. "What'd you do? Where'd she go?"

Hex studies Coal's growing alarm. "It was created with Halloween's magic. It wasn't real, Coal. It was *magic.*"

"Don't talk about our baby that way, sweetheart."

Hex's eyes bulge. "Our *what?*"

"I was already thinking of names."

Hex massages his temple with a long-suffering sigh. "Again, it was not a real cat."

"You killed our child. So heartlessly. I'm not sure I like this side of you."

"I have no idea what I've walked in on," Iris starts, "but this feels about right. Random magic. Coal being dramatic. What else have I missed?"

Coal drops into the chair behind his desk. *Now* I see it hit him, that he's at *this* desk as the official leader of Christmas.

His jaw tenses, his persistent happiness wobbling.

And, true to my brother, he yanks up a beaming smile after half a millisecond and plunges onward. "First of all, I'm Santa now, so show some respect, Lentora."

Iris's eyes flare. "The fuck?"

Coal launches into a recap of everything that's happened this morning.

At the end of it, he looks at me, and I can see him remembering my reaction to Dad's news, how we haven't gotten to talk about that yet. I give him my best *don't do it now* silent plea, and he rolls his eyes with a *fine, but later.*

Iris is staring at Coal's desk, cradling her jaw in one palm.

"Shit," she grumbles. "And I thought my morning was busy."

Coal's brows dip. "Easter prep? I didn't mean to drag you away from—"

"It's fine. I'm not the only one in Easter with responsibilities." But I know both Coal and I clock her strain.

Coal had extended a special invitation for Easter to join the winter Holidays collective after all the shit went down with Dad. We'd thought King Neo had been sucked along by Dad's lies like most people, and he was, but not enough to jump onboard Coal's New and Improved Christmas plan. Instead, Neo used the excuse of not being a winter Holiday and pulled back from his former heavy associations with Christmas, throwing himself into preparations for the upcoming Easter season. Meanwhile, Coal's been relaying to me what little Iris tells him about how the different factions within Easter's court are grumbling over Neo's weakness in letting our dad manipulate him, how Iris was unable to *lock down* Prince Nicholas, and other such fuckery that's all an excuse to slowly force out her family.

All the stuff she's trying to keep afloat is why she switched to online classes, why I don't see her around university anymore—and why I wanted so badly to give her a happy ending too. She deserves it, deserves it so deeply my chest aches. I hate that I not only couldn't give it to her, but that I messed up our friendship in the process.

It wasn't entirely selfish on my part, wanting us to be together.

Iris doesn't linger on the knowing stares both Coal and I give her, and I can't help the weird mix of gallows' humor camaraderie. What would Iris and I even have to talk about if we *were* still talking? She doesn't want to talk about the political shit in Easter. I refuse to talk about my parents or anything that happened with her or my waffling position in Christmas. So, that leaves . . . the weather?

Iris's lips float up in a real smile. "Congratulations, Coal. Really."

He beams. "Yeah. It hasn't sunk in yet. I gotta say, this theft is inconvenient to the massive party I would have immediately thrown."

His tone counters his words the same way his hands do, thumbs flicking at each other in a nervous tic. Hex catches it too and threads his fingers into Coal's.

"There will be a celebration," Wren adds, phone pinched between her cheek and shoulder. "We will need to show everyone that a sudden transfer of power is in no way a sign of weakened leadership, but proof that Christmas is moving in the right direction. Particularly if news of this joy theft gets out."

I didn't realize it was a possibility that people might see these developments with Christmas and cry that we're fucking things up. Everyone's been supportive of Coal's plans. None of our court has voiced displeasure.

But the joy theft on top of Dad taking off . . .

Coal hums. "That sounds like a problem for Tomorrow Coal. Hell, maybe Next Month Coal—for now, Iris? What do you know about St. Patrick's Day?"

Iris straightens. "My father met their king once or twice, but no negotiations ever developed. He's a pompous ass, so I'm honestly shocked he didn't get along better with Easter and Christmas."

"They haven't reached out since Easter's rather public parting from Christmas?" Coal asks.

Iris's face screws up in part humor, part exhaustion. "While the autumn and winter Holidays may be in neat little collectives now, the spring Holidays are *content in being independent.* So says my father. The most we interact with is Valentine's Day because of Lily's impending wedding drama, and they're not even *spring,* really, are they? But no, we don't check up on one another."

Coal leans around Iris. "Wren, can you pull up profiles for the reigning family of St. Patrick's Day? I've got an idea."

"Of course." She ends her phone call and attacks her tablet.

"Okay. So." Coal pops his tongue. "Christmas is going through all kinds of changes. We're evolving. So it wouldn't be too unusual for us to suddenly be interested in visiting another Holiday, start dialogue through outreach. Yeah?"

I smirk. "Aw, your Yale is showing."

"Shut up. But say I go to St. Patrick's Day. Say I'm there to foster support, yadda yadda—while secretly investigating why that Holiday is trying to screw us over. I find proof that they did it, confront them, and get them to give us back the joy they stole before it becomes an issue with the winter Holidays collective."

"You don't think they'd be suspicious?" I ask. "*They* know they're screwing us over. And suddenly Christmas comes calling, wanting to be friends?"

"And I know that I don't give a flying fuck if they know we know." Coal takes the tablet Wren hands him and flips through what looks like dossiers. "Let them be awkward and uncertain about our intentions. Maybe they'll slip up. It's good that they'd be a little on edge."

"You could visit other Holidays as well, to serve as a cover," Hex says, but he doesn't hide his reservation.

"There we go. This is a totally normal leader thing to do, right? A goodwill tour."

But Wren, lingering by the desk, clears her throat. "As the reigning Santa, and still leading the ongoing meetings with the winter Holidays collective, when would you propose such a tour?"

Coal's jaw dips open. "Ah. Shit."

My heart kicks up, the familiar relief of finding something I can do that's beneficial. All the other tasks I've managed to glob onto have been measly and paper thin. But this? It'll *matter,* and the part of me that's always two stressors away from a tension headache relaxes a smidge.

"I'll do it."

The room looks at me.

"I'll be an ambassador," I expand. "My term at school is almost over; I can finish up my courses early. I'll visit a few Holidays."

I'm still a part of Christmas. I'm not just moping along the edges, the spare gravitating around the heir.

My own callousness makes me recoil. I hide it by running a hand through my hair, but my eyes catch on Iris, who's watching me maybe too closely.

Coal grins. "Perfect! Look at us. *Diplomats.* We're so mature."

He passes me Wren's tablet.

"Here—study up on their family," Coal says. "We'll figure out some other Holidays to ship you off to as a cover, and we'll research them too. We won't go in unprepared like when Halloween came calling."

"Oh, but your face when you saw me in the ballroom was priceless," Hex tells Coal with a teasing smirk.

"I'm pretty sure I haven't unknowingly kissed anyone from St. Patrick's Day." I look at the first profile, one for St. Patrick's Day's king. Around Dad's age, Malachy Patrick looks like a standard white businessman. It says he was the younger brother of the former king who died five years ago; the crown should've passed to that guy's son, but it was decided that the heir wasn't ready to handle the responsibilities. Malachy was originally an entrepreneur who owned—still owns—one of the largest whiskey manufacturers in Ireland, Green Hills Distillery. He's unmarried, no kids, so on and so forth.

"You never know." Coal waggles his eyebrows at me. "But you don't have my level of decorum. You wouldn't handle such a shock to the system with nearly the same level of grace."

"Ha. Sure. We both know, of the two of us, that you're the more level-headed"—I swipe to the next profile, the heir—"*holy flipping fuck.*"

I convulse like I got electrocuted, head to toe.

"What?" Coal tries to lean over the desk to see what I'm looking at.

My breath dissolves in lungs gone to stone. It's all I can do to gape up at Wren.

"Who is this?" I point at the screen. The screen that clearly says *Lochlann Patrick, Crown Prince of St. Patrick's Day* over a picture, but horror is rising, rising up my throat so I can't stop myself from going, again, "Wren, who the fuck is this?"

She blinks in veiled offense. "Pardon me?"

"Sorry. Sorry. I—Wren—*who is this guy?*"

"That's their crown prince, Lochlann Patrick."

"No," I tell her.

"No?"

"No."

"Kristopher, I'm quite certain—"

"No. No, you see, that cannot be their crown prince. *He cannot be their crown prince.*"

I laugh. It isn't funny. And I drop the tablet onto the desk so the room can see the image.

Red hair. No beanie, the strands pushed back across his head in a slick wave. Pale skin, freckles, gray eyes. He's smiling now, not glowering, which accentuates the shit out of his cheekbones, and it's a headshot but he's in a suit, not a tank top.

He's also not covered in Cambridge blue tinsel.

Coal, Hex, and Iris are all staring at me like I was the one who spontaneously created a black cat in midair.

"Kris." Coal leers. "*Did* you kiss someone from St. Patrick's Day?"

Chapter Three

"No. I—*I know him.*" My voice is creaky and shrill. "He goes to Cambridge."

"Okaaaaay." Coal drags out the word, confused, and I dig the heel of my palm into the bridge of my nose.

"We were in something of a . . . conflict."

"Conflict?" Coal grunts. "Wait. That study room thing?"

Just do it. Like a Band-Aid.

"He stole a study room from me," I hear myself say, and it sounds so goddamn absurd that I hate myself all over again. "So I sort of. In revenge. Filled the whole room with tinsel."

Coal's office is dead quiet.

"And filmed it." I drag my phone out of my pocket, eyes shut, and by muscle memory, I pull up the video.

Not that I've watched it a profuse amount. I just know where I stored it. That screenshot staring up at me, gray eyes framed in reflective blue tinsel strands.

I press play and swivel the screen towards where Coal, Hex, and Iris are standing. The office fills with the muffled sounds of the study hub's laughter.

The video ends.

"That was *you?*" Iris chirps.

My eyes pop open. "What?"

She digs her phone out of a pocket on her dress and flips through screens until she shows me a tabloid site, one of the outlets that covers all Holidays, *24 Hour Fête*. Magic goes into keeping these news sites separate from the normal world, and until a few months ago, when Coal severely cut our press coverage, they featured the Claus family more than anyone else.

Unluckily—or maybe luckily?—neither Coal nor I frequent these poison sites.

The page Iris is showing me has its own video of that guy stumbling out of the study room. It's a different angle, but there he is drenched in tinsel, there he is flipping off someone in the crowd—me. But my face isn't in the shot and it isn't clear who he's mad at.

The headline: *St. Patrick's Day heir ensnared in hazing scandal.*

I snatch her phone and scroll through the article. It alleges that Prince Lochlann is connected to hazing at the university.

Can he be trusted with as much power as King Malachy has given him? the article asks.

Half of me wants to laugh. And I do. A dry, humorless gasp, because it was one idiotic moment that involved *tinsel,* and this reporter is blowing it up to be *hazing*?

Maybe using Cambridge blue tinsel was a mistake. Well, doing it *at all* was a mistake.

"You knew about this?" I gape at Iris.

Her eyebrows are nearly at her hairline as she takes her phone back. "Only people like *you*"—she gestures at me, Coal, and Hex—"who refuse to read the tabloids don't know about it. The St. Patrick's Day royal family has never been in the spotlight, so this? Their crown prince comes out of nowhere with a scandal, *and* it turns out he got passed over for the role of king? It's made Lochlann into the paparazzi's next fascination."

The article did sound the way tabloids used to talk about Coal, dissecting how irresponsible he was, how unworthy of his station.

It almost makes me like Lochlann out of solidarity against tabloid bullshit.

And I started it for him. *I* did this to him.

"*Fuck,*" I groan. But my stomach turns to concrete and sinks straight to my toes. "Oh shit. This is bad, isn't it? Like, bigger picture bad. Christmas attacking St. Patrick's Day?"

Hands grab my cheeks.

Coal beams at me.

"You tinsel-bombed the St. Patrick's Day Prince," he says. "I have never been more proud of you in my life."

His joy butts up against my dread like oil on vinegar. It's comforting, in a way; this has always been our dynamic. Me, silently panicking about a thing; Coal, finding that same thing hilarious.

"For fuck's sake, Coal—"

"You *tinsel-bombed the St. Patrick's Day Prince*. This was almost an act of war."

"*I know*—god, get off me—hence my appropriate response of *oh shit*."

Iris passes her phone to Coal. "No one's connected Kris to it, but it's certainly being framed severely."

"I don't think he knew who I was," I try.

Although—*how* didn't he know who I was? My face used to be plastered all over Holiday tabloids.

Coal scans the article. His humor droops, and I can see the same thought occurring to him that I had, how familiar it reads.

"Vultures, all of them," Coal mutters to the screen.

Hex is scanning the article now. "This *is* a far better reason for why Christmas is so abruptly interested in visiting St. Patrick's Day."

My whole face gets lava hot.

Oh no.

"Given the impact of this . . . tinsel scandal," he continues, "it would be far less suspicious to have you go there to mend fences. And you wouldn't have to visit other Holidays to perpetuate any cover."

"This incident did screw up the guy's image," Iris says. "I don't know how he actually is as a person, but—"

"He *actually is* a douche." But as soon as I say it, I wince.

Whether he's a douche, I feel bad I caused someone to be smeared like this.

Unless he's stealing from us.

Then fuck him.

I scrub my hands over my face, and when I drop them and meet Coal's eyes, I might as well be translucent.

"You don't have to do it," he assures me. "Wren—figure out a way for me to go."

I'm not the only one who gives Coal a *the fuck are you doing* look.

"I appreciate it," I tell him, jaw tight. "But I can do this."

"Yes, you can," Iris agrees gently. I'm looking at her before I can think not to. "You can fix this. And be great in the process."

"Is it? Fixable." I bite the inside of my cheek.

Iris's eyelids flutter. "Of course it is."

Coal still looks like he wants to protest, fire in his eyes that isn't just for this situation. It's from Dad's departure, but where that's a problem he can't solve, this is.

I love him for it. But I flat-out refuse to let him take on everything. Hell, up until a few weeks ago, I refused to let him take on *anything* if I could help it.

I've been floundering to stay relevant in all the changes he's been making, and those insecurities double back on me now, sighting the underbelly of my weaknesses with lethal precision thanks to the image of Dad walking out now too.

My throat thickens.

Coal wouldn't do that. I *know* he wouldn't do that.

I'm being childish. All these fears, all this anxiety—fuck it *all*.

I nod at my brother. "I appreciate your offer, but it's fine. Besides, you'd go to St. Patrick's Day to apologize for my behavior, *without me?*"

Coal cringes. "Ah. You mean it wouldn't be convincing to show up in Ireland all, 'Trust me, Prince What's-His-Butt, Kris is torn up about the whole tinsel attack. He's so sorry he sent his *brother* to apologize for him.' Yeah." He clears his throat. "Not the best move."

Severity falls over him so quickly that my face relaxes.

"But Iris is right," he says. "You—"

"What?" She frowns at Coal.

He frowns right back. "What? I said you're right."

"I'm sorry, still didn't hear you." She cups her ear. "One more time?"

He catches on. "I said Iris is the pinnacle of humility and we should all aspire to emulate her poise."

She folds her arms with a satisfied nod. "Continue."

Coal, smirking, refocuses on me, and that smile helps temper the way he says, "I do think you'll be good at this. Being our ambassador. Getting to the bottom of our stolen joy."

"Sucking it up and apologizing to a jackass," I grumble.

"I believe he's a jackass. I also believe that you're incredibly capable of figuring out what's going on." Coal's vicious grin returns. "And send me that video. I'm going to put it in one of those digital photo frames and set it above my fireplace."

"Piss off."

"And I'll engrave it to say *Baby's First Political Incident.*"

Hex laughs, and Coal whips an adoring look at him that's so love-laden it forces me to turn away. God, they're freakishly good at creating immediate intimacy in public.

Turning angles me at Iris.

I never stared at her that way. The way Coal looks at Hex.

She deserves someone who will.

Her smile is timid. "It's nice to see you. Even under the circumstances."

"It is?"

Her head tips, braids falling over her shoulder. "Yes. You idiot. You're my Claus boys. When it's just Coal, all I get are jokes and his messy nonsense."

"Excuse you," he pipes in, one thumb hooked in Hex's belt. "There is nothing nonsensical about my mess."

Iris rolls her eyes as if to say, *See?*

I try to smile, but end up dropping my chin and scratching the back of my neck.

"I'm sorry," I tell her. "You deserved better than—"

She punches me in the chest.

I jerk away. "What the—"

"Stop apologizing. Don't take care of me. I don't need you to take care of me. What do *you* want, Kris?"

My gaze swings to Coal and Hex, heads close, talking quietly and smiling like fools in love.

What do I want?

Coal asked me that a few weeks back. What I wanted to do, really do, like I had any other choice than to be a Prince of Christmas. And yeah, sure, at one point I'd dreamed of going to school to learn more about books, but that was a pipe dream; and yeah, sure, at one point I'd been neck-deep in my writings about happy ever after, but Cambridge crushed any time for frivolous art, and I've broken myself out of longing for that happy ending.

So now? What do I want?

"I—I don't know," I say.

Iris hesitates. Watching me. Waiting.

"*You* deserve better, too," she whispers. "I wish you'd know that."

Discomfort builds, makes it difficult to speak. I don't know what to do with the way she's looking at me. Pity, but not; sorrow, but not.

I deserve better?

She can *see* me, right? Sweats that smell like coffee and bags under my eyes? The guy who brought a full-fledged PR nightmare down on someone whose only crime—at that point—was not giving up a study room?

"When do you need to get back to Easter?" I ask.

"A few hours, latest. Why?"

What the hell. "Stay for lunch? I miss Renee's cooking, and I know you do, too."

"Yes!" Coal springs away from his desk. "Stay. You have to stay. Kris asked, so the awkwardness is over."

Iris shakes her head in amusement. "Subtle, your brother is not."

"It's one of his many charms." I push my hair back, tugging at the strands. "But—lunch?"

She considers. "Only if you promise to start texting me again.

There have been like two dozen insane made-up words my professors have tried to pass off as English. I kept a list."

I crack a smile. "I wanted to figure out a way to send you a photo of that guy. Before I tinseled him."

Iris arches one eyebrow. "Mm, he is dreamy. Those cheekbones."

"Right?" My eyes pop wide and I fumble. "I mean, no, not the dreamy bit. He opened his mouth, and any dreaminess went full nightmare."

Iris's arched eyebrow sharpens. "Uh-huh. Sure it did."

She's teasing about me finding another person attractive. Which isn't something we *ever* did before, so the fact that we can now . . .

Maybe things between us will be okay.

And not just okay, but better.

Woah there, let's not get ahead of ourselves with that kind of positivity. I might sprain something.

"And this is why I didn't send you his picture for . . . what's the media of the moment?"

"You'll laugh."

"Probably."

"Mosaic."

"That's not a bad—"

"Using multicolored googly eyes."

I do laugh. Enough that Coal and Hex and even Wren shoot identical surprised looks at me.

Am I that much of a sad sack anymore?

Iris has her phone back out and she pulls up a photo, shows it to me, and I laugh all over again. It's—well, there's no other way to describe it.

It's a mosaic of Iris's sister made out of multicolored googly eyes.

I'm sure she loved being immortalized this way, all proper and dignified as she is.

"That is the single most horrifying and hypnotic thing I've ever seen," I say. "How do you have time for this?"

"I make time." She shrugs. "How do you blow off steam between your classes?"

By picking fights with guys who turn out to be Holiday royals, apparently.

Iris shows the picture to Coal and Hex.

"Oh. My. *God*." Coal waves at Wren. "That's the only format in which I will accept an official Santa portrait. Make a note of it."

Wren blinks slowly at him. And does not make a note of it.

Iris grins. "I needed something silly after my unintentional deep dive into Russian Orthodox iconography."

"Yeah." I chuckle again. "I can see that. So—you'll stay for lunch?"

She turns her grin on me. "Do we have a deal?"

I smile. "Yeah. Deal."

"Then I'll stay."

"And we can review the other members of the St. Patrick's Day family," Coal adds. "Make sure Kris hasn't viciously assaulted anyone else they're related to."

"It was hardly a *vicious assault*—"

"Wren." Coal ignores me. "Can you send him the profiles for—"

My phone pings.

His jaw drops. "A few hundred years ago, you'd have been burned as a witch."

She makes a noise I swear to god I've never heard from her. It takes me a beat to realize she's *laughing*. "Thank you, Nicholas. I appreciate that."

I reach across the desk and shove the side of Coal's head. "I'll see about getting my classes wrapped up early before we have lunch. When am I leaving?"

Wren poises her finger over her tablet. "When would you like to? I haven't reached out yet."

"As soon as possible." Get this over with.

It's manageable, if I break it down: go to Ireland to apologize, tail between my legs. Figure out who is stealing joy from us, even though there's no way it isn't someone as arrogant as Lochlann. Stop him from stealing from us. Get him to pay us back.

I suck in a stabilizing breath, wading through my bubbling emotions to find one last, lone island of resolve. I owe it to this guy to give him the benefit of the doubt after my prank and this subsequent tabloid mess. Maybe Lochlann isn't the ass I remember. Maybe he was locked in his own Week Five Blues episode too. Maybe it's the St. Patrick's Day King who's screwing over Christmas and Loçhlann doesn't even know about it.

My thoughts swivel sharply back to Dad.

Nope. Not thinking about him, or Mom, or anything but *this*.

Not that *this* is much better.

And that's how I find myself in the Claus Palace foyer with a suitcase at my feet and a scowl on my face five days out from March 17.

It couldn't have been a quick visit. No, oh no; the moment St. Patrick's Day heard I wanted to *apologize* for my *behavior,* it skyrocketed from a quick weekend bounce-over to *Wait a few weeks and come for the full splendor of our Holiday.* Which isn't surprising—the tabloids have been having a field day picking apart Lochlann's life, according to the summaries Wren gives me. They go off speculating wildly about any gaps in his history, and are doing their darndest to paint him as an immature wild child.

He's definitely their new golden boy of paparazzi fodder.

When we announced my visit—and the reason for it—there was a brief shift in the articles, wherein few people believed I was actually both involved *and* the perpetrator of the tinsel incident, because *Prince Kristopher is usually so reserved.* As though I'd lie about this.

So I'm now due to spend five days in Ireland, prancing from St. Patrick's Day event to event, proving to the press that the tinsel was a harmless prank between *friends,* not something that Lochlann had any fault in.

Not only do I have to apologize, I have to pretend that Lochlann and I were and still are the kind of pals who tinsel bomb each other. While, of course, I'm really there to figure out who's stealing from us.

What could go wrong.

The delay of me going to Ireland also means that St. Patrick's Day has spent these three weeks siphoning joy from us. Which could be another reason they pushed my visit, to allow more time to suck up our magic. They're taking small amounts now, according to Marta, but it's grating to know someone is actively hurting our Holiday and we have to let them.

The amount we're planning to use as repayment to the winter Holidays shrinks each time another chunk is stolen, and if we don't figure out who is doing it and stop them, we'll have to tap into the joy we need to keep Christmas running. Which means things like monitoring the wishes of the world's children, creating toys, and even keeping our whole North Pole compound hidden from the real world could be at stake.

It's giving us a taste of what it was like for the winter Holidays Dad stole from.

Coal was right; it is karma. Karma for all those years Christmas spent draining other Holidays of their joy. But we're trying to *undo* all that; if anything, it should be our dad who has to swallow his pride and fix this. That's way too much to ask, though.

I muted all texts and messages from him, but Coal told me he sent a photo. Of him and our mom. At a pool bar.

That's the most we've talked about them. Coal's tried a few times, but I can't. I won't. It doesn't matter. They're grown adults; if they want to spend time together, the hell do I care? And, bonus, Mom hasn't texted me the whole time Dad's been with her, so really, this is a good thing for everyone.

I roll my shoulders, trying to work out the permanent kink in the back of my neck. My jaw is clamped so tight the beginnings of a headache palpitate across my skull.

"Unclench your jaw, Kristopher," Wren orders without looking up from her screen.

Coal's right. She is a witch.

I obey. It doesn't help.

I tug at the tie around my neck, trying to free even a millimeter of space. At least the rest of my ensemble isn't overly formal—relaxed blue pants and surprisingly comfortable brown shoes, a simple pale green button-up under an emerald cardigan, the tie an interweaving plaid of green and red. Subtly Christmas, subtly St. Patrick's Day. Our stylists are going to become experts at tying Holidays together.

Wren deftly clucks her tongue at my continued fidgeting. "If you mess up that Eldredge knot, I will personally garrote you with it."

"That's a risk I'm willing to take. I can't fucking breathe."

She gives me an unimpressed stare.

"Sorry. Nerves." I drop my hands and try to compartmentalize the choking grip of the tie.

"You don't need to breathe," Wren says. "It isn't on the itinerary."

My stare is flat. "Fantastic."

"Do you know what *is* on the itinerary?"

"Yes." No. She sent me a copy, I took one look at it—five days of festive activities culminating in a Dublin St. Patrick's Day parade—and haven't opened the file since.

The one solace: I know many of these activities will involve beer.

"What *is* on the itinerary," she continues pointedly, "is a detailed explanation of your daily stylings to coordinate with the arranged events, and today's specifically says *Eldredge knot.* I will make sure you present the proper visage of Christmas for this first introduction, because I know you will grossly neglect the outfits I picked out for your remaining days."

I snort but clear my throat to hide it. "I don't know what you're talking about."

"Mmhmm." Wren's eyes drop to my suitcase, and she gives a sad headshake like she can read the assortment of pun-heavy Christmas shirts I stuffed in when the stylists left. But if I'm going to spend almost a full week trapped in Irish hell, I want to be comfortable. And passively witty.

Wren smooths down a stray curl that's escaped my topknot and surveys my outfit for the fourteenth time. "All right." She checks her watch. "As soon as your brother arrives to see you off, we can leave."

I tug at the tie again before giving up and pinning my hands behind my back with an impatient huff.

"Purge your system of that attitude now, Kristopher," Wren warns. "You won't get—"

Saving me from another lecture on the importance of my ability to lie, Coal hurries down one of the wrapping staircases that frame the foyer. He's got winter Holidays meetings this afternoon, and like my mix of St. Patrick's Day and Christmas, his outfit is a diplomatic blend: a white shirt with a red sash, likely for St. Lucia; a blue suit jacket emblazoned with silver designs of candles, Hanukkah; and a sprig of holly in his breast pocket for Yule. There are other Holidays in the collective, but those are who he's meeting with today.

"I'm here, I'm here," he says, fastening the cuff on his jacket. "And look at me—very nearly on time."

"Early, actually." Wren waves at staff near the door and they begin setting up the necessary magic to travel. "We aren't due to leave for another three minutes."

Coal comes to a shuddering stop. "Wren. Are you *managing* me?"

"Nicholas, it is quite literally my job to manage you. Have you not noticed that you are always precisely on time, even when you claim to be running late?"

Coal's mouth drops open. But I watch his mind work. And his mouth snaps right back shut.

I chuckle. "Well, damn. You've cracked my brother. Can you send me a list of the cheat codes you've figured out?"

"Of course."

"There's a whole *list*?" Coal chokes. "Manipulation, in my own court! The *betrayal*—"

"Say your goodbyes." Wren heads to the door, and Coal comes up alongside me.

"If she sends you that list, I want a copy."

"Throw away that digital photo frame and I'll share it." He really did put that tinsel video in a frame after he pulled a copy off the tabloid site.

Coal blanches. "Never."

"Then no list."

"Traitor."

"Gonna excommunicate me?"

"Shut up. Or what is it you posh Cambridge boys say? Piss off."

"Be nice or I'll make these talking points I'm working on for your next meeting just twelve bullets of how amazing your brother is."

Coal frowns, the mood crashing. "You aren't supposed to be working on anything for me right now." He shoots Wren a look over my shoulder. "Kris is officially off any other duties while he's in Ireland."

I don't bother arguing. I'll keep doing what I've been doing and ignore him by working through Wren instead.

"Shit." I shake my head. "It's terrifying that you can do that."

"Do what?"

"Become . . . *this.* The Christmas King, so quickly. It looks good on you."

It does, but it's been a slow rollout of publicizing it. Coal refused to let Wren plan a party announcing his new title until the winter Holidays collective is figured out, so once it all comes together, there'll be some big shindig celebrating Christmas's new direction from every angle. That doesn't stop him from embodying his role now.

Coal grabs the back of my neck. "And *this* looks good on you. Being our ambassador. The more I think about it, the more it makes sense. We *should* be visiting other Holidays. There should be a lot more collaboration outside of established alliances, or at least awareness and understanding. And I do think you're suited to this."

The chasm of anxiety that's been opening more and more since last Christmas closes a little bit. See? I have purpose still. I have things to contribute. I have *worth,* goddamn it.

My smile comes more easily. "Don't get mushy, I beg of you."

"I'll get mushy if I want to." Coal squeezes my neck. "You said twelve bullet points of how amazing my brother is? Number one, how you helped me out last Christmas. Number two, how you've always been the one to help me out. Number three, how considerate you are—"

"Okay, Wren?" I turn away, face aflame. "I'm ready to—"

Coal grabs me in an overly clingy hug, practically wrestling me to the floor. "Number four, how dependable you are; number five, how generous—"

"Shit, Coal—okay, god, I love you too! Uncle, uncle!"

He lets me go and is reaching to mess up my hair when Wren seizes his wrist.

"I am not above garroting you as well, Santa or no," she tells him.

He missed that part of the conversation, so he squints at her, but slowly pulls away. "Understood."

"All right. We're traveling in five—four—" She moves back to the door.

I face Coal one more time. His teasing has helped alleviate my stress, like always.

"Once more," I whisper.

He smiles. "Unto the breach."

"Two—one." Wren points at the door. The mistletoe, the staff, it's all set up, and on a wave of magic that warms the air and lifts the hairs on my arms, the door opens.

Coal nods and I move to stand next to Wren, who holds the door open for me.

Just get it over with.

I step forward, hauling my suitcase. Wren snatches it from me with a scowl that reeks of how I *broke etiquette.*

The door shuts behind us.

And we're in Ireland.

The foyer of this castle is older, more worn-in, than Claus Palace. The overall colors are weighted and dark, with gray stones exposed along the walls and floor, and panels of red-brown wood capping the high ceiling, a heavy background for an iron chandelier. The smell to the air is the musk of ancient things with something earthy beneath it, damp petrichor richness.

Off to the side, a half dozen photographers wait from Holiday tabloids, already snapping photos and mumbling notes into recording devices.

They'll be at every event we do over the next five days.

I'm hit with memories of all the times Dad ruined our outings by using them as PR stunts. Image was everything: look how beloved King Claus is; look how powerful; look how irresponsible Prince Nicholas is; look how nonexistent Prince Kristopher is.

My nerves strain, twisting even more.

Will parading around result in the press backing off on their smear campaign against Lochlann, or is this playing into their bullshit? It'd die down eventually, right, if Lochlann stayed out of the spotlight?

"Welcome to our humble castle."

An internal clench grabs my body at the sound of his voice, that lilting, upward roll to his words.

Opposite the door, at the edge of the foyer, Lochlann waits, bookended by two women. I fight to keep my eyes on his, but unwittingly, I dip down, taking in his choice of outfit in one quick swoop. He's in a corded ivory wool sweater, the sleeves rolled to his elbows, and I know its intent is to represent his home, but all I can think is that he's trying to look like a ginger Chris Evans from *Knives Out*.

He *does* look like a ginger Chris Evans from *Knives Out*.

Motherfucker.

His pants are simple, brown, and he has no other touches of color on him, and I hate that Wren tried to bridge our differences through my outfit. I should've come in roaring Christmas absurdity. Red and gold and candy canes and a star on my head. Oh shit, I should've worn a terrible sweater with *tinsel* on it—god, missed opportunity, massively.

Lochlann tips his head when my eyes return to his, victory flashing across his face, like I lost a power play.

I channel my reaction into clenching my fists, not constricting my face, which remains smooth, pleasant.

What are the odds he's forgotten I called him hot?

Wren softly clears her throat next to me.

I pull in a deep breath and cross the room.

"Prince Lochlann." I stop in front of him. "I'm pleased to be here."

Well I'll be damned, that almost sounded genuine.

I recognize the two women with him from the files Wren sent me: Lochlann's younger sisters, Fionnuala and Siobhán, both at Trinity College in Dublin, twenty and eighteen, respectively. Fionnuala is studying political science; Siobhán is undecided. Fionnuala likes singing and animal rescues; Siobhán likes fashion and football. Their mom died when all three of them were young, and their dad had a heart attack five years ago, which was when their uncle became king because Lochlann was deemed unfit. The press have come up with dozens of reasons as to why, but no real cause was officially given.

And I also know a smattering of useless tidbits about Lochlann now. He's a year older than me, twenty-two; he is indeed studying art history at Cambridge, which does not congeal in my brain—he's the heir of St. Patrick's Day, and he's in the *art history* track? He also has a degree in business from Trinity that he got at *sixteen,* some kind of prodigy. His list of likes was as vague as the ones for his sisters: painting—which, duh, art history—and whiskey. If that's what we're doing, my whole personality is writing and self-doubt.

The only one from their immediate family I don't see is the King.

It also hits me how empty this foyer is. If we were five days out from Christmas, our palace would be in utter chaos—staff running everywhere, preparations in tumult. But the castle is silent, and all the rooms that open off this one are empty, no flurrying bedlam of an imminent Holiday.

Did they clear everyone out for me?

Why?

Lochlann stands in the position of figurehead with ease, that wide, placid smile on his face, the same one from his headshot. Performative. I get it; I'm performing, too.

But god if it doesn't spike my animosity.

His gaze holds on mine for one too-long pause before he extends his hand towards me. We're supposed to be playing up a charade of already knowing each other—and he might have known who I was anyway—so he doesn't introduce himself, just says, "Hello again, Prince Kristopher."

I shake his hand.

Cameras flash. My smile stays amiable.

His grip tightens. He has calluses on his fingers.

I squeeze right back.

"I don't think you've met my sisters." Lochlann extricates his hand from mine and motions to them. "Princess Fionnuala. Princess Siobhán."

Fionnuala has short hair, red like her brother, and she's almost as tall as he is, but less filled out in a simple black dress, with even more freckles splattered across her pale skin. Siobhán has long blonde curls and a compact stature, wearing a bright pink dress all sleek and fitted, and she's smiling sincerely where Fionnuala is fuming. I recognize that expression; she hates me for what I did to her brother.

Well, that's fair. Honestly, if someone had done to Coal what I did to Lochlann, I'd hate them, too.

I nod at his sisters and look back up at Lochlann. "Christmas is excited to see the full breadth of St. Patrick's Day." I toss out one of the many phrases I wrote that Wren approved as decently polite. "I'm eager to spend these next five days in your Holiday."

"Yeah, we have quite a full schedule arranged for this visit." Lochlann winks at me. "If I remember, you're quite the fan of schedules, eh, boyo?"

My smile flickers.

Lochlann throws his arm around my shoulders and spins us to face the journalists. My muscles arrest at the feel of his body pressed to mine, but I hardly get a beat to react.

"Let's buck off this formality a bit," he says to the paparazzi. He smells like that cologne again, spicy and expensive, with the same undercurrent of chemical bitterness. "A few weeks ago, Prince Kristopher and I had a wee bit of a misunderstanding at our school. Wouldn't you say so, boyo?"

Stop it with the fucking boyo. "A gross misunderstanding. Yes."

"Oh, gross indeed. Now, what's the real reason you've come to my Holiday?"

His gaze burns the side of my head.

Panic seizes me. Did he guess that I'm here to investigate him and his family?

But he's beaming down at me.

"To apologize," he says into my face.

I go even more rigid. "Well. Yes. That is the purpose of this whole—"

"Oh, no. No, hardly. The events of the next few days will be to enjoy some time together, St. Patrick's Day and Christmas. But to-day, this right here? Ach, the people want your apology!"

He throws a smile at the journalists, and one of them melts, blushes at his princely charade, traitors. They have their cameras ready, recorders out.

My mouth dries and it's my turn to burn the side of Lochlann's face with my gaze. "You mean—"

"Apologize," he commands. "To me. Now."

I knew it was coming. But he's *demanding* it. I haven't *offered* it. And there's a spark in his eyes that says he knows exactly what he's doing.

Apologizing is why I'm here. This is what Coal needs me to do. Eat crow.

That reasoning is suddenly hard to see clearly.

Because right now, being in Lochlann's presence, that heavy, choking wave of pretentiousness quaking off of him, I'm livid.

I don't *get* livid in a way that doesn't turn into depression.

Except, it seems, around him.

He still has his arm around me, a pinning vise, so I throw my arm around him too, playing up this buddy-buddy bullshit.

Then, to the journalists, "What happened in the library study room involving Prince Lochlann was nothing more than a harmless prank between friends. But I am sorry, Prince Lochlann, for the negative spin it put on you."

That's the apology I wrote. Simple. Effective. Done—

"And?" Lochlann presses, talking out of the side of his mouth.

I fix him with my sweetest smile. "And what?" I hiss.

"And that's na good enough."

All smiles. Happy, grinning, friendly smiles for the cameras.

"You can't be serious."

Lochlann laughs like I said something funny. He tips his head closer to me, eyes on the journalists, and growls for only me to hear, "You're lucky I do na make you get down on your knees and beg. Though you did call me *hot,* so would you enjoy that, hm?"

My whole body goes molten so aggressively I get dizzy.

It fades, tapped by a slow drain of fury, head to toe, and with that drain goes my thinning resolve.

He wants a performance?

I'll give him a performance.

"And," I say to the journalists, "our misunderstanding in the library was entirely my fault. Prince Lochlann was merely a harmless, ignorant—"

His grip pinches on my shoulder. "All right, now."

"—witless, I mean, unwitting, victim. I am honored to spend these next few days with him to draw light to what the press should be focused on: St. Patrick's Day's magnificent grandness. Their outstanding generosity. Their kind, welcoming, marvelous spirit that I have seen reflected so beatifically in Prince Lochlann himself."

A few of the journalists blink at me, mouths slightly agape.

I hear a rumble in the deep of Lochlann's chest. Annoyance.

A pause for pictures. Smiling still.

"Was that the apology you had in mind?" I whisper up at him. "Or should I go on about how all the rainbows in Ireland point to the pot of gold in your asshole?"

Those fingers on my shoulder are going to leave a bruise.

The muscle tics in his jaw. "You have na yet begun to repent," he mutters.

"I agreed to *apologize,* not repent."

"You're in Ireland. That's what we got here, repentance and Guinness."

I angle for the reporters off to the side, smiling, and saccharinely tell him, "I will make your life a living hell these next five days."

Lochlann rocks my shoulder and stage-laughs again. "Now, boyo," he whispers to me, "how would that look for these nice reporters when you came here to be my wee bitch?"

My nostrils flare as journalists start asking questions about the events we'll be doing.

I did try to play nice.

But I'm going to get proof that he's the one stealing from my Holiday.

Then I'm going to go Christmas nuclear all over his St. Patrick's Day ass.

Chapter Four

Questions answered, pictures taken, Wren leaves, and so do the journalists. But the stiffness of performing carries over to dinner in an appropriately medieval dining room with the same dark wood beams offsetting the bright white walls. A long polished table way, way too big for four people is set with places for Lochlann, his sisters, and me.

Across from my seat, Siobhán darts looks at me. Fionnuala deliberately does *not* look at me.

And Lochlann, to my left at the table's head, sits so rigid that I wonder if he's having a muscle spasm.

I rip off a hunk of soda bread and stuff it in my mouth so I have something to do that isn't talking until I can get my head to settle.

First *boyo*. Now *bitch*.

Him and his motherfucking accent, I swear.

And also screw this bread, holy shit it's good.

In our painful silence, a butler emerges from a side door and sets a first course in front of us. It's a bright green leek soup that is also maddeningly delicious, savory and creamy. I eat quietly, not even letting my spoon hit the bowl too loudly, because it feels like another ploy for victory. Whoever talks first loses.

I take a mouthful of whatever the butler poured in a squat glass on my right.

Oh shit.

Whiskey. Straight whiskey.

Of course it's whiskey. What the hell did I think it was? It's *brown*, for fuck's sake.

My tongue burns where I hold the whiskey in my mouth and it's everything I can do not to choke, eyes watering, throat contracting—

—until I realize Lochlann's watching me.

He clocks that I've got a gulp of whiskey I can't swallow and his face lights up like a Christmas tree.

Challenge so strong I can feel it bruising my skin, he lifts his own glass and downs the whole damn thing in one go.

Don't give in. Don't bow to his juvenile taunting.

Except this is alcohol, so it isn't exactly *juvenile,* which means it's a fully *adult* taunt and not matching him would let him win more than resisting on principle would.

Yeah, that's a strong argument.

Regardless, I force the gulp down, a cough welling deep in my lungs, but I will die before I admit how much I hate strong liquor.

I toss back the rest of my whiskey before I can psych myself out.

Holy fucking shitballs goddamn.

I'm not sure where I find the fortitude to hold in my wheezing gasp, but it's good to know that when I need to, I can completely control my faculties.

The butler materializes from nowhere and refills both our glasses.

Great.

Lochlann's gray eyes are pinned on me. Making indentations in my face.

"You all right there?" he asks, not bothering to hide his chuckle.

My neck is bulging against my too-snug tie, throat on fire and eyes tearing, and the only solace is that he talked first. "Fine," I manage. "Where's your king?"

I want to subtly insert that Lochlann is *not* in charge, not really.

The warmth of the whiskey streaks in lightning arches through my chest.

Well.

That's okay then.

Lochlann lets his glare hang on me, and when he smiles this time, it's significantly less performative and more annoyed.

"Off on business. He'll be at the St. Patrick's Day Dublin parade, though, if you're so keen to meet him."

"I get you all to myself, then." I give another beaming smile and throw it at the princesses too. "Along with your sisters, of course."

Lochlann rolls his eyes. "Fucking show pony," he grumbles.

"Sorry?"

He looks straight at me. "I said you're a fucking. Show. Pony."

I laugh, totally humorless. "And yet, you *claimed* to have no idea who I was in Cambridge. Wouldn't a *fucking show pony* like me have registered in your memory more?"

Did you actually know who I was, you dick?

"You might've," he snipes, "only I did na expect an esteemed Prince of Christmas to be slumping round with coffee-stained sweats and scraggly hair. So you'll have to forgive me for not automatically recognizing Your Highness."

My neck aches with how tightly I clamp my jaw.

Okay. Yes. I was a bit . . . underdressed that day.

But I twist to rip into him when Siobhán bolts up straight.

"Will you be running in the race tomorrow, Prince Kristopher?" she asks in a rush, like she's been working through possible questions and finally figured out the best one to start with.

Lochlann drops his eyes from me, pushing soup around his bowl.

My smile for Siobhán is real. "You can call me Kris."

"Kris," she echoes. Then she leans in like she's got a secret. "They'll never tell you themselves, but you can call her Finn, and him Loch."

"Siobhán," Fionnuala hisses. "Christ, you're such a wain, don't be nice to him."

"Loch, huh?" I turn to him with a grin. "Can I call you that? We are such good friends, after all."

He's not looking at me. He's staring down the middle of the table and licks his bottom lip in a clear, unbridled glower. So, his ability to fake this propriety lasted all of, what, an hour? I'm tired too, but I can do this all day, buddy.

"Of course." He faces me, says slowly, "Kris."

I sit up, an irritating itch rolling down my spine. "Loch."

He white knuckles his whiskey glass.

"So, Kris." Siobhán shifts in her chair. "The race tomorrow?"

I should pretend I read the schedule and know what she's talking about, but the whiskey is starting to make my head a little fuzzy. Me and my zero tolerance for anything harder than 8 percent alcohol.

"What race is that?" I ask.

Siobhán leans her elbows on the table. "The 5k charity race? There's a festival around it too."

"He's na running." Finn cuts a direct look at me, her first since we sat down. "He canna be arsed to raise money for youth services and after-school programs."

I blink at her. That sounds . . . not nearly as performative as I'd expected for our first event.

"Of course I'll run for that." If it was Coal, hell no, that boy couldn't run up a staircase; but I can do a 5k no problem thanks to my one moderately healthy coping mechanism: hitting the gym.

Finn seems unconvinced. "Really? I would na think Christmas would give a shite about giving *back* to people rather than taking *from* people."

"That reputation is exactly the thing my brother and I are trying to undo," I say civilly.

"Christmas has been terrorizing other Holidays for *years*. What exactly do you think you can do to make up for that, *Kris?*"

I stare at Finn, trying to tell myself not to take it personally—my Holiday was a piece of shit for a long time to a lot of different people.

"We're trying," I say again. "It's no excuse for—"

Finn's on a war path. "Living up your privileged arse off the magic you stole from other Holidays—"

"Christ, Finn, get off it," Loch cuts in. "Not everything has to be a bloody fucking crusade."

Finn snarls at him, but surprisingly relents, sinking into her chair and shooting me one last glare.

After a moment of silence, Siobhán gives a strained laugh. "Finn is our moral compass, as you can see."

"She's not wrong," I admit.

That makes Finn glare at me all over again, expecting a fight, but I grab another cup in front of me.

"It will take a long time to undo what Christmas has done." I fiddle with the glass. "My brother and I didn't know how to counter it. Turns out it just took a few moments of reckless bravery to get started. And diplomatic outreach to other Holidays."

I bat my eyelashes at Loch.

He works his lips, and the whiskey tunnel-visions my focus on that repressed snarl so I take a drink before I think to check which glass I grabbed.

The whiskey. Again.

Loch sights it, hunter to prey.

He picks up his own glass and knocks it all back easily.

I don't have to do it. I *know* I can't win a drinking contest with any-one, least of all someone who's downing whiskey like water. I don't think he's on his second glass like I am—I'm pretty sure the butler's been refilling his more, and Loch's eyes aren't even bloodshot.

My whole face squints to double check.

Yep. They're clear.

And gray.

Who has gray eyes? Is that a real eye color?

Loch's expression pinches into revulsion, likely at the way I'm studying him. So to cover, I suck back my glass of whiskey, because *that's* a smart move.

But this time, I'm not able to choke off my reaction, and I splutter a wet cough into my lap.

Classy, Kris.

Real top-shelf levels of self-preservation going on here.

Loch snorts. "Canna handle your whiskey, boyo?"

"Would you stop with that *boyo* shit." I wipe my mouth with a napkin.

"Consider it part of your penance. Boyo. Though I prefer Coffee Shop, I think."

"Fine, then. *Shamrock.*" I drop the name and wait for a response.

Loch's fuming glower is unfazed.

Siobhán picks at her bread and singsongs *"Awkward"* into her lap.

"See now, *boyo*." Loch leans back in his chair, chucking his spoon into his bowl with a clatter. "This is why I'm having a wee bit of trouble taking your earlier apology serious."

"Loch," Siobhán tries.

Finn is smirking at me. Like I deserve whatever's coming.

"You do na seem at all remorseful," Loch continues. "You seem to be the same stubborn prick you were in that library."

"Funny," I snap back. "I was thinking the same about you."

Ohhh, here's the whiskey coming out to play. Mix that with the incendiary fury Loch unleashes in me, and I should excuse myself from the table until I'm sober out of fear for what I might do without inhibitions.

But see above re: the whiskey coming out to play.

Oh boy, does it wanna *play*.

Loch launches forward, red starting in his neck and rising up his cheeks. "Do you have any idea the mess you made for me? You saw the goddamn tabloids?"

"Yeah, I saw the tabloids—and do *you* realize that I did come here to apologize?"

"I do na want your *pity*, Coffee Shop."

"Not pity—I felt *bad* about what I'd done to you. And I *was* going to apologize. Properly. But you had to go and jackass-up that confrontation—" Did I say that word right? *Confrontation*. Yeah, we're good. "So you're right, my apology didn't come off as sincere because you reminded me of what a self-righteous dick you are. And you know what? Turns out, *I'm not actually sorry*."

He darkens. "Why are you here, then? Go on back to Christmas if you hate me so much."

"I made a commimit—" Fuck. "Commimim—" Fucking whiskey fuckity fuck fuck—

Dark amusement flashes in Loch's eyes and I hold up a finger at him.

"*Commitment*," I get out. "I made a *commitment*, and I honor my commitments. So I'm going to stay in St. Patrick's Day until your Holiday and I'm going to be all smiles for the cameras and every tabloid that circulates is going to think we're the closest of friends, and not a single second of it has to do with *you*. I'm just the best liar you've ever met, and I fucking hate the tabloids thinking they can manipulate anyone. Even someone who's an asshole."

I barely manage to keep from fist pumping that I got all that out with only one tongue blunder.

Kris, 1—Whiskey, 0.

Or, er, maybe more like half and half.

The butler waltzes back into the room and trades our soup bowls for the second course like this is a totally normal dinner service and two of his charges aren't yelling at each other.

A pile of herbed mashed potatoes covers a chunky stew, the beef so tender it disintegrates on my fork. Rosemary and garlic explode over my tongue, creamy butter from the potatoes, a savory-umami symphony from the stew.

Fucking hell, why is their food so good?

They're the enemy. This should taste like dirt but I'm making a mental note to ask Renee to incorporate more Irish fare into our meals and I hate tipsy me for being a food whore.

We eat in silence. Again.

Utensils clink.

The butler refills our glasses and I am truly winded by how much whiskey Loch is putting away; meanwhile, I had two glasses, piled in meat and potatoes, and the edges of the room are still carouseling. At least he doesn't make his every sip a challenge. Only when *I* drink does he need to show off.

Last course. Finally. Dessert, crumbly shortbread with a martini glass of something brown and creamy.

"Is this . . . chocolate milk?" I can't help but ask.

Siobhán starts to answer when Loch jumps in with, "Yeah. Chocolate milk. For the shortbread."

He's obviously lying. They wouldn't poison me. Would they?

Fine. Whatever it is, it can't be worse than the whiskey.

I pick up the martini glass and, holding his gaze, I chug it in three quick swallows.

More whiskey.

It's Irish cream.

Loch sips his glass delicately with a wicked leer. "Sorry, boyo. *Irish* chocolate milk."

I sit there for a second, trying to guess how much whiskey was in there, then, a beat later, *feeling* how much whiskey was in there.

The room is a little brighter, a little warmer, a little spinnier.

"Fuck me," I groan to my plate.

Loch doesn't hesitate. "Only if you say please."

That warmth intensifies, the spin gyrates more.

All that sugar and whiskey and my sensitive reaction to alcohol? I am going to be hungover tomorrow.

And then run a 5k.

Awesome. Just. Fan-fucking-tastic.

And I haven't asked any of my esteemed fellow diners a question even adjacent to finding out if they might be the one stealing joy from us. No, I've been too busy picking at Loch and getting properly sloshed.

Well. Today has been a comedy of errors, hasn't it?

Somewhere in my soul, my guilt grows several more roots, but I won't feel it until tomorrow morning. I'm locked in this state of suspended sensation and I really should drink more whiskey. All the noise in my head is . . . muffled. Like the alcohol is holding a pillow over my self-contempt's face.

Distantly, I can hear that self-contempt screaming to pull myself together, but oh no, I can't make out what it's saying, how tragic.

Loch slams his hands on the table and shoots to his feet. I flinch so hard it's a full convulsion.

"I'll show our guest to his room," he tells his sisters.

Finn's eyebrows leap up. "Are you sure?"

"Dead on. We'll be fine."

"We will? Ha." I press my fingers into my temples. "He's going to throw me into the moat, isn't he?"

"No." Finn smirks icily. "Only because we do na have a moat."

I laugh. And have a disconnected thought that they could kill me, very easily, right now. The three of them. Maybe the butler'll help.

Siobhán smiles at me again, pleadingly. "He will na throw you anywhere. Will you, Loch?"

Loch presses a hand to his chest. "On my honor, he will live to see the race. I would na deny myself the chance to beat the Christmas Prince."

"It's a *family fun run*," Siobhán enunciates. "Remember. *Fun*. We'll be seeing you tomorrow, Kris. It was lovely to meet you."

She stands in tandem with Finn, so I mirror them, hands planted on the table as the room goes upside down then right back up.

Holy shit, Irish whiskey is strong. Do they know how strong it is? They should warn people about how strong it is.

Siobhán leans over the table, that conspiratorial glint back in her eye, and I decide I like her, that she couldn't possibly be the one to screw over Christmas. Her brother got all the severity and dickishness; she's pure sunlight.

"For what it's worth," she whispers, not low enough to be private, "I thought the tinsel was right funny."

"Siobhán!" Finn smacks her arm.

"What?" Her grin scrunches her nose. "No one ever gets to take the piss out of Lochy."

He looks like he wants to dump the rest of his Irish cream on his youngest sister's head.

"Leaving. *Now*." Finn grabs Siobhán's arm, and they both press kisses to Loch's cheeks as they funnel out of the dining room.

Loch stays rooted against the table. Maybe he's drunk too, just hiding it well.

"Lochy," I mimic Siobhán.

Me saying it is even more hilarious than her saying it, and I splutter laughter as Loch's eyelids pulse.

Loch leads me out of the dining room and I pad along silently, not trusting myself to speak again. It's hard enough to walk without toppling into side tables as he winds us through the castle.

The lights are low, the walls dabbled stucco with that heavy cherry-red wood stretching in beams across the ceiling. Occasional tapestries show scenes of Irish history and landscapes, the stone floor covered in mismatched antique rugs, making the castle cozier than Claus Palace. Homier. Like everyone who lives here is required to sit in front of a roaring fire and read for a few hours a day, and I definitely don't hate that idea.

"That was Colm," says Loch. "If you need anything, ask him. Do na bother me."

The butler. "Colm. Got it." And then, plowing through my rapidly degrading filter, "Where's everyone else?"

"Eh?"

"Your staff. For St. Patrick's Day? Shouldn't there be other people getting ready for—"

"We do na have other staff." He faces forward, and I push a little faster to walk alongside him.

"Is this St. Patrick's Day's base of operations?"

"Mm."

"Then . . . you don't have anyone helping you bring a whole Holiday to the world?" I let my disbelief show.

Something passes over Loch's face, a flicker of tangled emotions until he lands on derision.

"Nah, boyo." He sneers. "That's what the leprechauns are for."

The toe of my shoe gets caught on a perfectly flat plane of carpet. "Lepre—excuse me?"

"Leprechauns. They're the ones running the show."

All Hex's eerie Halloween shit churns against my drunkenness to severely screw with my head.

Sweat prickles on the back of my neck. "You—you're joking. You're joking? Shit, I'm drunk." I squish my eyes together and suck in a deep breath like that'll purge my veins of this gunk, but when I look back up at Loch, his grin is ripe and wild.

The hall around us is spinning, but his smile is a fixed point.

"Of course I'm joking," he huffs. "You got elves prancing about the North Pole?"

"No. That would be ridiculous. Obviously." *Thank god.*

Silence falls, and I'm reminded that I got exactly *nothing* out of this night, no hint at who might be behind Christmas's stolen joy, and ah, there my self-hatred is, finally rising up through the alcohol in a shattering fragment.

I scratch my forehead as Loch takes a left. "That's something Christmas and St. Patrick's Day have in common, then."

He looks at me like I'm a moron. Which is fair in this moment. "Not having legendary creatures? Rather sure that's what all Holidays have in common."

"Yeah. Well. I—" I'm trying to transition into what *else* Christmas and St. Patrick's Day might share, like, I don't know, *joy*—not the smoothest transition.

We pass a room, the doors thrown open. Loch heads up a staircase across from it without pausing.

I, however, come to a full stop.

My body is all limp and tingling. My brain, a fogged mess.

I step into that room, drawn like a magnet, and the breath gets vacuumed out of my lungs.

"This," I say, not even sure if he followed me in, "is your library?"

Holy.

Actual.

Fuck.

The library in Claus Palace is my favorite room in the place, the overlap of a ski lodge during a blizzard and a lounge in a cottage.

But this room? It can't even be called a room. It's the Cambridge Library gone full medieval fantasy. It's all the best elements of castle grandeur thrown into a blender with thousands, *thousands* of old leather volumes and newer glistening spines organized into wrapping tiers of balcony shelves that stretch two, three, *four* stories above me. Night is falling fast so the few massive iron-paneled windows I can see from here do little to light the space, but that makes it even more impressive, gothic accents hanging in the shadows and hidden corners.

"Yeah," Loch confirms behind me.

"This is your library." I whirl on him. "What were you doing in Cambridge's library?"

He jerks back. "Studying. Or I was trying to."

"You could have been using magic to hop over to *this* whenever you wanted, and you chose a study room like *that*? What is wrong with you?"

Loch's shoulders stiffen. "Do *you* use Christmas's magic to fund your study sessions? Christ, Mary, and Joseph, you wasteful bloody arsehole."

"*I'm* the asshole? I'm not the one who hunkered down in that room *illicitly* when I had literal *paradise* in my *house*."

The abruptness of being in a room like this while well past tipsy absolutely *wrecks* my barriers, letting a tidal surge of emotion through.

This is how I felt when I stepped into Cambridge's library my first year and had an entirely different major lined up alongside a naive resolve to do something for *me*.

Wonder.

That's the feeling.

Like all these books hold possibilities and if I pick the right one, I'll get swept away somewhere better and *righter* and truer.

I tear my hands through my hair, yanking it out of the topknot, letting it hang down loose and messy because an ache is rising up the back of my head. I tug at my damn tie and manage to get it undone enough that I can take my first non-gasping breath since Wren forced me into it hours ago.

"Fuck." I spin back to Loch. "Just—whatever. Where's my room?" I need to lie down. I need to not be—not be in *here,* with these books, with these little slivers of potential I gave up.

When was the last time I wrote something that wasn't a school paper or stuff for Christmas? When was the last time I read something that wasn't a research text?

Oh my god I hate whiskey so much.

But Loch doesn't move, studying me in the light that has fully shifted into blurry nighttime gray.

He pulls out his phone and switches on the flashlight. "C'mon."

And he heads off, not back out into the hall, but deeper into the library.

I hesitate.

Then follow the flashing of his phone's light.

He doesn't go far before he stops beneath the wrapping balcony. With the hostility of someone who would rather be hurling breakable objects at a wall, he yanks books off a shelf and shoves them into my chest.

I stagger, make a cradle of my arms, and he piles books in it.

"What are—"

"You're gonna be down here anyway, yeah? And I know in that fancy-ass international relations track that they sure as hell are na having you lot read good shite."

My mind cartwheels over the fact that he knows what track I'm in. But I know what track he's in too. Shut up, whiskey.

"So if you're gonna use *my* library." He grabs one last book, adds it to the pile, but doesn't let go of it, hovering over me in the yellow-white beam of his flashlight. "You gotta read the literature that matters."

I glance down at the spines, willing my spinning eyes to focus. "Oscar Wilde. William Butler Yeats. Bram Stoker."

"Irish—"

"Irish authors. I know. I was in the English track for a term."

I hear the words. Feel their echo.

And go impossibly still.

I never told anyone I did that. Not even Coal. He assumed that I was always in International Relations because Dad forced me to, and I never corrected him.

And I just admitted the truth to *Lochlann Patrick,* of all people.

So when Loch asks, hesitantly, "Why'd you switch?" he's close enough that his exhale billows across my cheeks.

I shove the books into his chest. "None of your business."

He pushes them right back. "The payment stands—you wanna use this library while you're here, you read these authors."

Fury rages. Bright. Piercing. And I remember every second of that term I spent in the English track. I remember why I *stopped* being in it, why I stopped writing, not because Cambridge consumed my time, but because—

Ah hell. *I do not think about this.* Ever. It's done. It's *over.* I have my whole real life lined up now—helping Coal with Christmas, being an ambassador, fulfilling these duties, so on and so forth, I don't need to think about that other shit.

But Lochlann. Fucking. Patrick.

Is standing here in this amazing library, trying to guilt me into reading these books with a smugness that's a permanent fixture on his face.

"Ah yes, the superiority of classics?" I snarl. "No other books are worthy? You aren't a true writer if you haven't read and loved these pinnacles of human creation? Stick them up your ass. Where's my room?"

Loch lurches back. Something on my face must finally break through his pomposity, because he snatches the books from me.

His expression fades to resigned annoyance and he drops the books on a table. "You're an ungrateful arse."

"I really don't care."

But he keeps studying me. He's frowning but doesn't look as pissed as he should, and the energy is—different. Like he's trying to work something out.

Without another word, he cuts around me to head through the library.

I follow, scowling at his back as we leave and file up the staircase.

On the second floor, after ducking down another long, dark hall, Loch shoves open a door.

"Here," is all he says before he marches away.

His silhouette fades into the shadows.

I push into the room and slam the door.

Pretentious *prick.*

My eyes barely see the room. It's small, a lamp on in the corner, my suitcase propped on a bench by an armoire. A canopy bed is arranged for the night and my brain picks that moment to go *leprechauns did the turn-down service* and I shiver at that horror movie image.

Alone, silence pressing in from all sides, my self-hatred rises up again, along with its ever-obnoxious friend, guilt.

I made a mess of my first night here, didn't I?

I dig my phone out of my pocket. There are a few missed texts— from Wren, chastising me in a mildly passive aggressive way for going rogue with the apology, and I manage to ignore my wince; but most are in the group chat with Coal and Iris, both of them asking me how it went.

I hit a video call with Coal before realizing I have no idea what time it is. It's after ten here, so what time is it at home? Ireland is ahead. Time zone math—

The call connects, showing the hazy outline of Coal in shadows. "Hang on, we're in the theater room. Sweetheart, can you get the light?" It pops on. "Thank *youuuu*. Okay. What's up?"

He takes one look at me and bolts upright in a black recliner. I can see other empty ones around him, so I'm assuming it's just him and Hex watching a movie. That I interrupted.

Ah, hello, guilt, there's always room for more of you.

"What's wrong?" Coal asks. "You're a mess."

I catch sight of my image in the self-view screen and yeah. *Mess* is accurate. Hair all disheveled. Eyes bloodshot.

"Sorry." I rub my face. "I should've texted first."

"The interruption is much appreciated, honestly," says Hex off screen. "Coal picked this show and I am regretting every second of it."

"I picked it for *you*! No, wait, Kris—what happened?"

I give the simplest answer. "Irish whiskey."

Coal gawks at me, so motionless I think the screen froze.

He snorts. "You idiot."

Hex drops onto the chair beside him. "You need me to leave?"

"No, no." But Coal looks at me, eyebrows twisting. "No?"

"No." I press my fingers into my eyes. "Actually. Never mind. Go back to your date." I start to hang up, but Coal waves his hand over the screen.

"Woah! Wait a hot second—tell me how it went. Even in those press shots, you and Lochlann looked like you wanted to give each other Colombian neckties."

Hex writhes in the chair. "*Coal.*"

"Colombian what now?" I ask.

Coal grins, cheeky. "We're watching *Hannibal.* Colombian necktie. Throat sliced, tongue pulled through. Necktie."

Hex mimes gagging. "This is the last time you ever get to decide what we watch."

My eyebrows pop at the half of Hex's face that I can see. "*You* are grossed out by *Hannibal?*"

"Right?" Coal jostles Hex's shoulder. "I picked it because here I thought *oh look, I can bond over a love of horror with my boyfriend, the Crown Prince of Halloween,* only to find out that *someone is squeamish.*"

Hex blushes. "Just because something falls under a general Halloween purview does not mean that I am required to enjoy it. I am far more of a thriller and jump-scares person."

"Your court will revolt."

"Oh yes, people are known to be furious when it's discovered that their leader does *not* enjoy watching people get maimed."

"Huh." I chew on my tongue. Which is a little numb. Which explains why everything I say feels pillowy. *Woooo,* alcohol. "Hex doesn't like horror. That's good to know."

Hex's attention pivots from Coal to me.

I smirk at him and his eyes narrow, but not enough to hide the laughter in them.

Coal yanks the phone away until I only see his face. "Don't use this knowledge to torment him."

"This is how Hex and I have bonded, Coal, and I finally have ammo. You can't take this away from me."

"Nuh-uh, we aren't getting off track anymore. Tell me how it went tonight."

Damn it.

He sits forward. "Wren said you and Prince Lochlann were *clearly uncomfortable in each other's presence.* And the photos that have already posted . . . *uncomfortable* is generous. The press seems to be buying what you're selling, but good god, dude, how do you suck at acting so much? You've been there, what, five hours?"

"Four and a half."

"Four and a half. And you look like *that* already?"

I hear the concern in his voice, and I know my brother—he isn't saying this accusingly. But I can't help the tug of shame that's more sobering than an IV of espresso.

"I'm sorry. I let Loch get to me. I didn't—"

"Loch, huh?"

My face gets warm. Er. Warm*er*.

"Are you friends now?" Coal presses.

"*No.*"

"But you're using a nickname."

"His sister told me to. He agreed. He's calling me *Kris*. This isn't that big of a deal."

Is my voice shrill?

"It *feels* like a big deal," says Coal. "You're yelling."

"I AM NOT—" I catch myself. Breathe. "I am not yelling."

"Okay, I'm confused. You're confused?" Coal asks Hex, who squishes close so he's in the screen again. "We're confused. Walk us through what happened. You get to St. Patrick's Day. Lochlann— *Loch*—greets you. Pictures in the foyer. You apologize—which, loved that video of the apology, by the way; I do *not* remember that many adjectives in your draft—then . . ."

I sit on the bed and fill in the rest. The dinner, the food, which was definitely the highlight; Loch's inability to have a single conversation that doesn't revolve around himself; then the library, his pretentious Irish classics; then—

"Wait." Coal is lying back now, his head on Hex's shoulder. "He saw you were interested in the library. And even after you guys screamed at each other during dinner, he showed you his favorite books?"

I yank my tie fully off and let it snake to the floor. "So?"

"*So* it sounds like he was trying to connect."

"No. There was some ulterior motive. You weren't there, you

haven't met him. He *exudes* this manipulative bullshit energy and I'm not having any of it." I sway as the drunkenness gets tired of fighting my self-reproach and gives up in favor of exhaustion. "But I'm sorry. I'll be better now, more prepared to field him. I won't keep dropping the ball and letting him get to me."

Coal shifts to give Hex a look I can't see.

"What?" I pull the phone closer. "What was that?"

"Nothing."

"That look wasn't nothing."

"I like looking at Hex. Don't climb all over me about it."

I might be crossing into paranoia territory.

"But"—Coal sucks in a breath—"you could get further in your investigation if you aren't constantly attacking him. You don't have to actively buy into his bullshit, but remember, *lie*."

This is all stuff I knew going in. I was *ready* to lie my ass off; I *knew* Loch unsettled me last time we met, so I should've been even more prepared.

Instead, I not only let him get to me, I let myself get drunk.

"It's still early here," I try. "I can fix this. I'll get answers tonight."

"No—Kris. I love you. Go to bed. You're drunk and tired."

"I'm fine. Totally sober. Never been more alert in my life."

Coal rolls his eyes. "Of course. You're a picture of angelic grace. And since you're so consumed by angelic grace right now, I'm going to tell you what to do, and you will *gracefully* obey me. One, you're going to *stop drinking whiskey, you lightweight dumbass.* Two, you're going to lay down and go to *sleep.* Three, you're going to pretend that anytime Lochlann speaks, all you hear are choirs of little kids singing Catholic hymns. Four, you're going to go to *sleep.*"

My eyes are shut and yeah, it'd be easy to lie back in the pillows, but I stay upright. "You said the last one already."

"It bears repeating."

"Mm."

A pause.

Coal sighs. "You're not going to listen to me, are you?"

I pretend to be tipping over onto the bed. "Falling asleep already. Can't talk. Love you. Good night."

Coal barely gets out a "Don't think you can—" before I hang up.

And because my inhibitions are still lowered, I pull up the text thread with Iris.

I started messaging her again after seeing her in Coal's office, but it's only been in response to her texts, nothing I've initiated yet.

Now, I flip over to some of the links Wren sent of the tabloid sites with their shots of Loch and me from earlier today.

Yeah. Wow. I do look miserable. Smiling, but my eyes are screaming, *Kill me*.

I scroll down, screenshot a pic of Loch, and send it to Iris.

IRIS
I never sent you his picture—he's a prick, but here, character study. How many googly eyes do you think it'd take to recreate those motherfucking cheekbones

IRIS
well look who's coming back into our little game with a ringer

On second thought, his ego definitely doesn't need to be fluffed any bigger.

She's quiet for a long time. Well, maybe like a minute or two, but I watch the ellipses pop up and go away and pop up again.

IRIS
hmmmmmm

i'll get to work adding prince lochlann to my character study sheet

get some sleep monsieur
ambassador

> Why does everyone keep
> telling me to do that?

What was that unnecessarily long *hmmm* for?

This whole day has left me swaggeringly exhausted, but there's no way I'll sleep more than a few hours tonight, if that. Coal and Iris don't know what they're talking about.

I mute my phone and dig a T-shirt out of my bag, a bright green one that says *100% That Grinch* in swirling red script. When I change, I immediately feel better.

Throwing back two preemptive ibuprofen dry so Tomorrow Kris doesn't hate Tonight Kris too much, I slip out into the hall.

I came here with a job. And goddammit, I'm going to do my fucking job.

That's all that matters.

Chapter Five

It's pitch black in the hall. No sounds come from any direction, so either everyone's gone to bed or Loch and his sisters live in a different wing. I vaguely remember the route he took to get me here from the dining room, but there were other passages that branched off, and a place like this has to be full of secret doorways and hidden shit.

I pull my phone out to hit the flashlight and swivel it up and down the hall.

Okay. Where would I put the joy meter or the king's office in a castle? Either is likely to have proof that they're stealing from us. Down, maybe? Basement. Dungeon levels. The most secure areas.

I head back down the stairs, shoes tapping on the stone steps. The library doors are still open, every bit of every hall I pass through drenched in darkness, and it hits me again how empty it is here, this massive place. And it's *freezing*—I hadn't noticed, but in my T-shirt I feel the full brunt of March in Ireland in a stone castle.

I shiver as I try doors on the first level, looking for a route to the basement. A few sitting rooms, a closet. One finally reveals a set of dark stairs that twist downward, looking so much like something out of a slasher movie that I go rock solid.

I hiss at myself and descend.

But I leave the door open behind me. Just in case.

Each step down has the temperature plummeting until I swear I can see my breath in the flashlight beam, goosebumps listing in waves up my arms and down my neck.

The stairs end at a long, echoing stone hall. And I hear . . . something.

A pulse. A haunting, echoing *thump-thump*.

My brain, of course, goes *It's a heart. They have a heart buried in the walls. Loch went Edgar Allan Poe on this place and that's sacrilege because Poe isn't even one of his precious Irish authors.*

But the beat congeals into music. Base heavy and pounding.

I follow it, keeping my steps quiet, and the farther I go up the hall, the louder the music grows until I don't worry about making noise. Any sound is being swallowed in "Iris" by the Goo Goo Dolls blaring from an open door on the right. White light spills out, cutting in a single rectangle through this dungeon gloom.

I turn my flashlight off, pocket my phone, and, breath held, I peek around the doorframe.

High ceilings tower over paint-splattered tarps on the floor. There's a canvas propped on the far side of the room, an absolutely *enormous* square at least eight feet tall with folded ladders leaning in the corner next to it. Various shades of red, orange, and green paint are smeared across the canvas in the haphazard organization of abstract art. A space heater gently raises the temperature of the room and the warmth licks at my face.

Loch is in front of that canvas, paint palette in one hand, using his thumb to stroke a line of vivid orange against a swoosh of red near the middle. His head bobs to the music, muscles in his back flexing.

He's shirtless.

And I glare daggers at the sculpted lines of his shoulders.

Of course he's jacked. It isn't enough that he's a prick; he has to have the body to match his self-esteem. Though I'm one to talk, I suppose, what with how I intentionally buy these Christmas shirts too small because yeah, okay, I spend a lot of time in the gym pretending that lifting weights alleviates my stress and I might as well show that off. How have I not seen him working out at Cambridge? I'm there often enough to—

I lean too far forward and hit the edge of the open door so it bangs into the wall.

Loch whips around with a panicked "*JESUS FUCKING SHITE.*"

Any other time, I'd laugh at how I got *another* one of those out of him, but I'm caught in the doorway of his studio with my arms splayed.

Loch flings the palette to the floor. "What is your problem? Jesus Christ, sneaking up on me like that."

He's defensive, voice shaky, and I'm shaky too, not having planned for any of this.

"I—" I clear my throat and take a single step into the room. "I was looking for Colm. You said to go to him if I needed anything but you didn't tell me where he is."

"Colm's on the same floor as you." Loch's talking too fast, voice unsteady. "Two lefts from your door. Only room in that hall. What do you need him for this late? Gotta have someone telling you a bedtime story?"

Don't take the bait. Don't. Do. It. "Anticipatory hangover cures."

Loch scrubs the back of his hand across his chin. It leaves a trail of red paint on the cliff of his jaw, streaked through his short beard. Matching smudges are all down his chest, his gray sweatpants as splattered as the tarp under his bare feet.

My gaze bounces up to his, cheeks heating. I wasn't—*looking* at him. I'm tipsy. And exhausted.

But he shakes his head, not paying that any mind. "And your first thought was *Oh, they store their help in the basement?*"

"I . . . heard the music."

Loch's head tips, like it hadn't occurred to him that anyone outside this room could hear his music blasting.

His eyes roll shut at some realization. "Useless magic."

I perk up. "What?"

But instead of answering, he looks at me again, and it's . . . different. That same pull of realization, but with a shadow of dread.

"You heard the music. It brought you here," he clarifies.

"What does this have to do with useless magic?"

C'mon, tell me you're stealing from us. Admit it and make this easier for us both.

Loch grabs a spray bottle from a side table and mists an area on his painting, pumping the nozzle more aggressively than needed.

"St. Patrick's Day's magic," he says. "It's useless. *Luck.*" He clicks his tongue in distaste. "Which I've always thought was a xenophobic attribute for our Holiday's magic to assimilate, *luck of the Irish* and all, but Siobhán's certain it leads us to *where we need to go.* As if luck canna be *bad* too." He waves at me. "As displayed."

I absorb this, mind switching gears noisily. "So—you—you're saying your magic made me hear your music so I'd come to you? That's what you were talking about?"

Loch puts the spray bottle back on the table. "I'm saying my headphones broke this morning, so I had to blast my music like this and now—you're here."

I scoff. "There's no possible chance your headphones broke because electronics do that sometimes and I happened to hear your loud-ass music?"

His aggravation deadens his stare. "Fine. Take the piss."

"Are you sure your magic isn't narcissism instead of luck?"

He turns to his canvas with a muttered "Arsehole."

I smirk at the back of his head.

Then hear Coal telling me that maybe Loch will be more forthcoming if I'm not attacking the shit out of him.

I'm usually way better at prioritizing what Coal needs me to do. Loch's ability to derail me is getting a little ridiculous.

Holiday magic manifests in increasingly bizarre ways, influenced by the beliefs and traditions people create as they celebrate. So, sure, it's possible Loch's magic could manipulate his life in terms of luck.

And if it's *bad* luck for Loch that led me here, then it should be *good* luck for me, right? Maybe his magic's pissed at him for stealing Christmas's.

The Goo Goo Dolls drone on in the proceeding silence.

I stuff my hands in my pockets. "An American band? After your display in the library, I thought it'd be all Irish, all the time."

That's not much less confrontational than mocking his luck magic.

He glances back at me and his lip understandably curls. "I'm not a monolith, ya wanker."

Like the Halloween Prince not liking horror. Still need to figure out how to use that to my advantage.

The song ends.

And immediately switches to "With or Without You" by U2.

I can't help the shitty grin that rolls across my face.

Loch blushes from the edge of his beard to his hairline, his kick of embarrassment reforming his face into the closest to sincere I've seen on him yet.

My smile reels back. A fraction less shitty.

"That was . . . poor timing." He clears his throat and crosses the room to punch off the sound system.

Silence drops with a heavy thud, the stone walls aching with the absence of noise.

Loch clears his throat again and messes with an area near the speaker—a sink, a cupboard, supplies stacked precariously along a paint-splattered concrete counter.

He shifts back with a glass of water and gets close enough to shove it at me.

Orange freckles decorate his torso. His arms. Like the droplets of paint sprinkled on the tarp.

"The start of any good whiskey cure," he tells me.

My nose curls at the paint-smeared glass. "I'm good."

"Do na go waking up Colm for him to bring you a glass of water. Take it."

"There has to be a better cure than water."

"How much have you had? Water?"

I lick my teeth. "Two ibuprofen."

Loch pushes the glass closer. "Proper nice that'll be on your stomach. *Drink.*"

I snatch the glass from Loch and take a gulp. When I swallow, I wave at my face. "Happy? Jesus."

"My lot in life is fulfilled."

I smack my lips. "It tastes like paint."

"It's acrylic. Ya won't die." But he chuckles. "Although, given your proven delicate constitution, you might be keeling over in a wee bit."

I weigh my options. Then chug the rest of it, dare accepted.

His eyes lower from mine, and I think *ah, yes, I've won . . . something,* until I realize he's watching my throat.

His awareness there is abruptly tactile, making my muscles jump with electric pulses.

I lower the glass.

He flinches and moves away to snatch up his paint palette.

I grimace at him as I cross over and dump the empty glass in the sink. He left streaks of paint on the cup that are now on my fingers, but there isn't a single paint-free towel to be found, so I settle for scraping my hand on my pants.

When I turn back for the door, the angle of the canvas changes enough that it catches my eyes.

I stop.

"Did ya need something else, then?" Loch bites, his back to me.

"That's—a face?"

He gets a posture I recognize, the grip of wanting to hide art. I feel that way whenever Coal looks over my shoulder while I'm writing. Like part of your soul is laid out, and you wouldn't mind sharing it one day, but in that moment, it hasn't grown a protective shell yet.

But his canvas is the size of a wall, so there's no hiding it, and Loch relents with a drawn-out sigh. "Yeah. 'Tis."

My eyes follow the flow of the paint blotches, the rhythm of the red and orange and the contrasting green. It's a woman looking over her shoulder with a wide, joyful smile, eyes round and glittering.

"Who is she?" I ask.

I can feel Loch's stare on the side of my face. My attention falls to him.

He's fuming. "None of your business. Yeah?"

It's what I said to him in the library.

Don't constantly attack him, I hear in my brother's voice.

"I'm sorry. I shouldn't have gotten defensive earlier. You were trying to be . . . nice. Maybe. I shouldn't have snubbed your favorite authors."

Loch's brows shoot up. "Those were na my favorite authors."

"But you—"

"I assumed you had na read a lick of Irish literature. Wasn't about to let you be both a prick and an eejit."

"Oh yes." I bare my teeth. "Three years at Cambridge and I'm still considered an idiot."

"There's knowledge and then there's education, boyo."

Loch extends his palette to me.

There's about two yards between us, so I give him a confused look.

"You paint?" he asks.

"Ha. No. I have a friend who does and I leave that sort of artistic expression to her."

"Nah, that's true—you said writing, eh?"

My face falls, mind flying back through everything I said in the library.

Fuck. I let that bit of information slip too. Just dumping all my secrets on this guy, aren't I?

Loch pulls the palette back to himself and waves at the canvas. "It's part of a series I've been doing for a final project. *Portraits of Ireland.*"

I'm more grateful than I can say that he didn't make me expand on the writing thing, but hell if I show him that. I nod up at the painting. "So who is she?"

"Not a clue. Saw her in Cork last year. She had this . . . light about her." He drags his hand through the air, encompassing the untouchable. "Wanted to capture it. Joy like that is the point of all this, eh?"

He eyes me again, and the challenge this time isn't *Come at me bro*; it's deeper than that.

This is likely the longest we've gone without yelling at each other. I want to point out that it's because I'm choosing to be the bigger guy, but I don't, and that feeds into my pride of being the bigger guy, and I'm stuck in an ego-loop.

"All this? You mean your Holiday?"

One half of Loch's lips cuts up. "Surprised I give a shite?"

"Not really. I'm reserving having an opinion about who you are in relation to St. Patrick's Day until I find out for sure. Fuck the rumors."

His tension goes to suspicion. "The hell you on about?"

"What? Nothing."

"You're being awful pleasant."

"You're mad that I'm not being a dick to you?"

"A bit."

"You're certifiable. I'm trying to be civil. Can *you* be civil?"

"I can be perfectly fucking civil."

"So can I."

"Well, awful good, then." He holds the palette back out to me. "Paint."

"What?"

"We're being perfectly fucking civil. And this is a perfectly fucking civil thing to do."

"I will screw up your painting."

"Impossible. It's abstract impressionism."

"Oh, okay, that makes perfect sense." That means nothing to me. "Why?"

His eyes go up and down my body. Not fast enough that he's trying to hide it, not slow enough to be suggestive.

It pins me in place. A transitory statue moment, like I'm allowing him to look at me.

"You can tell a lot about someone by the way they do art," he says. "I wanna see what kind of person you really are."

"How will I see what kind of person *you* really are?"

Loch's smile is ferocious. "Nah, you owe me first. Maybe this is why my magic brought you down here." He steps closer, palette extended. "Paint."

Stubbornness wends around us.

Fine. It's his art at risk here. I have nothing to lose.

I grab the palette and dip two fingers into the orange paint. "If I screw up your painting, remember, you made me do this."

"There's no wrong way to paint."

I step up to the canvas. Most of the white where I can reach easily is covered, but a few clean bits poke through. I have no idea what the intention behind those blank spaces is, but I choose one at eye level and put my fingers on it. Two dots of orange are left behind.

"Jesus, Mary, and Joseph," Loch hisses behind me. "You love proving me wrong, eh?"

"What?"

"*That* is the wrong way to paint."

"Oh, piss off."

"You made two *dots* in a flow that's all curves and motion."

"Well, maybe I'm more artistic than you." I wave up at the rest of the canvas. "There's too *much* curve and motion. You need something solid."

"Back up."

"What?"

"*Back up,* boyo. What's the first thing you see now?"

I take a few steps back, fingers coated in paint, palette level on my other hand.

My eyes immediately go to those two dots. It's all I can see. Two dead spots in palpitating, dancing waves.

I roll my eyes and return to the canvas. The dots are almost dry already; I scoop up more paint and try to add a curve over them that matches the rest.

It does not match the rest.

It's somehow just a line.

More paint on my fingers, I reach forward again as Loch stomps up behind me.

"Christ, you are wrecking it." He wipes his hand off on his sweatpants and grabs my shoulder, the arm I'm using to paint.

I whip a glare back at him. "What are you doing?"

"Relax. You're too stiff. It's translating. The paint can feel your stress."

"I'm not stressed." But I growl it through my teeth, so that kind of negates it.

His eyes hold on mine. "Must be some other reason you're tenser than stone."

"I work out a lot. I was hoping you'd notice."

Loch sighs, exasperated. "Course you would. Preening like a fucker."

That was almost the exact thought I'd had about him and his physique.

It shocks the hell out of me when I laugh.

Catches him off guard, too. His eyebrows pinch and he looks all over my face, a quick sweep, searching. Analyzing? I feel suddenly like a portrait subject.

He clears his throat and juts his chin at the canvas. "You're gonna fix this. Now *relax.*"

His thumb pries into my shoulder, and I can feel under his strength exactly how stiff I am. I always know, I always have a headache on the precipice of splitting up my skull, but he hits a spot and my eyes bulge. My hand sags and I roll my wrist, stretch my fingers.

God, that's good.

Wait. What the—

Loch reaches in front of me with his paint covered hand. The curve of each fingernail is caked in it, something more permanent than the splotches on the rest of his skin, like he paints so much it's an enduring part of his body now. Those fingers shake, but I could be imagining that, maybe my eyesight is still a little whiskey-loopy; or maybe I'm the one rocked, not sure why he's standing so close. And touching me.

Or why he's wrapping his hand around mine where it's lifted in the air.

His other hand keeps pushing into my shoulder, thumb kneading that one knot like he'll force it to submit. Warmth hits me, not the space heater, but *him,* a velvet frisson that carries the scent I now attribute to him, that rich, spicy cologne with a sharp chemical smell—which must be paint-related, sealant or varnish. All of it this time is battling with a whiff of exertion sweat, and I realize I'm holding an inhale like I'm dissecting his scent.

I exhale forcefully through my nose.

The angle puts his face right next to the shell of my ear. His voice goes limp when he orders, "Relax for me, boyo."

But *relaxing* is out of my capabilities at the moment. Hell, even *thinking* is out of my capabilities at the moment.

I'm stagnant. A morbidly fascinated spectator in my own body as I let him put my fingers back on that orange line. He drags my hand down, bends it, knuckles twisting, until we milk the line into an arch that flows with the rest.

"There," he says. It doesn't have his expected croon of victory or his usual pompous control. I can both hear and feel the scratch of his words like they're struggling to roll out of his throat. "Was that so hard, now?"

I'm staring at the curve we made.

Not at his hand cupping mine, both lifted in front of me. And I'm not fiercely aware of his other hand vise-gripped on my shoulder. Or the curl of his breath on the underside of my jaw.

I'm not aware of any of those things because I'm hovering outside all this, watching, drowsy with thoughtlessness.

Loch strokes his fingers down the back of my hand, leaving trails of mixed orange-red-green.

My head slants towards him. A robotic motion. I stop there, the full scald of his exhale burning my cheek.

And he steps away.

A ruthless knot ties deep in my stomach and wrenches me back into my body, stiffness returning to my shoulders and neck.

I drop my arm to my side, hand in a fist.

I'm exhausted. On the razor-thin edge between drunk and hung-over. Having come off a day of emotional volleyball. *Because of him.*

Coal's insistence that I go to sleep makes a lot more sense now. I had no business trekking around the castle in this condition.

I'm crushingly aware of Loch behind me, his miring gaze on the back of my head.

But he barks, "Now get to bed, boyo."

"Bed?" is the only thing that comes out of my mouth.

"When I beat you in the race tomorrow"—his voice is a little rough—"I do na want it to be because you're tired and hungover. I want it to be because I'm better than you."

The paint from his fingers is drying on the back of my hand.

I should snap back at him. But I don't. I'm being the bigger person. That's right. I'm choosing not to take his bait.

I keep my eyes on the floor as I crouch to set his palette on the tarp. "Yeah. See you tomorrow."

"And drink more water."

That jars my defensiveness when I'm a foot from the door. I don't look at him, but my lip curls, and all I can think to say is a childish "Make me."

Real smooth.

I know he's smirking at me. I *know* he's smirking.

I bolt back into the frigid dark of the castle's basement hall like plunging into an icy lake, a crash of sensation-shift, hot to cold. I stagger, catch myself on a corner in the dark.

That was . . . weird. Right?

That was weird.

He did this to throw me off, didn't he? Was this another power play?

But it . . . why did it *work*?

Oh, I am in no condition to answer that.

I'm going to go to sleep. I'm going to go to sleep, and in the morning, it won't be weird. It'll make sense.

Yeah.

In the morning.

Chapter Six

I do not feel terrible when I wake up the next day. Mild headache, slight nausea, but overall not as shitty as I expected.

I shower in the room's ensuite. The water scalds away most of my headache—until I see the paint on the back of my hand.

My eyes follow the lines of the multicolored strokes.

That whole thing last night had to have been a power play, and I was strung out enough to waltz right into it. He remembered I thought he was hot and used his . . . *hotness* against me. He was in his element, that painting studio; I fell into his hand. Literally.

Well, not today.

I'm halfway through pulling on my running gear—the schedule says to change here, not at the race, then meet in the foyer at eight—when I smell . . . breakfast? Bacon, for sure.

My slight nausea goes *oh-ho, we are not so slight anymore* and rampages up my throat.

I shove my fist against my mouth. For fuck's sake, do not barf before a run.

I follow the noxious fumes to the door, open it, and find a breakfast tray on the threshold.

A quick glance tells me the hall is empty; it's barely six thirty, and while I'd blame my sleeplessness on the time change, it's entirely because I don't really sleep anyway and more passed out in restless turmoil for a handful of hours last night.

I grab the tray, knock the door shut with my hip, and deposit the tray on the desk. It has a pitcher of water and, under a metal cloche, I discover a plate piled with thick-cut bacon, scrambled eggs, scorched tomatoes, mushrooms, and a giant scoop of baked beans.

The smell smashes into me like a battering ram.

I slam the cloche back down and rock over the desk with another gag. "Oh, no—"

There's a note next to the pitcher.

Hangover Cure. DRINK ALL THE WATER.

In that curling, cursive script I recognize from the study room door.

Did he—

Did Loch make me *breakfast?*

I swallow again. Hard.

Sending me this is diabolical.

I am not going to throw up. As long as I get out of this room. Like, right now. God, the smell.

Loch is the actual devil.

I'm the first one in the foyer by a long shot, having to escape my room and all, so I catch up with shit I missed on my phone.

A few texts from Coal, making sure I didn't do anything dumb last night. No comment.

Messages from Wren too, updating me on today's schedule and expectations.

More in the group chat between Coal and Iris, Coal saying how he's started planning for his combined *I am Santa now* slash *announcing the winter Holidays collective* party. Iris jumps in with how her sister hasn't finalized a date for the wedding that was supposed to happen weeks ago between her and the Valentine's Day Prince, but Easter prep is swamping them all anyway, so whenever the Christmas party happens she'll try to *make an appearance.*

Coal's already responded that he'll hold off on any parties until after Easter so Iris can not only be there, but also be *mentally present.*

I assure Wren I'm on top of things—*I'm ready to go early, I'll be on my best behavior; I'll finish up the latest meeting talking points today too, what else can I do?*

Then I fire off a few texts to Coal—*do you need anything for the party; the missing joy hasn't caused problems with the other leaders yet has it?*

I click on the last of my notifications—

—and every hangover symptom intensifies in a sickening furor.

Mom texted me.

A sour tang burns the back of my tongue, head pounding angrily.

It's a photo. The one Coal said he'd gotten from Dad before I left for Ireland, of him and Mom at a pool bar.

MOM

MOM
Kristopher, you obviously didn't see this photo your father sent. If you had, I know you would have responded.

Your brother did not respond either.

Why haven't you spoken to him yet?? You said you would get him to talk to me.

Your father is here. Nicholas is the only one who still refuses to move on. You know how much I love all of you, and you haven't gotten through to him yet.

You are behaving petulantly!!

Why can't you both be happy for me??

My hand shakes, and that shaking travels up my arm.

If I don't acknowledge her, she'll keep texting.

She'll keep texting anyway.

I click on the response window.

Saw the pic. You look happy.

Well, Dad does. Mom looks annoyed, honestly. I don't think I've ever seen her happy in my life.

I pocket my phone before I can see if my message is read, the ache of nausea churning now and my headache on a warpath.

A lifeline comes when footsteps precede someone entering the foyer. Something else to focus on, thank god—

I flick my eyes up too fast. The room rocks violently and I squeeze my eyes shut.

Goddamn headache. Goddamn nausea.

Goddamn texts.

"You have tattoos?" I hear Loch say.

Well. He's a distraction, at least.

I tip my head and squint up at him. No pulse of nausea this time. Baby steps.

He's outfitted for the run too. Black tights, his thumbs hooked in the sleeves of a form-fitting gray fleece hoodie, the color almost the exact shade as his eyes. His beanie is a bright, cheery green with a white shamrock.

I stare at his tights. His sleeves. I've got tights under loose running shorts, but my baggy tank suddenly seems like a dumb idea, given that the 5k is *outside* and it's going to be cold. At least I thought to shove my hair up into my own beanie.

Mine is far superior. It has a T-rex in a Santa hat eating a small group of fleeing elves.

"Yeah?" I roll his words back through my head as I connect the way his rather severe stare is hopping from one of my shoulders to the other. "Oh. Yeah. A few."

Ha, a few. I spend so much time at a tattoo parlor in Cambridge that I should have a plaque on the chair.

The tattoo on my left shoulder is an abstract swirl of black and gray tribal designs. It was my first one, and after I got it, Iris mocked me ruthlessly, saying how if I was going to get art permanently inked on my body, it should be meaningful and not *the same base-ass tribal stuff most gym-rat dudebros get*.

I wasn't even able to argue, because my whole thought process with it had been *Oh, tribal swirls, badass, do it.*

So for my right half-sleeve, I asked Iris to help me with the design. That one has two pine trees set against snow-covered mountains with wrapping script woven through them. I'm half sure she worked her name into the mountain range somewhere, but I've never been able to find it.

Loch leans closer to my right side. *"Once more unto the breach?"* he reads.

Yeah, I should've worn sleeves.

My eyes shut again and I rub the skin over my nose. "The product of the year I started university and had way too much freedom and equally too many emotions about said freedom."

Oh, talking is somehow as bad as looking up quickly.

I bend forward, elbows on my knees, breathing in through my nose, out through my mouth.

Maybe if I get Coal to respond to that photo, she'll—

No. Stop. I don't want him to have to deal with her.

This race is going to suck.

"You look ill," Loch notes.

"Your pillow talk leaves something to be desired, darling."

He kicks my chair and I choke down a heave.

"Fuck off," I moan pathetically.

"Did you eat?"

My nausea now has far less to do with whatever alcohol I had last night, but that comment earns him a full, searing glare. "Hilarious."

"You did na eat? Did you see the tray?"

"Oh, I saw the tray, and your joke was received. What do you want, a medal? You win that round. Now stop talking about food."

"Christ, but you are a gobshite, aren't you?"

"A *what?*"

"A gobshite," a new voice says. Finn, walking into the foyer, trailed by Siobhán. Neither are dressed to run, both bundled up in wool coats and scarves. "A fool. What'd he do now?"

"Canna handle his whiskey and thinks he can do this run on an empty stomach," Loch says.

I cradle my head in my hands. "I'll be fine. Let's *go*."

"You won't be fine. Colm!" Loch ducks out of the foyer.

A different presence hovers over me.

On a deep breath, I stand to face Siobhán.

"He's na trying to hurt you," she promises.

"Eh, maybe a wee bit," Finn adds with a grin.

Loch saunters back in and slams something into my stomach.

My vision goes starry. "Oh my god. I hate you," I choke out.

"Eat this," he orders.

A granola bar, a bag of almonds.

Okay, better than baked beans, but—

"And here." He adds a water bottle into my hands.

"All right, *Mom*."

"I'm serious, Kris. I'll na have you puking in my car."

My brain stutters.

On him saying my name.

And a second time, on *car*. "We're driving to the race?"

"Well, yeah."

"Why not use magic to travel there? It's in *Cork*, isn't it?"

"Mm."

"That's like a two-hour drive from here!"

"Hence the ungodly hour we're up." Finn accepts a travel mug of something steaming that Colm produces. He gives one to Siobhán as well, another to Loch; he has a last one that he tries to hand to me, but Loch snatches it.

"Ah-ah. Food and water first."

One of my hands is outstretched for the coffee, the other holding the food and water bottle to my chest.

"You're denying me caffeine," I state, to be sure I'm understanding what will be put on the police report as my motive.

"Oh, I know how much you love your caffeine, Coffee Shop, but *ya need to eat*. Water too."

Inch by inch, I lift my glare to Loch's face. "Give me. That coffee."

"Eat. Your food." He holds my coffee back far enough that I'd have to basically wrestle him to get it.

Siobhán and Finn watch us like they're at a tennis match. Or the Hunger Games, in Finn's case.

"Fuck you. Fuck you *so much*." I rip open the granola bar and tear off a bite and chew, and gag, and keep chewing until I swallow. The bite miraculously stays down. I unscrew the water bottle and take a few gulps.

I hate that my stomach does feel a little better. "Have I earned my coffee?"

Loch relinquishes it to me, and I'm so desperate for it that I almost miss the way his voice serrates over the words "Good boy."

My body jolts.

A spurt of coffee launches out of the mug's mouthpiece and hits my wrist. The sting of pain from the hot liquid is about a thousand degrees cooler than the gush of napalm that chutes from the base of my skull to my tailbone.

I gape at Loch. "What did you—"

"You do na know how to fight a hangover?" He cuts in like he said nothing of importance, and maybe he didn't; maybe I misheard *boyo*. But the scalding of my nerve endings doesn't think I did. "And you call yourself a Cambridge lad."

My throat is desert-dry.

I take a long drink of coffee. It doesn't help.

"I—I know how to treat hangovers," I stammer.

"Clearly. You seemed to be doing so well for yourself. Did na you ask me to get you a proper cure?"

"I—" No? Not really. I asked him to tell me where *Colm* was and that was a cover for—

I didn't even find the St. Patrick's Day joy meter last night.

FUCK ALL OF THIS.

I clamp my hand around the coffee mug, all that napalm bubbling into anger. I need to move, I need to run, I need to sweat and ache and push myself to dangerous physical limits.

"Can we leave now?" I ask Siobhán. She's literally the only person in this family I can stand.

Her eyes flash between me and her brother.

And she gets a look on her face. Like she's connecting something.

But it's Loch who says, "We're off."

He shoves past me to march for the door, his arm bumping my mug. Another spurt of coffee hits my shirt.

I stand there, glaring into the middle space.

I'm going to commit a murder at a charity 5k family fun run.

That is not how I thought I'd ruin my life. But I'm good with it.

I don't understand anything about St. Patrick's Day.

Loch drives us from Castle Patrick to Cork. *Loch* drives us. Not a staff member. No magic used. The oddness drops into all the other oddities, their empty castle, their lone butler, their absent king.

What is going on?

We ride the long two hours in silence, me in the back with Siobhán, Finn up front with Loch. The two of them talk, and Siobhán chimes in occasionally, but I sit there and eat my almonds and keep my gaze everywhere except on the rearview mirror, the way Loch always seems to know when my eyes land there, because his crash into mine.

The Irish countryside rolls around us, tiny two-lane roads swapping for highways, framed by potent, wet greenery and a rising blue sky that swells to neon and vivid by the time we get to Cork.

Hills descend us into a city split by waterways, the lowering tiers sprinkled with multicolored cottages and buildings in red, peach, fuchsia, and blue. Flags and streamers and pennants wave from *everywhere,* a veritable assault of St. Patrick's Day festivity, that green, white, and orange flag plastered to walls and windows, cars and streets. We weave through town, cross a bridge, and follow a stream of people that grows and grows.

Loch parks in a garage and we pour out. It's *freezing*, but I'm too much of a stubborn ass to admit I fucked up with my choice of shirt, so I blow into my hands and actively suppress my shivers as we take stairs out of the garage.

I twist alongside Loch in the stairwell. "I thought the point of all these events was to be seen by the Holiday press."

Loch arches an eyebrow. "Yeah?"

"So why the private drive? Are you trying to avoid them?"

"Oh, they'll find us, no problem."

"Then . . . I'm confused."

"That's na even a wee bit surprising, boyo."

"Screw you."

We hit the ground level and a park opens around us, foliage lush and ripe even in the dead of March. It's like all the plant life surges back to riotous emerald for this. Did the King use some of St. Patrick's Day's magic for it?

Tents and booths are speckled throughout the park, more vibrant punches of orange and teal and pink. Signs are wedged into the grass, dozens of them, all advertising Green Hills Distillery. Why does that sound—

That's the distillery King Malachy owns.

I frown. The prevalence of the signage makes it look more like a festival for Green Hills rather than a St. Patrick's Day charity race.

Finn pushes between me and Loch. "I'll be in the speaker's tent. I assume you're gonna miss my speech?"

"Always, lovey." Loch gives an insolent smile.

She flips him off over her shoulder as she weaves into the crowd.

"Speech?" I ask.

Siobhán loops her arm with Loch's, her nose already pink in the chill air. "Finn always gives a wee talk. She's on the charity's board."

"And every year, she manages to make a worthy cause sound dull as old scissors," Loch says.

"Be nice," Siobhán counters. "*I'm* gonna support my only sister."

"That's why I have two of you. So I do na have to be so loyal."

She smacks the back of his head. "Keep on with that attitude,

Lochlann, and I will na be at the finish line to cheer you. I'll be there for Kris."

Loch raises his eyebrows. "Pardon?"

I smirk.

"Oh, maybe I should do that anyway." Siobhán's smile is toying. "I might hit a shop and make up a big lovely banner with his name just to see ya get that crease in your forehead. Oh, yeah, that's the one."

My smirk blows into a wide grin.

Loch shoves her. "Get off, maggot."

She skips away, hands in the pockets of her deep green coat, blonde hair a splash of light as she vanishes into the festival.

I lean towards Loch. "So, in case there's any confusion, I like her best."

I say it to egg him on, as per usual, but something retracts in his eyes. Or hardens, maybe? It's a shocking enough change that I pull back and feel like I should apologize.

Which is annoying.

"Donna be goin' after my sister," he barks. His accent churns so thick that I almost think he's speaking in Irish.

"I . . . had no plans to."

"Well. That's the first sensible thing you've said this whole trip."

"Your accent is almost unintelligible when you're really angry."

The skin along his cheekbones goes as red as his beard. "I am not angry," he enunciates.

"Okay, that's worse."

"What's worse?"

"You not having any accent at all."

He rolls his eyes. "Let's get signed in."

The race tent is set up not far into the park, and other runners are queued in front of it, waiting for bibs. We join them, and more oddness cracks through—we're standing in a line. I get that there are tons of normal people around, but shouldn't there be an area for the St. Patrick's Day ruling families? No one's even calling out in greeting to Loch. Not that that's too unusual, this being such a big event, but surely *someone* here knows the Crown Prince of St. Patrick's Day?

And there's so many signs for Green Hills Distillery. A massive one hangs on the back wall of this sign-in booth, the logo an illustration of gently sloping emerald fields. The slogan is written around it in bold, square font: *Tradition. Heritage. Legacy.*

My nose curls. Those words all basically mean the same thing?

"What is with your uncle's distillery?" I ask.

Loch shifts on his feet, glaring at the sign ahead of us. "The King sponsors this event. Kind of him, eh?"

"I thought he was only going to be at the Dublin parade. Is he coming to this event too?"

Loch laughs. It's as cold as the wind.

"Are you going to expand on that?" I step with him when the line moves. "Why your uncle's so absent? Why we drove here instead of"—I cut a glance at all the normal people—"instead of using *other methods?* Why your castle's so damn empty?"

Loch folds his arms over his chest and stares off into the festival, expression shuttering.

I grunt. "Fine. I'm sure Siobhán will tell me."

That yanks his focus back to me so assertively my back seizes, shooting me upright, at attention.

"Don't fuck my sister," he snarls.

I balk. "We went from me maybe flirting with her to *fucking* her? Again, *I have no plans to.* Flirt or fuck. But shouldn't Siobhán be the one to have a say in this?"

"Not if her say is choosing a pompous pretty boy arsehole who struts around like he's god's gift."

I don't miss a beat. "Aw, you think I'm pretty?"

He doesn't either. "Do you still think I'm hot?"

That shuts me up. Briefly. "Do you want me to, if I was flirting with your sister?"

His jaw tenses. Silence falls again, and the line moves forward, carrying us with it. But that silence lengthens, grows heavier, pushing in an uncomfortable knot against my chest.

"She's not my type, anyway," I add.

Loch cuts a look at me, one brow cocked. "What is your type, then?" he asks slowly. Then adds, "Since my sister is na good enough for you."

"You're *mad* I'm not interested in her now? And you said I'm infuriating."

"Bet you go for the upper crust Cambridge sort. Trust funds and their da's credit card. Is that what you thought I was?"

"Yep. You caught me. I'm superficial to the max. A materialistic douche, inside and out. But you're assuming I was interested in you."

"It was na an assumption. You told me so."

My cheeks heat. "As an artist, you should know the difference between appreciating an aesthetic and actual interest."

Loch snorts. "You did na answer the question."

The line shifts forward.

What is your type, then?

"The fuck if I know," I mutter.

"You do na know?"

I grimace at him. He holds, showing what could be sincerity.

He really gives a shit? Why?

"I have a friend I thought I was in love with," I say, and immediately hate myself for telling him this at all. But I'm supposed to be *bonding* with him, right? Luring him into something like friendship. "And it was a whole years-long pining fiasco. It'd been . . . it'd been something that was *supposed* to work. We're both Holiday royals, prince and princess happy ever after shit."

Loch scratches the back of his neck. "Do I know her?"

"Iris Lentora. Easter."

"Ah. I've heard of her."

"Anyway. I got drunk. Confessed my feelings. Realized halfway through that I was in love with the idea of a fairy tale ending, but I wasn't in love with *her*. So that's my type, I guess. Fantasies."

All those fantasies have someone else in them, though. But I have no clue what type of person I want them to be—I only know what type of person they *should* be. Someone kind and calm because I'm such a mess, and I need that balance. Iris was the blueprint; I think I was interested in my other two exes because they reminded me of her, and she was who I was *supposed* to want, so I went after them for that familiarity. But I don't remember being upset when it ended with them, and even this mess with Iris—I miss her friendship, which we're repairing, but I was never brokenhearted. Just humiliated and ashamed.

Have I ever been interested in any of the people I've been with? Or did they . . . fit a mold?

I refuse to keep talking about myself in this capacity so, distantly, down a long, echoing tunnel, I ask, "And what's Prince Lochlann's type? Snobbish and endless credit cards?"

We're next in line, the group in front of us arguing over who gets what bib number.

Loch chuckles. "Dead on. Spoiled Cambridge lads with trust fund money to burn."

"I don't buy that for a second."

His eyebrows go up.

"Because you think *I'm* spoiled and stuck up," I explain, "and you treat me like you want to strangle me with my own intestines half the time—"

"Lovely image, that."

"—so I honest to god cannot imagine you giving the time of day to a guy who's spoiled and superficial. I think the stress of being in a relationship with someone like that would give you an ulcer."

"I'm Irish, boyo. Talking shite is how we flirt."

"What kind of guy are you into, then? For real? What kind of man would sweep Prince Lochlann off his feet?"

There's a pause. Long enough that I know I don't imagine it. It drags across that spot on the back of my hand.

But his humor slides away in an abrupt rush. "Certainly not hopeless romantics like your sorry arse. That's what you are? A hopeless romantic?"

"I guess—"

"So you will stay away from Siobhán."

I recoil. "Jesus, the more you order me around like that, the more it makes me want to woo her to piss you off."

Loch doesn't say anything. He sure as hell *looks* like he wants to, like there are a hundred threats rolling through his head and he can't decide on one.

The group in front of us leaves and Loch shoots forward to accept a clipboard from a race attendant. I reach for one too, but he smacks my hand away and scribbles out a form for me.

"What is your problem?" I snap.

He attaches one bib to his sweater and slams another against my chest, arching over me as he presses the paper to my thin tank top.

"Cover up that coffee stain on your shirt, *again,* ya clumsy arse."

"*You* bumped *me* this time—"

"I have a job to do. Stay away from me 'til the race."

And he cuts off into the crowd. Leaving me there, holding that bib, scowling after him.

Is he seriously mad about me and Siobhán?

There *is* no *me and Siobhán.*

Jesus motherfucking Christ in a shithole.

I stick the bib to my tank—Malachy's distillery has a logo on this too, god, overkill—and dive after him.

As I elbow my way into the crowd, I spot the first group of Holiday reporters clustered in with regular ones. I recognize some from the events they covered in Christmas. A guy from *Holiday Herald;* a reporter and a photographer from *24 Hour Fête.* They're hanging back like they do when we're all in public, which is a relieving buffer, that they can't be all up in my face without arousing suspicion and breaking the *keep our worlds separate and private* rules.

But they spot me, and they spot Loch ahead of me, and I watch them take shots of us as I follow him.

The path he takes weaves deeper into the festival, behind the race registration tent and away from the gaggle of reporters. When I get about two yards behind him, we're lost among normal people and I'm close enough to call out to him, but he slows his pace. Here is where the festival goers congregate, kids darting between legs and people milling around booths that sell food and hot drinks. Signs

for Green Hills Distillery are rampant, and there's a giant tent farther down hawking bottles of its whiskey.

But the booth Loch ducks into displays rich maroon wood carved
into sea creatures. He goes right up to an older guy and they exchange friendly hugs before talking animatedly, hands waving, all
smiles.

I stop a few paces outside the tent, too far to hear what's being
said, and I'm unsure of why I even care to catch up with him.

But I stand there. Watching like a creep as they chat, then Loch
nods goodbye and heads to the next tent, this one selling watercolors.

The process repeats: he greets a person, I'm guessing the artist;
they talk and laugh; then he heads to the next tent, and so on.

Coal can often be found bouncing from person to person at our
events. He knows absolutely everyone's names and random facts
about their lives. So this could be that, and these people could be
linked to Loch's court somehow.

Something doesn't sit right, though.

Why isn't Loch making sure reporters see him interact with people? My whole apology was to prove that he isn't the irresponsible,
scandalous prince the headlines say, but he didn't even stop to let
the Holiday press get any shots of us at the race tent, and he hasn't
once glanced around to see if they're nearby now. They aren't.

I let him pull ahead in the crowd, losing him in the people and
noise.

My sternum tightens and I rub it absently.

I could ask one of the people he's talked to what he's doing. But
what if they aren't part of the Holiday world? Then I'm the weirdo
stalking this guy for no good reason.

Or, here's an idea: I could ask Loch himself.

Psh. *Hell* no.

I angle for the speaker's tent to find Siobhán and see if she'll give
me answers, but an announcer calls all racers to the starting line.

Later, then.

The race begins on a blocked-off road that runs parallel to a wide river, its water a flat, still mirror for the swath of blue sky. The opposite bank shows the descending tiers of hills that wove us down into Cork, and the route ahead is lined with ivy-wrapped trees that cut halos of shadow through the piercing sun.

I fall in with the other racers, stretching and jogging in place. It helps warm me where I'm still freezing, but I don't feel it as much.

I do, however, feel him come up next to me and begin stretching too.

I don't say anything.

Siobhán and Finn are off to the side with the spectators. Siobhán gives me a thumbs-up; Finn sees it and elbows her to stop.

A starting gun pops.

"Don't trip, boyo," Loch says and takes off.

I bolt after him.

It's a 5k; it's absolutely idiotic to lead at a dead sprint.

He isn't being idiotic.

Until I jog up alongside him.

He increases his pace.

So I do, too.

We bob through the other runners, who throw us confused looks as we gain speed.

First him a little.

Then me a little more.

He passes me, so I push faster, and soon we're well ahead of the other racers, and I'm definitely no longer cold, sweating sheets in the thick, chill air.

The river path bends to the right, snaking through a cluster of buildings so damn quaint I forget I'm supposed to be kicking his ass and he gains a few yards on me.

I shove on, lungs burning, and fuck, I am going to hate myself tomorrow. Seems to be a reoccurring pattern in Ireland.

The road inclines and I can't stop my gasping, winded moan.

Loch glances over at me. He's sweat-slicked too, just as winded, but his smirk is cutting. "Struggling?"

"You wish." Oh god this hill can screw itself.

"First whiskey," Loch pants, "then hangovers. Now running. What *can* you handle?"

Oh-ho. *Ooohhhhh*, that's it.

I break into a sprint and we're not even halfway through the race yet. Loch huffs at my burst of speed and matches me, and we crest the hill as it finally levels out. Rowhouses blow past us, the river on our left at the base of an ivy-covered hill, and we run like we're being chased by something, like we're both absolute morons.

The path curves and a castle pops up on our left. Looks like it'd normally be a tourist stop, but a water table is set up in front of its closed gates with a few race volunteers already holding paper cups out for us.

"Blackrock Castle," Loch wheezes as he snatches one, downs it, and nods his thanks.

I bypass the water. "You sound tired."

"Just getting started." Loch cuts an accusatory look at me. "You didn't drink, boyo."

"You can take"—I have to break to gasp—"each time you call me *boyo*"—smack talk while sprinting, all of this is a bad idea—"and choke on them."

Loch laughs.

It's bright and shattering and *real*, not weighed down by the weirdness of our fight earlier, and as we leave the castle to glide down into a parking lot, the path drops. I *see it* descend, but that information doesn't make it to my brain, sticking against the dam of his laugh.

I trip head over ass and go crashing down the road.

Chapter Seven

My knees smash to the pavement, jarring my body so bad my teeth clack. I try to catch the impact by rolling onto my shoulder at the last second, but the momentum carries me flipping one more time until I land on my back in the grass at the edge of the path.

And I just lie there.

Because yeah. This seems about right.

I already knew my body was going to hate me tomorrow, but it's *really* going to hurt now. Pain flares up both my legs, my shoulder is burning, something on my temple is wet—

"Kris!" Loch skids to a stop, doubles back, and drops to the grass next to me. "Holy shite—Kris, are you all right?"

My lips set in a grimace.

"Fuck," is all I can get out, refusing to feel the full brunt of the pain I know I should be in.

"Sit up—slow, go slow. Christ, Kris, you're—ah, shite." Loch's hand is on my back and he can't seem to decide which injury to be more horrified by, the cut on my temple or the gash through my shoulder or the burns on my knees where my tights ripped. Everything's bloody and the cut on my temple leaks down the side of my face.

I'm sitting up, but suddenly the ground seems a little closer than it was before—

"Kris! Stay up, lad—here." He rips off his beanie and presses it to the cut on my head.

I wince at the sting. "You could have used my beanie."

Loch goes momentarily stiff. I think he blushes, but his face is already scarlet in the exertion of running.

"Yeah. That woulda made more sense." He licks his lips. "Here, hold this to your head. C'mon, to your feet. The water table'll have first aid. Up, now. Slow."

We're down the hill where the water table volunteers can't see us yet. It's bad enough that Loch bore witness to this obscenely graceful moment, but we get to bring other people into my humiliation now, too. Awesome.

"Oh, the paparazzi will love this," I say, or more moan, because Loch bodily hauls me to my feet and *ow*.

He loops my free arm over his shoulder, my other one dutifully holding the beanie to my cut.

"Do na worry about that. Come on."

My mouth opens to say that of course it's easy for *him* to say that, he's not the one all banged up thanks to his own stupidity—but then Loch bolts his arm around my hips, crushing my body to his.

It's so he can hold on to me. Keep me standing upright. Because my legs are jelly.

I feel all his muscles that I saw last night. Feel them pressed against me, around me. Straining.

We head up the path, mostly by his support.

My pulse swerves wildly. *"Spare Claus Beefs It at Cork Race, Saved by Lucky Charms in Shining Armor."* Do I have a concussion? I think I'm babbling.

I don't *babble*.

Loch gives me an odd look.

"The headline. That the paparazzi will write. When they see us like this."

"That's na important right now, Kris. We're almost there."

"You're saying my name a lot."

"Should I go back to Coffee Shop? Shut up, now."

We're both a sweaty mess and my heart is thundering like mad. Loch's heart is going too, the echoes of it shaking his chest where it's pressed to me.

"Your heart's racing," I hear myself whisper.

We crest the hill and he pauses to readjust his grip on me. Up ahead, I spot flickers on the road. Other racers. The volunteers at the water table can finally see us, and someone calls out; but Loch's gaze pops down to mine.

I let the beanie drop away from my forehead.

There's something unendurably intimate about looking into someone else's eyes within a certain distance.

I have a concussion. I have to have a concussion.

The next words that come out of my mouth are, "There's a rim of green around your pupils."

Loch exhales. A staccato pant.

"You should've eaten more. You're woozy," is his response.

He starts us off again as two of the volunteers reach us. They offer to take over helping me, but Loch assures them he's got it.

A sweep of caustic awareness washes over me: relief.

I don't want anyone else holding me like this.

We make it to the water table. The volunteers not only produce a first aid kit, but they also get the race's on-call doctor to head up. Loch lowers me into a metal folding chair behind the table while we wait for him.

I toss the bloodied beanie in the trash and reach for the first aid kit—to find it in Loch's lap.

He's crouched before me, ripping open a box of bandages and antibiotic ointment.

My face sears with heat. "I can handle this on my—"

Loch gives me such a rebuking glare that I lurch back on the chair. The impact of my spine hitting the metal forces out a breathy "Sorry."

Sorry?

I mean, I'm used to apologizing for my very existence a lot, but—*sorry?*

Loch's glare softens.

"Do na apologize, Kris. Just stay still." He readies a sterile wipe. "Might sting."

And he gently dabs at the scrape on my right knee.

I watch him, jaw gawped open.

The volunteers are busy getting water to the next wave of racers. Loch's doggedly focused on bandaging me. So no one sees the seismic shift happening across my face; I can feel the stunned stretch of my expression, but I can't stop it. Can only stare down as Loch finishes one knee by soothing his thumb over the tab of the bandage, an anxious scowl on his face.

He takes my other leg in his hand, brushes the frayed edge of my tights aside, and ghosts his fingers over my kneecap as he checks the wound.

I had no idea, *no idea,* how sensitive that part of my body was.

The heat from my blush sizzles across my chest. Burns, burns, goes atomic as it settles in my gut.

What . . .

What's happening here?

A cart drives up as Loch's bandaging my other knee, so it's the doctor who steps in and dresses my temple and shoulder. And thank god for that—I'm not sure how much more of Loch's ministrations I could've handled.

The doctor checks the response of my eyes to light and a few other tests until he nods definitively. "No concussion. You're lucky. Fall like that? But it's superficial wounds. You'll be fine."

Lucky.

No. That's—no. I'm reading into things. *Lucky* would've been not tripping *at all.*

"No concussion," I repeat dazedly.

Loch is behind the doctor, and his anxious rigidity goes out with a grateful breath.

So I'm the only one mortified.

Everything I said to him. Everything I *felt.* With nothing to blame it on but myself.

Loch guided me up the road. He put bandages on my knees. It wasn't anything *sensual* to him; he was being helpful, Mr. Hero.

Well isn't that the cherry on the shit-cream sundae that's been this whole day. Past two days. Every moment I've been around Loch since we collided with each other in Cambridge.

"Good, then." Loch sounds winded. "Thank you, doc."

The doctor packs up his supplies. "You lads can ride back to the finish line with me?"

"That'll do," says Loch.

"No—what? Why?" I shove up from the chair. The cuts on my knees burn, but I'm not dizzy anymore.

Not from my injuries, at least.

Loch eyes me like maybe I do have a concussion. "You are na finishing the run, Kris."

"*You* can finish the run."

"Do na be faffin' around—get in the cart."

"Faffin' around?"

"*Wasting my time.*" Loch rounds on me, rage kindling in his eyes. "Get your arse in that cart and do na go tryna tell me to *leave* ya."

I meet his rage. Anger for anger. "Gotta get those paparazzi pics, right? Repair your reputation?"

That's what this is. What it has to be.

Unease floods my system, desperation to hear him confirm that that's his only concern, to redraw that line in the sand between us.

Loch might have been mad before.

He's *livid* now.

"Get in. The fucking. Cart." He wheels off without another word.

The doctor is already in the driver's seat, waiting none too awkwardly while we yell at each other. Loch hauls himself in the passenger side, the whole cart rocking.

I drop into the seat behind him and glower at the scenery as the doctor takes us to the finish line.

The blocked-off two-lane road is bordered by dead shrubs and spindly trees that haven't gotten the memo about this being for St. Patrick's Day. A crowd looks on from either side of the road as I climb out of the cart, and cameras flash. The Holiday reporters keep their distance, but they get plenty of shots of me all banged up and Loch hovering nearby.

Siobhán and Finn rush up to us.

"Christ, Lochlann!" Siobhán smacks his arm. "You actually tried to kill him!"

"I did not!" Loch looks in horror at the reporters. "The bastard tripped himself."

"Do you want me to go tell that to the journalists?" I nod at the reporters. And wave. Because fuck them. "Tell them how Prince Lochlann valiantly swept to my rescue?"

Finn snarls at me. "Do na use that title here! You eejit, we're in *public.*"

But Loch rounds on me, face red, eyes wild. I can't place it at first, it's not anger; amorphous emotions push and pull him, and he centers it all on me.

"You got *hurt,* Kris," he spits, like I might've forgotten. "This is na a joke."

Worry.

He's worried. For me?

No. Right? No, that's not—

A shout rips through the air. Not from any of us.

Off to the side of the finish line, a fight has broken out, bodies in a tussle of fists and kicking legs.

"Shite." Loch tears off without hesitation and I pitch after him, but Siobhán grabs me, and Finn gives me a withering glare.

"He can handle this," Finn snaps. "You're in pieces."

She isn't as unsettled as she should be. There's a *fistfight,* at one of their Holiday events, a place that should be all joy and happiness—and Finn seems tired. Siobhán drops her eyes to the ground.

Meanwhile, Loch is centered in the conflict, and I recognize that telltale flick of his hands. He's using magic—not to stop the fight; our magic can't change a person's choices. But it can, if needed, lighten spirits.

Which is generally something a *king* should do, and on a much grander scale.

But their king isn't even here. His advertisements are, though.

Doing what Loch is doing should be wildly unnecessary. His uncle should have this covered, blanketing everyone at this festival, everyone celebrating St. Patrick's Day, in a feedback loop of joy and goodness and light. I get that the King might not be at every event we go to, but the people generate joy, he uses that joy to enhance their happiness, and it builds and builds everywhere people are celebrating his Holiday.

The press swivel from taking shots of me all ripped up to getting pics of Loch in the crowd.

"What is going on here?" I ask, breathless.

Finn glowers at Siobhán. Who glowers right back.

"Ya both are stubborn arses," Siobhán barks at her sister before she turns to me. "Our uncle is a right prick."

"Siobhán! It's none of his business."

"It's *my* business, and I'm na about to let the chance at Loch having a real ally pass by."

My face widens in surprise.

"Now, Kris." Siobhán's sweet smile is marred by the first show of anger I've seen on her. "To be fair, our father was a right prick in his own way, too."

"Jesus, Siobhán. You're on your own." Finn walks away, towards the fight that's now settling.

I stay focused on Siobhán. Who sighs and folds her arms.

"We've had a long run of prick rulers for St. Patrick's Day," she says. "Our grandda and da weren't cruel, just poor managers. No vision. But our uncle keeps a tight hold on the magic, hoards it all up."

A few police are intermingled with the crowd around Loch now. The doctor has his medical kit back out.

"This happens a lot? *Fights?*" I can't stop the disgust from warping my voice.

Siobhán nods with a wince. "Our uncle does na use his magic as he should. The attitude gets . . . muddled."

"So St. Patrick's Day is running out of magic?"

"We've quite a lot of it. But our uncle's a greedy son of a bitch who uses all our magic to make the luckiest business decisions for his distillery, claiming it's an Irish company, so its success is *imperative* to St. Patrick's Day's success. It's all fucked. Finn and I get no magic; Loch barely gets enough to do—well, that." She waves at her brother. Who doesn't appear to be using magic now, as the fight's stopped; he's got his hand on someone's shoulder and is talking to them, posture gentle and soothing.

"That's why we drove here instead of using magic to travel," I connect.

"Yeah."

My lungs grip tight. For all Dad's jackass ways, he never limited our magic. He threatened it, but we always had enough. Which turned out to be because other Holidays were being forced to give us their magic. So, perspective and all.

But I feel a pulse of empathy. For Siobhán. Finn.

Loch.

"Is that why you don't have staff at the castle?" I ask.

Siobhán shrugs. "With our uncle keeping the magic for his distillery, we got less and less to *run* our Holiday. The staff and court've been slipping away for years. Malachy gives magic to the ones he wants to keep close, but the rest have faded out, and we do na have magic to help with the resources we need in the castle."

"Wait. You're saying no one runs St. Patrick's Day? What does your uncle do?"

"Fucks off in Dublin with his distillery. Shows up at the big parade every year to let people adore him, as if he deserves any of it. Pops in on occasion to check the joy meter and yell about how he does na have enough magic." She scowls at one of the Green Hills Distillery banners. "Oh, and plasters his adverts on every event *Loch* coordinates. Like this race? Malachy'd canceled it years ago. But Loch started it up again last year, and it was a big success. Malachy got right livid with Loch for daring to go against him, but he let Loch keep this race on account of it bringing in more magic. Only he took credit for it, slathering his distillery over everything."

A picture is starting to form. And it isn't at all what I expected. It makes my heart rate spike, or maybe it never calmed at all from the run and fall, so it's banging even harsher now, quaking my chest apart.

"But Loch should be king," I try. "Why isn't he?"

Siobhán's eyes dip over my shoulder.

Loch is talking with a police officer. The press are hovering near him.

"He took it hard when our da died," she whispers. "He's always carried too much. He's a brilliant idiot and an artist to boot so he's doomed to burn out one day. Uncle Malachy used that against him, pushed our court to believe he was *unreliable*. Loch was so young, plus reckless and silly, before Da died, so they believed Malachy. *Loch* believed Malachy. He surrendered the rule on the idea that Malachy would give it back once Loch's *worthy,* but we know now, that'll be never. Which is a heap of bullshite—you saw all the artists' booths there, yeah?"

She points to the area behind the race registration tent. Where I'd seen Loch talking to the vendors.

"Before Malachy canceled this event, it was a charity race. When Loch brought it back, he got the organizers to bring in local artists, made it a proper large fundraising festival. It's a celebration now, with Irish artisans and musicians. Loch does stuff of that sort all across the isle while Malachy takes credit. He runs circles round Malachy."

I press the pad of my thumb between my eyebrows, fighting down a headache—from my fall, from the tension in my shoulders, from this finally making sense in the worst way possible.

I really, really wanted Loch to be the thieving jackass.

He could be. Maybe he's stealing Christmas's magic to compensate for his uncle's stranglehold. But wouldn't Loch be doing more with magic then? He's barely using anything.

Malachy's the one stealing from us, isn't he? His own Holiday wasn't enough anymore.

"So—" I shake my head and lower my voice. "That's what my being here and all this press shit is—he's trying to change his court's opinion of him to take back the throne?"

Siobhán looks skyward, pleadingly. "Let it be so. Finn and I both were shocked off our arses when Loch told us he'd planned you coming for the week, and planned more having the tabloids so involved. He's not told us his reasoning because he's a grumpy fuck, but we're hopeful this means he's *trying* to replace Malachy." She glares at me. "I know you've got no reason to give a shite, but you're here, and so help me, Christmas Prince, if ya bring more stress on my brother—"

She stops. Considers. "Do ya know what happens to a body when it's buried in a peat bog?"

"I . . . I do not."

"Well. Make trouble for Lochlann, and you'll find out firsthand. I told ya this for a reason. Ya need to understand him. He lets Malachy take credit and walk all over him, and Finn and I are proper *sick* of people thinking the worst of him. I like you, Kris. You could be good for him. Getting him out of his head like ya do."

Good for him? We're not friends, and we damn near kill each other in every conversation we have.

I thought Finn had the whole terrifying-sister angle on lock. But the real threat is Siobhán, hiding behind that bubbly façade.

I manage to clear my throat. "I don't want to make things harder on anyone. But I'm not sure how useful of a . . . of a *real ally* I can be."

"Hm." She considers me, her eyes toying. "You've got a point. You are a right eejit sometimes."

"Okay, that's harsh—"

"Why'd ya trip on the road, eh? It's a paved path." Her eyebrows lift expectantly.

I think she means that only a dumbass would trip on flat pavement. But I remember Loch's laugh. The way it'd sent me toppling over. I scrub a hand over the back of my neck. "Fine. I relent. I'm an *eejit*." She grins and jostles my shoulder.

Finn and Loch come back, both looking exhausted. But Loch's exhaustion sharpens as Siobhán peels away from me, and I see the echo of our fight about me not trying to sleep with her.

He glares at me.

I hold that glare, but I don't return it.

He drops his eyes first.

"I've had about enough of Cork," he says to no one in particular. "Home?"

"Yeah." But Finn dips her head back dramatically. "Ah, Christ, the car is gonna *reek* with you two in it. Canna you find somewhere to shower first?"

"I do na *smell*." Loch snags Finn and jerks her head down to bury her face in his armpit.

"Get off me! *Fucker!*" She flails, landing a fist to his stomach, and he lets her go with a laugh.

"We'll pile 'em in the back and open all the windows." Siobhán points at Loch, who spreads his arms and moves as if to tackle-hug her too. "Do na touch me, ya wanker."

"Ah, but Siobhán—deirfiúr bheag—" He lunges, and I stumble away as Siobhán ducks and squeals and the two of them tear across the road, hopping through the crowd, angling for the carpark.

It leaves Finn and me to trail them, and when she gives me her usual frown, I become aware of the stupid grin on my face.

"Siobhán threaten you good and proper if you fuck us over?" she asks.

Well, *Finn* definitely can't be the one stealing from us because, god, the irony of *me* fucking *them* over.

I nod.

She eyes all my injuries and shakes her head in disgust. "See if ya can get to the car without falling on your arse."

And she quickens her pace to walk off without me.

Which is fine. I need the time to . . . breathe.

My phone is in the car. So I can't text Coal and ask him what I should do, and I don't want to text him while we're all in the car together in case someone sees.

So for now?

I'm on my own.

The knot of pressure in my chest matches the one currently radiating pain up my neck.

What is it with the rulers of Holidays fucking off their duties so the heirs have to step in? Loch and I should start a club with Coal and Iris.

At the car, Finn claims the driver's seat and Siobhán sits next to her, which leaves Loch and me to crowd into the back, all the windows thrown down in the frigid March air. That won't last long. But we do stink.

And this car is *tiny*.

I didn't realize it when I was sitting with Siobhán. Loch has to bend his long legs practically to his chin, pivoted with his hip towards me to give Finn enough room to put her seat back. I squish in next to him, doing my best not to touch him, my body shoved up on the door like I'm trying to scale it.

Finn drives us off, the chilly air buffeting my face. I close my eyes. My body aches, every wound throbbing with the beat of my blood. The one granola bar and bag of almonds I've eaten today is rapidly making my stomach revolt against the rest of my body.

Something cold touches my knee and I jerk.

Loch chuckles. It's a water bottle.

I note the small unzipped cooler between his feet.

"You did na drink enough during the race," he says.

I take the bottle. "You are way too concerned with my water intake."

"I would na have to be, if you'd drink enough of it."

He produces another granola bar, a bag of carrot sticks, sandwiches, and passes some up to Siobhán and Finn too.

A handful of snippy comebacks pop to mind.

But all I say is "Thanks."

Shit, I need to sleep. Like, really sleep, but I doubt even this level of exhaustion will result in anything more than a few restless hours tonight.

We eat in silence, the car quickly going arctic, and I regret my tank top all over again. But my stomach is full now and I close my eyes again and lean against the open window, focusing on how the icy wind rolls into my lungs, crisp and cool.

His uncle is screwing him over. Worse than my father ever did, at least in the way he treated Coal and me. If I got proof that Malachy is the one stealing Christmas's magic, what would happen? He cares about smearing Loch so much, making sure their court is against him—would the scandal of people knowing that Malachy's a thief be enough to not only get Christmas's joy back, but also force him to give Loch the throne too?

Could my presence here help undo Loch's bad reputation—not

necessarily with the press, but with his court? That was the point, right, to set the story straight about his *hazing incident.*

Or he could have organized my being here to cover up stealing Christmas's magic? Maybe he's hoping he can find out how much we know about the theft.

The thought doesn't come with the annoyance and hatred I expect. It's . . . deflated.

I *saw* Loch at the festival. How he was with those vendors.

And how he was with me, when I fell.

I want his uncle to be the one screwing us over.

My own thoughts catch on themselves, trip and tumble into silence. *Why?* a voice whispers. *Why do you care whether Loch's the thief?*

After about thirty minutes of riding while holding myself angled away from Loch, straining all the muscles I abused today so I don't bump into him, I put my hand flat on the seat to prop against it and give my torso a break.

But my eyes are shut.

And I don't see his hand already on the cushion.

I feel it now, though. The edge of his wrist against mine.

My body goes even tenser. Concrete solidified.

Pull away. It was an innocent mistake. *Pull back.*

But a second passes.

Two.

And it rapidly barrels past the time when I could yank away and claim it's an accident and now, now, I'm actively touching him, *barely* touching him, and the beat of blood in my injuries channels to pound, pound, pound over my heart.

It's an accident. He touched my knees earlier, and that meant nothing, so this, this means—

His finger moves.

Hooks with mine.

Holy shit.

The icy wind thrashes against my face and chaos ratchets to boiling in my head, it's haunting me, that juxtaposition, cold to hot to cold—

I hear his voice, the memory of it. Echoing. Echoing.

I'm Irish, boyo. Talking shite is how we flirt.

Holy.

Fuck.

Has he been *flirting* with me *this whole time?*

And. Oh my god.

Have I been flirting *back?*

No. No way. Flirting is telling someone they look nice, or smiling at each other across a room, or anything that leaves a fuzzy feeling in my chest, not—

Not heat so intense I don't think there's a part of me that isn't blistered anymore.

Not tension so potent it creates its own gravitational pull.

That's not—that isn't—

Oh my god.

THAT'S WHAT THAT IS?!

My mouth opens. I gulp the wind. But I do not move any more than that.

Only I do.

Bullets of that cold-hot-cold are firing down into the root of my stomach, and I chase them. I am stripped of all thought again, a being of appetite only, and that appetite wants more of this sensation, *hot-cold-hot*—

I work my hand under his and twine our fingers together.

What am I doing.

I'm suffocating is what I'm doing. I've passed out from my injuries and I'm unconscious right now.

Loch's fingers tighten on mine. His thumb strokes over the back of my hand and I launch stratospheric.

There is nothing deniable about this. No rationalizing it off. It's such a thing outside myself that I'm forced to sit here in excruciating mental silence and endure his hand in mine. The roughness of his palm, a callus between two fingers, probably from a paint brush.

This is so childish, isn't it? Holding hands. This is playground bullshit. It shouldn't be—it shouldn't *be*—

But it's *everything.* His touch is on my hand but it's all over my body, and those bullets whizzing through me, the aching thuds of my pulse, *all of it* swells together in a detonation that is physically agonizing to not react to.

My eyes split open. And I twist to him; increment by increment, I'll find an excuse in his face. My mind will start working again and I'll see the reason I did this and it'll be something—something— that makes *sense*—

I get as far as looking at the seat between us when Loch pulls away.

He drops my hand and cocks his shoulder to me and clears his throat, scratches his jaw. His beard bristles on his fingertips.

There's paint caked in his nailbeds. Specks of green. Orange.

I stare down at my palm. Empty.

No thoughts.

But a feeling.

Rejection.

Another. Stronger. Feral and out of control.

Confusion.

I tuck my hand into my lap.

"*Shite,* close the windows!" Siobhán shrieks. "I canna take it any-more. It's *winter,* Christ."

Finn hits a button and all the windows go up.

No, I need that air, fuck, *fuck*—

One arm curled up on the car door, I make myself as small as possible, nonexistent.

Loch shifts. My eyes dart over to him. I can't stop it.

His head is angled at the window, but he dips his eyes to the side. Towards me.

Goes back to staring out the window.

I watch the muscle in his jaw, under his beard, constrict, stay clamped.

Hot-cold-hot.

My hand is still on fire. The brunt force of the sun scorching every line in my palm.

I spin away from him and shut my eyes and do not think, not at all.

Chapter Eight

We're pulling into the drive for Castle Patrick when Loch, Finn, and Siobhán all get alerts on their phones.

It takes me until that moment to realize I haven't checked mine. I grab it out of the seatback pocket and see about twenty missed texts. The latest few are Coal chastising me because he saw the press shots so *TEXT ME BACK YOU MORON why did you have bandages in those pics??*

Wren also messaged me. There are a few links to recent tabloid articles; Loch intervening in the fight at the finish line has overshadowed my injuries. A few reports speculate that Loch *caused* the fight, while others saw him using magic in an attempt to stop it.

Anger spikes at the assholes who're trying to lay more blame on Loch.

Which is . . . weird. Feeling angry on his behalf rather than *at* him.

None of that is Wren's concern, though; she asks if I'm okay, and wants to verify what happened, *in case Christmas needs to make a statement.*

Before I can respond to anything, Loch grumbles, "*Shite.*"

He says it with such a punch of horror that I throw a look at him.

He does not look at me. "Siobhán?" he asks.

She's staring at her screen. "*Fucker.*"

"What?" Finn finishes parking and wrestles her phone out.

"What happened?" I ask.

Siobhán frowns when Loch doesn't answer.

"Text from Colm," Siobhán explains. "Our uncle is paying us a visit."

"Ah hell," Finn curses.

My eyes widen. "When?"

"Now." Loch pops open the door and launches from the car.

I haul myself out and hobble after Loch into the castle, pretending my injuries don't hurt as much as they do.

By the time I stumble into the foyer, Loch is talking with Colm. When Loch's eyes slide to me, he looks, briefly, ashamed.

"Thanks, Colm." Loch pats his shoulder and hurries down the hall. He's trying to avoid me.

Fuck that.

I limp after him, biting back a wince, and just about match his pace. For a few halls.

"I almost got a concussion today," I call to his back, several paces ahead of me. "Stop making me run, jackass."

He staggers to a halt at the base of the stairs. There's a beat where I'm shuffling closer to him and I think he's going to bolt again, but he stays, shoulders drooping in resignation while his hands stay fisted.

I almost, *almost* say *good boy.* But my throat, thankfully, refuses to let those words out.

Face flushed, I come up alongside him. He's glaring at the steps.

"So?" I press when he stays quiet.

His jaw's going to fracture at the rate he clenches it. "So?"

"Your uncle?"

"It's none of your concern."

"Yeah, it is."

"How do ya figure that now?" he asks the stairs.

"I'm here as an ambassador from my Holiday and haven't met the King of St. Patrick's Day. So it's mildly my concern." And I want to see this fucker for myself. "Are you going to talk to him now? Where is he? I'm coming with you."

Loch finally does look at me. But he must see the logic in my reasoning, because his nostrils flare. "He's in his office. Told Colm to get a supper ready for us all to have, *as a family,* but that's sure as fuck na happening. I'm showering then I'm gonna talk to him. If you are so invested in meeting him, be outside your room in twenty minutes."

The girls come up the hall behind us. "Loch?" Siobhán calls.

"Twenty minutes," I say to him, and I don't give him a chance to renege. I dart-hobble past him up the stairs.

"And take some pain tablets," he shouts after me. Then adds, muffled by the stones, "Gobshite."

I shove into my room and yank out normal clothes while texting my brother.

COAL

Sorry. I'm alive. Everything's fine. I tripped like a dumbass. I'll call you tonight.

COAL
HE LIVES!!
kris. KRIS. surely you have five minutes to text back your king and brother
KRISTOPHER
pretty sure this is treason

I take a second to assure Wren I'm fine too—and tell her that Christmas should, in fact, make a statement.

I quickly tell her about my fall, how Loch helped me. I tell her how he *was* intervening to *stop* the fight—I don't mention his magic use, since that seems to be a touchy subject, per Siobhán. Basically, I write an impromptu press release via text so Wren knows to spread the truth of what happened regarding both events.

That's what I'm here for, isn't it? To make his reputation better. This is my job. One of my jobs, at least.

Wren responds with a thumbs-up, so it's as good as done.

I take the world's fastest shower. A blue sweater, jeans, and those brown shoes from the first day, nothing snarky or irreverent, not for this. My bandages survived the shower, so I leave them and throw my wet hair into a topknot, and I'm back outside my room with minutes to spare.

Loch's already walking towards me from up the hall. His frantic clean-up has produced shower-slicked hair set off like a flame by a black turtleneck sweater and tight black pants tucked into boots.

He sighs heavily. "Dinna change your mind?"

His whole demeanor is stiff and alert, survival mode coupled with a deep, pulsing inner fury, and a little fear.

He looks how I know I do when my father is around.

"No. I didn't change my mind," I tell him.

Loch sighs again and keeps walking. He leads me a few halls over, past half a dozen closed doors, to one that's more nondescript reddish-brown wood.

He doesn't knock. Just swings the door open.

The office is a sprawling testament to the overall medieval style of the castle, with a mahogany desk in the center and heavy, dense navy curtains pulled back to show the late afternoon landscape. Bookshelves cover every wall, old antique things more for orna-mentation than use, their shelves holding leather-wrapped tombs with gilded edgings, framed photographs, and other decorative knickknacks.

Behind the desk sits the guy I saw in Wren's profiles.

Malachy Patrick.

He looks like a Wallstreet prick who talks in finances and hedge funds and investments. His suit is probably more expensive than most cars, his pale skin bronzed in a fake tan, his gray hair perfectly coiffed.

Loch stops across the desk from him, hands against his spine. "Uncle."

Malachy glances up from a tablet in his lap. "I told Colm I'd be seeing you at—"

His focus pivots to me.

One dark brow curves over deep-set eyes, an intentional shift of both his attention and attitude.

"Ah. Our esteemed guest," he says mildly. His accent is softer, almost English, like he's forcing it to not be thick.

I don't step forward for any formal introduction. I should. But I hate him, the feeling growing more potent with the way Loch's fists are knotted behind his back.

Malachy sets his tablet on the desktop, rises, and buttons his pin-stripe suit coat. Every move is gradual, taking charge of the room by making even mundane acts look calculated.

"How are you finding your time in Ireland, Prince Kristopher?" He props his hands on hips. "Is Lochlann being an *attentive* host?"

I only see Loch twitch because I keep him in front of me so I can watch both him and Malachy.

"Yes." I stare at the side of Loch's face.

He doesn't turn away from his uncle.

But he subtly shifts to the left. Between me and Malachy.

"Did you invite him to accompany you when meeting with me, Lochlann?" Malachy asks. "Keeping him close, are you?"

Malachy holds Loch's eyes for one second. Two.

He wouldn't like that his nephew is trying to correct a negative press assumption about him. Is he pissed that I'm here, helping Loch?

Good.

"I'm here as a representative of my Holiday," I try. "There's nothing to—"

"Oh, I know very well why you are here." That intent gaze oozes back to me. "To prove that my nephew is something he is not. Or maybe to prove that he is *exactly* who the press thinks him to be."

I frown. "Excuse me?"

"Don't—" Loch starts, but Malachy clicks his tongue.

There's something in the way Malachy looks at Loch. Like he's holding a leash, and I have a sinking feeling that if he tugs even a little, Loch will go from a firestorm of stubbornness and personality to acquiescent and beaten.

I almost reach for Loch. To—what? I want that connection severed. Want that leash broken.

But Loch ignores all of this. "Why are you here, Uncle?"

Malachy flicks his hand dismissively towards the door before unbuttoning his suit coat and sitting back down. "As I said, I will see you tonight at supper."

"No. You can talk to me now. What do you want?"

Malachy's eyes go from his nephew to me with a shitty smirk. "In mixed company? Are you quite certain?"

Loch says nothing, an internal war waging.

Malachy's face hardens. He doesn't even look at me when he says, "You are dismissed, Prince Kristopher."

How many times in my life has my dad said that to me? Ejected me from conversations, situations, events, press shots, and I went, letting Coal handle it all. Dad's mask of congeniality was always more convincing; Malachy doesn't even pretend to not be toying with us.

My lip curls. "No. I'm good."

The contemptuous glare Malachy gave Loch is now pinned on me.

Loch places himself directly in Malachy's line of sight. "Kris. You do na—"

"I'm not just here because of the press situation." I push around him, in front of Malachy. "Christmas has been removed from many Holidays for too long and we're seeking to start conversations. To discuss what we all have in common and pool ways to fix issues that involve things like organization. Politics. Joy."

Malachy nods. "Yes, let us talk about *joy.*"

My heart kicks. But his amusement is a warning light.

Malachy angles his tablet towards us, swiping through screenshots of paparazzi nonsense. My arrival here. My apology. Photos of the race.

He stops on shots of Loch in the crowd during the fight, calming everyone down.

Air hisses out of Loch next to me. A pained grunt.

"Kris," he whispers. "Leave. Please."

I whip a look back at him. His eyes are wide.

I haven't heard him *plead* before.

It's wrong, seeing him like this, posture bowed, submissive.

I'm stunned enough that I nod before I can summon energy to argue.

One more second of watching his eyes. Of waiting for his posture to change, a flicker of an opening I'd use to stand my ground.

But there's nothing. Just—*this.*

"It was a pleasure to meet you, King Malachy," I say numbly, facing Loch.

When I do turn, Malachy's analyzing this interaction, and his amusement seems to deepen. I don't know what we gave him, but it feels significant.

Self-hatred roils in my chest. I spin on my heel and leave the room, even with half of me screaming to not let Loch be here alone.

All I can see is every fight Coal and I had with our father, every moment Coal took the impact of his anger, the worst of his focus—and that time when Coal thought Dad was going to hit me.

It's impossible for me to go far. I don't even close the office door all the way, just hold it in the seam, knob twisted, ready, waiting.

Loch must suspect I'm still nearby, because he switches into Irish. He doesn't want me to listen.

Well, I'm sorry, but that's not going to work.

I haven't used Christmas's magic at all since I've been here, but I tug on the constant connection I have to it that I've wholly taken for granted.

"—broke up a fight," Loch is saying. "I don't know what you think—"

"Don't play dumb with me," Malachy snaps in Irish too, all pretense dropped. "You used magic. We had an agreement, you selfish piece of shit."

The hair rises on the back of my neck. I damn near stomp back in there, held at bay only by Loch's immediate "I did what I had to do." A flicker of his usual confidence returns. "What *you* are supposed to do."

"And *I* cut you off. I let you and your sisters stay in this castle. I even let you carry on with these little events, *and* I fund much of them—"

Yeah, so he can slap ads for his distillery everywhere. Real altruism right there.

"—yet you repay all that by stealing from me—*again?* Did you not learn your lesson last year?"

"You want to save face, don't you?" Loch's voice is remarkably calm. But calm in a way that's holding back dread. "If things go like this too long, attitudes unmonitored and our people *forgotten,* the court will get suspicious. It isn't enough to run events half-assed this way. We can't—"

"Stop accessing my magic. If I catch you in more situations like this"—there's a smack, and my vision goes white before I realize Malachy's tapping the tablet's screen—"you'll see how fast I throw the three of you out on your asses. You'll be begging for my forgiveness."

"You're the *King*," Loch implores. "How long do you think you can sustain this? Do you even realize what you're destroying—what our people lose year by year that we allow—"

"I thought you'd realized how kind I've been to you, Lochlann. I thought you'd realized how much more you have to lose. *Do not mess with me,* you ungrateful little fucker."

"You're the King," Loch says again, breathless. *"Act like the King."*

"This is your only warning."

Silence hangs.

I feel the absence of threat along with the sizzle of transportation magic, and I realize—Malachy is gone.

My hand is so tightly clenched around the knob that when Loch pulls on the door from the other side, I don't let go, don't bother trying to hide that I was here the whole time.

I shove it open and he flinches back.

His face is red, eyes glassy. Behind him, the room is empty—

Except for a small bunch of clovers next to the desk, growing out of the carpet.

I freeze.

That wasn't there before. Remnants of St. Patrick's Day's transportation magic?

Like the one left in Christmas.

If they know clovers get left behind when they use transportation magic, then they know they left at least one when they fled Christmas after installing the device on our Merry Measure.

So whoever it was—Loch or Malachy—they know they left a clue behind.

It *was* hidden, and no one noticed it until I did, so maybe they took that risk. Or maybe they tried to cover their tracks when they left, but missed one clover . . . just bad luck.

I yank my eyes away from the clover patch, but Loch hasn't noticed my fixation on it.

He grunts in exasperation. "I told you to leave," he says, back in English.

"I left the room," I say. In Irish.

His eyes go wide, round and horrified.

"I wanted to know if he . . ." I switch back to English, then fumble. "If I needed to come back in."

I watch his mind work, rolling through the conversation, trying to figure out if he said anything I shouldn't have heard. But I stay in the doorway and I'm only livid *for him* and he seems to realize that with a shattering, slow blink.

"Why would you've come back in?" he asks.

"To help you," I answer stupidly.

Loch's wonder goes to suspicion. "You do na seem surprised by what you heard. Siobhán. She told you about Malachy?"

"Don't be mad at her for it. But yes."

Loch cups his hands over his face and scrubs, hard, trying to wipe away the past few minutes.

"Are you gonna move?" He waves at how I'm taking up the whole doorway.

I step out into the hall.

Loch doesn't leave, though. He studies my face. Looks up at the ceiling with another sigh, but this one seems self-deprecating.

"Get drunk with me," he orders the space above my head.

My mouth pops open. "I—"

He cuts around me to head up the hall.

I watch him get a few feet ahead. Tautness is strung through his shoulders.

"That was na a question, Coffee Shop," he calls back.

I follow.

Chapter Nine

Loch winds through the castle, back down past the dining room, and into a long, silent kitchen. The whole middle is taken up by a rectangular butcher block island, pots hanging over it that glint polished copper when he flicks on a light. Every inch of space has the same ancient feeling as the rest of the castle, only this room is hung with centuries of food prep, spices in the air, flour worked into the smoothed wooden surfaces and the terracotta floor tiles and the wall-sized fireplace at one end.

Loch crosses to that fireplace and crouches in front of a cupboard near it. Bottles clink as he rummages through its contents.

"If you pull out more whiskey, I'm leaving right now," I say.

He's halfway back up, a bottle of whiskey in his hand. The label is definitely not Green Hills Distillery.

"Will na you let me have my vices in peace?" he moans.

"I watched you down like four glasses of that shit and you were barely tipsy. You said you wanted to get drunk."

"'Tis na *shite*, ya tasteless prick." He thinks. "But that's fair."

He bends back down, and hesitates.

"I'm gonna get my drink of choice for when I wanna be good and pissed," Loch says to the liquor cabinet. "But you canna mock me for it."

"I passionately do not agree to that," I say and spot a pantry in the recessed shadows next to the fireplace. We'll need something to eat. Drunk goal or not.

The pantry is mostly empty. Cans of food, some baking supplies, a few shelves of essentials.

Our chef would be *appalled*—this close to their Holiday, and they're not fully stocked?

But they don't have the funds to fill it, do they? Enough to keep up appearances, whatever Malachy deigns to give them. And they don't have people to provide for, either. Just a visiting Christmas Prince.

Heart in my throat, I sort through the meager food stuffs until I find two clipped bags of crisps on a shelf.

By the time I get back with them, there's a bottle near one end of the butcher block island.

I chuckle. "Whipped cream vodka?"

Loch sits on a barstool. I grab the one across from him and he cracks open the bottle.

"Laugh it up, boyo, but my logic is proper brilliant. Sláinte." He takes a swig. "You see, it does na taste quite like rubbing alcohol, but it does na have the syrupy shite that guarantees a bloody awful migraine."

He offers it to me. I make a great show of cringing as I take the bottle.

"Sláinte to you," I say and drink.

The rim is warm from his lips.

I swallow forcefully.

"You're in no position to laugh at my drinking choices." Loch grabs the bottle back from me. "Hating on Irish whiskey like that. I should throw you outta the country."

"I'm more of a beer guy."

Loch sputters on the next drink and shoves to his feet. "Why dinna you say so? Christ."

"Where are you going?"

"Wait there."

By the door we came in, Loch yanks open a fridge and hauls out two bottles.

He returns, pops the lid off one on the island's edge, and hands the bottle to me. Smithwick's ale.

"Oh, yeah, beer and vodka," I note. "This is going to end well."

Loch opens one for himself and retakes his seat. "That's the point, eh?"

I barely get out the start of a question when he cuts me off.

"I dinna know you spoke Irish." He unclips a bag of cheese and onion crisps, but his hand's shaking a little.

"I don't."

He gives me a flat stare.

"I mean, it was magic. Unless I'm actively choosing to use magic to translate what you're saying, I don't speak a word of it."

"So you were spying on me intentionally?"

"Yes." I don't try to cover. I hold his gaze and let the silence stretch, stretch, god it has to snap eventually, but his eyes go from suspicious to soft to—to—

I grab the vodka and take a long gulp because there's a realization that's swiftly fighting up through my chest with clawed fingers and once it gets into my head I am not going to be able to ignore it anymore. But for now, I can keep it down, choking for air in vodka and ale.

"It's good Christmas's magic lets me do that," I add. "Half the time, it's the only way I know what you're even saying."

Loch barks a laugh. "Fuck off. My accent is the pinnacle of sexy."

"Yeah, that's why Dublin's the city of love? Or wait, no, that's—" And I use magic to help me rattle off a stream of French. I'm getting tipsy and I want to see his reaction.

He has the vodka at his lips again. It holds there, his amusement careening into shock.

His cheeks pinken. "Neat trick," he says into the bottle.

He sets it down without taking another drink, but his throat fluctuates.

I almost reach for my phone. Almost ask if I can take a picture of him and send it to Iris because that, there, that bob of his neck—something about it is worthy of being immortalized. In googly eyes or any other medium.

"Still." He drags the back of his hand across his chin. "My accent's a helluva lot better than yours, French or no. What you got going on, eh? Some American English inbred bullshite even though Christmas is in *Greenland,* which never made sense to me anyway. You lot could have your North Pole reputation without freezing your arses off. Bit of a pigheaded commitment to your mythos."

The vodka is starting to take me and the beer is joining in so all I can do is laugh.

Loch smiles.

Mine slides right off, the way condensation's dripping down my beer bottle.

"What's going on with your uncle?" I whisper.

It kills the levity. Stabs it dead in the chest.

Loch picks at the label on his beer with his thumb. "You heard. He's a bastard."

"I gathered. But I mean—"

"I know what you mean." He leans back and blows out a heavy exhale, and with it his armor unravels, showing exhaustion, and worry, and regret. Such potent, raging regret that I don't know how I missed it before, glowing through the smallest cracks in his sarcastic, piss-taking exterior like molten embers burning him to ash.

He swallows more vodka. Winces at the taste, or himself.

"No one takes my Holiday seriously," he says. "No one's given a shite about us in generations. We're the Holiday of drinking and partying and green fucking beer. My father believed that, and his father, and half our court. They do na take themselves seriously— what hope have we ever had, to *be* something?"

"*You* don't believe that." Not a question. A fact.

Loch takes another drink of vodka. Jesus, he's going to finish half the bottle at this rate—I snatch it from him but just hold it.

"No," he whispers to the table. "I do na believe that."

Then he looks up at me with a burst of energy, so *alive* in an intoxicating joy, I feel spotlit by his passion.

"It's a celebration of our people. A celebration of their survival in the face of political and religious instability. In the face of starvation and oppression and the fucking English's attempts at genocide. It's everyone from Queen Medb to Grace O'Malley to Mary Robinson. It has na always been that, I know, and there are problematic parts to be sure. I mentioned earlier *the luck of the Irish*? The phrase itself came from racist pricks who thought Irish success could only be because of *luck*, rather than any *skill*; but even that's na fair. We do have luck, in our folklore and pantheons. We were built on luck long before arseholes bastardized it. St. Patrick's Day has become the one thing we agree on even when we're divided, even when we're scattered across the globe. So we embrace the bad with the good, because you would na only see someone as the shite they've overcome, but as the fact that they did overcome it at all. My Holiday is a uniting thread of who we are and what we're capable of and I—"

He stops.

Drops back against the barstool in a limp heap.

"And I have no power to make it what it deserves to be because Malachy's pouring all our joy into his *motherfucking* distillery. That's what he does with it, uses magic to make his business *lucky*—Siobhán told ya?"

I nod.

He mimics me. "I've tried so hard to harness our magic, at least the luck when I can, but I have so little of it. It does na always *listen* to me, and when it does, it—"

"It breaks your headphones so wandering Christmas princes stumble into your studio?" I offer.

He snorts. "Useful, eh? I do na know what to do with magic scraps. And last year." He licks his lips, leaves a wet sheen that is a beacon. "Last year, I was right fed up. I have some access to our magic; the transfer to Malachy did na take like it should, so my control of it will na fully separate, despite his best attempts. And last year, I'd had it. I used what I could to try to make our Holiday better. I organized festivals and restarted events that'd fallen by the wayside. It wasn't a lot, but it was *something*. And Malachy—he became our guardian after our parents died, and they left us some money, but he's the *King* and this is technically *his* castle. Our family bank accounts, all of it is his. So he pays for everything, for Siobhán and Finn's schooling— I got a scholarship—but if he pulled that money? We would na have enough to keep this up. Already Colm's here on mostly his own dime, gets room and board. Malachy let go all the staff last year after my stunt. Holds it over our heads now because of my stupid attempt at making things better."

"Does your court know what Malachy's doing?" I ask. "Do they come to events?"

"Nah." He drinks more of his beer. "It's been years since they were involved in the running of anything because Malachy pushed 'em all away. If they do go to events, he knows, and appeases them so it all *looks* aboveboard. He puts money into the successful events so he can take credit for doing his damn job, and the Holiday still happens, eh? It carries on. It isn't *grand* though. It isn't what it could be, on a global scale—we have a decent time here in Ireland, but around the world? The Irish diaspora suffers the most, and I canna even make sure people *here* get what they need."

I sip the vodka, tongue sweet with that artificial whipped vanilla flavor. "You should show them. Your court."

Loch's eyes go hesitant. "What?"

"I saw you in the crowd today. Not just with the fight—the artists you talked to before the race. Siobhán told me how you set it all up. How anything good that comes out of this Holiday is because of you."

He blushes. *Blushes.* His cheeks go vibrant red, the tip of his nose rosy.

"Siobhán," he hisses.

I'm stuck on his blush. Utterly captivated by it.

My lips fumble, but I clear my throat. "You should invite your court to the castle. Or to Dublin for the final big parade. Confront them before Malachy gets a chance so you can show them how hard you're working to cover where he's lacking."

Loch gets a bemused look on his face. "You sound like Finn. But what would I show them? That I can help festival organizers coordinate? Malachy's done a good enough job of making sure the court thinks I am exactly what he says, someone untrustworthy."

"But you wanted me here to help that," I counter. "You wanted to show that the tabloid lies were just that, *lies.* I could've apologized and left, but you wanted me to stay for the full Holiday. Why?"

Loch scowls, but he directs it at his beer bottle. "I told ya, you can leave if you hate it here so much."

"That's not what I meant. I meant what are you hoping to get out of me being here for this week? You want the Holiday press to write good shit about you, right?"

He shrugs, sheepish almost, worrying the inside of his cheek.

Then he drags a hand over his chin and his lip curls, anger, not at me, directed . . . somewhere out, but also somewhere within. "I do na want Malachy seeing he can use the Holiday press to further take my legs out, yeah? I figured, if I make a splash with addressing this first incident, Malachy'll be less inclined to pile on. The press getting fixated on me like this was chance, but I do na want it to be intentional in the future."

My head bobs slowly. "And Malachy let you arrange this? Isn't he worried, with the press being so involved, that opinion could turn against him?"

Loch grunts at his beer bottle. "He knows he's got us pinned, my sisters and me. He knows we'd bow to him."

"But you *are* trying to change things with your court. How they see you. You just aren't going to act on it beyond your reputation?"

Color drains out of Loch's face and he seems to realize in that moment everything he's said, like he wasn't fully in control of himself.

He drops his head into his hands. "Ah, Christ. This has to be some treasonous act, pouring my guts out to you. In my defense, there are few people I can talk to about this shite. My friends at Cambridge obviously do na know about—" He waves a hand, gesturing at what I assume is our whole Holiday hidden world. "They have strong opinions on various types of abstract art, but St. Patrick's Day? They think I'm loopers talking about it as much as I do. Still though, you do na need this."

"Yeah, I do. I get it." Hell, how many times already have I caught myself thinking *I don't talk about this with anyone* as I'm in the process of talking about whatever it is with *him*? What makes it so easy for us to talk to each other? "Besides, I'm a bit of an expert in treasonous acts, actually."

Loch's brows concave.

"Coal—my brother—and I sort of overthrew our father last Christmas." I tip my beer bottle as I talk. "He was stealing joy from other winter Holidays. We put a stop to it by rallying them to stand against him."

"Yeah, I know that." He snorts. "The news made it all seem quite civil. I did na know *you* were involved."

"Surprised?"

"Of course." He forces a grin. "Is that why you agreed to stay for the week? To foster treason in unsuspecting Holidays?"

I don't pick up his attempt at humor.

I'm here because someone has been stealing Christmas's joy the same way we stole from other Holidays.

I thought it was you.

But it's Malachy, isn't it? It has to be Malachy.

I could say all of that. This is a natural opening. I'd know it's Malachy for sure and I could pursue investigating him and maybe Loch would help.

But he has a helluva reason to steal from us, his uncle cutting him off like this. Just because Malachy's an ass doesn't make him guilty.

And just because things are shifting between me and Loch doesn't absolve him.

As much as I know all that, I know even more that if I brought up the theft right now, I'd see the truth in Loch's reaction.

This is the reason I'm in Ireland at all, the whole point of my visit here. Coal needs me to do this. *Christmas* needs me to do this.

So why can't I get my mouth to open?

I suck down more beer, but my throat is dry, each swallow an effort.

Loch frowns when I'm quiet too long. "Kris?"

I shake my head, hoping my face doesn't give away everything reeling inside of me.

Do it. Ask him.

"How did Malachy convince you to give up the crown?" I hear myself ask. "He's so villainous he's almost a cartoon."

It's the vodka. It's the beer. It's—it's not *me.* This can't be me, this person who made a conscious choice to *not* do the thing my brother needs me to do.

I don't want to know if Loch's stealing from us.

Not tonight.

Guilt is tart and vile in my stomach and I take another drink to counter it.

Loch chuckles at my question, and I'm not sure where the tension is coming from, but it's creeping over me like an inbound tide.

"My da had just died. I was vulnerable. Malachy convinced our court that I was too unstable, too insubordinate." He swipes the vodka and chugs a mouthful. "Maybe he was right."

"Like hell he was right." The back of my neck burns.

He gives me a wry look, but doesn't argue, and doesn't agree.

"My dad passed Christmas to my brother," I tell him without thinking. Is that something I can spread around yet, before Coal's formal party announcement? Eh, add it to the list of my problems for tomorrow. "The woman who runs our Merry Measure said—"

Loch sputters a laugh. "Your *what?*"

"Christmas's joy meter. The Merry Measure."

"Is everything in Christmas a pun?"

I grin. "If I have any say in it, yes. But when the woman in charge of our joy meter oversaw the transfer, she said it had to be willing and joyful to work. Maybe, because your transfer of power to Malachy wasn't entirely willing or joyful, it didn't take fully, and that's why you still have access to St. Patrick's Day's joy."

Loch's eyebrows rise into a sardonic twist. "I did already come to that conclusion on my own."

"Then—" I scrub at my face, fighting for clarity. "The transfer never entirely took. So what's to stop you from . . . taking back control from Malachy? Basically cancel the initial attempt at a transfer, since it was never completed? You wouldn't need Malachy's participation likely, since he isn't in full control and was never supposed to be."

Loch's face throws me into quaking silence. Eyes wide, lips parted, brow furrowed.

"You've likely already tried that," I say to my nearly empty beer bottle. "Of course. It was dumb of me to assume you wouldn't have tried everything. I—"

"No."

I frown up at him.

He's watching me in that absorbed way he's done a number of times now, like he can listen to my inner thoughts if he focuses hard enough, can see straight into my soul if he wills it. And god, I *feel* that, his lidded-eye gaze an overhanging thunderhead.

"I have na tried that," he whispers. "What you're suggesting is a coup."

"Maybe I am here to instigate treason."

Loch finishes his beer, plunks the empty bottle onto the table, and scrubs his hand over his mouth. "This day has been too long to entertain a *coup* on top of everything else. And *Christ*"—his eyes go from the bandage on my forehead to the one now hidden under my sweater—"you have to be feeling like shite."

I shrug. "The vodka is doing wonders, honestly."

He bends across the table, reaching for the bottle.

I pull it back.

"Kris." He cocks his head, chastising. "I should na have even let you drink."

"I'm not broken. You aren't in charge of taking care of me."

"Who does take care of you, then? It sure as hell isn't *you*."

"My brother is excellent at—" Well, no, he isn't. I take care of *him*, and that's part of the reason he's pushing me to do different things, because I spent so much of my life being the one making sure *he* ate enough and slept enough and drank enough.

No one does that for me.

Until.

I stare at Loch.

The realization I'm fighting rises up, up, pounds on my swollen throat with angry fists.

I take another drink of vodka.

Another.

A third, to be safe.

Loch snatches the bottle from me. "Jesus, you're gonna vomit."

"Vodka isn't whiskey." That doesn't matter; a lightweight is a lightweight. "I'm perfectly fine with—" My body chooses this moment to hiccup.

Loch cuts a smile. "What's your brother excellent at?"

"Oh. Um. Drinking. You'd like him. He's got the same burdens as you and channels them into unfunny humor the same way."

"He's who that tattoo is for, eh?" He points at my right arm.

I gawk at him. Click my mouth shut. "Yeah. How did you know that?"

My stomach swoops at all this talk of Coal. Once negotiations are over, the other winter Holiday leaders will expect repayment to begin, and we won't have enough joy for it, and Coal will be the one who'll have to face them. I have *one job* to help him, and I can't even do that right.

Loch's cheeks are pink again. "He's the only one you really talk about. Well, him and that girl of yours, Iris."

"She's not my girl," I quickly correct. Then, "What did last night tell you about me?" Still abrupt, pinched throat making everything tight and desperate.

"What?" he asks, airy.

"You said you can tell a lot about someone by the way they paint. What did it tell you about me?"

Loch pushes to his feet.

I flatten my hands on the cold butcher block. Hold my breath. Like any movement will break whatever spell this is or yank me back to soberness and I am in a fuzzy, gilded, vodka-induced haze and I don't want to leave.

But he crosses to the sink, pours two glasses of water, and places one in front of me as he sits again.

He drinks. Watches me over the rim.

"It's more telling that you called yourself the *Spare Claus* today," he says.

Blood rushes to my face. "It's a tabloid headline—"

"Na. It isn't. See, I've read the tabloids, and I—"

"I'm sorry." It topples out of me. Half genuine. Half wanting him to stop this course of conversation. "For the tinsel incident. I really am. I never intended to hurt your reputation or give your uncle further cause to undermine you."

Loch's face gentles. "Now that's a sincere apology, boyo. But we're talking about *you* now. And I never once saw the press refer to you as *spare* anything. Is that how you see yourself? Or is that how your brother treats—"

"No. Fuck no. Coal would never."

"So why'd you call yourself that?"

I take a gulp of water though I want more vodka because this will sober me up and the only way I can answer his question is to be drunk.

"I am the spare."

Loch scowls. "Nah, you aren't."

"No. I—I'm the backup. The background. The one who's been so focused on other people getting their happy ending that I have no idea what I want my own to be. And now Coal's set. He's got his boyfriend and Christmas and he doesn't need me anymore, not like he used to, so I could do *anything*, and I'm floundering because *what the hell am I supposed to do*. I built my life around making sure other people were happy. I even went to Cambridge and kept going in this shitty track out of some childish dream that it'd earn my father's—"

That catches me. Not in embarrassment; I'm caught in realization.

I squint at Loch. "You're in the art history track."

"Yeah?"

"Why?"

"I like it. I got the scholarship, so I went."

"But—you also have a business degree."

"Ah. That." Loch stretches out a kink in his neck, and again, I'm hit with the need to take a picture of that neck, the way the muscles expand, retract, even under his black turtleneck. "That was my own attempt at winning my father's approval. I do na regret it—it's sure as hell helped me manage things that Malachy drops. But I realized, after my da died and Malachy snatched the throne, that the only thing I could control was my own happiness. I dinna want to give up on St. Patrick's Day, but I wanted to have a . . . balance." He shrugs. "I am na always great at it. Siobhán and Finn will testify to that. But I'm at Cambridge now for *me,* because it reminds me that I do have power outside of Malachy."

I stare at him long after he stops talking. That's a mentality that I've never been able to grasp, one I've been seeking for years. To do something for no other reason than I *want* it.

"I have no idea what to do," I whisper. "I have no idea what I want."

Loch watches me unravel at the island and I press a fist into my forehead as the room spins.

"That vodka. Is hitting me." I clear my throat. "You're right. This day has been too long—"

His hand lays over my other one where it's splayed on the table.

My eyes go wide. I lift my head because I want to see his face this time.

His eyes are bloodshot. He sways a little; or maybe I sway, the sky is dark beyond the windows. What time is it? I have no idea. Time doesn't exist. There's only whipped cream vodka and the way Loch's fingers follow the lines his smears of paint left yesterday, down the delicate skin on the back of my hand.

He launches up from the barstool.

I stand too, tethered to his movements like a reflection.

He comes around the end of the island. My body shifts to follow his, then he's in front of me, his heat pricking goosebumps down my arms.

"You do na know what you want," he says. Asks.

"No." The word wrenches out of me. "What do you want?"

A smile. It's shattering. Earth-destroying.

He curves down, breaking the height difference in a graceful arc, and rubs his lips across mine.

It's barely a kiss. It's a question. It's the start of something, one of those endless lines of possibilities that ripple out from me, only this one gleams and pulses and shows me the way until I get to that realization I've been fighting and I stand face to face with it.

I want him.

God, do I want him.

I let it explode over me, but what comes isn't destructive, it's a web of refracting beams the way the kitchen light is going into streaks at the edge of my vision, giving me a centering focal point around which everything else is ombré rays.

I shove onto my toes and kiss him back.

Loch whimpers in the core of his throat and meets me before I've even come up all the way, lips punishing and devouring and severe.

He tastes like vanilla and bitter hops and I'm gulping him in the way I drank up the frigid breeze from the car window. Like it could shock the thoughts from my head, the stress from my body, the chaos from my soul. And he does, with each palpitation of his lips on mine, I'm taken to the basest form of a primal existence. He sucks my tongue into his mouth and his beard abrades my face and it's all a throughline straight to every individual nerve ending. I make a noise that he counters with his own delicious moan and he's not just peeling me apart now, he's obliterating.

I never knew kissing could be *this*. Could be the fervor of every argument, the passion of every lashing that tongue has given me verbally, but in a way that melts my insides and I feel golden.

His hands are on my jaw, clamped around my head, holding me in place like I might evaporate—I might, I am, he bites my lower lip and my blood is turning to champagne bubbles. I grab onto his sweater against his hips to anchor to this plane of existence, but I'm *touching his hips,* those arched hills, that deep V I saw in his studio, and I whimper pitifully.

We twist and I need the support of the island at my back, his body boxing around mine, his height transforming to consume, swallowing me raw.

"Kris." He morphs my name into a melody, lilting accent dripping from each letter he speaks into my mouth. "You're all I've been able to think about for weeks. The only thought in my head is what your face will look like when I take you apart—like this, like this right now, you're perfect."

He hefts his hands under my thighs and I swear to god all the air in the room vanishes. It's nothing but electric ozone as I'm lifted, slammed to sit on the edge of the island, legs spreading to belt around his waist.

There are stars shooting all around, supernovas thrown into ruin by the way he works his lips across my jaw, laving, sucking, drawing an abstract curve with his mouth the way he paints them with his fingers. Those fingers. Those *fingers*—they're tangled in my belt, tugging, and I rock my head back and I'm so drunk and he feels so *right.*

"Perfect, Kris. Christ, look at you, spread out for me. So fucking good."

His praise hits my veins rapid-fire, my breaths heaving faster— holy shit, I've never been this close this fast. I rock against him, not caring at all that I'm devolving into greedy little moans that get lewder when his hard cock grinds against mine, but I *am* greedy. I am greed and gluttony and proof that these sins are deadly.

I can feel his grin on my neck. The flick of his tongue. "You like that, eh? Me telling you how good you are."

"*Mmmf.*" I try to speak but language is gone.

He puts a kiss in the divot under my ear, his words echoing in its hollow. "You are, Kris. So good for me. Look how well you react."

He bites my neck and I struggle for something solid but the world is sweaty and honeyed.

I want to be good for him. I want to be the *best* for him—all my existence whittles to that need.

"I canna concentrate on anything when you're around," he whispers. "I just want to taste you, I just want to do this to you—"

Bottles tip over behind me; one shatters on the stone floor. It makes me jump, and Loch, wrapped around me, turns to marble.

I match him. Still tied up in his gravitational pull. The pause gives me space to breathe, gasping, whiny breaths.

Loch presses his forehead to the curve of my shoulder. "*Shite.*"

He shoves back off of me, putting so much space between us that I'm immediately hit with a blast of cold in his absence. I shiver, splayed out on the table, arms propping myself up, legs wide.

"I should na have done that." He's looking at the floor. He's flushed and his hair is sticking up on the side and I don't even remember touching his head, but my hand feels it, that texture, the way my neck echoes the burn of his beard.

That's what I feel. Roughness, a scour on my heart from the regret painted so clearly across his face. It's him pulling away in the car all over again, except this time, everything he said is draped over me in contrasting silk. *So good for me, you're perfect—*

"Loch," I get out. My throat is wrecked. My body is a disastrous collision of mismatched pieces.

"I should not have done that," he says again, more forcefully, and he marches down the kitchen, rips open the door, and leaves.

It's all I can do to stagger off the island, legs gone to liquid, heart banging around my rib cage in ardent, aching thuds.

Glass crunches under my shoes. The bottle was empty, at least.

And I focus on that.

The glass everywhere. The crisps spread on the island. The half-full bottle of vodka.

Blearily, I pull my phone out and take a picture of it all.

I come back into myself midway through cleaning up.

We just made out, and he ran off, and I'm *cleaning up his kitchen*.

I hurl the dustpan I found back onto the shelf. It hits with a clang and I slam the cupboard and I—I—

I don't know. I don't know.

I should know.

I *do* know.

I know that his kiss tasted like all the dreams I waxed on about in the writing I don't do anymore, the words I wove while trying to imagine Iris but all I imagined was a fantasy, an ending.

He tasted like those fantasies.

He felt like those endings.

It's him.

Chapter Ten

I lurch out of the kitchen, 45 percent certain I'm leaning to the left like I'm on a listing ship.

My hip bangs into a doorframe.

Okay, 70 percent.

But I am 100 percent certain that I have never been this drunk in my life. The kind of drunk where I'm back in my guest room with no memory of walking there and I'm holding my phone and staring down at a link I don't remember opening. It's a tabloid site, a picture of Loch and me at the race's starting line, not looking at each other in a way that's even more potent than if we'd been staring into each other's eyes.

The caption is something about us being *buddies*.

I drop to the floor, my back against the edge of the bed. Fingers shaking, I pull up the thread with Coal, vodka in control of my faculties so I fire off a text to him before the rest of me can catch up.

PEEP, MINI CANDY CANE, AND THE BEST CLAUS

> how bad would it be if i kissed the guy who stole from us

My head hangs back against the mattress. The room is a merry-go-round of the too-bright overhead lights, spinning and spinning, and it smells like *baked beans* in here—

My phone rings. Not a text. A video call.

The vodka answers.

"First of all," Coal says immediately, "you not texting in your normal proper format is the most terrifying way I've ever been yanked out of a meeting."

I didn't—what did I do? "Fuck. Sorry—"

"Don't apologize. Secondly—you know you texted the group chat, right?"

Oh, nothing sobers up a person faster than realizing a drunken mistake.

I swipe away the video chat screen and check the text thread and—yeah. Yep. I did that.

Iris responded with a bunch of question marks.

With trembling fingers, I move the video call back over. I'm pale and stricken in the self-view screen, and Coal immediately goes reassuring.

"Hey, it's fine," he tells me. "You know Iris is cool."

"But she and I—I didn't—shouldn't have—"

"Kris. I need you to breathe right now."

So I do. That's what I'm good at. Doing what others need me to do. Right? That's my *whole problem.*

Coal sits down somewhere, and I recognize the wallpaper behind him.

"Are you in a hallway?"

"Do you want me to go back in and take this call in a room full of winter Holiday reps?"

He said that already. *Yanked out of a meeting.*

"Fuck, Coal, you did not have to call me!"

"Kris—"

"Oh my god. Do they know why I'm in St. Patrick's Day? The real reason? They found out, didn't they? And what have I done to help anything? Oh *fuck*—"

"*Kris.*" Coal leans forward, shoulders hunching around the phone. "That meeting had nothing to do with Christmas's joy. We won't start any repayments until after the winter Holiday collective treaty is signed, which won't be until negotiations are done, which are still looking to go for a few more weeks. We're good for now, I swear. We have time. *Breathe.* Tell me what happened."

My eyes flutter shut. The vodka is seemingly satisfied with the path it's led me down and is now having *words* with all the beer in my system. Churning, vomit-type words.

Or maybe all that roiling is from the taste of Loch on my tongue.

"Kris," Coal says again, softer. "What happened?"

I screw my thumb and finger into my eyes.

"Can I guess?" he presses.

I nod, sure, go for it—

"Did you finally realize that all that hatred you felt for Loch was actually you wanting to bang him?"

The look I give Coal's face on my phone is every building ounce of shock that's been welling from the moment I touched Loch's hand in the car. "*You knew?*"

"Of course I knew. No one hates someone for *breathing* like that unless they're trying really, really hard not to be turned on by them."

My moan gets mangled in a laugh.

Coal's face settles, patient. "Are you okay?"

"I'm drunk." I chuckle, and a dam breaks. "I fell down a hill because he laughed. Oh, I met his uncle, the St. Patrick's Day King—he's *massively* fucking over Loch in a way that would make Dad proud. And then." I choke, throat swelling in sharp response to the sting in my eyes. "Loch kissed me in the kitchen."

"And—you're not happy about that?" Coal's voice is cautious, trying to feel me out.

"*No.* I shouldn't have let him do that. Coal, he could be *stealing from us.* I've been fucking up this entire investigation from the start, all because of, what? *Him?* What kind of asshole does something like that? I came here for a reason, and this was *not* that reason. I'm so sorry, I—"

"Kristopher—"

"You guessed it had happened though—you knew. What else do you know?" I cling to my phone, willing Coal to spill all my own secrets out at me. "Why did you know I'd fail at this? What do you know that you aren't telling me? Who am I? Oh, fuck, that's a pathetic question. Oh my god. Oh my *god.*"

It's too hot in here and I'm in this stuffy blue sweater still and suddenly I'm on my feet, tearing open the door, lurching sightlessly into the dark hallway.

The air is immediately colder and that helps but it isn't enough.

"Kris—hey." Coal moves, too, stands and jogs down his own hall-way. "Hang on. I can come to you. I should've done that to begin with—why do I never go to *instantaneous transportation magic* before literally any other solution? Let me—"

"No, no, I'm fine."

"You're not fine."

I twist down the staircase and barrel forward, into the library. "*I'm fine.*"

"Kris. You're having a panic attack."

"*I do not have panic attacks.*"

The library is black, the moon and stars outside muted by clouds, and I drop to the floor and spread out on my back between a few shelves of books.

It's *frigid* in here.

The cold, cold air demands my heart slow down, freezing my lungs solid so I stop gasping and can take actual breaths. My limbs are a little numb, but the sting of the cold works sensation back into them too.

Coal's in his room now. A light pops on, and he says something muffled to Hex. A door opens, shuts, and Coal sits on his bed and I stare up at him, phone held over my face.

My eyes are wet.

"Kris," he starts. I think his eyes are wet, too, but why? I'm fine. He's fine. This is *fine.* "I'm sorry."

"Don't apologize—"

"Shut up. If you don't want me to come kick your ass in person, then *shut up and listen.* Okay?"

I nod.

"I'm sorry I'm part of the reason you feel like you don't know who you are," he says. "But—"

"You *aren't,*" I cut in. "Coal—this isn't what—"

"What did I say?" His voice is stricter than I've ever heard. And *that* shuts me up, the severity, a force of presence he's always capable of but rarely, *never* shows.

"You may feel like you don't know who you are," he continues, "but *I* know who you are. You're kind and considerate and you've got the biggest heart of anyone I know, and you're probably already thinking of ways to help Loch with his uncle. You're artistic and sensitive and strong, and there's a reason you became my rock. But you're allowed to be soft, too, and selfish. And I think that's where you're struggling, not knowing where to start with choosing stuff that's for *you*. Why did you think you loved Iris?"

I sniff. "Don't. Don't make me talk about her."

"Dumbass, I will *come over there* and hang you upside down if you don't—"

"Jesus. Fine. I should have loved her, okay?"

"Why? Who said?"

"Just—everyone."

"*Who?* Specifically? Who looked at you and said, *Kristopher, you need to fall in love with Iris?*"

My mouth hangs open. And I have no answer.

"You assumed it was what people expected of you?" Coal guesses. "Do you remember during Christmas, when Hex first got here, I asked what you wanted to do with your life?"

Yes. "No."

"Liar. You almost told me. You *almost* said something, then you deflected. What were you going to say? What do you want to do?"

Alcohol is a cruel, tricky truth serum, because I fully intend to play up having no idea what he's talking about when instead I say, "I want to write a book."

I do?

I did.

Forever ago. So long ago it's the wish of another person, and I'm shocked it's still living within me. And it is, *living,* because saying it out loud fills me with a buzzing sensation, the same champagne fizz as when Loch touched me, like every moment without this is stasis.

I used to write books. Silly little stories. Coal read a few, and I even let Iris read a few too, and she—god, I forgot all about this. She drew characters from one of those books for me, two kids at a summer camp in what I vaguely remember as being pretty much a direct Percy Jackson rip-off. I still have that picture somewhere, because it meant the *world* to me, to *see* these people I'd made up in my head.

Coal shakes the phone. "Kris! God, *yes*. Yes, okay? That's *amazing* and you should. I remember you used to write stories all the time. All your happily ever afters."

I close my eyes and a tear leaks down my temple.

"And tonight," Coal continues, "when he kissed you. Did you kiss him back?"

"I should've used tonight to question him about the joy theft." I throw words like shields. "I *chose* not to do that, Coal. It was an intentional decision I made and I fucked over our Holiday all for— all for—"

"I would've been pissed if you had asked him about that."

My eyes fly open.

"Did you kiss him back?" Coal repeats, punctuating each word.

Numb, I nod again.

"I think that was the first time in a long, long while when you did something because *you* wanted it. Not because it fulfilled some requirement you felt was put on you. And I'm proud of you."

I flatten my hand over my eyes, tears stinging as sharp as every observation he lays down, every uncompromising truth because he knows me as well as he knows himself. And there's comfort in that, so much comfort in that; this isn't something I'm making up. If my brother sees it too, it must be real.

"In all that writing you used to do about happily ever after," Coal continues, "did you ever think what being happy would actually feel like?"

"None of those things were supposed to make me happy."

I hear the words. I'm not sure who said them.

"What?" Coal asks. His voice is low. I'm still covering my own eyes, can't see him, can't face myself.

Something's building, I'm so sick of revelations tonight, I can't handle more, *stop*—

"None of the things I tried to do were supposed to make me happy. They were supposed to *work*."

A sob grabs me. Cuts off anything else I might add.

"Work how?" Coal asks softly.

There were guidelines when I was younger. Those storybooks I loved so much. There was a collection of fairy tales, all the old-school ones. *The loyal, duty-bound prince and his sweet partner, happy ever after.* Do this and this and this, and boom, a perfect life.

The kind of life where—

Fuck.

The kind of life where my mom would come back.

If I got this storybook perfect life, she'd come back.

Coal hisses in a breath.

I said that last part out loud. I can't regret it, because with it comes a groundswell of an unburdening, washing away.

"It's so dumb." I'm ripped to pieces over how pathetic my voice sounds. "That I do this. Why I do this. Fuck, I *know* nothing I do will bring her back, but—"

"I know," Coal whispers. "I know, Kris. I'm sorry, and I—god, I hate her so much. I'm so sorry she's hurting you."

This was all wrapped up in Coal's own personal revelations a few months back. The deep, eternal scars that our mother leaving put on him. I was so proud of him for recognizing that and starting to heal, while I'm falling apart because I thought if I built some antiquated perfect life, not only would Mom undo what she did, but no one else would have a reason to leave.

I altered my whole being into shapes that fit voids in everyone else's lives so they'd *stay,* so my life would look perfect, so I wouldn't be alone again. But I never asked myself what shape I wanted to take.

"For what it's worth"—Coal's voice is strained—"it wasn't a bad goal. You wanted to be happy. You still do. Somewhere along the way, you lost sight of what would make *you* happy in favor of what you *thought* you should do. This dream isn't working for you, is it? So maybe it's time to try a new dream."

"That's the problem." Another sob comes, a whimper that echoes in the wide, empty room. "It's all too *big*, and what if I pick the wrong thing again?"

"Kris, you don't have to figure out who you are in one moment. Certainly not a drunk moment, god, I beg of you. Just start small. See what comes together. Keep making choices because *you* want them, not because you think anyone expects it or it'll make someone else happy. None of this is for anyone other than *you*."

"I came here to do a job, though. I came here to—"

"You can do that. Like I said, we have time until the missing joy becomes a real problem, and you've already made progress in finding out about his uncle being suspicious. You have a few days left. And honestly, if you end up spending your time in Ireland making out with Loch and doing nothing else, do you think I'll give a shit? I mean, I do, in that I definitely care about not pissing off the winter Holidays collective, but it's impossible for me to not make sure *joy* is my priority. And your joy? Top of the list. Always has been."

If I wasn't already a blubbering mess, Coal's words would have pushed me over the edge.

"What if he's the one stealing from us?" I ask. "What do I do then?"

"Just . . . be cautious, I guess. But I don't think you'd be this twisted up about someone who was a thieving asshole. No matter what happens next, keep choosing yourself. Promise me you will."

"I don't know how to do that. I tried, tonight, with—with Loch, and—"

And he walked away.

I should not have done that.

Coal picks up on what I don't say. "It didn't end well?"

I shake my head.

His demeanor changes. Stiffens. "Did he hurt you?"

"No. Not—no." Yes. He did, but not like that.

"Was he drunk too?" Coal asks.

"Yeah."

"Then tomorrow's a fresh start. For both of you. Try to talk to him. See if you can get some clarity on the situation without alcohol or stress clouding things. Even beyond this kiss, I think he's doing something for you. Whatever's forcing you to face these truths about yourself is worth pursuing."

He's right.

Loch is the first person I've interacted with who hasn't immediately made me think about what he expects of me, what he needs, who I can be for him. It's been nothing but fighting each other from the start—I mean, I'm thinking of how to be what he needs *now*, like how to help him with his uncle, but it isn't at the sacrifice of any part of me. It's what I want to do.

Coal hums. "No more thinking, okay? Go back to your room and go to sleep. Actually—" He squints. "Where are you? Did you stumble out somewhere safe or do I really need to come get you?"

"No. I'm fine. I'm in the library." Something occurs to me. Like a barrier lifted, and I can feel things that happened more fully. "The library I was in with Loch, where he gave me those books. I should've known then. It was like a scene from a queer *Beauty and the Beast*."

Coal laughs. It urges a smile onto my face and I'm so relieved for it.

"Go to bed," Coal says. "For real."

"Okay."

"Do not fall asleep on the floor of the library. And hey. Look at me."

I do.

His face takes up most of the screen. "I love you, dumbass."

I roll my eyes in a miserable attempt to hide how much it means to me. "I love you too. Asshole."

"Pissant. See? I can use that word now, too."

"Good night."

"Good night."

I click off the video call. The library drops into blackness around me, and I lie there on the carpet for another long, shuddering breath.

Then I lift my phone again and send Iris that photo I took of the mess in the kitchen.

A few seconds pass, and she texts back.

IRIS

IRIS

i'll make a mixed media artist out
of you yet

saw your other text. you doing all
right?

how'd the bottle break?

> How'd the bottle break?
> How did the bottle break.
> There are a few couches around an unlit fireplace about two rows
> up, back by the door. I make my way there and collapse on one. It's
> stiff and meant for formal sitting, not a sprawling guy drunk off his
> ass, but I'm too strung out to care.

I'm fine. Thanks.
Sorry I texted the group chat.
Meant to only bother Coal
with my mental collapse.

IRIS

so you were going to send me
the pic of the shattered bottle,
then nothing?? like i wouldn't
have known something was up
anyway

i'm free right now. call me? we can
talk about it

Thanks. But I just got off the
phone with Coal, so I'm all
talked out.

IRIS

it's been a pretty interesting
progression of photos you've

sent. first the one of loch. now the
broken bottle.
what's the next one gonna be?

My reaction is to tell her—jokingly, the way I would Coal—to
fuck off. Are we there yet? After everything else tonight, why not
find out?

The next photo will be me
lovingly flipping you off.

IRIS
eh, derivative. you've got more
photographer potential than that

Are you seriously critiquing
my text photo dump?

IRIS
like a fine wine babycakes

A noise warbles through the library a beat before my fogged brain
realizes I laughed. It settles in my chest, real and warm.

Just for you, I'll try to make
my emotional breakdowns
form a poetic, complete
story arc.

IRIS
that's all i ask
but seriously, take care of yourself,
okay?

I drop my phone onto my chest and lay there, arm thrown over
my head.

Coal told me not to figure things out in a drunk moment. Iris got me thinking about poetic resolution, which is the *opposite* of what I should be doing now; forcing my life to fit a certain mold is what got me into this mess. But maybe that's not what poetry is? Nothing beautiful is ever forced. So what pieces have I missed, what path am I already going down that I haven't noticed because I've been too busy trying to make other paths work?

Okay. Short introspection moment.

What do I know about myself?

One. I like writing. I miss it. I miss it so much that I think that's part of the ache that's always in my chest—I miss doing it for *me,* not to drone on about the economic and political ramifications of the Jacobite party against Robespierre's rise or other dry-ass bullshit that I *do not care about.*

Two. Well, One-A. I really hate school. Like, deeply, passionately loathe it.

Three. I want to kiss Loch again. I want to kiss him again and again and I want to find out what he was going to do when he was trying to take off my belt. I want to know if he always talks like that when he's kissing or if he was drunk, because if that's what he does when he's sloshed then whatever that tongue of his can do sober is going to completely annihilate me.

Four. Four. Is there a Four?

Well. Three things is a start.

Why did Loch say he shouldn't have done that? Why did he pull away—twice, in the car and in the kitchen? Maybe he was picking up on my uncertainty? Everyone else sure as hell seems able to read me.

I'm starting to lose consciousness. In and out like my breath, brighter then darker, hazy then still. And I want to make a decision, have a plan for the morning, but all I can do is close my eyes.

Chapter Eleven

"Christ, Kris! There ya are."

Awareness grabs on to me and the worst headache known to man lodges itself behind my eyes.

Directly after, waltzing through my body like a triggered orchestra of pain, comes an ache in my legs and tremors in my muscles and everywhere, *everywhere,* I feel the brunt of the physical exertion of yesterday's run along with my graceful faceplant down the hill.

"Holy shit," I moan and tug the blanket up over my head.

. . . did I have a blanket last night?

I crack an eye open. The scratchy library couch is under me, but a thick quilt weighs me down now, warm but smelling of storage mothballs.

Siobhán shakes my arm and my moan devolves into a doleful whine.

"You gonna make a habit of waking up in our castle hanging? It's getting a wee bit racist, Kris, not gonna lie."

Hanging? Hang—hungover. Ah.

I sit up, eyes in slits.

She's fully dressed. And in a coat. And morning light is pouring through the far windows, lighting up the library in a pale haze.

"What time is it?"

"Time to *go* is what. We're waiting on your sorry arse. Thought the leprechauns got ya."

Slowly, I glare at her. "You all need to stop joking about that."

"Joking?" She crosses herself. "I do na joke about leprechauns."

I give an unimpressed blink.

Siobhán grins. That grin wavers and she holds up her phone, showing a white screen so fast I don't catch what it is. "Interesting bit of reading Christmas put out 'bout the race."

Bit of what?

My contorted face is question enough.

Siobhán stuffs her phone back into her pocket. "The statement Christmas put out over Loch helping you yesterday, and his role in the fight. Shot those bloody speculations right down. Made Loch look real grand in it all."

The texts I sent Wren. She must've polished them up into a press release and sent it out already. Of course she did.

"Oh." Why am I blushing? "Well." And I shrug stupidly.

Siobhán beams at me and crinkles her nose. "Ah, don't hide it, Kris. We're winning ya over, I know we are." Her smile softens one last time. "Loch sure as fuck will na thank ya himself, the stubborn prick, but thank you."

Damn this blush straight to hell. "You're welcome."

It's no big deal. It's what I'm here for—what *they* think I'm here for. But that's all I can get myself to say.

"Now get your arse up and change, you reek of—" She sniffs. "Is that whipped cream vodka? Christ, Loch did this to ya. I shoulda known."

That blush goes nuclear.

Everything rushes back over me—the kiss, my call with Coal and texting with Iris, passing out here.

The kiss.

The kiss.

The—

My eyes catch on the table next to the couch.

There's a glass of water. Two pain pills. A bag of crackers.

The heat building in my body floats into my cheeks.

I'm painfully aware of the silence stretching between Siobhán and me, but I feel drunk again for an entirely different reason.

"Give me ten minutes?" I squint up at her.

"Five. And that's generous." She swats the side of my head and spins out of the room.

I take the pain pills, down the water, and eat a few crackers before I leave the library. What's the event today? Pretending to like

Loch at these events for the tabloids will be a whole lot easier now that I actually like him, *like him* like him, and I freeze once I'm in my room.

That effervescence from last night is everywhere, my veins and my gut and my chest as I inhale.

I like Lochlann Patrick.

It's overtaking all my senses like a megaphone announcer got ahold of my amygdala, *I like Lochlann Patrick.*

But my rational side remembers, quite vividly, that I don't know what he's thinking. I held his hand in the car, but he pulled away. He initiated the kiss, yeah, but he *stopped* it, too—then he brought me hangover and pain cures in the library, and covered me with a blanket. So what does *that* mean?

Shit.

I'm in all sorts of trouble.

I ignore the Wren-approved outfit for today—she *labeled* my sets of clothes, good god—and throw on a T-shirt and jeans. New bandages in place, I make do without a shower, grab my coat, and get down to the foyer in an absolute hurricane of new sensations that a twelve-year-old would be more equipped to handle. As is, I feel half out of my mind.

Attraction was always so soft with other people. With some of them, I'd find myself having to actively remember *Oh yeah, I like them.*

Which, in retrospect, should've been pretty telling.

In my defense, liking people that way was easy and calm, and I *wanted* easy and calm. I wanted simple and drama-free and steady.

Now, I'm wondering if I ever wanted that, or if I thought it would make me happy as a contrast to how torn up I always am about my other life stressors. I thought the balance to being in a constant state of anxiety was peace; but what if it's chaos? Not fighting my own chaos or trying to tamp down my emotions, but leaning into it until I'm yelling and he's yelling and honestly, it's *hot.*

Maybe liking someone *should* be this caustic, a long, slow, silent death.

He's standing off to the side of the foyer already, going over some papers with Colm, and he's wearing a black wool coat with the collar popped, the cut of it hugging long lines that feed to his hips, down his legs, and his hair is set in an intentionally messy spray. I can't hear what he's saying but his lips move, and I watch those lips, feel their impression on my neck.

This is.

Going to be a problem.

He also doesn't look even a little bit like he woke up with a hangover.

Dick.

"*Finally*," Finn drones and stands from a chair. "Let's *go*."

Loch stiffens.

His back to me, he nods his thanks to Colm, dismissing him.

I give Colm a smile as he passes. Loch said he's here on his own, since Malachy stopped paying his wages. If Dad had done that to us, would Wren have stayed with Coal and me?

Colm leaves, and I face Loch. "Where is the event today?" *What* is the event today, I almost ask.

"It's down in our wee village here," Siobhán says. "Not a long drive. We volunteer at it every year, a music festival. And *dancing*, eh, Lochy?"

He gives her an unamused smirk. "Oh yeah, I'm breaking back out my reel shoes, did na I tell you? Headlining today."

"Reel shoes?"

Loch almost looks at me. Catches himself, his jaw bulging.

Okay, I don't like this.

He walks out of the castle without another word, the bright light of morning wrapping him up.

Finn follows.

Siobhán rolls her eyes in a huge arch. "What'd I tell ya? He's a stubborn prick."

My confusion doesn't abate. "Huh?"

"He's ashamed you had to make a statement about the race at all. Does na know how to function when anyone helps him. He treats

Finn and me the same when we do anything even a bit nice for him."
She hooks her arm through mine. "Stubborn. Prick."

Is that the reason? That can't be it. "Is he really dancing today?"

We walk out to see Loch and Finn already loaded up in the car,
Loch driving this time, Finn next to him.

I intentionally ignore the way my stomach sinks with disappointment.

"Ha! No, he has na danced in years," Siobhán says. "We all used
to, though."

We slide into the car and she pats his shoulder in front of her.

"But Lochy was the best dancer, weren't you?"

He starts the car. "That wall of trophies in my room did na win
themselves."

Siobhán leans into me. "He's lying. He was fucking awful."

"Oh, you're one to talk," Finn jeers. "Nearly breaking your ankle
every performance."

"At least Mam and Da dinna have to *beg* me to stop."

"Dancing is part of our heritage," Loch mumbles to the windshield. "I wanted to be good at it."

"Stick to painting, lovey." Siobhán pats his shoulder again. "Oh! A
few of your paintings will be down in the village, eh? That'll make a
good setup for you two and your whole press nonsense. You'll show
Kris your art, yeah?"

My eyes go to the side of Loch's head.

I know he knows I'm looking at him. His hand flexes on the
steering wheel as he pulls us out of the castle's drive.

"He's already seen my art," Loch says. Definitively.

"I'd like to see more of it." My voice comes out softer than I mean
it to.

Loch's eyes dip to the side. He refocuses on the road and doesn't
say anything.

Siobhán gives me a shrug, and I sink back against the seat, staring
out at the passing scenery, foliage and the occasional tree and stone
fence breaking the hilly landscape.

Deciding that I like Lochlann Patrick is not the hardest thing I'll have to do, turns out. It's finding out what he thinks about me.

And now that that's in question, I'm pinned to the seat in pre-emptive dread.

What if he pulled away because he realized it was a mistake to kiss me? Or what if everything that happened yesterday was a by-product of his stress over his uncle and his Holiday and had nothing to do with the way he feels about me?

Or what if he is the one stealing from Christmas, and he pulled away because he feels guilty for it?

I close my eyes, dropping back into my self-disgust like an old friend.

The rest of the drive passes in silence, made awkward by the way Loch is actively *not* talking, and even Finn gives him occasional weird glances at the way he takes corners too aggressively.

The village is quite a bit smaller than Cork, but decked out in the same orange, white, and green decorations, banners, and pennants and people wearing all manner of vibrant scarves and hats. Green Hills Distillery ads are similarly plastered everywhere. Booths are set up along the main street, with larger tents off between clusters of trees, all of it in the sleepy stretch of a festival starting to get going.

"We're home by one." Loch parks in a lot off the main strip.

"One?" Siobhán echoes. "We usually stay far longer."

"I got work to do at the castle," Loch says too quickly. "I canna be arsed to spend a whole day down here. This festival is a quarter of the size it once was, anyway." He glowers at it through the windshield, and his anger peels back, goes to sadness. "We will na need all day."

She leans forward. "That does na make it less worthy of our support. We know this. We've talked about it."

Finn grunts. "He's being a donkey's arse to pout. Heap of good that'll do us."

Siobhán glares at her. "Do na be insensitive to—"

"I'm not *insensitive*." Finn spins in her seat, facing Loch. "This isn't any different from our usual shite situation, is it? Unless your stance's changing on what we *can* do."

Loch's jaw is clamped so tight it bulges by his ears. Through gritted teeth, he says, "You know it's not that simple."

"I know *you* think that. I know you're na gonna capitalize on the wee bit of *good* press you've finally gotten." Finn snaps her scowl from Loch to me, and I gape at her when she looks at me with something like appreciation.

But Loch stays quiet, unreactive, and she grumbles at him.

"Fine then. But do na discount what little we can do. We can help out the organizers like usual. The musicians you recruited—they're here too, yeah?"

He doesn't respond.

"They'll wanna see you," Finn continues. "They'll wanna thank you for getting them in. We know you've got *work to do* at the castle, but you've got work *here* too."

"She's right," Siobhán says. "We know you do na want to anger Malachy, but start at least taking credit for what you do."

Loch drops his eyes to his lap. "I will, yeah," he says with no inflection.

"You're a stubborn bloody arsehole," Finn retorts, and Siobhán gives me a look like *See?* "Some of our friends from school are gonna be here, so if I'm na back by one, I'm having this concept called fun that you should look into. Our Holiday needs to bring *joy* and I'm gonna make sure it does."

She climbs out, and Loch rubs his fingers across his forehead with a defeated sigh.

I linger, lips parting.

Siobhán gives me an imploring look and juts her head at the car park around us.

Would he listen to anything I say anyway? All it'd be is a reiteration of what his sisters said.

I relent and open the door.

Finn is jogging off for the booths, waving at someone, and I watch a group cluster around her. I could join her; but I lean on the trunk while Siobhán and Loch talk.

The car doors open and shut a few minutes later.

Siobhán's smile is bright as she rushes to join Finn and the group.

Which leaves Loch standing beside me.

"You should invite your brother to the event tomorrow," Loch says without preamble.

I twist to him. "Why?"

"It's an evening up in Belfast. Pub hopping, mostly. Invite him. And his boyfriend, yeah?"

I study him. His face is too calm.

"None of that answers *why*?"

He's staring off at the festival. "You'll enjoy Belfast more with him. And today, even—the three of us volunteer at this festival, but you are na expected to do that with us. You should meet Siobhán and Finn's friends. They'll show you a real grand—"

"Are you trying to get rid of me?"

He hesitates a tad too long, now forcibly keeping his eyes on the booths and waving banners. "No."

Ah, okay, I can still get mad at him, that's good. "Is this because of the statement I had Christmas release, or us making out in your kitchen?"

His face sets on fire. Embarrassment—and anger. His jaw locks in hard and his eyes stay fixed to a spot in the distance like he's in a trance.

He says nothing.

My lip curls, and I huff and shove my hands into my pockets. "Great. That's great. Really classy. So what do you need me for today? We find the paparazzi even though you don't plan on using your repaired reputation at all, then we part ways so you can go off acting like last night didn't happen?"

Loch stomps away. Fully leaves the conversation.

"You son of a—" I rush after him but he whirls around and I come up short, nearly slamming into his chest.

"Do na talk to me about last night," he growls. Finally looking at me. Furious, cheeks scarlet and eyes aflame, but looking at me.

"What if I *want* to talk about last night?" I ask.

He huffs, breath hot on my face, a contrast to the cold air wrapping around us. "There's nothing to talk about. I told you, I should na have done that. It was a mistake."

There's a rip in my chest. An abrupt, jagged hole.

I cling to anger to stop that rip from pulling me in half. "A mistake?"

"Yeah."

"It was a *mistake?*"

"Are you thick? *Yes.*"

"Bullshit." I fight hard not to sound anxious. "You can't have said the things you did on a spur of the moment fuckup. You thought about doing that. You *wanted* to do that to me. You—"

"It was drunken weakness," he cuts me off. "I canna handle another mess right now and I should na have opened the door to take on *you.*"

From the moment we met, we've been picking at each other. Insults, jabs, even some too-direct accidental hits where I've noticed us both immediately backing off in unspoken agreement.

This is decidedly *not* that.

He thinks I'm a mess?

That word attracts others and piles them in an immovable blockade. *Mess. Selfish. Disappointment. Why can't you do anything right?*

I gape at him, feeling the blood drain from my face, fingertips numb.

Loch must realize his own words in seeing my reaction.

His eyelids pulse. "Shite. Kris—"

I walk away, not even sure where I'm going, but I duck around Siobhán and Finn's group and head into the main strip of festival booths.

Some are prepping food, roasted potatoes and fried pretty much everything, and it makes the air cloyingly decadent. I walk, and walk, until I come to a small green space nestled in an alleyway.

I canna handle another mess right now.

I should na have opened the door to take on you.

My heart races, aching with each too-fast thud, and I rub at my chest but nothing eases.

That's exactly what I'm always terrified everyone in my life will see.

That I'm a mess.

That I have nothing to offer.

There's a bench nestled under an arching tree and I scramble to sit— —and look up at one of his paintings.

It's been printed on a massive poster that covers the whole side of the building opposite me, complete with info for the festival highlighted over the bottom. This one is two people dancing, done in the same style as the painting in his studio, showing them from the shoulders up, twisted to some mute melody. They're smiling, a captured, fleeting joy.

I stare up at the wash of colors, purples with pops of red, every stroke in motion.

He really is a talented jerk.

The ache in my chest throbs and a wheeze rattles in.

Fuck Loch. Fuck Ireland. Fuck all of this.

But I *can't*. Not yet.

I pull out my phone, vision blurring until I blink enough to clear it. My drunken text to the group chat is the last one in the thread. I delete it, then start again.

PEEP, MINI CANDY CANE, AND THE BEST CLAUS

You are all cordially invited to come rough it with me tomorrow. Party it down, Belfast-style.

COAL

i'm always up for a party.

to what do we owe the honor of gracing you with our presences?

i assume by all you meant that I can bring hex too

I would never dare part you from your emotional support boyfriend. Of course, bring him.

Iris? Can I pry you away from Easter prep insanity?

IRIS
yes, thank you, fuck i need a break

Easter stress isn't eating you alive?

IRIS
it's fine

That's all she says. For a solid minute.

Scrap Belfast, Coal and I will come kick your court's ass for you. Who do we need to throw down?

COAL
YESSSSS let me at em

IRIS
is it a good image for santa to beat people up

COAL
oh

IRIS
honestly, it's the same stress it usually is, and getting sloppy drunk with you fools is exactly what i need. though i appreciate the offer and it would be admittedly hilarious

to watch coal try to punch
anyone

COAL

excuse you iris i am incredibly
intimidating in fights, nay, i am
LETHAL

> What data points are you
> basing this conclusion off of?

COAL

have you seen me, i am a badass,
no data points needed

> Aw, he's a sweet kid. Let's
> keep him.

IRIS

maybe if we give him a stable
home we can train the delusions
out of him

COAL

why do these text chats always end
with you two ganging up on me

Talking with Coal and Iris unleashes the same warm comfort as
it did last night.

If these two idiots love me, I can't be that much of a mess, can I?

A shadow falls over me.

I look up at that painting again.

"They're coming tomorrow," I say to the air in front of me. "So
you won't be stuck with me."

"Kris." His voice is rough. Supplicating. It's unnerving. "I should
na have—"

I stand, cutting him off. I'll be damned if I look at him again.

Maybe ever. "You had the right idea. We only need to be around each other for press shots. But—"

Now I do round on him. I meet his eyes and yeah, I regret it instantly, but I point at him and try, try, *try* to shove aside my hurt.

"—you should invite your court to Belfast tomorrow, too."

It's not what he was expecting me to say.

Loch flinches. "What?"

"You're going to be doing the same stuff there that you've done at the other events, right? So *show them.*"

He sucks his teeth. "It's na as impressive as you eejits keep making it out to be. I have contacts; I connect people with each other. That's nothing but—"

"You need to show your court that you're better than Malachy. You need to start getting them on your side so when I leave and your image is better, you can *use that.* You're doing all this stuff for your Holiday, and it's admirable, but you're not protecting St. Patrick's Day, are you? No matter what you do behind the scenes, you aren't really fighting for it."

He looks like I slapped him. Hard.

Now we're even.

He shudders out a breath. "I do na have anything worthwhile to show my court. The things I do are not—"

"For someone who acts like he's the greatest thing to ever walk this earth, you have no idea how amazing you are, do you? No wonder your sisters are fed up with you. God, you're so much like Coal, it makes me want to scream."

Loch's expression spasms. "Like your brother?"

"Yeah. A dumbass who's whining about how he doesn't do enough is just that—*whining.* He annoys *everyone* in his life with his refusal to accept the fact that he's *actually capable.* So do me a favor, and do your sisters a favor, and *stop* with this whole act of not being worthy of your court's support. I know Malachy's gotten in your head, but fuck, dude. Just. *Fuck.*"

Eloquent. Really.

There's a reason I write, and Coal's the one who talks.

But I've said a lot of nice things to a guy who's screwing with my emotions, so I duck around him.

Loch grabs my arm.

He's wearing that spicy cologne again that I know now was an instant turn-on and I hate him so much.

"I'm sorry," he whispers. He sure as hell *looks* sorry. Brows hooked up. Lips parted. "I should na have said what I did."

"I don't care." I do. Shit fuck, I do.

"And . . ." He stammers. "Thank you. For what you said, what Christmas said on my behalf. You did na have to make a statement like that."

"Yeah, I did." My chest swells, so I throw up this barrier hard and fast. "That's why I'm here. Speaking of, where are the paparazzi? We should—"

My phone buzzes. I yank it out because it's easier to deal with texts than him—oh look, other people need me, not just you, you jackass.

But the moment my eyes hit the screen, scalding horror crashes down on me.

My mom's calling.

Chapter Twelve

Frantic, I think back over our texts—I've been responding. Haven't I? Plus Dad's with her, so she's getting attention.

The last time she called me was over a year ago. She gave me shit for not being able to get Coal to talk to her; Coal then came to Cambridge and subsequently also gave me shit, but more lovingly, when he found out I hadn't left my room in a day or two.

But I'd been sick.

A little.

I'd been sick *with guilt* over the fact that I couldn't be what Mom needed. Sick over the fact that a little voice was whimpering in the back of my head, *If you could do what she wants you to do, you could fix her; but you can't, you're a fuckup, and it's no wonder she left you.*

My spiraling panic holds me in place so long that her call ends before I can decide whether to answer.

"Kris?" Loch tries to get my attention, leaning down, but when I don't look away from my screen, he steps closer. "Christ, Kris—you're pale. What's wrong?"

A few seconds later—I've barely caught my breath—my phone pings.

A text.

MOM

MOM
Sweetheart, your father and I are renewing our vows on the island this weekend. I expect you and Nicholas to both be here.

Holy what?
My vision whites out.

I fight to keep from absorbing any of this yet, especially as texts pour in, one after another, not giving me time to respond, even if I could:

MOM

Do not deny me my children at such
an important moment in my life.

You should be able to do this one thing
for me. Do not be selfish, not now.

SAY SOMETHING

Kristopher, I've only ever wanted
you to be the best you can be. This
behavior is NOT that.

It should not be this difficult for you
to do the right thing.

"Kris?" Loch is in front of me.

My hands are trembling again, but I manage to copy Mom's first text about the vow renewal and forward it to Coal.

COAL

Did you know about this?

A second later, he tries to call me.
I decline it.

Not now. With Loch.

What the fuck?

COAL

it's bullshit. we aren't gonna go
and i didn't want to stress you out.

call me when you're free. please.

fuck, i told her i was responding on
behalf of us both, i told her not to
fucking contact you.

Coal talked to her?

Coal talked to her.

He said he'd be the front line of defense against our parents for me. But he—

He talked to our mother.

It's both a weight and the lifting of a weight in one, opposing forces dragging me in two.

All the months, *years* she's spent guilting me into getting him to talk to her, and when he finally does, she doesn't say a goddamn thing about it to me?

I want to pace, want to run, want to *move*. But my body stays motionless, internally vibrating, every organ and muscle shuddering. I put my phone against my forehead and breathe. Try to breathe, at least, but the air gets trapped in the back of my throat until I cough, yanking in breaths that go nowhere. I breathe in, in, in, I can't breathe out—

Loch eases me back onto that bench. "Bend forward," he orders. "Elbows on your knees. Breathe—*out,* too, Christ—wait here."

He leaves, and by the time he rushes back, I've managed one breath, maybe; the alley is spinning, that painting in front of me, all purples, reds, the green of the grass too—purple, red, green—

Loch sits and catches me as I topple towards him. "Kris! Shite—"

He rights me and something cold, *freezing,* lands on the back of my neck.

A second passes, and whatever it is starts to feel the good kind of cold, shocking the panic from my nerves.

A breath goes in. All the way. And all the way back out.

Another.

"There ya go." Loch holds that cold thing on my neck with one hand, has his other locked around my forearm, thumb rubbing soothingly against my coat. "Kris—what happened? Is everyone all right? Do you need to go back to Christmas?"

"No. No. I'm—"

"Christ, boyo, do na say you're fine."

A laugh squirms out of me. It's humorless.

In lieu of having to explain, and probably because I'm still weakened and unstable, I find myself showing him my mom's text thread.

His eyes glide over the screen, and his expression transforms, emotion spreading down his face so I can track each muscle change that pushes him from concerned to furious.

"Your mam speaks to you like this?" he growls.

I snort.

His eyes whip to me like I might be hysterical. I probably am.

"She must know your uncle," I say before I can think not to. I wince. "I didn't mean—"

"Shut up, Kris." He adjusts the thing on my neck, his fury not banking, not exactly, but becoming something I can't put a name on. "What a matched set we are, eh?"

I gawk at him.

How dare he say that to me? We're not a set at all. Yeah, we have shit in common, but *he's* the one who put a stop to it, and now he's sitting here looking at me like he wants to go to war on my behalf?

Holy shit. *That's* what that look is.

Loch pulls the thing off the back of my neck—a bag of ice. "You feeling better now?"

Hardly.

But I motion at the ice in his hand. "How did you know to do that?" Some of my anger recedes. "That was . . . useful."

"Finn gets this way." He pauses. Clears his throat. "Do na tell her I told you that. She'll rip my balls off."

I pocket my phone and drop my head into my hands, relishing air going into and out of me unobstructed.

My panicked reaction to my mother has never been that bad in public before. Breathing is sometimes a struggle, sure, but getting so dizzy that I very likely would've ended up on the ground if Loch hadn't caught me . . .

It is possible my brother was right and I do have panic attacks.

I NEED TO STOP
HAVING REVELATIONS
ABOUT MYSELF

AROUND LOCHLANN PATRICK.

His other hand is still on my forearm. He squeezes, and it shoots off a ricochet of fire up my body.

I'm supposed to be mad at him.

But I feel hollowed out.

"I'm not sure what I would've done if you hadn't been here," I admit into my palms. "L—"

I almost say *Lucky you found me,* trying to get back on level ground, but—*did* his luck magic lead him to me? At the exact moment my mom pulled this shit.

My hands drop, jaw tight.

His wonky magic needs to back the fuck up, I swear to god.

"She shouldn't speak to you like that," Loch tells me. It's a delicate brush on the side of my face. "She does na deserve you."

Oh, fuck him, fuck him and his *empathy* and his calm, steady presence.

"She doesn't deserve a mess?" I glare at him.

His face slackens. "I did na mean it."

"Come on. Let's get those press shots."

I shove to my feet and I do *not* teeter, I do not get dizzy.

Loch stands too, his hands out like he might need to catch me again, but I refuse to need his help anymore.

There's hardly any space between us. The warmth off him is a barrier wrapping around me and I think, maybe, he'll say something else. Something . . . more.

He deflates.

I walk off into the festival, an ache rising up the back of my neck as he follows.

The Holiday paparazzi, a few of them, are outside the largest tent where a fast, uplifting overlap of fiddles permeates from within.

Loch angles us for the entrance, ignoring them.

But I come to a halt.

The reporters are ready, cameras grabbing shots of other people too, to keep in line with our world being hidden.

I don't know if it's the emptiness of being emotionally drained.

I don't know if it's Loch's maddening combination of pushing me away and supporting me.

But I find myself walking directly up to the paparazzi.

"Kris?" Loch realizes I haven't followed him and pivots after me. "What are you—"

"Hey. You're from *24 Hour Fête*?" I stop in front of one reporter I recognize. Not enough to know or care about the guy's name. Coal probably knows, but they're one reason our lives sucked so much. Now here they are, ruining Loch's life the same way, making it easier for Malachy to keep control of his Holiday and feed Loch lies about who he is until he *believes* them, he sits there and thinks he's a screw-up, thinks he can't do anything right—

My eyes burn, but I hold my ground.

The reporter's surprise shifts to interest almost immediately. His gaze cuts around before he goes, "Kristopher," no title, no weirdness to give anything away in public. The fiddle music helps drown us out too.

"Asshole," I say back.

The guy's brows go up.

The other reporters, three of them, have recording devices out now.

Yeah, *Prince Kristopher* doesn't act like this. *Prince Kristopher* fades into the background and *Prince Kristopher* is a nonexistent, anxiety-riddled pushover.

Well, maybe I'm sick as fuck of being *Prince Kristopher.*

Loch leans close to me from behind. "What are you—"

"I've learned a lot from my short time in Ireland," I say to the reporter. "Mostly that first impressions are hardly ever right and often conceal a far more complex story. We do ourselves a disservice by only seeing things through one narrow lens. Loch taught me that, how St. Patrick's Day is generally dismissed as a Holiday of drinking and green beer, but it's a Holiday of Irish cultural heritage and unification. We never get to see that part because we're taught to focus on the headline-grabbing bits—like you've done with Loch. He's loyal and dedicated, and he does more for this Holiday than anyone knows *because no one ever reports on that.* You've been following us around these past few days and you've been obsessing over him for even longer, but have you paid attention to what he does? To who he *is*? Stop being so lazy and try reporting the *truth* for once."

I spin away, leaving them slack-jawed.

That did nothing to vent any of my shit and only made me feel *more,* feel *stupid*—

Loch grabs my arm. I fight him off, but he keeps ahold and hauls me into the tent.

The music slams into us, what was muffled by canvas now roaring. He drags me over to the side, towards a group of tables that are empty because everyone is dancing, the tent packed with people centered around a stage up front. No one looks at us, no one bats an eye; the reporters don't even follow us in. I'm still unused to Holiday events not somewhat centering around the ruling family, and the anonymity is jarring.

We weave through the tables until we're in the farthest corner, then Loch rounds on me.

He's still holding my arm, and despite the layers of clothes, the skin there goes to froth.

But he doesn't say anything. He wants to, his mouth bobbing, and him being on the back foot brings him into focus, the man behind his facade.

Suddenly, seeing him like this isn't upsetting. It's a privilege.

"You didn't have to do that," he says quickly. A toppled rush.

Heat crawls up my face and I drop my eyes to the floor. "Probably made things worse." I relive everything I said and wince. "Shit. I shouldn't have—"

Loch tightens his hold on my arm and I look back up at him.

His eyes coast over my brows and dip down, to the space between my parted lips. That awareness zaps through me, brings my body to attention in an involuntary lurch.

The fiddle music rises and rises, then crashes in a slam of percussion.

"Do you dance?" he asks.

My head tics in confusion. "What?"

Without taking his eyes off me, he nods at the crowd, the noise of the tent, the cadence of celebrating, and repeats, "Do you dance?"

That's what he's asking? That's what he wants to talk about?

I go along with it, barely, the words feeling heavy on my tongue. "Irish dancing? What do you think?"

He grins. That asshole. Grins like that'll make everything okay.

It doesn't.

It definitely does *not*.

Nope.

Shit.

"I can teach you," he tells me.

"Can you? Finn and Siobhán seemed to think otherwise."

"They would na know talent if it kicked them in the shin."

"Which you probably did, according to their estimation of your talent."

He smirks. "Ah, go on, have your fun slagging me off."

My eyes widen. "*What*-ing you off?"

"Slagging. Like—eh—taking the piss. Having a laugh." His smile is insufferable, sharp and manic. "What did you think it meant, boyo?"

I think it means you're messing with me again.

I wait for even the barest gloss of self-preservation to crackle in my chest. Like any amount of *I shouldn't let him off the hook so easily,* and I'd be out of the tent so fast.

But nothing comes.

Now that I'm giving myself permission to be selfish, that apparently also means I've lost all common sense.

"Sure." My voice is clipped. "Teach me to do an Irish dance. God, this'll be good."

He locks his hand on the back of my elbow. His cologne is a drug and so is how angry I am, how exhausted from that shit with my mom, how confused because he still feels like a soft place to land.

Loch steers me into the crowd, not quite dragging me like he did a bit ago, and I hate how much I like him taking charge.

On the stage, a band draws a riotous song from their instruments and dances as forcefully as the people below, sweaty and grinning. There doesn't seem to be a designated dance floor, just a free-for-all of fun, and Loch stops us a few paces within the crowd, the sheer, un-adulterated *force* of the joy around us nearly knocking me off my feet.

Some of the people closest to the stage are wearing traditional Irish dance outfits, decorated emerald vests and bodices over frilled skirts and leggings, though they don't seem to be performing, merely enjoying the song like everyone else. Most people are trying some moves, laughing when they land a step, laughing more when they falter. Legs kick and hands spiral in the air and a group of four people merges, parts, reshaping across the floor in a fluid ebb like the song is physically guiding them into geometric designs.

Loch comes up alongside me, the hard plane of his chest down the length of my arm. I get halfway to facing him and stop so he's beyond my eyesight.

The song transitions to a new one, still uproariously fast and saturated with happiness. The crowd cheers and more people pour inside to dance until there's enough bodies packed in here that the two of us won't be targeted for sucking too much.

He adjusts his hold on me until I face him.

The music blares around us, its potency a cocoon.

Loch walks into me, forcing me backwards, and I'm hit with such a vivid overlay of the way he pressed around me last night that I trip. But he grabs my other arm and holds me steady, and we're two stones in a sea of dancing and kicking. The crowd's joy and laughter thuds against our stationary bubble, relentless, determined for us to feel this joy, for us to laugh too.

My hands come up, fisted against his chest, the tempo of his heart going so fast my knuckles rattle. I think we should be dancing, or moving, or doing *something*, but when my gaze connects with his, there's only one thing I want to do and I'm not sure it's something we should do with reporters lurking around.

But his eyes intensely darken on me, and yeah, yes, I would kiss him in public. I'd kiss him anywhere. I'm stretched bubble thin for him.

I move in closer, chin angling up, but the moment I do, I *feel* my own stupidity, pushing too far in a drive of need, not reason. None of this has been driven by reason, and I hear everything he said to me in the parking lot paired alongside my internal monologue from last night when I chose to kiss him over doing my duty, a Greatest Hits rebound of my screw-ups the past two days.

But I'm here, face tipped up to his, *hoping*.

That darkness in Loch's eyes withdraws as he rolls them shut in a grimace.

"Kris," he moans, and the music tries to dampen it.

I get whiplash with how fast I go from wanting his tongue in my mouth to being livid with him. "Don't. Just—don't."

I try to pull away, to leave with my pride intact—*ha,* pride? I barely know her—but Loch keeps his clawed-finger grip on my arms.

His look is pleading. But firmer. Resolved. "I did na mean what I said," he repeats. His lips curl on themselves and he pulls in close, but it isn't charged. "I've fallen in with a whole parade of direction-less dipshits, and I know what being around the wrong people can do to our positions. And I canna—"

"So I'm a *directionless dipshit* now?" I jerk back, face on fire. "Fuck you for—"

"No! Christ, Kris, I'm saying *I'm* that for *you.*"

It's so much the opposite of what I thought he was saying that I can only stare.

"That was what I meant earlier. I did na mean to say that *you* were a mess. I was angry at myself—I have too much going on with my Holiday. And then you said—" He groans, and the air alters to make room for it. "You said you do na know what you want. That's fine, it's fine, Kris. But I canna be the one to help you figure it out. I canna give you what you need."

"Did I *ask* you to help me figure anything out?" I demand.

"Was it na a mistake to you?" Loch asks. He isn't accusing. He sounds dejected. "Tell me it was na a mistake for me to kiss you. That I dinna get blindsided by my own stress and spring that on you when you *told* me you did na know what you wanted."

The skin across my chest is too tight.

He looks so ashamed, so pissed off *at himself.*

"It wasn't a mistake," I tell him.

Loch's self-admonishment doesn't change. "What was it, then?"

"It was—"

It yanked me out of a half-life I'd been living.

If I don't kiss you again I feel like every nerve in my body will wither away.

That single kiss was more transformative, more vast, more excruciatingly important than anything that's ever happened to me and you're the most noble, caring person I've ever met, and it breaks my heart that you don't see that what you're doing is so spectacular.

In some alternate universe, I say all of that.

But in this one, I hear those thoughts as if from a distance, and I hear what Loch said, and it rotates into focus.

One kiss.

We had *one kiss.*

All this shit building up in my throat sounds a helluva lot like a love profession, which is *categorically insane.* He has so many problems going on with his Holiday, with his uncle, and I admitted my uncertainty to him last night. And, oh yeah, I'm *investigating him.*

He may have said he didn't mean to call me on being a mess, but he wasn't wrong. I mean, the fact that I'm wobbling back and forth like this is proof enough. The fact that I basically threw myself at him again, even with him saying it'd been a mistake, validates all of this.

To my silence, Loch gives a resigned nod and lets me go. "I'm sorry, Kris. I should na have kissed you."

"Wait." Even saying that comes out choked, garbled. I'm drowning in unsaid words.

"I have to make rounds."

Wait—

The crowd parts for him.

And I stand there, trying to catch my breath, a hundred versions of *No, it wasn't a mistake, kiss me again* lying limp and useless in my throat.

It was a mistake though.

Wasn't it?

My phone buzzes, spiking my anxiety, but it's Coal, asking me to call him so we can talk about Mom.

I don't want to talk about her. I don't want to give another second of thought to her.

But that's my problem. Never talking about it. Never acknowledging it. Until it's become such a beastly, hulking part of me that I'm a scrambled mess who has no idea who he is *because of her,* because of how I've repressed the shit out of my every response to her.

Is that why I couldn't get myself to say anything to Loch? I never address my own problems. I avoid, and deflect, and ignore.

But I'm *tired* of being that way. I'm tired of wallowing in not knowing what I can do to be useful, to contribute, to *matter.* I'm tired of feeling like I'm bobbing along, waiting for something to give me purpose and make me happy, mercilessly at the whims of time and fate.

I plunge into the crowd and angle for the exit, only to remember the journalists I told off are likely still outside. Thankfully, there's another exit across the tent, and it dumps me out in an empty path between this tent and another that's blasting guitar music.

It's nowhere near time to head back to the castle, but it was, what, a twenty-minute drive? I could conjure up some mistletoe and find a doorway to get there, but I can walk that. I *need* to walk that. I need to *run* that, but I'm in dress boots and jeans.

I set off through the festival, walking through the cold March air. I hurry past booths selling crafts, more woodworking and paintings, woven bags and jewelry, musical instruments and photographs of dancers. Green Hills Distillery has another tent I avoid, though I would've heard if Malachy was in attendance.

How many of the other vendors are here because of Loch? What else has he been doing to compensate for being unable to affect his Holiday through magic? He's an impromptu talent scout and coordinates cross-festival interactions. What would Coal and I be able to do for Christmas if we had no magic? Like maybe bake cookies or some shit? And here Loch is, getting spotlights on parts of his Holiday, his culture, all on his own.

I cut up the road we took to twist down into the village and hike my way into the Irish countryside.

My fingers itch. Stretch absently in my pocket.

I pull out my phone. Swipe to a notes app.

And write.

Chapter Thirteen

I'm *writing* again. Journal-type shit shorthanded on my phone, but it's a start, and that start blossoms long-dormant flowers throughout my body. By the time I jog into the castle, sweaty and winded with my coat thrown over my shoulder, I feel more like myself than I have in way, way too long.

Colm is coming out of the dining room when he sees me hurry in. His eyes drop to my T-shirt—pale blue, with a debonair monocled snowman over the words *Kiss My Snowballs*.

To Colm's credit, he doesn't react.

"Prince Kristopher." He glances behind me, clocks that I'm alone, and his brows go up. "Is everything all right?"

"Yeah, I—" I stop.

The castle is empty.

Well, just Colm.

Which means that office is empty now, too.

I nod. "Yeah. I wanted to come back early. Can you text . . . uh, Siobhán, tell her I'm here? I don't want her to worry."

Colm studies me in that way staff have where they seem able to see through bullshit.

"Of course." He bows his way down the hall.

I pocket my phone. Writing can wait—I need to find that joy meter. Loch or Malachy, it doesn't matter.

I toss my coat on a chair in the foyer and head for the office. Is it Loch's office, or is it Malachy's? I can't imagine Malachy does any work here. But if the joy meter is anywhere, it's gotta be there.

The halls wind around me, silent and chilly, and I shiver, arms pricking with cold.

The office door is shut. I stop in front of it, warring with whether there'd be any magical protection. Knowing Malachy's stinginess, doubtful.

So I grab the knob.

It's unlocked.

Huh. That's . . . lucky.

I look around like a physical manifestation of Loch's magic is going to pop up and give me a mischievous wink.

Why would Loch's magic be helping *me*? Unless it'd somehow help him.

This is a dumb coincidence. Loch didn't lock the office because we left this room in a hurry last night, so he probably forgot.

Yeah. That has to be it.

I've never been so glad Christmas's magic is straightforward. A few days in St. Patrick's Day, and I'm a conspiracy nut.

I slip inside and shut the door behind me. My heart thunders for a solid five seconds as I stand inside, waiting for something to happen.

Nothing does, and I exhale, long and slow.

I have no shame left at this point, so I dive right into snooping. Maybe there's an agenda on the desk that says *Malachy's Calendar: 1 o'clock, be an ass; 2 o'clock, steal Christmas's joy.*

But the first thing I see is a notebook with a bunch of stapled business cards next to notes in Loch's handwriting that say things like *fifth generation lace maker* and *on a music scholarship—watch senior capstone show.*

There are several notebooks like it. And schedules for festivals happening across the isle, performers in attendance, who needs assistance, if Loch's able to help.

I glare down at the books.

This is why I'm all jumbled up inside. He had to go and be this honorable, infectious, passionate son of a bitch with soft, full lips and abs that put me on my knees.

"You're a goddamn dumbass, Claus," I mutter.

The drawers hold office supplies, files about updates to the castle and money transfers between Malachy and Loch for minor upkeep and school tuition.

Hands in fists, I head to the nearest bookshelf. This is an old-as-shit castle; they'd have hidden passages, right?

A tremor of excitement scuttles up my spine as I search along the bookcases for cranks or anything telling.

Please have a hidden passage.

Please be something cool to help this day not feel like such a disaster.

The books are old and decorative, fancy versions of classics like the *Odyssey* and *Frankenstein*. There are framed pictures of Loch, Finn, and Siobhán way younger, smiling with two older people—their mom and dad.

I linger over one picture, a gap-toothed Loch with Siobhán on his shoulders in front of the castle, both dressed like they'd come from an Irish dance, outfits as green as the hills with intricate gold threaded designs. Their mom is next to them, arm around them both, all smiles.

He looks so innocent in that picture. Weightless.

I don't have a single picture with my parents like that. The best is a family photo right before Mom left. Coal's making a weird face because Dad yelled at him, and I'm trying not to cry because I *hated* when they fought. But Mom looks perfect, she always did, put together and not a hair out of place, even if we were falling apart.

I shake the emotion away and keep searching.

A few feet down, a gust of air catches me off guard.

It slips through two of the bookcase panels, and I stop, feeling the crack. There's definitely space here, along with a hinge three feet to the right for a door to swing open.

Even though there's no one else in the room, I resist doing a fist pump.

Hidden passage.

I move along the shelf, try a few books or random items that might be levers. Nothing.

Should I push on it? It wouldn't be that easy—

It is.

I shove on the edge, and something clicks, the door rebounding and swinging open as a magnetic latch releases.

Now is when my guilt chooses to rear up and go, *This is a bit invasive.*

But if I can get proof that it is Malachy stealing from us, then Loch can use the scandal to push out his uncle. It benefits him, too.

No. If I can get proof, I'll use it to *help Christmas.* We'll force Malachy to give back what he stole.

Don't think about Loch.

Don't think about what I can do for him, who I can be, to get him to want me.

I push open the door until light from the window on the opposite side of the office shows a space barely big enough to be considered a closet.

At first I think I found an air conditioner or heater. It's no taller than I am, a hodgepodge of iron fixings and gears, more functional looking than the Merry Measure in all its steampunk grandness.

But there's a familiar series of gauges across the front, tracking inputs, outputs.

I bend closer. The input needle swivels to the max; the output needle is in a state of drain. Malachy, pulling joy to feed his business's success. That asshole.

Carefully, I search around the joy meter, looking for—I don't even know what. One of those attachments similar to the one on the Merry Measure? They'd have to have put a gadget on this one to act as a receiver for the one in Christmas.

Ah.

Wedged in at the back is a little box exactly like the one left in Christmas, brass and about the size of my fist. There's a readout display on this one, a date and time stamp. The last draw was yesterday. Or . . . it's not shut off, is it? The light on the one in Christmas was green, but this one has a red light on top.

I reach for it. I can unplug it and take it back with me.

But then whoever installed it will be alerted that we know, and nothing about this tells me the *who.*

I pull my phone out and shoot off a picture of it to Coal, asking him to check that it matches the one in Christmas, but I'm almost certain they're identical.

There's a switch on top next to the red light. I bend closer—*On/ Off*. It's in the *Off* position.

Malachy could have turned it off when he met me yesterday; he could've been worried I was getting close to realizing what he's doing. Maybe he's intending to turn it back on once I leave.

Or maybe it's Loch.

I scrub at my face, giving myself a beat to feel how that fits in with everything that's happened.

It could still be Loch stealing from us. His uncle refuses to let him have magic for what he needs to do, so he's taking some from Christmas to bridge the gap. He funnels it into their joy meter and draws it out before it can get sucked up into Malachy's pull, and he uses these small amounts to do what he can to spread joy during his Holiday. I've only seen him use magic once, though. But he would be doing it sneakily, wouldn't he? If he's stealing from us, and his uncle would flip shit again.

Shouldn't I feel, I don't know, *betrayed* if it's him?

All I really feel, staring down at that device, is grief. For the notebooks on Loch's desk full of how he's fighting to make up for what Malachy lacks. For the distraught look on his face when he said I deserved better than him.

I found proof that St. Patrick's Day is, in fact, stealing from us, regardless of who exactly is the culprit. I've given the paparazzi plenty of material to counter that tinsel incident, so I can leave now, and not have to deal with any of these terrifying, too-massive-too-fast feelings. Coal can decide how to proceed with confronting St. Patrick's Day and getting our stolen joy back, and I can burrow into my duty-laden existence of following him around like a purposeless, sulking shadow.

Or.

Or.

I check the hall for Colm, then slip out and shut the office door behind me.

COAL

COAL
got the pic you sent, and while i'm
hella impressed by your grade-a
sneaking skills, CALL ME. dude.
fuck this magic shit for a second.
we need to talk about mom.

> No, we absolutely do not.
>
> I'm still not sure whether it's
> Malachy or Loch, so I'm going
> to hang around and see what
> evidence I can drum up.

COAL
how are things with loch?

That being his response makes my chest sink.

> Not great.

COAL
what?? since when??
okay i'm putting pause on my
suspicion of him cuz i was
beginning to think that he was
fucking you over while he was
fucking you over just to throw you off

> Ew, Jesus, Coal
>
> So, wait, now you're not
> suspicious of him?

COAL
well yeah because if it is
loch then he'd still be messing
around with you to keep you busy,

right? has there been more
kissing? so maybe it is the
uncle

> You're saying that the only
> possible reason Loch would
> be into me is to distract me
> from figuring out his evil
> master plan? Wow, thanks.

COAL

you know what i mean asshole

wait HAS there been more kissing?

kris

you're not responding.

i'm going to kick his ass tomorrow

tell me what happened or all i'll
be able to focus on is flipping his
face inside out and wearing it like a
halloween mask

> Hex is right. No more Hannibal
> for you.

I jog down the stairs and stop outside the library.

Do I want Coal to come raging in here tomorrow all defensive?
No. Definitely not.

So I lie through my teeth. Er, fingers, as it were.

> There has been no more
> kissing because it literally
> happened last night and
> we've been busy since then.
> He's at a music festival. I
> fucked off to go investigating.

> I don't know how I'll get proof
> of who it is though. Malachy
> doesn't have any of his

private stuff in this castle.
I think his setup is in some
swanky office in Dublin.

COAL

due to personal reasons i'm gonna
have to ask you not to go breaking
into an office in dublin

I wasn't suggesting I do. I just
don't know how to get proof
that it was him so we can
bring him down.

COAL

i'm worried about you.

i'm worried that mom rattled you.

I'm fine. We're not going to
their vow renewal. I should
block her number.

COAL

YES YOU SHOULD.

don't hate me but i think you're
doing exactly what we talked
about last night. that you're on the
verge of sacrificing pieces of
yourself for what you think loch
needs from you. that you're hoping
to find proof that it's his uncle
stealing so you can bring him
down for loch.

I almost text back that that's not what I'm doing. Or that nothing happened, everything's great, don't worry, tomorrow in Belfast will be fun, all of us together.

I started writing again.
Just a little. But I'm going to
do more.

COAL

HELL YES KRIS!!

that's great dude

be careful. if you wanna come
home now, we've got enough to
work with. you don't have to stay.

i don't want you getting hurt

I know. I appreciate it. I'll be
careful.

I step into the library and . . . think.

I have no idea how to find proof that Malachy did this. *If* he did this.

Do I need proof? If it is him, he has to suspect my real reason for being here. So maybe I lie?

When I see him at the Dublin parade in a few days, I can let him know that I have proof. That I found something while I was poking around the castle, and trap him into admitting that it was him. I'll try to record it so I can have his documented confession. And if it isn't him, then he'll think I'm odd and pushy, no harm done.

Which would mean, then, that it is Loch stealing from us.

I could skip all this elaborate scheming and confront Loch instead.

These thoughts are a Ferris wheel. I need to know who is stealing from us—I could ask Loch—I don't *want* to know if it's him—I want it to be Malachy—I can't investigate Malachy from here—I could ask Loch—and around we go.

An ache thuds across my forehead, burrows deep into my temples.

In another act of selfishness, I mentally table all this and go in search of Colm.

About an hour later, I'm back in the library, now bent over a notebook I got from Colm, when Loch storms in.

"The fuck did ya think you were doing, leaving without a word like that?" he shouts.

I don't look up from where I'm seated on the floor at a coffee table, head in one hand. My other fingers are fully cramped around a pen. I've been writing pretty much nonstop, stream of consciousness bullshit, the same type of stuff I'd typed on my phone while walking back from the festival.

I wrote about how mad I am for the way I've conformed to limitations I put on myself.

I wrote about how hurt I am for what my mother has done to me.

I wrote about what it would feel like to be alone, to be truly left.

I wrote, and I'm rusty. Most of it sucks.

But I'm *writing* again.

I cross out a word. "I asked Colm to let Siobhán know."

"That was *forty minutes* after I realized you were *gone*, Kris. I nearly tore apart the festival searching for you."

"Why were you searching for me?"

"I—" He stops. Stammers over his rampage, and it makes me look up at him.

Seeing him is the final nail in my *I'm confused* bullshit.

I'm not confused.

I'm a mess, and I've got shit to work out, but about him? I'm sure.

His anger, though, *is* confusing, infuriatingly so. *He* walked away. *He* was the one to put a stop to this, so he has no right, no *fucking right*, to reprimand me.

But I stay calm and refocus on my notebook. The words blur, so I pretend to write something. "I can't imagine what else you needed me for. The paparazzi got what they wanted, didn't they? My role was fulfilled."

"Your *role*?"

I shut the notebook and climb to my feet. "Yeah. My *role*. You don't get to—"

Siobhán rushes in. "See! I told ya he'd be in here. Kris?" She clocks my posture, Loch's, the tang of our fight on the air.

God, we do fight *all the time,* don't we? No wonder it was so obvious to Coal.

"I'm sorry I worried you," I say. To his sister.

Siobhán frowns. "You two are being fucking weird."

"Here." I scrawl my number on a sheet of notebook paper, rip it off, cross around Loch, and slap it into Siobhán's hand. "In case I wander off again."

"Kris." Loch snaps my name like a dressing-down.

"I'm tired." I flip absently through the notebook. "I'll be in my room. Still haven't recovered from yesterday."

My eyes go to his.

I don't want him to see how much each of his rejections has hurt. I don't want him to think I've been holed up here entirely because of him. I'm not sure what he sees though, what I'm showing him.

I'm headed for the door when my gaze catches on something.

"Ah." I tuck the notebook under my arm and swipe up the stack of books from a side table.

Loch grunts as I slam them into his chest.

"Pulled these out of your vast collection," I say. "I was happy to find that your library wasn't all dry-ass classics. You said you can't give me what I need, but maybe I can give you what *you* need. Some actual *joy.*"

They're books I loved when I was younger. Books I read when I was at the peak of my writing obsession, when I was *so certain* all these happy endings could be mine if I . . . if I was *more.* And yeah, this is what started me off on my fucked-up belief system, but at the time, I was so innocent in my joy, and *that's* what I miss more than anything. To be happy and not analyze why.

Loch fumbles the books in his hands, eyes fastened on me, not a shred of anger left now.

"Kris," he tries. "I—"

But I leave, and get two feet out of the library when Siobhán yells something at him in Irish.

I don't bother using magic to translate. I get up to my room and drop into the desk and keep writing.

And it turns into writing about him.

The same vein as the shit I used to wax on about over Iris. Only it's more pointed, and the places where I'd get stuck over her, they flow now—like the framework was in place, but it'd refused to congeal because it was waiting for that final piece. For *him*.

For that stubborn prick.

I should send it to the reporters. An exposé on Lochlann Patrick from the inside, who he *really* is. I'd have to tone it down rather significantly; this is opulent, flowery writing, words I haven't gotten to use in years because there's no room for them in academic papers or political documents for Christmas. Words like *diaphanous* and *graze* and *ephemeral* and *ravage* and even *sloppy,* because there is poetry in mess, too.

I write, and write, sculpting reality into something imperfect and beautiful.

I don't come out of my fugue state for a long, long time, breaking back to the surface with a gasp. My back screams from being bent over, stomach roiling with hunger and eyes going slightly crossed. They burn when I grab for my phone to check the time.

After midnight.

A smile rises.

In spite of the pain, I feel *good*.

There are missed texts from Coal and Iris about tomorrow's details for Belfast. They're planning off of Wren's original schedule, so I give a thumbs-up at the where and when we're meeting, then scan the rest of my notifications.

There's a text from a number I don't recognize.

UNKNOWN
You didn't tell me those books you
gave me were so fucking sad

I launch to my feet, good feeling evaporating.

That *asshole*.

> This number was for your
> sister. For emergencies.

UNKNOWN
This is an emergency. Look
outside your door.

Frowning, I open the door to see a dinner tray on the hall's carpet. My stomach rumbles at the smell of braised meat and potatoes.

Next to it, in a neat stack, are four leather notebooks under an unopened package of cushion-grip pens.

Heat burns up my face.

Fuck him.

I juggle the tray and writing supplies, nudge the door shut with my hip, and set everything next to the notebook Colm gave me.

Then I stare at my phone for a few seconds, aggressively beating my fingers on the desk.

He can text me, fine. He can leave me food and . . . unnecessarily thoughtful gifts.

But he doesn't get to choose how I save his number in my phone.

THE ACTUAL DEVIL

> I'm not even hungry.

THE ACTUAL DEVIL
Yeah you are, boyo.

> What did you mean the books
> were sad? Which one did you
> start with?

I know before he even has to say it.

Most of the books I found were ones that spurred my happy ever after bullshit. A collection of fairy tales, a few longer novels.

But there was one.

One book I found in his library's shelves, and I included it in that stack, buried it down at the bottom, because while it broke me as a kid, that break is a part of my foundation.

THE ACTUAL DEVIL
Bridge to Terabithia.

If I had any doubt about his magic being based in luck, good or bad, I don't anymore.

Mom started reading that book to me before she left. Part of my childish beliefs once she was gone involved *she has to come back, she didn't finish the book.*

Once it was clear she *wasn't* coming back, I went ahead and read it myself.

Two kids create a fantasy world in the forest behind their houses. Two kids, full of hope and imagination, driven by wonder and freedom and belief.

One of them dies.

And yeah, sure, there's a lot of deep literary discussions that came from this book, but as a young kid whose mom had left in the middle of reading a book I hadn't known would end tragically, it was a one-two punch of grief.

My eyes sting again. I've been staring at the notebook too long, that's all.

THE ACTUAL DEVIL
I started to suspect how it would end, so I skipped ahead and I cannot believe you would give someone that book without warning them.

First of all, YOU SKIPPED AHEAD? Sacrilege. Sentence: a painful, public flogging.

Second, how did you suspect the ending?

THE ACTUAL DEVIL
The book had a vibe about it. I
dunno.

> A vibe? You guessed that
> Leslie dies based on a vibe?
>
> Where the fuck were you
> when I was seven, your vibe
> could've saved me a lot of
> heartache.

THE ACTUAL DEVIL
You read this when you were
seven?? Christ, that explains a lot.

> You have no idea.
>
> And stop texting me. We're
> staying away from each other,
> remember? I wasn't starting a
> book club with you.

THE ACTUAL DEVIL
You should be so lucky to have me
in your book club.

Eat your dinner, maggot, I've got
reading to do.

It's a clear sign-off, but I stare at his text far longer than I should,
my heart in a suspended state of racing.

All the words I wrote today roll around and around in my head.

It's easier to write. Always is.

So I send one last text.

> You were right earlier. I am a
> mess. But you said you are
> too. It wouldn't be easy, and
> I don't think you want easy.
> Neither do I.

Chapter Fourteen

The next day, we're not due to leave for Belfast until after lunch, so I spend the morning filling up the notebook Colm gave me. I don't use the ones Loch left.

But I use the pens.

C'mon, they're *cushion grip*. I'm only human.

I stay at the desk in my suite rather than trek down to the library. Because it's comfortable.

Not because I'm a coward.

I also don't turn on my phone.

Again, because I am definitely not a coward.

I'm just, like, conserving battery life or some shit.

Only I finally do have to turn on my phone when Iris, Coal, and Hex are supposed to show up, and I gotta face the results of my dumbass text last night at some point.

There are no missed texts from Loch.

I open the thread with him. The message I sent last night is read. Unanswered.

Fuck this guy.

There's a bunch of shit from Coal and Iris—Iris has been counting down by the half hour for the past three hours like we haven't seen each other in years. But this is the first time we've all hung out since before my Christmas love declaration, isn't it? So maybe it is a big deal.

Wren sent me some more tabloid links. Less than after the race because nothing *scandalous* happened at the music festival, but these articles are markedly less clickbaity. They talk about how Loch spent most of his time with a few different musicians, and one reporter uncovered that many of the new artists were there because *Loch* arranged it. There's not a whiff of negative speculation to be had, no mention of Loch screwing anything up. No mention of me yelling at the paparazzi either.

One article ends with a question. *What else has Prince Lochlann been doing behind the scenes?*

I switch back to my text thread with him. Still nothing. Has he seen these articles? Does he care? Why do *I* care, if he's such a stubborn asshole?

Fuuuuuuuck.

I tear through my suitcase and throw my anxious energy into looking as dead sexy as humanly possible. There's one shirt in particular I've never worn because the innuendo is a little *much* even for me, and it's the tightest thing I've ever bought—a sizing mistake, actually—but it'll show off every muscle in my chest and arms.

Not that I've taken interludes from writing this morning by doing impromptu push-ups in my room.

There's a lot of denial floating around.

I tug the shirt on. It's bright cherry red. With a candy cane in the center. And the words *I'll Lick It For You.*

I start to pull my hair up, but then leave it down so it hangs past my jaw. My black jeans are appropriately tight, too—I want this fucker to suffer.

But that's all I can do. I'm not as into styling as Coal or Iris, so I stand in the bathroom and survey myself and hope it's enough to make Loch stew, because I know whatever *he* wears is going to make my inner thoughts be the equivalent of a keysmash.

My phone buzzes, rocketing my heart nearly out of my chest, but it's Iris.

If Loch hasn't responded to what I said by now, he isn't going to. Just. Accept that.

PEEP, MINI CANDY CANE, AND THE BEST CLAUS

IRIS
WE'RE HERE GET YOUR ASS
DOWN TO THE FOYER

I grab my coat and race out the door. I have no reason to be nervous. But if Loch is down in the foyer first . . . or, god forbid, Siobhán . . .

It feels like two worlds are colliding and the idea of that fallout is *terrifying.*

In the foyer, Coal, Hex, and Iris are there with Colm.

I should have asked Coal and Iris to dress me. Hex, too. They're all decked out as befitting a night of pub hopping in Belfast. Iris is in a sequined purple dress with knee-high boots, heels so sharp I legitimately fear for her ankles; Hex is in one of those corset vests that Coal *will not shut up about;* and my brother has chosen to wear gray on gray with a gray scarf, understated but giving appropriately pub-happy vibes.

While I'm in *jeans and a T-shirt,* the fuck was I thinking?

Iris squeals and jumps on me. Colm excuses himself from talking with Coal, who then leaps into the hug, nearly shoving us all to the floor.

My chest releases, stress unable to keep its stranglehold on me with them around.

"Good god, you guys, it's not like I've been off at war." I'm grinning as I disentangle from them. But I have missed them—I've missed *this,* this easy friendship.

I nod at Hex, who looks potently relieved not to have been part of the tackle-hug situation.

Iris hooks her arm through mine. "Based on your texts, I wouldn't be so sure. It's been a bit of a battlefield here, hm?"

"Battlefield?" I blink innocently. "What? No. All I do is lay around and drink whiskey and regret it immediately. It's been smooth sailing—"

"Kris! Introduce us!"

Finn and Siobhán are at the threshold of the hall. Siobhán is dressed similar to Iris, in a short pink dress and boots, while Finn is in ripped jeans with a thick black sweater sporting strategic holes to show a shiny silver tank underneath. Her more casual outfit helps balance out the scale of fashion on my side and I relax a little.

Until she eyes me, head to toe. "I see why you called in reinforcements now."

My eyebrows slide up. "What?"

"You've given up your sham of professionalism and need someone else to represent your Holiday." She waves at my shirt.

Siobhán elbows Finn. "Be nice. Kris, you look"—her veil of cordiality wavers—"very, ah, comfortable."

"We're going *pub hopping*. It's hardly—". But I stop.

Finn's right.

We'll be photographed; I'm here as a guest of St. Patrick's Day.

And I'm wearing a shirt with a blowjob joke on it.

Finn catches the horror my face must show and bursts out laughing.

My jaw drops. I don't think I've made her *laugh* yet. At least, not without an underlying air of murder. Even Siobhán gapes at her.

"Christ, you're easy to rile." Finn slaps my shoulder. "It's funny. If people canna handle your shirt, they *definitely* canna handle today's aspect of our Holiday. Getting proper shitfaced. Keep your depraved clothes."

Siobhán rolls her eyes. "Make up your mind whether you're plotting his grisly end or accepting him. I canna keep up with your mood swings, Finn."

She ignores Finn's responding mew of offense and turns to the group behind me.

"Welcome to Ireland!" she says brightly. Iris is closest, so Siobhán grabs her in a hug. "I'm Siobhán. That's Finn."

Am I imagining the way Finn's face is red? It wasn't red when she was laughing at me. So—

She does not go in for a hug with Iris like Siobhán. She extends her hand instead, board-stiff. "Ah, yeah. Easter? Iris Lentora?"

Oh.

Finn is *blushing*.

"Yes." Iris accepts Finn's hand. "Nice to meet you."

Finn shakes her hand.

Again.

And again.

Iris squints at her.

Finn drops Iris's hand and leaps back like she saw a mouse. "I, er—"

I wave at Coal. "And this is my brother, Coal, and Hex, from Halloween."

Finn cuts her eyes to me in a look of bare relief at the shift in focus. It damn near makes me jump spastically too, but I smile at her.

Siobhán hugs them both, and even Hex relents at her effusive joy.

As the foyer fills with the jabber of introductions, an out-of-place jolt rushes up my spine, hips to hairline. I turn, seeking it out—

Loch is off to the side of the hall's entrance, arms folded, a bag hooked around one wrist. He's in another Aran sweater, this one a deep blue that sets off coppery undertones in his hair and beard.

Goddamn those sweaters. Like he's a sexy, mysterious lighthouse fisherman.

I catch the pulse of him checking me out too, but his face sets with an intense throat-clear before I can figure out his reaction.

Everyone pivots to him with such a myriad of various intentions that I'm shocked he doesn't tip over.

Siobhán rushes to him. "This is my brother, Loch—oh, you brought it! Excellent!"

She takes the bag from him and pulls out—paint bottles?

To my confused look, Loch's eyes glimmer with mischief, finally a little more like himself.

"You did na think you could go to Belfast without being proper done up, did you?" He nods around the room. "'Tis a pleasure to meet you all."

I point at everyone mechanically. "Coal. Hex. Iris."

Loch smiles at each of them. Stops on Iris.

He swivels back to Hex and, in an awkward burst, tells him, "You lot owe your Holiday to us."

There's another beat of silence.

Hex cocks an eyebrow.

"St. Patrick's Day started Halloween?" I clarify.

Loch clears his throat again. "Ah, no—Ireland. Originated in the festival of Samhain."

Hex appraises Loch, letting the moment stretch in silence again. I can't help thinking Hex is fucking with him on my behalf, and my chest warms that for all the ribbing Hex and I give each other, he's got my back.

Finally, Hex smiles. "I'm not surprised you know that. We have started to bring the roots back into popularity, but most people still don't know of Ireland's influence. There is credit due to Scotland and England too that we—"

Loch frowns. "Pardon?"

Hex's eyebrows lift a *tad* too naively as he says, "Well, Samhain is not solely Irish, is it? It's Gaelic, and extends into parts of Scotland, England—"

"*England?*" Loch licks his teeth. "Go way outta that. Halloween came from *Ireland,* lad. Those other bits are poor imitations."

In the midst of this, Coal sidles up to me and nudges my arm. One look, and he doesn't even have to ask it. *You all right?*

But I don't want to—can't—answer here, so I nod at Loch and Hex now debating England's contributions to Halloween versus Ireland's. "You're not going to defend him?"

"Nah. He's hot when he gets all fired up over his Holiday." A pause. "Hex, not Loch." Another pause. "Although—"

"You sure you're okay to be away for the evening?" I cut him off. "No pressing winter collective business?"

Coal snorts. "Oh, the other Holiday leaders *insisted* I leave. They all wanted a break too. Apparently—get this—I'm a *workaholic. Me.* Mister Barely Maintaining a C Average. The other leaders demanded a break from the, and I quote, *obnoxiously thorough meetings.*" He's grinning. "They're great people. This collective's going to be fun."

My smile is true and glowing. "I'm glad you've found your calling, Santa."

He shudders. "That still sounds wrong."

Hex is beaming in his innocent yet maniacal way, and Loch laughs, mildly horrified, so this feels like as good a time as any to think about something else.

"Okay." I clap loudly. Siobhán has finished laying out the paints on a side table and I motion to them. "So—are we doing arts and crafts or what?"

Loch pivots to the paints. "Belfast is basically a precursor for the big Dublin parade in a few days, so you gotta go all out." He picks up a jar of orange paint and a small foam brush. "Face painting. You can tell how good a time you had by how fucked up the paint is at night's end."

Iris bounces. "I'm in!"

She joins Siobhán at the table and picks out colors. Finn trails her like a puppy; I honestly have no idea who Finn even *is* now, her whole demeanor all soft and wilted.

Coal loops his arm around Hex's waist. "I'll paint you if you paint me?"

Hex hums uncertainly. "I am not sure I trust you not to paint something obscene on me."

"I'm happy to do it for you both," Loch says. "Kris can attest. I know my way around a paintbrush."

"I haven't seen you use a brush," I note. "You know how to use your fingers, though."

I *hear* what I say as I say it.

Mixed panic and horror knot in my throat and my gaze collides with Coal's. His face takes on a look of such bliss, oh the gift in the euphemism buffet he's been given.

To my eternal surprise, my brother tips his head demurely. "Thanks, Loch. But why don't you help out Kris?"

That is definitely not the worst thing he could have said, yet it shoots that panic-horror mix down into my gut.

Coal drags Hex to the table, promising none too convincingly not to debase him.

Loch's eyes are on the floor by my shoes. "It does na need to be elaborate. A few strips of orange and green, you're good."

"Are you sure you want us doing this? Doesn't it feed into assumptions about your Holiday you want to undo?"

Loch looks at me. A quick impact, emotions rapidly flickering over him, surprise and gratitude, then it all dissolves in a small grin.

"This is na an assumption about my Holiday. It's just become one of the biggest parts. It's still an aspect I will na deny."

"Yes, I can see how it'd be heartbreaking not to celebrate the impending headaches and projectile vomiting."

"That's only you, boyo. Some of us know how to drink good and proper."

I smirk. I can't help it. "Piss off."

When I reach for the jar and brush in his hand, he waves me away.

My stomach tightens. "I can do it myself."

"Nah. You *don't* know how to use your fingers."

Heat bursts over my face. And I so badly want to say *you have no idea what my fingers can do.*

"Just hold still, ya eejit." He pockets the brush, opens the jar, dips in a finger, and glides paint across my cheekbone before I can object. Not that I would have.

I stop moving. Stop breathing. Held there with his finger on my face, the hand with the jar propping under my chin and angling me up to him. I stare at his eyes even though he's pretending to be focused on getting more paint, putting a second stripe under the first.

I wrote so many things about him in that notebook upstairs. I wrote and wrote and I could recite it to him now. Would it help? Would it change how he sees us? But my brother and Loch's sisters are giggling over paint behind us, and my throat goes dry.

"Are you going to let me paint you?" I ask. It comes out rough and low. "It's only fair."

Loch hesitates, muscles stiffening up his arm, in his neck. "I, eh—I will na be coming with you tonight."

My lips part, brows scrunching in confusion.

Siobhán hears him. Finn too. They stop what they're doing and frown, and I'm staring up at him the same, three fronts of unspoken questions he responds to by swapping the orange paint for green and working on my other cheek.

"What are you talking about, dearthár?" Siobhán asks.

Iris, Coal, and Hex are working with the paint, but they watch us none too subtly.

Loch exhales like he's preparing to free-fall out of a plane, and the rush of air makes the paint drying on my skin contract, a jerky spasm of sensation that scrapes along my nerves.

"I have guests coming tonight." He finally looks at Finn and Siobhán. "Aislin. Tadhg. Eamon."

Those names mean something to them. They gape at each other, then back at Loch.

"You invited them here?" Siobhán asks.

"Who?" I look between them all.

"They're each the head of a branch of our Holiday," Finn tells me, her eyes on Loch, analytical.

Loch invited his court here?

Relief fizzes through my chest in a geyser burst. He's going to show them what he's been doing. He's going to explain to them how wrong Malachy has been about him.

He's finally taking charge of his Holiday.

Loch's face is an odd, sickly mix of pale and red.

Siobhán tosses a paint bottle back on the table. "When are they arriving? We'll go change to—"

But Loch holds up his hand. "No. Go out to Belfast. Keep the schedule. This is—it's na a—" He falters, mouth opening and shutting, before he swings his attention to Coal and Hex—and me, briefly.

He stands straighter. "I'll be talking to them, then they're off, probably to Belfast too. It will na be a long meeting. So go, have a presence there. I'll handle this."

Finn and Siobhán stare at Loch in concern, excitement—and anger, from Finn.

"You were na gonna tell us?" Finn hisses.

"I just did."

"At the last fucking minute."

Loch turns back to me, adds another green stripe to my cheek like nothing's wrong. "It's na a big deal. You've been wanting me to do stuff like this, haven't you? So let me."

Finn glowers at the side of his face before she rejoins Iris at the table, obviously ignoring her brother now. Siobhán follows, glancing back at Loch once or twice like she wants to argue, but she holds her tongue.

"You invited your court here," I whisper.

Loch's fingers twitch on my face. He purses his lips. "Do na talk. You'll wreck the paint."

"You invited them here," I say again. I have to, I *have* to make him feel this.

I smile.

Loch flinches, eyes cutting across the millimeter of space between his fingers and my lips.

"Do na look so smug," he mutters, but there's no annoyance in it, just a choked yearning I think he meant to cover up.

It damn near kills me to ignore it. "Are you kidding? The mighty Lochlann Patrick *listened to me*. My face might be stuck looking smug forever."

"It was na *you*." He shifts uneasily. "Finn's been getting on my arse about all these same things for years."

My smile goes sly. "But why'd you do it now? What made you finally reach out to your court?"

Loch doesn't speak. He screws the lid back on the paint jar and studies the marks his fingers left on my face.

His eyes go to the small bandage on my forehead. The reminder of my fall.

With a grimace, he ignores my question. "Be careful tonight, yeah? No more injuries."

"Worried about me?" My smile's failing so my words come out coarser than I mean.

Loch flexes his hands on the jar, veins bulging in his wrists, up the backs of his arms where his sleeves are rolled to his elbows.

He looks in pain.

Siobhán bounds over. "You ready? Look at you, Kris!" She touches the drying paint on my face.

She has a messy shamrock on one cheek. Iris has stripes that vaguely resemble the Irish flag. Coal and Hex have matching bands of orange and green that run from ear to ear across their noses, and Finn has a single thick band of orange down one side of her face.

I honestly don't even know what Loch painted on me. I don't care.

"We're driving?" Siobhán asks—with a pointed look at Coal. "It is a trek—"

"Ah, Siobhán, no—" Loch starts, but she's pouting at my brother, who is obliviously looking down at Hex, tucking a piece of hair behind his ear.

"It's not every day we have such esteemed guests with transportation magic," she says, loud enough that Coal does hear.

"What now?" he asks, and I step in.

"We'd be happy to get everyone to Belfast," I say. That much magic won't break us.

Coal blinks. "Oh. Yeah. Yeah! Christmas is more than pleased to extend this offering as thanks for St. Patrick's Day's invitation to—"

"Don't overdo it," I cut him off.

He shrugs. "Hey, I'm a diplomat now—you can't shut that shit off. Loch knows what I'm talking about."

Loch seems stunned that Coal is joking with him. "It's hard to live a split life."

Coal conjures some mistletoe. As he approaches the nearest door to set it up, I stay with Loch. Siobhán does too; Finn's the only one who keeps her distance.

Siobhán squeezes Loch's arm. "You'll let us know how it goes, yeah? Do na make me pull it from ya." She pauses, and her joy falls. "You owe us that at least. We could've helped. We're in this too."

Loch wilts. "I know." He yanks her into a hug, face resting on her shoulder. "I know, deirfiúr. I did na mean it as a snub. I—"

His eyes hit mine.

"I owe it to you," he whispers to her. "To fix what I broke."

She pulls back and swats him in the chest. "You broke *nothing*, Lochy. This is all Malachy and his shit." She smiles, happiness and sunshine again. "Now go and show them how great you are. Go and show them how *worthy* you are."

One half of his lips tips up. "Thanks."

She winks at me as she slips over to grab her coat off a wall hook.

Loch stuffs his hands in his pockets, tension winding between us, within us, a rebound of unsaid words and unfelt emotions.

"You are," I tell him, throat welling, "worthy of this."

Even if he's the one stealing from Christmas. Is that where his reticence is coming from? Or is it just who he is, someone incapable of accepting praise?

Regardless, I'm not going to make room for his discomfort. He's going to know how great he is if it kills him, because even if he is the thief, I've seen why he had to steal from us. It doesn't make it okay, but it makes it understandable.

Expectedly, Loch cringes and drops my gaze.

"Enjoy Belfast," he says, then he's gone, hurrying up the hall.

My heart does a hard twist, lurching me forward a step.

But Coal's next to me, and he throws his arm around my neck before I can do something stupid, like run after Loch. "Don't let him sour your day. We're here, and we're going to have *fun*."

The Belfast street where Coal takes us is packed, old black cobblestones crowded with people just like us, faces painted, but taken further too—massive green hats and shamrock headbands and bright green coats. Storefronts around us are mostly pubs, doors thrown open and various bands competing for airspace with screaming fiddles.

This seems to be the epicenter of the festivities, which is why it isn't surprising when the Holiday paparazzi find us after about twenty minutes of walking around. I clock them snapping our pictures, but I don't feel that usual twist of offense or repulsion. What will their speculations be about why Loch isn't here?

Siobhán and Finn transform into our tour guides—Siobhán willingly, Finn halfheartedly, still upset about Loch, but she at least seems distracted by Iris. We start at one pub and let the night carry us up the road, from bar to bar to a brief stop at a street vendor for flaky beef pasties, then back into it, until it's a fog of music and laughter and bodies getting progressively looser.

Which is how we end up at one pub that's playing the greatest hits of Irish musicians, and the crowd belts out each one like singing is giving their livers a pep talk. There's a giant chunk dedicated to The Cranberries, and Iris downright *screams* when they start playing "Zombie."

I've lost track of how many glasses of whiskey she's had—she'd make Loch proud, honestly—but she jumps up from her chair at the table we've crowded around and sings alongside most everyone in the pub. Siobhán joins her, and Finn sits there and laughs and takes video blackmail.

Coal and Hex are making out. Unsurprisingly. Coal isn't even drunk—he doesn't really drink anymore since Hex, and I think he's the only one clocking that I keep ordering soda. But with the night wearing on, they're fully consumed in each other as the band croons about what's in your head, in your head, zombie-ie-ie ohhhh—

I cup my hands over my mouth and whoop up at Iris and Siobhán as they screech the chorus, and I can't remember the last time I laughed this much, this deeply.

Iris grabs my arm and hauls me to my feet. "I know you know this one!"

So I join in, arm in arm, and Finn catcalls us, and for a moment, I feel like I'm watching myself from far away. The noise of the pub fades to a droning hum and everything slows way down, like moving through molasses.

I don't know where to start with fixing my internal mess. Or if I'll ever be able to fix it. But I do know that I'm overthinking like *all of it,* and if I want things to be different, I can't sit around waiting for them to change.

So I lean close to Iris and whisper-shout into her ear, "I started writing again."

Breath sucked in to belt the final lines, she whips her head at me so fast her braids smack my face.

"Oh my god!" She jostles my shoulder. "I loved your stories!"

"Remember what you did for them once?" This delirious wish is a hundred wants crashing together, forcing me to keep going. "You drew my characters?"

Iris's grin widens, her eyes a little unfocused, and I wonder how much of this conversation will stick.

"Of course!" She giggles. "Oh my god. I was, what, fourteen? They were probably awful."

"They were awesome and I loved them." The music swells, deafening, so I lean closer, heart faltering. "Do you think you'd do that again? If I wrote a book. Do you think you could draw things for it?"

She cocks her head.

"I mean—I haven't even started writing anything book-like yet," I stammer. "It was a . . . just a thought. I loved your art. Still love it. And I think—I don't know. It could be cool to collaborate on something like that? I know book illustration is a whole separate thing from book writing and it would probably never amount to anything, but I—"

Iris throws her arms around my neck. "Yes! Of course. Fuck yes. That sounds like fun."

I squeeze her back. "We could both use some fun, I think."

Iris leans away to bookend my cheeks with her hands. Her whiskey-loopy gaze focuses on mine, drifts away, refocuses, and she laughs. "There are more of you than I remember. But the real you is *riiiiight*—" She boops my nose. "Here."

"We should have had this conversation when you were sober."

Her eyes get round. "Oh *no*. Oh *no* oh no. If"—she hiccups—"if I don't remember this tomorrow, ask me again. Better yet—wait."

She shrugs me off to dig out her phone, taps away on her screen, and a second later, my phone vibrates in my pocket.

PEEP, MINI CANDY CANE, AND THE BEST CLAUS

IRIS
future iris this is past iris
draw for kris
it is his dreeeeeeeeam
a book a book a book

Her face is totally blissed-out. "I will probably be confused by that text tomorrow. But you can remind me and tell me there are no take-backs for drunk promises."

"Um. There should definitely be take-backs for drunk promises."

Iris shoves her finger against my lips. "Ah-ah. Shush, you. No take-backs. We're gonna—" Another hiccup. "We're gonna write a *book* together, my friend. You will write the book. I will draw the book. OH MY GOD!" She smacks her hands on my face again, her expression collapsing into pleading adoration. "You *like* my art?"

Wow. She is skillfully barreling from drunk to shitfaced.

"I really do, Iris," I say, and her round eyes get teary.

"Kris." She sniffs. "I—even with everything that happened. I want you to know."

Oh god. "Iris—we don't have to—"

"No. Kris." She tips my face so our foreheads are pressed together. "Kristopher. Even with everything that happened. You are going to be great at drawing things. I will teach you *so* much."

I pause.

Then snort. "That's not what—actually, that's fine. Thank you, Iris. I appreciate that."

She shoves my face back, rocking me like a bobblehead. "I'm *serious,* Kris. You'll be such a good artist. We'll be artists *together.*"

I definitely could have timed this conversation better. "You're very drunk."

She giggles and throws her arms around me again. "I *know.* Isn't it *great?*"

The song ends and up kicks one by The Script. "Hall of Fame."

Iris flails to Siobhán with a gasp so loud half the oxygen gets yanked out of the room, and they both bellow out the lyrics.

A hand grabs my arm.

It's Finn, and that shocks me enough that I immediately feel like someone must've died.

"What?" I shout over the music.

"He's a stubborn arse," she tells me. "But you got him to talk to our court today. Siobhán was right. You are good for him."

I gape at her. Fully open-mouthed staring. "What?"

She grimaces. "Do na make me repeat the nice thing or I'll vomit."

"She's into art too." I nod at Iris.

Finn's face goes stricken. "Eh?"

"She's into art too," I say a little louder. Iris is enraptured in singing. "If you point out unusual things, stuff she could use as inspiration, she'll eat it up."

Finn gawps at me. "Thanks," she says, sounding winded.

"Thank you."

She punches me. And I think I finally cracked her over to my side.

Coal pops up from his chair, sending Finn startling backwards, and *shrieks* the chorus to "Hall of Fame."

I bust out laughing and point to Hex, sitting primly on the chair Coal vacated, sipping a glass of water.

"Your regularly scheduled make-out session is over, I take it?"

Coal bats the side of my head. Fuck, everyone's handsy tonight.

But he gets a deeply serious look on his face and sings the lyrics as if they're a ballad, directing all that cheesy energy at me. I try to grab Hex to put him between us but the little shit slips out of my hands like an eel. Coal snatches a fork from the table to use as a microphone and goes full-on serenading, and fine, that's what we're doing tonight?

I sing right back at him, matching his weird energy, and he breaks in belly-deep laughs. His laughter yanks me over the edge, and I have to catch myself on the table to stay upright in my own hysterics.

I open my arms to this simplicity. Maybe everything can be this simple, too. As simple as accepting it, not overthinking, not worrying, and whatever backlash comes, I can stand strong knowing that I did what *I* needed, what was true to *me*.

It's past three by the time Coal uses more magic to send us all stumbling exhaustedly—and, in some cases, drunk off our asses—back to the foyer of Castle Patrick.

Iris leans heavily on Coal, her eyes shut, nearly asleep on her feet; her face paint is utterly wrecked, smears of green and orange muddled by sweat and exertion. Siobhán is Iris's mirror on Finn, and I realize—only two of us got hammered? Well, damn. Did we fail this particular St. Patrick's Day outing, then?

I give Coal a side hug, trying not to disturb Iris. "Going back to Christmas?"

My voice is rough from all the screaming, ears ringing in the heavy silence of the foyer.

"After I drop this lightweight in Easter." He hefts Iris, who groans.

"She drank half her body weight in whiskey," Finn pipes up. "While I dinna see you down a single drop. She's officially Irish now, whereas *you* are an interloper."

"Fair point." Coal salutes Finn. "It was nice meeting and then instantly going pub hopping with you."

Finn waves him off. Siobhán whines into Finn's shoulder, and the two of them make their way deeper into the castle.

Hex smiles at me. "You are staying here, then?"

"Wow." I smirk. "Coal, you sure can throw your voice. That sounded just like Hex."

Hex rolls his eyes. "I told him you would see through that." He leans in to give me a quick hug. "I, at least, understand why you are staying. You are not alone in your pursuit of doing the right thing."

"I'm not against him doing the right thing," Coal whispers. "I don't want him doing *the right thing* for the *wrong guy*." He glances around, and even though we're alone, Coal lowers his voice. "We have proof that the device we found in Christmas matches the one connected to their joy meter. Come back to Christmas, and we can strategize about how to approach both Loch and Malachy to get our joy back. You can be done."

Hearing Coal say that, I know exactly what would happen: Malachy would pin it on Loch. Make him take the fall.

I exhale. "I told her about writing again."

Coal's eyebrows go up. "Told . . . who?"

I nod at Iris. "Told *her*. That I'm—wait, what did you think I meant?"

Relief droops Coal's stance. "Shit, dude, I was terrified for a second you were talking to Mom again. God, don't do that to me."

"I didn't—no. Fuck no. I wouldn't."

"So you did block her number?"

My lips part. "I will."

"*Kris,*" Coal groans. "Hex, would you do me a huge favor and turn my brother into a scarecrow so I can *pummel him without remorse*?"

"That is not even sort of something my magic can do," he says.

"Block. Her. Number." Coal adjusts Iris to punctuate each word with a finger in my chest. "Dad too. That's my job now. That's how I protect you. So let me protect you, dumbass. I can handle them."

"And I can't?" No, I can't, but I can't let *him* know that. Even if he already does.

Coal sighs. "I know you can. But you don't have to. Block their numbers, Kris. Please. And whatever you do here—"

"I know. I'll be careful. I won't get hurt. I promise and swear and from henceforth do vow and whatever it takes to get you three out of this country."

"Oh, woe is Kris." Coal throws his head back dramatically. "He has people who care about his well-being!"

"Go home. Go to sleep."

"Yeah, yeah." Coal conjures mistletoe into his palm. "*You* go to sleep too. First, *block their numbers*. Then sleep."

"I swear."

"You're such a dumbshit."

I grin. "Love you too."

They leave. And the castle is now unbearably quiet, achingly without noise, like the stones are absorbing even stray brushes of wind.

I drop my coat on a hook in the foyer and head up the hall, steps muffled by the thin carpet.

My body stops by a door. I don't let myself think about why.

I push into it and drop down the spiral stairs. At the bottom, I can already feel and hear music. It's moodier this time, full volume John Legend reverberating as I inch forward.

The door to his studio is open.

Chapter Fifteen

The wall-sized canvas he was working on is gone, replaced by a smaller one—well, *small* comparatively. It's taller than he is, and it's mostly blank, the outline of shapes in a rough pencil sketch, a few clusters of preliminary colors, this one looking to be greens and gold with accents of red.

He's shirtless again, those paint-splattered sweatpants slung low on his hips. Standing in front of that canvas, one arm acting as his palette this time with globs of paint all the way up to his elbow, he dabs at the paint, wipes some on the canvas, back and forth in frantic motions so I know he's channeling all his anxious energy into this.

I knock on the open door loud enough to cut through the music.

He suspends in the motion of reaching for the top corner. Every muscle along his bare shoulders winds so tight he looks liable to sprout wings.

Slowly, he pivots to face me.

I drag one hand across my mouth, wishing I'd thought more about coming down here, wishing I'd grabbed that notebook and looked back over things—

I'm here. Be here, damn it.

I step into the room.

Loch goes back to painting. "You're drunk. I do na want you to do or say anything you'll regret when you sober up. Go to bed, boyo."

"I'm not drunk."

"Yeah, I buy that. Out in Belfast for how long? With that girl of yours."

"Iris? I'm pretty sure she would have entertained the idea of going home with Finn if she hadn't been so drunk herself."

That earns me a startled frown. "Finn?" He swallows his surprise with a grunt. "Good on Finn, then."

But he resumes painting, focused on one particular streak of green, fingers going over it, and over it, and over it.

I take another step forward. "How did the meeting with your court go?"

He twists his hand to dig his knuckle into a smear of paint. "Fine."

I could push him, call him on his bullshit, but he knows that answer isn't enough. He knows in the way he drops his hand with a growl that devolves into a sigh.

"It was good," he expands to the canvas. "They—they had no idea what I was—" He clears his throat. "They know now. What I've done. Most of it."

"What about Malachy?"

He shrugs and mixes a few paint colors in a new spot on his arm. "I did na tell them how they should feel about Malachy. I . . . gave them the truth on my end. It's all I can do."

"But it's still *big*. I'm proud of you."

Loch's shoulders go to his ears. "Shut it, boyo. Just—don't."

"Your sisters will be too. Well, after Finn gets over it. What you did today, opening up to your court—I'm really—"

"Go to bed," he says abruptly, a whip-crack of command.

I recoil. "I'm trying to—"

"I know what you're trying to do." He wheels around, streaks of green, blue, and red across his face and torso, as much a part of him as his freckles. Does the paint on my face look that chaotic now, that smeared? "And I do na know how else to tell *you* that I will na do this to you. I will na be some cruel awakening for you once reason comes back in. *Go to bed*."

"You wouldn't be an awakening."

He snorts in disdain and spins back to his painting.

I close my eyes, trying to pretend I'm writing. That these words are coming out of my fingertips, not my lips. "It wasn't a mistake. When we kissed. I couldn't say that because of how much it meant to me, which is dumb, I know. I should be able to tell you. But I'm *terrified* of you. I'm terrified that you see the same broken shit in me that's made other people leave because I'm a fucked-up mess and what do I have to offer you? God, Loch. Look at what you're doing. Look at who you *are*."

I pry open my eyes. He's still facing the canvas, his arm frozen, head cocked to the side.

"You aren't an awakening," I whisper. "You're the whole dawn. And I can't believe I ever thought I'd seen the sun before you."

He arches into the canvas, hand coming down to scrub at his hairline, so when he turns, a polychrome paint streak bursts through the shock of his red hair. That's what I focus on, the blur of colors all across his body as he closes the space between us in an angry, stomping rush.

Everything in me goes pliant, ready for whatever his reaction might be—please don't throw me out, please don't fucking throw me out—

His hand clamps around my neck.

I'm assaulted by his scent, dumbstruck by that expensive cologne and whatever paint chemicals are imbedded in his skin. Maybe that chemical twist shouldn't smell so good, but it all combines to be him in the peak of his element, and it's sexiness embodied.

My pliancy becomes submission, wide eyes and hands splayed as he keeps walking, walking, and I stumble backwards in his grip until my spine connects with the wall.

He presses the full length of his body against mine and uses his grip on my neck to tilt my face up to him, the paint slick and slipping between his palm and my skin.

"You're a goddamn poet," he snarls down at me, livid, "and I dinna stand a chance."

He kisses me, and the world goes ultraviolet.

He kisses like he's furious, all open-mouth attack that yanks the air from the very bottom of my lungs. I don't match his energy for once, I don't meet him in fury and rage; I stay malleable because the unarguable force of his storm is buffeting me like smacking hurricane waves and I am so eager to get sucked away by that chaos. Let it take me, let all of him take me, and somewhere to my left his speaker is blaring out a song I don't recognize, lyrics about fire, about lions, about roses.

He pulls back, lips tearing off of me. "Kris." It's furious still, but tinged with regret. "I need to tell you something first. I—"

I try to kiss him again, to shut him up, but his grip on my neck is relentless and runs a current of thrill from my shoulders to my groin.

"Tomorrow," I say.

His brows twitch together.

"Not now," I beg, and I don't even care that I am begging. "Please. Tell me tomorrow."

His gray eyes sift through mine, red-rimmed in his heightened emotions, or maybe he drank tonight—but he doesn't seem drunk at all. He looks clear-headed, for good or for bad.

The clarity makes his shift from confusion to realization obvious.

His eyelids flutter in self-deprecation. I recognize that emotion so well.

"You should want someone better," he tells me.

As good as confirmation. A red flag jabbed into dirt, ripping through roots and life.

I have one last chance to take the higher path. One last chance to do what I came to Ireland for, to stay safe in my miserable little world of order and duty and self-imposed rigidity.

"I don't want better." My thumbs dig circles into his hips, marking this spot, this moment. "I don't want a fantasy. I don't want sweetness. For once in my life, I want to be ruined."

I see in real time the way he processes what I say.

Wide open shock.

And then.

A zeroing in. A full-system reset that fixates him on me with a singular, agonizing look so primal as to be animalistic. Hungry, and barely restrained, and in it, all my final vestiges of anxiety dissipate because *he wants me.*

"Yeah," he whispers. "I can do that."

He releases my neck to hook my shirt with his fingers, and then it's up and off and this room isn't at all cold but I shudder in the rush of being hit by another ruthless, thrashing wave, ribs contracting around unusable lungs.

Loch makes an absolutely shattering rumble in his chest, a growl that prickles goosebumps of anticipation up the backs of my arms. His fingers coast down one of my shoulders, following the exposed art across my pec—mountains, fang-like crests that ripple into the valley of my sternum. He jumps that valley to trail the other side's tribal designs up to my shoulder, the barest fingertip touch that draws every bit of skin he ghosts over like iron filings to a magnet. His eyes plummet to the spreading branches of holly over my stomach, the leaves drawn to knife points as sharp as the mountains. Two of the bows frame my pelvis, extending beneath the edge of my boxers, and that's where he stops, making another shattering rumble that sounds like anguish.

"Christ, Mary, and Joseph. These tattoos. Your muscles. It's like you're formed of all my weaknesses."

"Am I?" I'm shocked I can speak at all for the lack of air in my body. "What else do you like?"

He spreads his fingers out on my stomach, and I can't think, can't breathe, his hand is flat on my body and I am undone.

"This," he says, his lips against my cheek. "This. This. This—"

"I have more." It squeezes out, some separate, hovering part of me. "Tattoos. More tattoos. You'll have to find them, though."

His hand stills. "*Kris,*" he beseeches, desperately messianic.

My mind goes to the huge tableau I have on my left thigh, how the art spreads down to my knee but, most importantly, up, *up* and up, and it hurt like a *bitch* to extend it where I did. But god, now, fucking *now,* I thank my past masochistic tendencies because I'm hit with the image of Loch licking the art on the inside crease of my thigh.

He grabs my neck again and his lips drop to my shoulder and he bites, hard. I cry out, scrambling for a hold on his arms, on his hips;

my fingers brush the molded hills of his abs and I die a slow, quivering death.

Why the fuck did I wear jeans that are so *fucking tight*.

"Kris," he says into the bite mark, the wash of his breath and the scratch of his beard oversensitive on the spot. I still have a bandage on my shoulder, and he lightly brushes his lips over it before sending those lips up to my ear. "What do you want me to do to you?"

I laugh. It's wheezy and delirious. "I—I don't know—"

He pinches my neck tight enough that I'm overly aware of my pulse throbbing, and when he drags his lips along my jaw and I twist to him, he keeps me down with a curling smirk.

"Asshole," I grunt.

His mouth comes in next to my ear until he sucks my lobe between his teeth and stars break and reform in the bottom of my belly.

"Tell me what you thought I'd be like with you, then," he whispers. "I know you thought about it, alone in that guestroom. Or in that shower? With my face in your head and your cock in your hand. Were we nice and slow, or did I fuck you until that filthy wee mouth of yours finally stopped talking?"

Holy shit.

I try to pull him closer, but he's staying resolutely back now, far enough that the only points of contact are our hands on each other's bodies.

"You did—" My supports are falling away. I'm left with an excruciating whimper. "Everything. Anything. I don't know. I—fuck, Loch. *Please.*"

I taste his grin.

"You're so pretty when you beg, Kris."

My hips cant towards him, but he's too far, and I need him, I need friction, I *need*—

"But *everything* is an awful wide margin." He nips my chin. "Tell me what you need, then."

Another whimper. "Please, please. *Fuck.* I need—goddamn it, *please*—"

I claw at his chest, gain a grip on his shoulders, but it leads nowhere with the way he's now studying my face, analysis that ends in a sultry chuckle.

"Ah, I think I know. You want me to decide, eh? You want me to take away the need to choose?"

My whimper this time isn't pathetic.

It's downright *groveling.*

I couldn't be more desperately needy if I was on my knees, but I nod—fuck. *Fuck.* Yes. To not have to decide anything. To not have to make any choices, no mistakes, no possible regret or guilt . . .

"Yes." I clutch his hand around my throat, the muscles in his forearm gone to marble. "Whatever you want, Loch. Whatever you want with me."

A jagged gasp tears out of him. A slurred, hissing "Jesus Christ."

He kisses me again, eating at me like he can consume me, and I hope he does. My pulse is going so fast I can feel it in places I never noticed before, my ankles, the inside of my elbows, I swear there's sensation in the tips of my hair when Loch unwinds his fingers from my neck to grate across my scalp and pull.

The paint on his arm and hands is all down my neck, spreading across my body in the wake of his groping. The idea of being marked by him like this wrenches a groan out of my core.

He echoes it and closes his eyes to breathe in deep—one long, slow inhale, his forehead fixed to mine. "Kris," he speaks against me, a catechism. "I need my mouth on you."

I nod. Nod again.

His fingers trail down my arms, link around my wrists, and yank my hands above my head, pressed to the wall. I pant at the force of it, breathing rough and unsteady as I meet his gaze in question.

"Stay," he hisses, then he's gone, dropping to his knees at my feet.

There is no shame left, not after the noises I've already made, so I look down at him with unabashed desire. Those fingers are hooked in the edge of my pants like when we were in the kitchen, only this time, my belt snaps open, button and zipper next.

His eyes grasp at mine as he wrenches my pants and boxers down my legs. The air hits me like sandpaper, my hard dick bobbing in front of him, and his gaze travels from my lifted hands to my chest palpitating in rippling breaths to—

His brows pinch, the intensity in his eyes folding into something new and back again, emotional origami as he looks at the tattoo on my left thigh.

I knew he'd see it.

But it grates even more than the air on my bare skin, more than the rawness of having my hands over my head.

The light touch of his fingertips to that ink makes me jump, startled by the softness. His thumb rubs soothingly, like he knows he spooked me, knows fully well he altered the mood.

"What is this?" he asks in a matching soft voice.

I look up at the ceiling, heart a battering ram against my ribs.

Sure, I could brush it off. I could tell him I don't want to talk about it.

But I've stripped so much of myself tonight. Holding this back would cheapen that.

"A scene from *Bridge to Terabithia*," I say to the industrial piping of the ceiling.

The tattoo is a forest with thick, lush trees, vines and plants and little glimmers that might be fairy dust. At the center, a rope hangs from the largest tree, the silhouette of a boy in mid-swing over a deep, endless black chasm. Halfway across, past where the arc of the boy's swing will take him, a bridge is caught in mid-formation, grand and glistening and straight out of a fantasy.

"This is you?" Loch touches the boy on the rope.

I hesitate before nodding.

"You're going to fall," he states. It isn't a question.

I glance back down at him. He still has his finger on my silhouette. Or younger-me's silhouette.

"How do you know?" I whisper. Not trying to deny that he's right, but honestly curious how he figured it out. Few people have guessed that. I tried to be flippant when I described what I wanted to the artist; I couldn't bring myself to have Iris design this one.

Loch's lips twitch in a shadow of his usual confidence. "Please, Kris. Art is what I do."

"It was the last book my mom read to me before she left." It's out of me like buckshot and I gasp, biting down on that show of emotion, but it serves as a spotlight. Might as well scream *this is deeply emotional for me.*

Loch analyzes the image again. Traces his thumb over the boy's silhouette.

He replaces his thumb with his mouth.

"Stand up straight." That commanding tone brooks no room for argument.

My chest releases, another gasp, this one of relief. If rawness is acid, then Loch's mouth is soothing the burn.

I drop back against the wall, hands still up, and there's only his mouth, that tongue, tasting every divot and swell of ink on my thigh until my trembling is from anticipation, not overstimulation. He works slowly, savoringly, covering the whole span of skin before his face presses into the very spot I imagined, the swath where the tree canopy curves up the inside of my leg. He holds there and breathes, the bristle of his facial hair rough, and I didn't know such a simple act could be so transportive.

He peers up over my body, leonine eyes and that wicked, cocky smirk.

"There ya are, Kris," he says, and I think he means to say it louder, but it comes out crooned so *Kris* ceases to be my name and becomes an endearment.

My mind clears entirely as he takes my cock in his mouth.

Immediate tight suction. Wet, intense heat.

He holds for a moment, tasting, adjusting, and I whine pathetically, hips rocking in the slightest thrust. It's a trigger; his hand starts working mercilessly at my base, pumping with his mouth in perfect, knee-weakening synchronization.

Oh, this is not going to last long, like, *at all*, fuck fuck *fuck*—

I try to control my breathing. Try to think about literally anything else. Like the paint in his hair. That color green. Think about paint and—not what he's doing with his throat—

My hands are fisted against each other, obediently above head, and the only things coming out of my mouth are pleading susurrations for more, for less, for everything.

He pulls back, stroking me slowly, a glow in his eyes, teasing pleasure. And I almost disintegrate right then, at that expression on his face and how it's targeted at me, for *me*.

"Look at you, Kris." His eyes drag over me again, heavier this time, pupils dark and predatory and visceral. "So sexy standing there, letting me play with you. So fucking *good* for me."

His strokes increase, faster, barreling me closer and closer—

"*Loch.*" I can't get out more than pinched, croaked noises. "If you—I'm going to—"

He shoves to his feet, keeping me in hand, and plants his other on the wall next to me. That unspoken statement of his control—that I would stay pinned to the wall like this, splayed out, while he's almost leisurely in his stance—is everything I never knew I wanted, to have given myself over to this.

"Too—" I writhe and gasp, all liquid groans. "Too soon."

He nudges my arm to make space next to my head, and his lips go to my ear. The barest brush of his tongue on the outer shell. "Boyo, what makes you think I'd be satisfied to only see you come once?"

I stop.

And let those words sink in.

Those voracious, beating words.

"For all you put me through," he purrs, hand shuttling over my dick, twisting at the head, lubed by his saliva and my own precum as the edge barrels closer and closer, "you can bet that hot ass of yours that I'll make you pay. I'm gonna turn you into a sated, sweaty heap on my studio floor."

My brain splits in half.

Half again.

I'm shredding into pieces.

I find one last flicker of composure squirming through me. "You put me through hell too, you son of a bitch." And then, "You think my ass is hot?"

He chuckles, deep, possessive. "You're gonna come in my mouth, Kris."

And he drops to his knees again.

Holy shit holy shit holyshitholy—

He sucks me down again and I manage one more labored breath before my body disintegrates, a rapid, relentless fire. He doesn't slow his rhythm, doesn't let up the suction so I can't help the wail I make, painfully taut. My hands collapse down and I jam my fingers in his hair, holding him in place to drag out the reverberations. He swallows obscenely and hums, content, *greedy.*

Slowly, he stands, a satisfied grin on his face. I haul him into me and kiss him, needing to taste him, the proof of what he did on his tongue. He opens for me, hands clamping to my hips until he pushes me back against the wall and tips his head away with a long, vulgar lick over his bottom lip.

"One," he says. "How many will it take to shut up that mouth after all?"

"God, you're a cruel ass." But I'm yanking at the strings on his sweatpants.

"You love it when I'm a cruel arse."

"Fuck you." I shove him back a step and topple to my knees, boxers and pants caught around my ankles, but grace was never meant to be a part of this. The wounds on my knees are barely healed, but the pain of dropping down on them is minimal—I'm a tunnel-focused creature of will and yearning, shelled out in a way I know I'll be craving for the rest of my life.

There is only this moment.

There is only me having to kiss every one of the freckles on his hips, lips smearing through paint to leave a trail of clumsy marks across the plane of his stomach.

His smug-ass look burns down at me, drives me faster, harder, until I yank his pants to his knees and I'm there, at the root of him, sucking his long, thick cock down without pretense.

One of my hidden talents: a complete lack of gag reflex, and even with how long he is, I have him all the way down my throat on the first thrust. I swallow, hold the muscles tight, and he actually, finally, gasps.

"*Shite,* Kris—"

The high of his gasp sculpts my focus to getting more of that noise out of him, which is a much-needed lighthouse. *Realizing* what I'm doing to him—the taste of him, the feel of him in my mouth, the warmth and the musk and the way he's rocking subtly into me—has me on the edge again, and I'll be damned if I give him another one from me so easily.

He grips my hair, at first gently twining it in his fingers, then wrenching it tight when I swallow on each bob of my head.

"Christ, Kris. So good, so fucking perfect on your knees for me." His panted words are juxtaposition, coarse silk, his thumb coming to rest on the edge of my mouth. "I knew your lips would look sexy wrapped around me like this."

I moan. *Fuck* do I moan, and I'm glad his studio is buried so damn deep in the castle.

My eyes water as I gaze up at him, his muscles writhing over me, his freckled skin coated in paint gone to wine-dark streaks. I understand in watching him, in memorizing the flow and twist of his body, why he paints. It's this, that's what he's trying to capture, the collision of ardency and rigidity in the way a body can be both wound to strain and sparking with motion.

His breathing escalates. Redness seeps across his chest, a brilliant cherry contrast under that paint, and he cradles my jaw.

"You gonna finish me off?" The question is a breathy gasp, a warning.

I don't stop, can barely nod, so I hum assent, take him all the way down, and hollow my cheeks.

A final shuddering gasp, his hands twisting in my hair, and he comes, the sensation of his release and watching, *feeling* him, shunting me into orbit.

I pull away, the back of my hand dragging over my swollen lips, and his eyes have gone glassy, half-lidded.

Emotions fight to surface, too many, too much, hitting me haphazard and making me aware of my bare skin.

"One for you," I say instead of anything real, and I cock my head, feigning listening. "Is that . . . silence I hear? All it took was *one* for the mighty Lochlann to—"

He dives down on me, brute force pushing me flat out on the drop cloth, our bodies connecting in a wave of delicious heat.

"Are you backtalking me, boyo? See how that works out for you, go on."

"Oh, I'm terrified."

He kicks his sweatpants off and I work my shoes and clothes away too, then he's back on me, the tarp cold against my spine. I kiss him and my body lights up in pyrotechnics when he splays himself over me, skin on skin that makes us both tremble. He alternates bites and kisses down across my chest, working in such a skillful rhythm of pain and pleasure that I thrust involuntarily against him, grasping, driving, and his weight bears down and digs right back.

He's brutal and he's sweet and he's one talented motherfucker in absolutely everything he does, and I relent and tell him that in some sort of fever. And he tells me, too, he talks until I swear the murmur of his voice is enough to shove me over the cliff.

But I'm off the cliff already, body and soul tumbling into cloudy ether. I've been falling for some time, helpless and weightless, a plunge in the moments where our eyes connect. I'm falling, falling, and he glides his arm under my back and braces me and I think, maybe, the final landing won't hurt.

Because he's falling too, and we're knotted up together, each a parachute, each in a terrifying free fall.

I wouldn't say I *wake up*, but I come out of some kind of coma with soft yellow light pouring down on me. There's a window high in the wall of Loch's basement studio, fogged glass that lets enough light shine through for me to take stock of where, exactly, I am.

On the floor. There's a pillow and a blanket—ah, yeah, he has bedding on hand for when he pulls late nights, he'd said.

Everything else slips back through me. Head to toe and up again in gradual, palpitating awareness, languid limbs and exhaustion, but the kind of exhaustion that's relaxed on a bone-deep level.

I force my eyes open wider. There's another pillow, but it's empty—

A silhouette comes into focus next to me, backlit by that yellow light.

He has one knee propped up, a sketchpad balanced there, a pencil in one hand and a half-eaten apple in the other. He's back in his sweatpants but covered in paint, and I know I am too; I can feel the chalky stiffness in my hair and all across my chest, legs, and arms.

"Hey." I touch his ankle. The easy contact reawakens every single sensation from last night.

His eyes glide down to me. There's a beat where we're looking at each other. One that stretches, stretches, and my body goes from limp in relaxation to springing with tension. I can't tell whether it's good or bad.

Until he smiles. "Hey," he says back. And points at a tray beside him spread with breakfast food and steaming cups. "Eat, boyo."

My chest warms and I sit up, blanket pooling around my thighs. I don't miss the way he makes note of it, and that tension cranks to passion. But I am hungry, so I take a scone and get one bite into it before I realize—

It's morning.

My eyes flare. "We have an event today, right? What time is it? Shit—"

Loch puts his hand on my knee, staying me from getting up. Even through the thin blanket, electricity sizzles, stops me cold.

"There is an event, but I talked with Finn and Siobhán. They can handle it. Another festival, nothing you have na seen already."

"But . . ." My mind is moving like sludge this morning. Thoughts come to me scattered and disproportionate like my brain isn't sure how to reboot after going *quiet* for so long. "The press?"

Loch's hand is still on my knee. His thumb moves over the blanket, rubs back and forth on me. "You've more than helped in that area. We can miss one day."

I scrub a hand through my hair. One whole side is caked with paint, plastered down the side of my head. "But you only talked to your court a few hours ago. Shouldn't you make an appearance at this event, reassert what you told them? We can—"

Loch leans forward and kisses me. He tastes like apples and mouthwash and it thoroughly shuts me up.

"I shoulda been clear," he whispers into my lips. "I'm na willing to share you with anyone yet."

"Oh." My face heats. "Okay."

"You should na worry about my court. About *me*. I have it handled now, I promise. I—" A rough, harsh swallow. "They know now most of what I've done is behind the scenes, anyway. I'll be at the Dublin parade, though, and that'll satisfy everyone."

"You'll confront Malachy there?"

He rests his forehead against mine. "Mm."

It's not exactly confirmation. But he pulls back and shoves my half-eaten scone against my mouth before I can ask more, and I don't want to get into details of Malachy while I'm naked.

"I will na have you passing out." His cheeks are stained pink through his own smears of paint.

"Bossy." I eat.

"You do na seem to have a problem with it."

I really, really don't. "Only when you—" I catch a glimpse of the sketchpad in his lap. "Are you drawing me?"

His eyes cut down to the sketch, and that blush along his cheekbones darkens.

Loch turns the book.

It's me, lying out on the floor, blanket around my hips, head to the side so it's mostly the line of my jaw and a scattered tangle of my hair on the pillow. He's drawn the paint across my body in the style of his larger canvas art so it looks even more like those are *his* marks on my skin.

The fire in my chest surges down to the base of my spine. I rest a fingertip where he's drawn the side of my face. "It's weird to see you do something more realistic."

"I canna seem to break this way of sketching. A downside of going to school for it."

"Downside?" I pick up one of the cups of coffee and the moment I take a sip, the rest of my mind kicks back on.

And even though I do want to have this conversation with him, the only thing I can think about is how he's wearing pants and I hate it.

Loch sets the sketchpad to the side and finishes his apple, waving it as he talks. "The mechanics of it. They're useful, but it gets me stuck in my own head a wee bit."

"Ah. You mentioned something like that—knowledge versus education?"

"There's knowing the steps, and then there's being *bound* to the steps. I do na regret taking these courses, but I wonder what my skill would be like if I did na have formulas clogging my brain. Structure is grand, but it does na often allow for the free flow of creativity and joy—and that's what it's all about for me. Just like our Holidays. Joy."

I lower the cup from my lips. "I know exactly what you mean."

Loch's eyebrow cocks encouragingly.

Discomfort presses against me and I shift under the blanket, legs stretching out only to fold back again.

"When I was in the English track, I went into those classes so eager. The things I was writing may not have been *good,* but they had a purity to them that I don't think I'll ever be able to recapture. And within the first week, I knew I'd made a mistake signing up for that track. The professors were so high on one specific way of writing, and they upheld it as gospel. We had to aspire to that style, or we were failures."

"The classics, eh?"

It's not surprising that he guesses. "Yeah. And I might have *liked* the books they upheld if they hadn't been such jackasses about forcing them on us. The first assignment I turned in—" My chest aches at the memory, but there's distance from that memory now, and I'm shocked that the ache twists into defensive anger, not resigned hurt. "The professor ripped it apart. In front of the class. It was a short story, barely a few thousand words long—and he *decimated* it, every word choice was wrong, every cadence of every sentence, the plot beats I'd chosen, it was too whimsical, it didn't take itself seriously, and on and on. And I sat there, letting him eviscerate me in public, because he was the gatekeeper of this art form, right? If I couldn't succeed here, I shouldn't write at all.".

Loch's hand is on my leg again. "That fucker. Christ. There's no construction in public humiliation."

"No. There isn't." I lock my hand in his and stare at that tangle. "So I switched to International Relations. And I hadn't written anything for *me* since. Until—until, like, two days ago."

"That's what you were doing in the library," Loch guesses.

I nod and look up at him.

"Colm said you asked him for a notebook. I'd—I'd hoped that was what you were up to."

A blush creeps across my face. "Thank you. For the other notebooks. The pens, too."

"Show me," he whispers. "Your writing."

"Oh, yeah, sure." I snort. "You want to read my rambling, stream of consciousness nonsense after not having written in *literal years?*"

"Yes." His eyes sparkle and he gestures around the studio. "You've seen my soul, in all its unformed pieces. I wanna see yours, boyo."

"My soul?" I laugh to cover the nervous hitch in my chest. "I don't know. It's rough shit. I'm not lying when I say it's been years since I've done anything *real* and I don't know if—"

"Kris." He squeezes my hand. "You do na have to show me. What that professor did to your psyche was a right fucked-up thing to do. The only way to get that arsehole out of your head is to keep moving forward. There is no greater measure of value than that which *you* give to a piece of art. And if the stuff you're working on is valuable to you, I wanna see it."

There is no fantasy, no alternate dimension, no manufactured fictional world where I do not fall for this guy.

I mean, our version of post-sex talk is about the structure of art, for Christ's sake.

"And you said I was a poet." My voice is delicate and brittle and very far away. If I talk too loudly, it'll break the hum of his words on the air, the net they're weaving around me.

He smiles, a gentle upturn of his lips.

That smile goes hard, though, and his grip on my hand tightens.

"But first," he says, "there's something I need to show you."

Tomorrow.

Tell me tomorrow.

Please.

The scone sits in my stomach like a rock. In too short a time, I've gotten used to giving in to what I want over what I need, and all I want right now is to tell him no, he doesn't need to show or tell me anything. If he doesn't, then I don't have to decide what to do with the truth and I can keep pretending this is simple.

But I bob my head in agreement.

And then feel the paint all over me again, the mess that is my hair. "I, uh—we should clean up first, maybe."

Loch's face transforms, a quick slip back into that feral possessiveness that ribbons through my body.

"Not yet," he says.

I pull at my paint-caked hair. "You'd make me walk around the castle looking like—well, looking very much like we had at each other in your studio?"

"It's only Colm here now, anyway, and he will na be about. I told you, Kris; I'm na ready to share you with anyone yet. And that includes washing my marks off you." He hesitates with a heavy breath. "I'll understand though if you'd rather—"

"Yes. I mean, it's fine. I can shower later."

His eyes brighten with relief, but his energy is off, a wall erecting. I know why. I do.

But I hate it, hate reality moving in so swiftly, hate the loss of an ease we only had for a few short hours.

He helps me to my feet and his gaze dips away respectfully and I hate that too. I hunt down my shirt, boxers, and jeans; they're balled against the door and I pull them on—

Only to stop with a wheeze.

Loch glances over. "Hm?"

"You asshole." I yank up my boxers and glare over my shoulder at him.

He frowns.

"There's paint everywhere. *Ev-ery-where,* Loch." I wave at my crotch. "You turned my dick into abstract impressionism."

A pause in which the only sound is the jangle of my belt.

He breaks first with a splutter but scrambles to cover it by clearing his throat.

I laugh too, and then we're both falling apart in a new way, clinging to laughter as a bridge through the conversation we know is coming.

I cross the room and kiss him over that bridge.

Chapter Sixteen

For once, it's a good thing that this castle is mostly empty—I'm a mess in my rumpled T-shirt and jeans, and Loch's half-dressed, and we make it about five feet up the hall before I'm kissing him again. His hesitancy is back, but he returns the kiss, hands plunging into my hair.

We pass the library and he's kissing me up against the door in an anxious rush and I throw my arms around his neck. This is how we're keeping warm in a castle in March, it's science.

We make it up to his office.

The door shuts behind us and the click of it in the frame pops this fragile bubble, I can feel its residue on my skin.

Loch's stance sharpens. He's actively not looking at me, eyes downcast on the carpet.

"Do you want to sit?" He waves at the chair, the one behind the desk.

I shake my head. I want to touch him again.

But I stay where I am, rooted in the middle of the room, and Loch grunts like he's decided something.

He crosses to the bookshelf. *That* bookshelf, the one with the hidden door I'm not supposed to know about.

I keep my face impassive.

He pushes on it. The door unlatches, and he shoves it open. "Here."

I draw closer, shoes padding on the carpet. He's staring at the joy meter in a trance. Like this thing is a nightmare and a dream all in one, and it has been, for him, the thing holding him back that will help him move forward.

He crowds in around it. The screen with readouts beeps as he hits a few buttons and a panel juts out of the side.

Coal and Dad put their hands on a similar one.

"Loch." His name kicks out of me.

"Malachy and I did the power transfer years ago," he says to the panel. The frosted glass is so harmless, a weird windowpane, nothing special. "But it never fully took. I told ya this. Transfers of power have to be joyful, and ours wasn't. I think—" He reaches a hand out to the screen, flexes his fingers, recoils. "I think you were right. Since the original transfer never took, the transaction's still in the joy meter. Lingering, incomplete. I think I could take it back."

My gut swoops.

Is *this* what he wanted to tell me? To show me? Not that he's been stealing our magic.

But I squash down that hope. God, I shove it so far down it wriggles in the base of my stomach.

"Do you want your sisters here?" I ask. "Do you—"

"No."

He looks to me, his eyes bloodshot, and his exhale shudders.

"Just you," he whispers.

I'm humbled into silence when, in a quick snap of action, he presses his hand to the screen.

Nothing happens. Outwardly. Nothing happened outwardly for Coal, either; it seemed to be a *feeling* he had. But I hold my breath, hold it and hold it until my lungs burn—

Loch lurches back, panting raggedly as he cradles his hand. His focus is on the joy meter as the screen slides back in, and he gapes, wonder mixed with disbelief.

"Did it . . ." I stammer. "Did it work?"

His response is small. Reedy. A voice spoken in the light after a storm. "Yeah."

The air is heavy with the force of what this means for him. He turns to me and I already have my hands up, ready for him—

But he catches himself.

And that pause is the final press down on the hope in my belly.

I expect it to vanish. For grief to surge in. Or—or *anger,* even, something negative, something painful.

But Loch meets my eyes and I feel grief, yes, but not for me.

He shifts back to the joy meter and bends down. There's a click, and he stands and holds out the device that's been funneling off Christmas's joy.

I take it from him, limbs stiff, motion automatic.

My gaze stays on his, though, and his shame breaks in a tumult of panic when I don't react.

"This is why you're really here?" He nods at the device.

"Yes," I whisper. "You left a clover behind."

He winces. He didn't intend to leave it, then. "I'll pay you back for every ounce of joy," he says quickly. "I'll make it up to you, I swear I'll—" He stops, eyes teary. "You're na angry, Kris?"

I fiddle with the device. It's easier than seeing another choice I'm making, and it might be the wrong choice—it *is* the wrong choice—but walking away is a wrong choice, too.

Maybe sometimes, a bad choice can result in goodness.

Because sometimes, a good choice can result in pain.

"I went searching for your joy meter that day I left you at the music festival," I tell him. "I saw the device on it. *You* planted the device in Christmas. Not Malachy."

His lips thin.

"You're na upset?" He sounds, honestly, baffled.

My throat cracks on a helpless laugh. "No. I should be, but—fuck, no. I'm not. I—" I bite my lower lip, heart beating hard. "We'll figure it out."

He said he'll pay us back. That's all we ultimately need from this, our joy back, so Christmas can pay the other winter Holidays what we owe them. Everything else, blame and repercussions . . .

He twitches towards me but catches himself again, and my gut knots up at his restraint.

"I need to touch you, Kris," he begs.

Don't ask. Don't ever ask. The answer's always yes.

My arms spread, and he dives in, face pressing into the bend of my shoulder. He clings to me so tightly, so intently, that every piece of my soul remakes itself to fit the way he holds me. I shouldn't want to conform to fit him, but it isn't like the way I'd get with other people—this isn't chipping away pieces of myself, it's like all my pieces bloom even fuller, vines reaching for the sun.

I'm hit with a careening bolt of terror.

It doesn't happen this fast.

I cannot have fallen for him *this fast*.

"Congratulations are in order," I say into his neck, hoping he misinterprets my racing heart, or thinks it's his own—his pulse is galloping under my lips. "King Lochlann."

He goes to iron, his grip on me crushingly tight for a moment before he loosens. I think he might push me away but he untangles my arms from his neck to plant my hands on his hips, one still holding that device. His fingers drape around my wrists and he rests his forehead to mine so when we speak it's in our own little cave.

"It'll backfire," he says. "Malachy will—"

"Malachy won't do shit. What can he do?"

"I—" His throat contracts. "He has access to some magic as part of the family, so he might na notice right away. But once he does, I do na know what he'll do."

"Cut him off completely. See how he likes it."

Loch huffs. "I canna—I will na be like him."

Fuck this guy and his sexy honor.

"Could you do me a favor," I moan, "and be like a *little* repulsive in some area? Just one. I don't even care what it is. I need you to not be so inhumanly attractive."

He chuckles, but it's pinched and thin. "I admitted to stealing from you. Is that na repulsive?"

"Not as much as it should be."

And god, if that isn't the truth. It *should* be repulsive, but it isn't, because he was stealing from us to sustain his Holiday, to fight against his uncle in a way I admire more than I can say. I can't even stand up to my mom about how she treats me.

"I do na deserve you," he whispers, his hold on my wrists tensing.

"You got lucky, I guess."

His laugh this time is more sincere, still tinged with disbelief, but he straightens and stares down at me with a smirk lingering on his lips.

It wavers. "This'll blow up in my face."

"No. It won't. You have Siobhán and Finn and Colm. You have your court coming around too."

He starts to argue, so I keep talking.

"You don't paint a whole picture at once, right? And I wouldn't write a whole book in a single moment. So let's take it word by word. What you just did, us, all of it. Word by word, okay?"

I can see arguments on the edge of his tongue, stalking his thoughts, his response.

So I kiss him.

He relents to my lips on his like I'm sustenance, cupping my jaw and opening my mouth and seizing control in a grateful, delirious attack. He kisses in promises and oaths and I accept every one, fingertips clawed into the muscles along his spine.

We break to gasp and I tell him, "Come with me."

His eyes are wet. He looks exhausted, the adrenaline crash after stress, so he nods without a fight and closes the bookshelf and I take his hand.

Half his mind is elsewhere, wrapped up in everything he's done, and he only realizes I've taken him to my room when we step inside.

"Kris?"

"Just—hang on." I toss the device from the joy meter into the chaos of my suitcase and grab the notebook I've been working on from the desk. My heart charges like mad as I flip through pages filled with my scrawled handwriting.

There are two things I could show him.

One is the writing I did about him. Mushy, embarrassing shit.

The other is . . . unbearable.

Don't overthink it. Don't linger.

Word by word.

I rip out the letter and hand it to him.

He takes it with a frown. But the moment he sees the top line, his eyes widen.

"Kris—are you sure?"

"You wanted to see something I've written." I sit on the bed because my legs won't hold me up anymore. "I want to show you this."

He lowers into the desk chair. "You wrote a letter to your mam?"

I shrug.

"Are you gonna send it to her?"

"No."

"All your encouraging me to stand up to Malachy," Loch says, "and you are na gonna send this?"

"It's different." I kick the carpet. "What Malachy's doing to you is fixable. My mother is . . . not. But processing what she did? *That* is fixable. So that's what the letter is."

He hums, maybe a little unconvinced, and folds his legs under him in the chair to read.

It isn't a long letter. I could barely stand to write even a few paragraphs. And I try not to watch him read—I open my phone, and there are about a dozen texts in the thread with Coal and Iris, complaining about her hangover.

No new texts or missed calls from my mother.

I pull up the thread with her. Messages fly by as I scroll, years of her abuse—that's what it is, I know now. *Abuse.* It was never a prelude to her coming back or requests I could obey to get her to love me. It was never anything but on *her* and I've let it go so, so long because I didn't want to admit how powerless I've been this whole time.

There is nothing I can do to fix my mother.

The paper crinkles in Loch's hand.

My eyes tear as I delete her text thread, flip over to her profile screen in my contacts, and block her number.

The chair groans a few seconds later.

Loch kneels between my legs. "Jesus, Kris, that ripped my heart out. You should send it. She should know what she did to you."

"She knows. She doesn't care. And that's why I wrote it—she'll never care, not really. She'll keep acting like nothing happened and we can pretend it all away without acknowledging all the shit she's dragged us through—"

"*Us. We*," Loch cuts me off. "You're allowed to feel this. Just *you*."

My eyes sting, filling too much now. A tear breaks free, tracks down my cheek. "She'll keep acting like she didn't do anything. To me. She'll keep acting like what she did wasn't cowardly even though she *knows* she hurt me. And even if she'll never care, *I* care, and I'm not going to keep acting like it's my responsibility to make up for what she did. This way"—I nod at the letter, on the desk now—"*I* get to acknowledge what she did. *I* get to deal with it. It's for *me*."

The sadness in Loch's eyes is so potent that it detracts from the way my own are hot and my breathing is cramped and my chest is straining.

"I wrote about you, too," I tell him. Talking to fill the void he leaves in his quiet sadness, something brewing in his expression that I don't like. "Really sappy, poetic shit. I wanted to send it to the reporters. Have Christmas release it, so everyone could read the truth about who you are. But you don't need something like that. You're showing everyone who you are on your own now, and you're doing this for *you*, not for tabloids or rumors. You helped me realize how okay that is, sometimes, to do things for ourselves. There is selflessness in being selfish."

Loch's eyes shut.

Something hovers over him, a shadow on a wall with no source. And it feeds into my terror all over again, that sharp, stabbing pain that this happened too fast and I remember what it was like for him to pull away. But there shouldn't be any more reasons for that, right? Everything's in the open now.

"Loch." I can't help that his name comes out imploring. I'm fraying, sleeplessness inching up over me. I cup his face, but his eyes stay shut. "Don't do this again."

"Kris—"

"I don't know what your problem is—maybe you don't deserve me, which is insane; but I sure as hell don't deserve you, either. So be unworthy with me, in this moment, right now. We're here. We have all day. I showed you part of my soul and we're next to a bed. So kiss me, you idiot, and be with me."

Now, his eyes do open, and god, that agony on his face is an arrow straight to my heart.

But he surges up and kisses me, and it's . . . different. There's no possession in it, none of that aggressive control. It's soft and savoring, his lips and the abrasiveness of his facial hair and it does something to the building fear in my chest, guides it away with a gentle hand.

Loch stands and yanks me to my feet with him. Then he's stripping off my clothes and his own in efficient silence, backing us into my ensuite and turning on the shower. The water heats while he kisses me, that slow drop of his lips over mine, and when the room is steamy he pulls me under the shower with him.

Clear marbles of water roll down his body, dragging streaks through the paint, pooling at our feet in rivers of gray. His silence in any other situation would feel off, but the way he looks at me as he works his hands in my hair, cleaning out the paint, is strung with such force that he doesn't need to speak at all.

The air fills with the spicy scents of shampoo and body wash and my eyes roll shut under the massaging tips of his fingers on my scalp. I let my own hands run wild, following the trails of paint, scrubbing them off his skin, lingering on the bend of his hips, that spot that will forever drive me out of my mind.

Forever. Not forever. Word by word. This moment, only.

He presses me against the tiled shower wall. His hands and mouth are reverent, moving with an artist's care, turning me into a dizzying masterpiece with lips sculpting the contours on my chest and stomach. He's wary of my injuries, washing them even more tenderly, and I hope the thunder of the shower covers the whimpers I make, deep, resonating pleas to my root.

"Fuck me," I tell him.

Mouth on my neck, he spasms, and I wish I could record the noise he lets loose. That hoarseness, that grind.

He pulls upright and it still feels like he's one thought from coming to his senses, but I can't be senseless alone. I know I should talk him through whatever is keeping him restrained, but in the wreckage of the past twelve hours, all that's left when his hands and mouth are on me is Edenic need.

I've been trying to let myself be selfish.

He is the pinnacle of that, pure living wish-fulfillment.

His forehead rests on my shoulder. Water pounds down on us, cooling slightly, but the warmth between us stays cosmic, the wild collisions in deepest space that create their own heat, create their own suns.

Feather-light kisses trail up my throat. When he gets to my ear, he exhales, and I feel it over me, in me.

"I'll prove myself to you, Kris," he promises. "I'll be worthy of you now."

He nuzzles the side of my head and groans, rutting against me in the wash of the water and the interstellar intensity. We're both steel-hard and the water eases the grind somewhat, but it's not enough, not now.

"Dry off and get on the bed," he commands, and every nerve in my body swerves online, a ruthless plunge of attention that banishes all other awareness.

The water squeals off behind me and I stumble out of the shower, grabbing the nearest towel and drying myself in half-assed obedience. We spill into the bedroom, both mostly drenched, but the bed swallows me up as he pushes me down on it and his body is there, stretched over mine.

He's not just wish-fulfillment, he's an intoxicant, and I'm blackout drunk on him.

Our dicks align and we groan simultaneously, riding the motion of a need that never went away last night, was never satisfied, the sweetest eternal decay.

"*Christ*, Kris." Loch pushes up over me and his look is so dark with need I can see galaxies in him. "Supplies?"

I squirm out from under him and he leans back on his heels to let me go.

But as I crawl off the bed, a sharp crack cuts through the room. I yelp.

"Did you—" I gape at him. "Did you smack my ass?"

His eyes sparkle. "Lightly."

"Lightly?"

"To get you to *hurry your arse up.*"

"How is that going to make me want to do anything other than dive right back into bed?" But I'm already rummaging in my suitcase.

Loch makes a strangled noise. I glance over at him, and he's watching me with narrow amusement.

"I canna tell if you're serious. Is that something you want?"

I shrug. "Not anything too painful, but I meant what I said earlier. I want whatever you want to do with me. *That*"—I motion towards the floor, back to his studio—"that was perfect."

It's a heavy admission. I hear it as soon as I say it, the power I'm giving him with this knowledge.

He's quiet. Eyes searching mine.

I'm worried I've fucked up the mood again when he smiles.

"I meant what I said too," he whispers. "I will prove myself to you. You give me too much trust."

That's so obvious I don't even have to agree. We both know it, feel it deep beneath whatever *this* is.

I toss a condom and a small bottle of lube on the bed next to him.

He clocks them and pins me with a stern look. "You had these awfully ready. Planned on fucking your time away here, did you?"

I kneel on the bed next to him and arch one eyebrow. "How do you know I haven't been?"

He works his tongue across his teeth, a slow build of that vulturine glare that is quickly becoming a physical necessity.

"Kris," he says, "has anyone else been touching you?"

Every part of my body shivers. Shoulders. Hips. My toes curl and I knee-walk closer to him, towering over where he's seated back on his heels. It lets me stroke my fingers through his beard and hold on to his neck, a brief power exchange.

"Why would you care about that?" I whisper.

He's *gotta* stop making noises like the one that rumbles in his throat. Halfway between a keening mewl and a growl.

The possession and need in Loch's eyes tell me he's letting me lean over him, letting me hold his neck, letting me toy with him. I shiver again, nerve endings swelling in the intuition of payback coming.

He rests his fingertips on my pec, drags them down, the lightest scratch over my nipple that makes them both pebble tight. "I care," he starts, that mewl-growl roughening his voice, "because I need to know where anyone else touched you, how they touched you, so I can do it better."

It should be enough. Teasing, taunting each other—that's what we do.

But I hear myself ask, "Is that the only reason?"

I want everything implied in his jealousy. I want everything hungering behind his control.

Loch stops with his fingertips over my belly button. His eyes stay on mine, reading me.

"It has to be the only reason," he whispers.

"Why?" I'm too revealed. Too exposed. It's pleading and childish and I *hear* that, but Loch keeps stroking his nails over my skin.

He leans forward, and I let him, until his mouth rests on my stomach. He inhales, exhales, warmth and coolness winding me up so I almost retract it, apologize for being needy.

But then he rocks his forehead on my chest. "Do you want me to say it's because I do na want anyone else touching you? Only me."

A mutinous gasp rips out of me. It gives everything away if I hadn't already.

Loch chuckles into my skin.

"Only me," he says again.

I shudder, another full body tremor. I can barely swallow around the way my pulse is thudding in my neck and I sure as hell can't keep up this game anymore.

"I usually have a condom in my wallet," I explain quickly. "Habit, always be prepared and whatnot. And the lube, well. I knew you'd stress me out while I was here, and how else would I relieve that stress?"

"And did you?" Loch's hand glides down my leg. Sends a quiver surging off in his wake. "Relieve stress right here in this bed?"

His smile holds daggers and immediately flips this dynamic right-side up. I'm still kneeling over him, but he's in control. He always was, and it crashes through me, freeing, weightless.

"Yes," I whisper.

"Tell me."

My lungs ache, chest and stomach clenching helplessly as he pushes a kiss to the tattoo below my abs, his eyes on mine.

"I—" My words come tangled, a frenzy. "It was like you said. Your face was in my head the whole time. Your voice. Your—*you*. Just you, Loch—I don't know how you didn't hear me crying out your name."

His pupils dilate, blowing wide, his upper lip curling slightly, the whole of his expression sending a pulse of warning over me.

"Oh, I will," he promises, and those wide eyes dip down my torso, mapping me, planning, and I hold steady for him.

My chest is hot. My cheeks, my arms, burning up under everything I've said and his gaze on me now.

He tracks that heat, the blush, and something in him breaks.

"You're so fucking *reactive*, shite." He crashes into me, teeth and tongue fighting themselves against my abs, and I grab his head and moan as he licks at me, bites at me.

His arm locks around me and in one quick flip I'm on my back again, hurtled into pillows that go flying, the bedspread flinging away at our agitated kicks. Loch's mouth beats down on me as ferociously as the blood beats at my veins as he works his way lower.

"How many different shades of red can I make you turn, eh?" He brands the question into the jut of my hipbone, bites a response where my thigh meets my groin. "Where else can I make you blush?"

"*Loch*." Zero to imploring in five seconds flat.

My fingers find his hair and latch in but he yanks me away.

"Ah-ah—hands over your head. There's a good boy."

Shit why is that so *erotic.*

I find handholds in the wooden slats of the headboard, eyes on the bed's canopy, breathing hard and jagged. Not looking at him, not being able to touch him, ratchets every sensation higher until my whole existence is the points where his lips and fingers stake their ownership.

He grabs my thighs and shoves them up towards my chest.

I was wrong, my whole existence also encapsulates inhuman cries that make me grateful the castle is mostly empty. How sound-deadening is stone? I can't care right now; no pretense, no build-up, his satin, venomous tongue licks over my hole.

"Holy *fuck*," I gasp and squirm, but Loch keeps me in place, his hands iron vises spreading me for him, holding me together.

He's ruthless here too—I shouldn't be surprised. Taking, taking, but his taking is also giving because with every lap of his tongue, every scratch of his beard on my thin skin, I'm begging incomprehensibly for more, and even then, he doesn't stop. He brings his fingers into play and alternates licking and stretching, plunging me into sensation without a break until I'm hanging by a thread.

When I'm sweating and frantic, he climbs back up my body to a symphony of breathy, throaty sounds from both of us. He's rolling on the condom and taking care of the lube before I can fight my way through the fog to do it for him. And it is a fog, I'm bobbing in a wide, endless rush of need and I know it will all be far too evanescent but he's made me *here* and that consumes me more than I've ever been consumed before.

Loch runs a hand up one of my arms, still over my head, still death-gripping the headboard. His grip clamps tight around that fist and he looks down at me; he could say something. He could kiss me. He could do anything, but he chooses to watch my face as he lines his dick up with my softened hole and pushes against the first tight ring. I feel his attention as much as the pressure, the give.

His breathing grates heavier, the only outward sign of him being as close to unraveling as I am, but he takes it slow, propped over my body with one hand on mine, the other on my hip, guiding me.

It's too slow, a gentle thrust in, pulling back, giving me a little more—it's not *enough*. All that need is shoaled up inside my chest until it bleeds out through the rest of my body and I'm writhing underneath him.

I don't let go of the headboard, but I wrap my legs around him and pull. "Loch, *please*—"

His hips snap forward.

Pleasure whites out my vision.

I hear the warbles of my cry like an echo. I feel the reverberations like the retreating crest of a wave, all white-capped foam and popping bubbles.

Loch holds, body strung taut over me, and my eyes find his through the haze, through the whimpers I think I'm making.

"Good?" he asks, concern etched in the slant of his brows, the focus of his pupils.

I nod, immediate, and yeah, I am whimpering, and it devolves to wordless pleading.

It's permission granted. It's a door opened. Loch takes my nod and my whimpers and his grin is extraordinary.

He drapes over me, one arm snaking around to hold me to him as he thrusts, broken grunts and firing pulses. Slow at first, then faster, tunneling into me, I'm well and truly gone.

"Shite, Kris," he moans. "You're so tight, *fuck*. Making me feel so good, look at you. Arch your hips, I wanna—there, Kris, *there*."

It's another unendurable contradiction: the way he holds me to him, tenderness; the way he fucks into me, aggression; but both those things are possession, aren't they? And I am, fully possessed, utterly his.

Nips of his teeth on the underside of my bicep are soothed with his tongue until he works his way over, breaks through the seam of my mouth with a vicious kiss. I hadn't even realized my jaw was tensed but I relent to him, let him in, rocking my hips to meet him.

"Loch, I need—I need—"

He changes the angle again and nails my prostate dead-center.

My head throws back in a shower of sparks.

His teeth sink into my exposed neck and he sucks, hard, scatters more of those sparks across my skin in another mark of his, replacing his paint. Each thrust hits me exactly right, embers flying wild.

His hand snakes between us and closes around my dick, pumping in time with his firestorm hips. "Let it out now, Kris," he orders into my skin.

My thighs are shaking, arms strung taut, every muscle straining, reaching, his cock drilling me relentlessly, I can't not obey.

Sensation releases me like cannon fire, a clawing shout and an explosion and I'm wrecked, spilling over his hand and streaking across our chests.

Loch's thrusts stutter. His face is buried against the side of mine and I hear him, babbled, senseless groans—no, words, words that slip through me like water before I can think to hold on to them.

"Mo chroí, mo chuisle, mo mhuirnín," then "*Kris,*" and his whole body tenses and quakes.

He doesn't give himself a chance to relax, he barely lets me breathe before his lips are on mine again, desperate, even more so now. He rocks steadily, almost absently, and I'm over-sensitized but I meet him there, gently pitching my hips with tiny, fevered grunts until we're twitching in aftershocks.

Loch pries at my fingers on the headboard.

"Touch me," he orders, and I do, I have to, arms damn near jelly but I curl them across his back and feel the sweat sheen on his skin, the rattling beat of his heart against his ribs.

The kiss settles from needy to savoring. Our lips are raw, our breaths pushing through in demanding gasps, but I can't stop, and he doesn't either, licking and tasting and *feeling,* I can't get enough.

I want to know the evolution of his kisses. How today's will be different from tomorrow or next month or five years from now, how the texture of his lips will change, how sometimes he'll be aggressive and sometimes he'll be this and I want to be able to track the differences like constellations. I want to know what it's like to kiss this man at every stage of his life.

Word by word.

It's too big to think of anything else.

But I want his forever.

I want it and I love him and I'm a goddamn moron.

Chapter Seventeen

My body is heavy and deeply relaxed, every limb sinking into the mattress in the density that comes on the border of sleep. A dream is there, something about paint splattered on a wall, fingers dragging through it—

Loch moves against me, and I come fully into consciousness.

I slept. And for the first time in I don't even know how long, I'm not exhausted.

I'm *happy.*

His head is in the middle of my chest, one arm slung over me, pinning me to the bed. His shoulders steadily rise and fall, the muscles down his back contracting and releasing in rhythmic breaths, the sheet draped across his waist.

As carefully as I can, I grab for my phone on the bedside table. It's barely morning. Of what should be my last day in Ireland. My room is a mess with the food trays we hauled up yesterday, most of the bedding is knotted around us, pillows scattered. Everywhere is marked by the undeniable signs that we did absolutely nothing all day yesterday except each other.

I scroll through missed texts. Nothing pressing.

Except that it's St. Patrick's Day, and the guy who should be overseeing this Holiday now is dead asleep on my chest.

I set my phone back down and brush my fingers through his bright hair. "Hey. Loch."

He stiffens, a panicked waking up, before he remembers where he is, who he's with, and channels that alertness into peering up at me.

A groan, and he drops his face to my sternum. "No. It's na morning yet."

"I'm afraid so."

He nestles into my chest. "Mm. You smell like me. My cologne."

I can't stop my dopey smile. "I probably smell like sweat and sex and need another shower."

"*Nah.* Stay like this." He glides up and kisses my neck and I'm inclined to agree with him, especially as his hand slips beneath the sheets and closes around my morning wood.

My back arches. "Shit, Loch, rabbits envy your stamina."

He laughs, reverberations setting off small earthquakes across my skin. "It's your fault, boyo. You're too hot. Had to go and be my dream guy made flesh."

His—his *what?*

I grab his chin and pull him up to kiss me, rolling us so we're on our sides, early light white and crystalline through the sheer window curtains. My heart chokes all the things I want to say, the questions I want to ask, and I kiss him because that's less terrifying and my head rings, rings, rings with those words, *my dream guy.*

We've said a lot of things since I came back from Belfast. This is *real* now, isn't it? We're together, everything confessed.

Why does it still feel like there's something being held back behind a bulging door?

"I'm supposed to leave tomorrow," I murmur. "But I could . . . stay. Help you settle things with Malachy. Or prepare for your coronation. You'll have one, right?"

"Yeah." Loch releases my dick and moans halfheartedly. "Finn and Siobhán will na let me escape without celebrating this."

"Good. They shouldn't." I pause. "Do you . . . do you want me to stay after today, then?"

Loch pushes up onto his elbow, dragging his hand up my hip, my side, to my shoulder, leaving a trail of shivers in his wake. "I canna be selfish," he whispers, eyes on the fraction of bed between us.

"No. You should be. Keep me here so I can be selfish, too."

His lips crack in a smile. But it's tainted again, that aching shadow that's been circling him since yesterday morning.

"You have no idea," he says to the mattress, "how selfish I've been already."

There's a knock on the door. A booming, insistent, *panicked* knock, and Loch's up and snatching on his pants before I can even twist free of the sheets.

He eases the door open a sliver as I'm stumbling through my suitcase, yanking out clothes that aren't paint-destroyed.

"What?" he snaps into the hall, and I frown at his back, the way he's a mix of terrified and angry.

"Malachy's here," comes Siobhán's voice. "He's screaming about our magic and *you* and—"

"Get down here," Finn barks. God, they've both come. "We'll keep him in the hall. Put some more clothes on."

Their footsteps thunder away.

Loch holds still in the barely open door. I rip on a shirt, but when he looks back, his eyes don't meet mine.

"I have to—"

"Go," I tell him. "Go. I'll meet you there."

"Kris." Now he does look at me. Through his anger and fear, he's pleading. "If I asked you to stay away—"

"I'd tell you to shut up, you idiot. Of course I'm going. Get dressed or I'll be down there first and yell at your uncle myself."

He crosses the room and kisses me. I rock into it, briefly thrown into an abyss by the demanding control of his mouth.

"You're a stubborn arse," he says, almost mournfully, but he finally leaves.

Loch beats me down to the foyer, racing in, tugging on another Aran sweater as I round the corner.

Malachy is standing under the blazing chandelier, red-faced and *screaming* at Finn.

"—told me about your little *meeting*. Eamon's asking questions now, questions he's never asked before. What the *fuck* was that meeting about? What the fuck do you think you've been—"

The moment Loch appears, his uncle rounds on him, and I'm sucked back to every argument Coal had with our dad. Every time I watched the two of them yell at each other and all I could do was stand there and hope to god Coal wrestled even a minor victory out of the situation. I wanted to intervene, *every fucking time,* but anything I could have said got stunned in terror so I was helpless to watch my brother take it all for us.

"*You.*" Malachy is all poison and fury. He's uncapped now, his hair mussed, eyes sunken, suit jacket unbuttoned and shirt wrinkled— what decorum he'd had last I saw him is fraying at the seams. "You owe me answers, you little shit."

Loch stops. His hands fist, and I hang back behind him.

Siobhán and Finn move off to the side together, both of them as wound as I am, watching Loch with tense jaws and wide eyes.

Finn's gaze slides to mine. She nods, once.

When I turn back, Malachy is glaring.

At me.

Loch steps between us. "It's over, Uncle," he says. He's talking fast. "I'm taking St. Patrick's Day back. This Holiday is *mine.*"

"The fuck you will. You think you can *take* it from me? Our court will—"

"Finally know that the position was never fully yours," Loch finishes. "I did meet with them. I didn't talk about you at all. All I did was tell them what *I've* done for our Holiday, and if that made them start questioning what was left for *you* to do, well." He shrugs. "And now, if you cry to them about how I *took* this Holiday from you, what do you think will be their first question, eh? They'll ask how I managed it, when the only way a Holiday can be transferred is through joyful willingness. When it isn't joyful, *this* happens." He points between them. "It's a fucked-up tangle of power that was so easy to undo, I canna believe it's taken me all these years to snatch it back. So go on, then. Tell our court the original transfer to you never fully went and I was able to pull it back. You wanna explain to them *why* it *didn't* take for you? That you manipulated me into giving up the throne?"

Malachy's face grows redder. He runs his hands through his hair in an aggravated, cornered lurch. "You've screwed up, Lochlann. You—"

"You'll tell the court you returned the throne to me," Loch says, calmer now, but I can see tiny vibrations in his clenched fists. "You'll tell them you finally decided it was time to pass it back."

Malachy's frantic rage pauses.

"Are you sure about this?" His tone is distorted. Like he has one last move to make.

All those little scraps of uncertainty swirl up, dust caught in a funnel cloud. The sense of something being off with Loch, something he wasn't saying, something lurking in the sadness of his eyes and the way he kissed me.

Unconsciously, I take a step back from him, to the side, so I can see Malachy better.

Malachy's eyes snap to me.

Loch dives between us again. "Malachy. *Get out of my castle!*"

One lip curls, a toying sneer that strengthens when Malachy asks Loch, "Did you get the Christmas Prince into bed like I told you to?"

I've never been punched before.

But his words are a physical fist socking me in the gut.

I realize too late that that question was bait. Bait I've taken by the horror and invasion I can't school off my face.

Malachy tugs his suitcoat over his stomach, a pathetic attempt at regaining composure. "Good play, Lochlann. I told you it'd be beneficial to have him here for the week. Now he won't seek repercussions for the joy. You can bend him over literally *and* figuratively."

"Don't you *talk about him*," Loch barks.

I barely hear him. Barely see Loch turn to face me, he must look pleading because his voice drops.

"Kris—"

Repercussions for the joy.

I look at him, and I should feel *something*, but every emotion bounces off a shield of numbness. Loch's face is blotchy and his eyes are round with all that shame he's been keeping at bay—that's what it's been. Every time he pulled away from me. *Shame.*

"You were stealing Christmas's joy," I state. "You were stealing it to help compensate for what Malachy wasn't letting you have. So you could keep your Holiday running. You were using it to *help* your Holiday."

Somewhere off to the side, Finn curses. It's far away.

Loch doesn't respond. He doesn't agree or assure me that's what happened. He stands there looking broken.

Malachy laughs. The pop of noise drags my focus back to him.

"Is that what he told you?" he asks. "*Allegedly*, who do you think acquired one of those handy little devices to siphon off joy? This prince no one trusts, who has no resources, who had to resort to stealing *from me* originally, or someone who has spent his life building the largest, most successful business in this country? I will give Lochlann credit where it's due; he was exceptionally quick to get on board. Though he wasn't successful at covertly installing the device in Christmas. Even so, the magic he stole went a long way towards paying off what he owed me. Again, *allegedly*."

Malachy is all I can see. A tunnel narrowing, narrowing until there's just his arrogant face while dozens of pieces shift around me, a kaleidoscope coalescing and parting only to reform.

I suspected Loch of stealing from us. I suspected Malachy of stealing from us.

I never thought it was *both* of them.

Both of them, doing it so Loch could repay what Malachy said he used last year.

Not to help his Holiday. Not some desperate way to fight back against his uncle.

They were working *together*.

I'm staring at Malachy, and I jerk my eyes away, unable to get my thoughts to stop pulsing around me.

Did you get the Christmas Prince into bed like I told you to?

"Congratulations on having St. Patrick's Day now, Lochlann," comes Malachy's snide voice. "I do hope this doesn't start your reign on a bad note."

"Get *out!*" Loch's shout rattles off the ceiling, but so do Malachy's footsteps as he crosses the foyer, opens the front doors, and leaves.

He's not been gone for a second before Loch closes the space between us.

"Kris." He's panting. "Look at me."

His command kicks into all the other times he's commanded me in the past twenty-four hours.

My eyes lift to his. Dutifully. Hopefully, *beggingly*.

"You stole Christmas's magic for your uncle," I state. "*With* your uncle. You gave our magic to him, and he put it into his business, not your Holiday. You didn't use any of it to help St. Patrick's Day."

He doesn't react at first.

I can't breathe.

It's the only thing that keeps me from yelling at him.

Finally, he nods, eyelids pulsing in suppressed misery.

"He told you to . . . to go after me." My voice is shockingly emotionless; it makes goosebumps go up my own arms. "He's the one who wanted me to be here for the week. He told you to get in with me, so I'd be thrown off from investigating the theft. So you could manipulate me. You were working with him the whole time."

Loch goes green, like he might be ill. "That's *not* what this—"

I hold up my hand, staying him, eyes holding on his, burning.

"Did your uncle tell you to go after me so you two could manipulate me?"

"He did, but Kris—"

I turn for the hallway.

"Kris."

He grabs my wrist.

I whirl back on him. *"Don't—"*

My shout cuts off. I don't know whether I want to scream *Don't touch me* or *Don't call me that*. The way he says my name, the way he's always said it, he might as well be saying *sweetheart* or *baby* or *love,* and I *can't* hear him say my name, not now.

"You didn't tell me." I've been operating on numbness up until this point, my voice finally breaks, my eyes heat.

He listened to me divulge all that shit about my mom, about realizing how abusive she is. I let him read her texts and that letter and he had the chance to *tell me* that he was using me.

But he *didn't*.

That's what's gutting me right now. I could've dealt with him and Malachy working together—probably. Eventually.

But he didn't tell me.

"I should have," Loch says, sounding rushed, anxious. "I dinna know how. Malachy told me to go after you, but that's never been what it was. Not from the start, I swear."

I want to believe him. Everything he's said to me. Everything I've said to him. I *want* to believe him, but all I can see is the lie hanging over our every interaction, a twisting toxic cloud braided through with the doubt I spent so long keeping at bay. The worry that I shouldn't give up my responsibilities and drop the ball on what Christmas and my brother needed so I could make selfish choices.

I made that selfish choice.

I took that selfish risk.

And he was lying the whole time. He had chances to tell me the truth, and he *didn't*.

Loch's holding my arm. He reaches up with his other hand and touches my neck, testing, then pulling me into him, and I concede, only with a lurching glare.

"*Let me go.*" I don't wait—I yank back, and he lets me.

Siobhán has her hands to her mouth, Finn scowls, the air is thick with ache and betrayal and I point at Siobhán.

"Do not let him follow me," I tell her.

"Kris." Loch tries to reach for me again, but I sidestep him and race for the hall to Siobhán's shriek of "*What did you do,* Lochlann?"

I don't expect she'll be able to stop him, not for long, so I tear through the castle, shove into my room, and lock the door. God, it's a mess, and it throttles me now, every memory in every corner—the bed, the shower, his hands on my body, his lips here, and there, and the words he said, their lingering pressure now a growing stone.

On autopilot, I stuff my belongings into my suitcase, eyes blurring. My chest can't take the weight and it splinters, actual cracks snaking along my ribs.

I went into this *knowing* it was him. But I got distracted by his cheekbones and his honor and his wild, artistic soul. And even when he told me he was stealing from us, it was okay—I rationalized it away because he had a noble purpose.

But stealing our magic to give to his asshole of an uncle? Not clarifying where that magic was going, that Malachy tolerated my presence here because he wanted Loch to manipulate me?

Letting Malachy blindside me like that?

The doorknob twists. The lock holds.

"Kris," he begs. "Open the door."

I don't say anything. I get my suitcase shut and I conjure mistletoe.

"*Please.*" He knocks. "Please don't—"

I use the door to the ensuite. I shove the mistletoe in and magic gathers around me and I don't think, I don't think, I *go*.

The door opens into the foyer of Claus Palace.

I race in, slam it shut, and drop back against it.

The foyer is empty, the lights low. It's like eight in the morning in Ireland—which makes it, what, five here? All the better, then, for me to slide to the ground, collapsing in the dark, my eyes snapping around like I can find a solution to what an absolute idiot I was.

My dream guy.

Prickling numbness starts in my fingertips, creeps up my arms. I cup my hands over my face to breathe into my palms but the rising panic makes me think of Loch putting that ice on my neck and guiding me down from the spiral.

I rock over my knees, suffocating, no way down this time, no path that's safe.

"Kris? Shit, dude—"

"Kristopher!"

Coal's footsteps thud on the stairs; Wren's heels clack up the hall to my right.

"You gotta warn us before you come back like that! All that new security we set up since the whole *break-in* thing needs to—Kris? What happened?"

Coal rushes the rest of the way and drops in front of me, his hands going to my shoulders, trying to get me to sit back.

"What's wrong?" he asks in such an unwavering tone that it eases me upright.

Wren is behind him, already dressed for the day, concern drooping her face. But she steps back, gives us space.

I roll my wet eyes shut because god, I'm such an idiot.

I say that, "I'm such an idiot. I'm such an—"

"Hey, hey—stop, breathe. What *happened*?"

"It was him. Loch. He was the one stealing from us. Which I knew, but I—" My head drops back against the door, body sinking, betrayal is an anchor and I am moored in place. "I thought he was doing it to stand up to his uncle, but they were working together. I was so stupid. God, Coal, I played *right into their hands*—"

"Wait—how do you know? What—"

Haltingly, fighting off that panic, I explain about Loch reclaiming his throne yesterday. Malachy coming this morning.

I leave out all the stuff in between.

Somehow, I think Coal knows anyway.

"Loch admitted he was stealing from us." My throat gets smaller, smaller. "But he didn't tell me it was *because of Malachy*. That he and his uncle have been working together this whole time, they planned to use me *this whole time*. He let me go on about—about how I felt and—I bet he was laughing at me because it *worked*. I did exactly what they wanted me to. I dropped everything. I told him I didn't care about the stolen magic. I gave up all my responsibilities here for *nothing*."

"Kris." Coal grabs my shoulder. He's in pajamas, hair flattened—I woke him up. Shit. *Why did I do this*—"Kris, god, look at me. *Stop*. You said he took back the throne from his uncle, right? So maybe he didn't have a choice before. Maybe—"

"Don't defend him."

"I'm not trying to defend him." Real fury surges up Coal's face. "I'm trying to find any excuse I can not to go back to Ireland and murder him."

My head hangs down, and Coal tugs on me again.

"Come on. Stand up. We're not having this conversation in the foyer."

"I woke you up. Go back to bed—I'm sorry I—"

"Shut the fuck up." Coal gets me to my feet. "How many times have you scraped my ass off the floor? So shut up and let me be the one to take care of you, because if I don't, I really will go kill the king of another Holiday."

I relent. He hauls me up the stairs, Wren following with my bag.

Until we get to the landing, and Coal whirls to Wren as a door slams off the wall behind us.

"New security system my ass," he hisses.

And then Loch's voice rings out. "Kris?"

He's here. In Christmas.

He's standing in the foyer, his eyes immediately locking on the three of us at the top of the staircase.

"Oh, over my dead body," Coal growls. "Kris—go. I'll take care of this."

But I stay rooted, staring down at Loch and the door open behind him, showing the entryway of Castle Patrick. He used magic to come here.

Christmas's magic, that he stole for his uncle?

I look away, jaw setting, eyes burning.

"I'll take your things to your room," Wren whispers, and she glides away.

Coal hits the bottom of the staircase out of the corner of my vision. "You've got a helluva lot of nerve, asshole."

"I know, I did na come here to—*please, Coal*—"

"Oh *do not address me like that,* you son of a bitch, not like we're *friends.*" Coal marches up to him and Loch takes a step back, hands up, and god, if Coal had a single violent bone in his body, I think he might hit Loch. "Get out of my palace before I freeze your ass into a snowman."

"He deserves an explanation," Loch says to him. To me. "Kris. You deserve an—"

"I said *get the fuck out.* He's not going to forgive you, you sorry—"

"I do na expect his forgiveness!" Loch shouts. "I said he deserves an explanation. You know he does. *Please.* Then I'll leave. Kris—I'll leave, I—"

"Fine."

My voice cuts over the room from where I'm above them, near the top of the staircase.

Coal holds for a second. He steps back, but he doesn't clear the way for Loch to come up the stairs.

Loch walks closer to the balcony so he's almost under me, and I feel his gaze fixed on the side of my face.

"Do you remember"—he takes a quick, rattling breath—"how St. Patrick's Day's magic has its basis in luck? For *months,* Kris, *months,* it told me to go to that study room."

That yanks my focus down to him before I look away again.

"So I went," he says. "I went, and some arsehole kept swiping it from me—but I went back, and back, and then . . . you. And fuck me, I knew as soon as I opened that door and saw you."

"You knew who I was even then?" I can't help the question, chest caving in.

"No, no—I meant I knew that I—" Loch's face reddens. "That you were what my magic was trying to get me to. *You.* And you were such an obstinate prick right from the gate, Christ, I could na help but fall for you."

"Explanation," Coal demands. "Now. You've got one minute, jackass."

Loch winces and scrubs a hand down his face. "Malachy was furious about the joy I used last year. It did na matter that what I used it for *increased* our magic intake; he wanted me to pay that magic back. He'd toss us out, cut off Finn and Siobhán's school, take everything we had left, if I did na get him more. We knew what had been happening in Christmas. Of any Holiday, you lot had joy to spare, and you would na miss a bit. He got the devices and I agreed. I'm sorry, Kris, and I was na lying—I will pay you back."

I drop to sit on the top of the stairs, staring blankly at the step below me.

Loch moves closer, speaking up at me. "I did na know who you were until your assistant reached out about your apology. Malachy pushed for you to stay longer, to make me figure out what you knew about the theft. And when I started to realize what I had done—I did na stop it when I should have. I thought my magic had been wrong, that you were na meant for me like that. I did na turn off the device until the night I kissed you, in the kitchen. But I knew the damage had been done—the damage was done before you even set foot in my castle. And I got to know you, and I tried, *tried so hard,* not to fall for you, but Jesus Christ, Kris, I was na lying. You are my dream guy."

"Stop," I whisper. No one hears.

"And I was terrified every moment I was with you, because I did na know how to tell you what Malachy and I had done, and I still don't. I do na know how to—"

I shove to my feet and lean over the banister. "You manipulated me. You *used* me, Loch."

"*No.*" He takes a lurching step forward. "Malachy told me to do whatever I had to do to get in with you. But Kris, nothing that happened between us was because of him. I tried to *resist* you because of him. And it all went arseways. I failed myself. I failed you."

"You didn't tell me. You let me find out like *that.* You asked me to—" My breath knots; I keep going. "You asked me to show you my soul, and you *let me.* You knew, *all this time*—fuck, Loch, how am I supposed to get over that? I *trusted* you."

He drops his head to his chest for one fortifying moment before he looks up at me, eyes glassy. "I should've stood up to Malachy years ago. But I could never . . . I could never fight through his shite. I was too much a coward. Until you. You did na let me be a coward, never believed I was for one second, and you finally got me to real-ize how much I had to lose by bowing to him." He makes a pained noise. "I do na expect you to get over what I kept from you, what I did. I do na deserve you to. But I am sorry, Kris, and you do deserve that. An apology. And you deserve to know that I will never forgive myself. I'm someone who hurt you and I'm despairingly in love with you and I canna bear to be both those things at once."

"You need to go," Coal says to him, but it's quieter. Unyielding, but calmer. "Now."

I'm frozen in this moment. Loch is, too, looking up at me, strain winding across his features.

He can't be in love with me.

Not this fast.

Not even if his magic brought us together.

Not even if I'm in love with him, too.

I can't be here anymore, listening to him, feeling this.

"Go back to Ireland," I rasp. "You have a Holiday to secure."

I walk away.

"Kris," he says. Then, louder, "Kris—"

"You're done," is the last thing I hear Coal say before I'm swal-lowed by the hall, hurrying for my room.

I get maybe two yards when I see Hex against the wall, arms around himself, wearing a gray robe with the hood thrown up.

"Don't," I beg. "Don't say anything."

He holds up his hands. "I was not going to."

But I'm the one who stands there, scowling at him, jaw working.

Hex's head tips, his dark hair spilling over his shoulder. After a moment of silence, his lips part.

"Months ago, I found myself in a similar position to yours, if you'll recall."

My scowl tightens, but Hex keeps talking.

"I ended up choosing my Holiday over your brother," he whis-pers. "A choice I regretted as soon as I'd made it. You have proven far smarter than I was. To choose him"—he nods back towards the foyer, where Loch has to be gone by now—"over your responsibilities almost from the start."

A laugh scrapes out of me. "This isn't *smarter*. This isn't—"

"If I had to choose again," Hex cuts me off, "no matter the repercussions, no matter the situation, no matter what was at risk for Halloween, I'd choose Coal. I'd choose my own happiness."

My glare finally relaxes, widening in confusion.

He shrugs helplessly. "My Holiday survived before me. It will survive after me. But I know now that I will not survive without him. So I'd choose him, and myself. Even if it makes no sense. Even if it hurts."

He smiles, but it's sad, weighted, and I know he knows we have that in common. The burden of overthinking, of self-inflicted responsibility.

"Do not regret choosing yourself," he tells me. "No matter what outcome is unfolding now—Coal is glad you did. We all are."

The heat building in my eyes, the tightness in my chest—none of it equips me to handle what he's saying, so I shake my head, refuting wordlessly, and walk away, faster when I hear Coal's footsteps coming up the stairs.

I get to my room and slam the door behind me; the curtains are shuttered, the lights all off. I bend double and tell myself I'm fine, I'm fine, *I'm fine*—

I'm despairingly in love with you.

The room shifts. I'm on my knees, head in my hands, and I *fucking hate him.* I hate that I can look back now and see the truth in every moment he pulled away, that he was trying not to hurt me, but I kept pushing. I *knew* something was off but I was so determined to choose what *I* wanted for once in my life that I refused to see what was glaringly obvious.

Here I thought I'd changed, when all along, I was falling into the same pattern as before: letting a fantasy override my common sense.

That's what I did with Iris.

That's what I did with my mom.

My gut sinks, my head spins, and I think I cry out, that blast of realization searing through me like a knife wound.

I only have myself to blame for this, my stupid, shitty fantasies and my stupid, shitty ignorance because I thought, for a second, that I could fix my mess. But it isn't fixable, is it? I'm right back where I started.

Only it *hurts* this time.

It hurts so much deeper than it did with Iris. This wasn't me trying to mold myself to fit someone else; this was me, all along, choosing something *real*.

What Hex said . . . it isn't that simple. I chose my own happiness, and it still ended disastrously because *I can't do anything right*.

Coal's hand grips my shoulder.

He bends down next to me and puts his arms around me and I hold onto him in the dark, not speaking. I will that silence to bleed into my scattered, tumultuous thoughts, but my brain is a ripped-out control box, all sparking electricity and thrashing wires that keep bringing me back to the same two things.

I'm in love with Loch.

And I can't believe I thought loving him would be enough.

Chapter Eighteen

Days pass in a blur.

The weekend comes, and I realize halfway through Saturday that Coal and I are supposed to go to our parents' vow renewal. Or, well, a prior version of me would have pushed for us to go.

But we don't. We don't even talk about it.

I have both Dad and Mom blocked, so whatever repercussions they rain down don't reach me. I want to ask Coal if they've contacted him. But I can't.

He does make us have a *brother night* Sunday evening, where the two of us haul up in the theater room and eat too much popcorn and candy and watch shitty movies.

It's when we're cleaning up the room that he stops, an empty popcorn bucket in one hand, eyes on the black screen. The theater lights are up.

"Is that how she always talked to you?" he whispers to the empty room.

My heart sinks. I don't need to ask for clarification or examples. They're in the set of his face, the harrowed look when his eyes find mine.

Whatever Mom's said to him about us missing their vow renewal, Coal's not hurt for himself. He's hurt realizing the depth of how she's treated me all these years.

"Don't—" I clear my throat. "Don't let her get to you the way I did. Don't let it go so long, okay? If it's too much."

Coal bats away my concern. "Oh, don't you worry. I let her *have it* the moment she tried to lay blame on me. That shut her up." He pauses. "I'm guessing you never talked back to her? Always took whatever she threw at you because you felt you deserved it."

I pretend to straighten the recliners we used. They're already in line.

"Kris."

The chair leather creaks under my hands.

Coal touches my shoulder. "I'm proud of you."

I look at him, deadpan.

He's not smiling. Not letting me brush this off. "I'm serious. I'm proud of you for putting up boundaries. I'm proud of you for protecting my brother. Because I kind of love him like crazy."

I chew the inside of my cheek. *Boundaries.* Is that what I did? It's what I *should have* done, years ago. But I let it go until just seeing a missed notification from her was enough to set me off on a panic attack. Which I do have, I know now; and Wren's hinted a few times at being willing to help me find someone to talk to about them.

But Coal shouldn't be praising me for doing what I should have done years ago. For doing what was my responsibility to fix: protecting myself.

Is this how Loch felt every time one of us would compliment him? Uncomfortable and deflective because, deep down, it wasn't heroic at all. It was the basest level of expectation, and we shouldn't be heralded for meeting it.

His refusal to accept praise was grating. *Wrong.*

Is mine?

Coal hugs me. No warning. Just his solid presence and a too-brief moment of peace.

"You'll believe me someday," he tells me. I cling to him. "And I'll keep reminding you of how brave you are until you do."

School starts again.

I should go back.

I don't.

No one says anything about it. Not Coal, not Iris. I ignore the emails I get about lectures and deadlines, and the decision to not go back passes over me so unobtrusively I barely notice it.

Coal spends as much time with me as he can, but he's stretched between final meetings with the winter Holiday reps, the impending treaty signing, and the combined coronation-treaty party for after Easter. Iris comes to see me too when she's able; and Hex.

I throw myself into helping Coal—to avoid Iris and Hex's pity, but mostly to atone for my screw-up. We know St. Patrick's Day stole from us; we know who, we know why. I expect Coal to come up with a gameplan for confronting them—confronting *Loch*—to get the joy back. I expect to walk into his office and for him to tell me, *Today's the day, we're going to confess everything to the winter Holidays collective and hope they forgive us for losing the joy we owe them.*

But he doesn't.

Negotiations carry on. Party plans are made. I fight to stay attentive during meetings, and anytime there's a task that needs doing, however mundane, I jump on it, hurling myself headfirst into all necessary writings, administrative duties, errant chores—hell, I even start coordinating with our head chef to dish out meals at the meetings. I'm desperate to be useful, shaking internally from the remnants of my earthquake, waiting for the aftermath rubble to crush me.

But then, about two weeks after I got back, we receive an invitation. To the coronation of the St. Patrick's Day King.

Along with that invitation comes another device like the one used to steal our joy, only this one, if plugged in, would transmit joy *to* us.

Marta plugs it in, and St. Patrick's Day sends back the joy they took from us almost instantly.

The need to atone darkens, warps, and the energy shifts every time I enter a room. Like I'm that sad, pissy dark shadow again that had to actively think *do not be a prick* to get through interactions without sulking. Everyone I'm near picks up on that, treating me like there's a fifteen-foot security radius emanating around me.

I try to rally. Coal needs me to buck up; Christmas needs me to get my shit together; if I'm not going back to school, I have to be *useful,* smile at these winter Holiday reps, why is it so hard? This is my future now. It always was. Fitting into whatever's needed of me.

My screw-up with St. Patrick's Day resolved itself. I didn't even have to do anything, did I? Loch gave the magic back. He probably would have anyway, if I had never gone there at all. He'd have eventually reclaimed his Holiday. He'd have eventually owned up to the theft; it's the kind of person he is.

I did nothing.

My self-loathing grows wings and loops around my head and my resting expression is a pained snarl.

So after a meeting where I'm supposed to be taking notes but miss half of what was said and Wren *sighs* at me—probably not in exasperation, probably in sympathy, but fuck both of those things—I march myself back to my room, self-imposed house arrest.

I rip out of the suit I'm wearing and drag on a hoodie and sweats. The ornate couch in my suite's main room is stupid uncomfortable, but I flop onto it anyway and pull out my phone.

My thumb automatically goes to the text thread I had with Loch.

I do not text him.

He texted. To apologize, again, and again, but there's been nothing since that first week.

Siobhán texted me too, apologizing on his behalf and wanting to still be friends and maybe I will, someday, but all I could do was text her that I'm fine.

I click off my phone and let it drop onto my chest.

If I close my eyes, it is like no time has passed. I could be back in my flat at Cambridge, trying to find the gumption to go to a class I hate, dreading every moment of every day coming at me.

And that familiarity is what finally slaps me upside the head.

The harrowing, aching *sameness* of slogging through my existence when I know now what it's like to be *me* again. It might've turned out to be a mess, but—within that mess, within those lies, I found parts of myself, didn't I?

I toss my phone on the coffee table and shove up from the couch, standing in the middle of the room, chest aching.

I don't want to feel like this again.

I don't want to be this person again.

But what do I do? I've gone into a state of detachment since I left Ireland because it hurts, but mainly I don't trust myself to react. I've thought I wanted so many different things—a happy ending with Iris, my mom to come back, *Loch*—but they were all *wrong* for so many different reasons, so what now?

My mind trips, crashes to its knees over one word.

Ending.

Coal asked me something a while back. *In all that writing you used to do about happily ever after, did you ever think through what being happy would actually feel like?*

It sure as hell isn't *this*. Miserable and on edge, like I've lost something, and every room I go into, I look around on instinct, expecting to see it—him—and I—

I slap my hands over my face and breathe into the hollow of my palms.

What does being happy feel like?

Not the ending.

The *after.*

What did I think I'd feel like after I got all those things I once wanted?

A barrage of words comes at me: content. Whole. Safe. Fulfilled.

It feels like lying on a bed under morning light and his sleepy weight on my chest.

It feels like my back cramping from bending over a coffee table, fingers spasming as I write and write and write.

I lower my hands, and my eyes snag on my desk across the room. I forgot to grab the notebook I'd filled when I left Ireland in a hurry, but my school shit is scattered from where I dumped it when I got back before Ireland, and I spot my laptop bag, right on top.

Why do I have to wait for an ending to give me those feelings?

Why can't I have any of that shit *now*?

I walk towards the desk on unstable legs, scramble through the clutter until I clear a space and ease out my laptop. I open it and pop it on and as it whirs to life, my breathing ramps faster, but something inside me settles.

I've been so obsessed with various endings giving me closure or happiness that I've neglected the journey to get to any of them. Like putting words into a story, word by word.

Why do the words that make the journey matter less than the words that make the ending?

I've spent so much time placing value on the end over anything else that I've missed so much going on around me. I've lost so many parts of me that I could have been enjoying rather than worrying how stupid mistakes would screw up some undefined future.

I'd started to get some of that back. With him. *Because of* him, and it aches like a wound now, but I can't lie around here and go backwards anymore.

What about the journey I'm on *right now?* What about *this* moment, the one I'm in? What can I do in this moment to help me feel content, whole, safe, fulfilled?

It wasn't just because of him. It *can't* have been just because of him.

I need to do this for *me.* I need that selfishness still. For a bit longer.

Once my laptop kicks to life, I drop down at my desk, pull up a blank document, and start writing.

It's mostly nonsense—at first. The same meandering thoughts I spilled out in Loch's library. Some of it coalesces into stuff about *Bridge to Terabithia,* decadent bullshit that rewrites what would have happened if that book had *not* ended so sadly. I dig out my old copy and reread it, and that sets me off on a frenzy of tearing through books I used to love but haven't indulged in for years.

When I'm not buried under stacks of books, I'm bent over my laptop, hands flying across the keyboard, chasing thoughts and seeing what congeals and letting myself *expand.*

I remember what Iris said a while ago, about what picture I'd send next in my text-photo-dump series. So I send her a shot of my laptop open to a document, and I look at it next to the one of the broken bottle on Loch's kitchen floor, and then the first one, of Loch himself.

The progression—Loch, broken bottle, writing—has me shutting off my phone before Iris can draw her own artistic conclusions.

Coal doesn't try to drag me to any more meetings, seeming to sense that I need time to do . . . whatever I'm doing. I imagine myself both a bird and an egg, building this nest of creativity around my unformed and delicate soul, nurturing it with stories I still love. I barely leave my room, but even in that solitude, I'm taking up more space than I've ever allowed myself.

I move and the air bruises.

Later—I'm losing track of days, but a *story* is forming, one I'm falling into with giddy abandon and I don't think I'd eat if Coal didn't bring trays of food, don't think I'd sleep if he didn't physically peel me away from my desk—the door groans open and I hear it enough to react.

"Let me finish getting this thought out," I mumble.

"That should be your next tattoo," Coal says. "Right across your middle finger, so you can flip me off and tell me to shut up efficiently."

I do flip him off, but I glance up.

My brother is in a suit. Dark wine red and cut to his lean frame, every inch of him styled.

Iris is with him, which shocks me enough that I spin around in my desk chair, but she's in a simple dress, not nearly as fancy as he is.

His style makes my mind race to the date, to events, to—

"The treaty signing? Give me ten minutes to—"

I'm halfway out of my chair when Coal shakes his head.

"It isn't the treaty signing. That's tomorrow. This is the opening reception welcome bullshit. And you're not going. I wanted to—"

"I'm . . . not going?" I push back the hood of my sweatshirt, a headache throbbing in my temples at the transition from writing to playing catch-up. "Why? I should. I can—"

"Kris." Coal cocks his head. "Don't worry about it. Today's event is a formality anyway. Iris came to hang with you."

Hang with me? Why would she need to—

Oh.

It's Loch's coronation today too.

I sink down into my chair. The cursor on my laptop flashes at me, and sensation creeps in now that I've broken out of my delirium.

My body aches from being bowed over for so long. My eyes are scratchy and dry. A million different emotions try to take center stage; all this writing has lifted a curtain and, for once, my self-loathing isn't the first to dive in.

"I'm glad you're here, actually, Iris," I say to my computer. "I'm working on that book. The one I sent you a photo of. The one I want you to draw pictures for."

She pads towards me and I feel her over my shoulder. "Can I read some of it yet?" Her tone is bright, encouraging. "You didn't even tell me what it's about."

Panic tightens my throat and the snap of my laptop shutting echoes in the room.

"It's—"

Not done. Not ready. It isn't perfect yet.

It probably never will be.

It's about a little prince who lives in a world of joy and wonder and has *everything.* He has a loving family and magic that can make candy canes and snow and his dad is *Santa Claus,* and yes, it's me, but it's also *not,* because this little prince gets to experience his world the way he should. He gets to see it through big, astounded eyes and feel everything with excitement and awe. He goes on adventures and gets to be innocent and curious.

I shoot to my feet again, sniffing hard against the prick of tears in my eyes. "Give me ten minutes, and I can be ready for the—" Damn it, what was it? A reception?

The rigidity in my shoulders winds tighter, and that ever-lurking dark cloud draws closer, pulled in so quickly through this protective shield I've started to build.

Do not be a prick. For this, for something that matters, *do not be a prick.*

I head for the closet, but Coal steps into my path.

"*Kris.*" He barks my name, and I stop. "Can you honestly say you're ready or even *want* to take on duties again? Stay here and keep writing whatever you're writing and I'll fill you in afterwards. Save your mental capacity for the signing tomorrow."

I don't want to feel this way.

I've taken steps to *not* feel this way.

But this is different. This isn't depressed, this isn't sluggish.

This is *infuriated.*

I don't get mad at my brother. I don't get mad at *anyone.*

Except Loch.

But this—this is a sudden, unstoppable eruption of feeling how many days I've spent locked in here, of calculating how many meetings Coal's let me miss, of the real life expectations crowding around me all at once so I pace away from him, back to him, scrubbing a hand through my unruly hair and my eyes go to my laptop and I want to *stay,* but I have to *go.*

Being in here has helped me piece myself back together.

But what good has it done?

And that's the struggle I always run into. The fact that what I need to be whole is *useless* to everyone else.

"I need," I start, looking at Coal, "to be a part of this. This is my Holiday, too. You said we were in this together."

Coal jerks like I slapped him. "We *are.* Missing a few things doesn't change that."

I continue across the room and dig into my closet, find a suit, a striped blue one Wren had me wear last Christmas that I remember not hating.

"Are you sure?" I snap. "It feels an awful lot like you're trying to get rid of me."

"Kris." My name comes on a wheeze from him. "You can't honestly think that I'd ever want to get rid of you."

"Why wouldn't I think that?" I *feel* how ridiculous this is, arguing with him while yanking on clothes, and I don't even care that Iris is in the room as I undress; and I *hear* what I'm saying like I'm suspended in a dream because I know, *I know* he'd never do this to me. But I can't stop, something is breaking out of me that I never thought would escape, and I'm not even sure who's talking at the moment, what part of me has control. "What else am I good for, if not standing at events like this and smiling for pictures? It's sure as hell the only thing Dad made me good for. Why wouldn't you eventually think that too?"

"Kris!"

"What else can I do for you? For our Holiday? What purpose do I even have? To sit up here and write about bullshit that doesn't matter? So I'll go to this fucking reception or brunch or whatever the hell it is, I'll go to a dozen stupid fucking events and plaster on a smile because god forbid I smile for *real,* god forbid I exist outside of being a prop for everyone else's entertainment."

Coal surges across the room. I'm half into the suit, pants on and the shirt buttoned to my stomach, and he grabs my arms and yanks me into a hug and I shove against him.

"Get off me—"

He holds me tighter, harder, until the pressure of his arms pushes a gasp out of my lungs, and that gasp is quaking and painful.

I see Iris, over his shoulder, and I stop fighting him.

She looks *furious.*

Iris marches towards me and Coal glances to the side to see why she's actually, physically *stomping* on the floor, and she uses that opening to shove me in the chest.

I stumble back.

"Stop talking about my friend like that!" she shouts. "God, Kris, I am *sick* of you talking about yourself like you don't matter. Like you have nothing to offer. Coal didn't want you going to the reception today because he *knows* whatever you're writing up here is helping you find

yourself again, and he didn't want to interrupt that. And I came because *you're my friend,* and I wanted to talk to you about what you've been doing. This was all the same shit you said after you told me you loved me, and you kept saying it even when I tried to tell you that you were wrong, *you are wrong.* So *stop it!*"

She shoves me again and I smack into the open closet door and hold there, gaping at her, all my anger wilting.

Coal's hands clench and unclench at his sides. It's unnatural for his face to look anything but goofy and smiling, so when he hits me with this heartbreak, it's silencing.

He nods at Iris. "What she said. Who cares if what you're doing doesn't help Christmas? Doesn't *contribute?* I've told you, Kris. I've told you I don't give a shit what you do as long as it brings you joy. You can be a part of this Holiday however you want, but if what you want to do, who you want to be doesn't fit in with a standard role in Christmas, then fuck it. You'll still be a part of this family, this Holiday. That will never, ever change. *Do what makes you happy.*"

A tear spills down my cheek and I let it fall, going limp against the closet door.

"*Are you* happy?" Coal asks, tentative; he takes a step closer. "I wanted you to start choosing things for yourself. This"—he waves at my desk—"is what I want for you, if it gives you what you need. Does it?"

Yes. No.

Almost.

I shrug, trying to get the rest of this shirt buttoned but my fingers fumble it.

"I think it will," I mutter.

"I want you at any event you want to go to—but Kris, what do *you* want to do, right now? Not for Christmas or me or anyone else. Fuck that, and fuck you for thinking that I don't want you to be a part of this. You'll *always* be a part of this. You can't escape me, ever."

Coal grabs my hand where I'm uselessly prying at the buttons.

"I'm not leaving you." He says each word deliberately. "Iris isn't leaving you. And you know what? I hate the guy, like I'm seriously considering assassinating him with an icicle—no one would know, the evidence would melt—"

"Coal," Iris breaks in.

"But I'm willing to bet Loch wouldn't leave you, either."

I flinch, shoulders hitting the door again. "He isn't—"

Coal ignores me. "You're worth staying for, Kristopher. *You.* Not what you have to offer people. *You* are worth it."

He's so sure. So goddamn resolved. I can't find it in me to argue, to shove aside anything he's said, because he doesn't lie. Not to me.

And so I let myself feel his words.

They drip down into my soul and gather in a sad, brittle puddle and I imagine a seed planting under them, something new and fresh, but it has roots, god does it have roots, and those roots pulse with that surety.

You're worth staying for.

"But he did leave," I whisper. "He left. And he lied. And I—"

"He didn't leave," Iris says. "*You* left him. He *followed* you. And yes, he lied about stealing Christmas's joy. He lied about his uncle's involvement. But can you honestly look at me and tell me you don't get why he did? I only know a fraction of what shit his uncle put them through from what Finn has said—"

"You talk to Finn?"

"—and even *I* get why Loch had to go to such drastic measures. Yeah, he should've told you. But is what he did something you can't work past? Do you think he is, at his core, a liar and a manipulator, or is he someone who got in over his head and made a dumb mistake?"

I wipe the back of my hand across my chin and shake my head because if I answer that, it all falls apart.

If I'd been in the same situation, would I have lied to him, too? To keep pretending for a moment longer, a second longer, that I wouldn't lose him? Yeah. I'd have lied. I'd have been selfish and a little cruel if it meant getting to have one more minute with him.

But I was wrong about something that should've been obvious.

I should have *seen* his hesitation and read it for what it was, but I willfully ignored it. Like I willfully ignored my mom's abuse, and how things never fit with Iris, and—

My eyes roll shut on an internal wince and *I'm so tired of myself.*

Iris cups my cheek in her palm. "You're afraid of people leaving you, but you aren't showing up for yourself, Kris."

"I'm going to ask you again," Coal says. "What do *you* want to do? Right now? Do you want to go to some boring ass welcome reception, do you want to stay and keep writing—or do you want to, I don't know, go to the coronation of a certain St. Patrick's Day King?"

The air leaves my lungs in a huff and my eyes fly open.

"That's why you both came," I guess. "Isn't it?"

Coal shrugs innocently. "I have no idea what you're talking about. This conversation happened naturally."

"I hate you."

"No, you don't." He grabs my shoulder. "And I don't hate you either. I *love* you. Iris loves you. So, Kris." He squeezes, hard. "What's it gonna be today? Whatever it is, we're with you."

I look, again, at my laptop. At the story, unwritten, waiting.

With a few keystrokes, I can create a happy ending.

But here, now? There's nothing I can do to guarantee a happy path for myself.

At least, not in this room.

"You talk with Finn?" I ask Iris. More direct this time.

She smiles. "She said he's miserable. His court backed him as king; Malachy tried to fight it, but Siobhán and Finn produced all kinds of receipts validating his greed, so he's fully out. And despite all that, Loch's miserable. I wonder why?"

Good.

Only it isn't.

I don't want him miserable.

"I won't pretend to know everything you went through with him," Coal says. "And I won't pretend to like him. But I know you were singing in Belfast. I got to watch you have *fun* and let go in a way I haven't seen you do in way too long. If you got to that place after a few days with him? It's worth figuring out what remains of the two of you. It's worth fighting for."

I drop my head into my hands and breathe for a second, the whoosh of air in and out of my lungs resonating against the roar of my pulse.

And then I laugh. Bubbling laughter that seizes me and doesn't let go.

"What's funny?" Iris asks, half smiling, and Coal is grinning too but his brows are pinched in worry.

"This is the second time," I manage, breathless, "that we've been in this situation. Last time it was Coal, talking him down after Hex left."

Coal barks a laugh. "Well, if this isn't the saddest friendship tradition ever: a relationship support group slash intervention. Remember when we used to go to bars?"

Iris folds her arms. "This *tradition* ends with you, Kris, because I'm learning from the two of you and your drama-filled bullshit. My happy ending will be normal and boring."

The levity is like a part in the clouds, a respite of sunbeams.

"The coronation is today?" I ask Coal, my voice small, stunted.

His eyes light up. "It'd be good for Christmas to make an appearance. But, alas, I'm beset by this welcome reception—who ever should we send in my place?"

Iris and Coal get me ready, because apparently it's *unacceptable* to confront someone you're in love with while wearing a half-wrinkled suit that's been stuffed in the bottom of your closet for three months.

They wrangle up a pressed forest green suit, low-slung boots, and a white shirt with no tie because I refuse to feel like I'm being strangled for this. My own anxiety will do that well enough for me. Iris and Coal fight about whether my hair should be up or down— down, they finally decide, and Iris does this thing to it with some volumizing spray so it's intentionally messy, not the *I got out of the shower and let it dry and this is what you get to look at* style I usually go for.

I focus on being simultaneously annoyed and impressed by their easy styling to distract from how nervous I am.

So I'm going to show up at his coronation. And . . . say what? I don't even know. I should write something down. But there's no time—I'm late as it is, so I'll have to speak from the heart, and we all know *that* will go over oh so well.

This is such a bad idea.

Iris hooks her arm with mine and we follow Coal down to the foyer of Claus Palace. Hex is there with Wren, and the two of them look surprised to see me out of my room.

Hex immediately guesses why with an abrupt grin.

"Good," he says as Coal hands me mistletoe.

"Kristopher?" Wren cocks her head, searching through her tablet like an answer will materialize.

"Kris is going to St. Patrick's Day for me," Coal tells her.

He stops me as I head for the door.

"And if anything . . . unfortunate happens again," he says, "you can inform the new king that I do have a foolproof way to kill him, and no one will ever find his body in a fjord."

I hug him. "Thank you."

He clutches me tight before smacking my shoulder blade and pushing me away. "Now go. No stalling. I know you and I know your overthinking—Iris, don't let him stall."

"Wait—you're coming?" I look at her.

"Of course I'm coming." She hooks her arm with mine again. "You think I'm going to miss you crashing Loch's coronation with a declaration of love? Over my dead body."

Coal throws his head back with a groan. "Ugh, don't make me play hooky from my own event!"

"I'm not going to *declare my love*." Am I?

My face is on fire.

"Nicholas"—Wren says his name in a chastising rush, like she's terrified he is going to fuck off and go to Ireland—"you are needed in the ballroom. Now. Please."

"I wasn't going to—fine, fine. Okay. Kris—*tell me what happens.* Like the *moment* it happens. Or maybe Iris, *someone,* update me, okay?"

I think I promise to, I think I say something else, but I'm at the door and using magic to take us to Ireland and oh, this was such a bad idea.

Iris drags me onward, and I go.

The foyer of Castle Patrick is packed with people. People I don't know, who likely don't know who I am, either—St. Patrick's Day's court and their extended families, I assume.

Seeing them warms a new emotion in my chest. Pride.

He did it. He really did get them to side with him. They're here, in support of him.

Fuck Malachy.

Servers rotate through the crowd, and from somewhere farther in, fiddle music plays.

Iris rejoins me from talking with a server. "Okay, they said the coronation happened already so this is like celebratory dancing and stuff. Loch's in the ballroom." She grimaces at me. "Good lord, Kris, your face matches your suit. Do not vomit."

"This was a mistake," I choke out. "I can't—I should call him. This is insane, right? Barging in here—"

"No, this is *romantic as fuck.*" She takes my face in her hands. "What did you used to write about when you were in love with me?"

All the blood in my body drains into my legs. "Wha—*Coal told you about that shit?*" I'm going to kill him.

"That's beside the point. What did you write about?"

My jaw sets. She pinches my cheeks together.

"Romantic crap, okay?"

"Romantic crap like *this,* hm?" She lets me go. "Make your own story. You deserve this sort of ending, Kris."

Her words quiver through me like electricity, crackling life into my limbs.

She points at me. "Go get your guy in a sweeping, event-crashing declaration of how much you want to fuck his brains out."

"God, Iris." But it yanks a laugh out of me.

She smiles. "Go. I'll be right behind you. Definitely not recording the whole thing."

"Oh, don't record it."

"Should've gotten me to sign an NDA. Now *go*."

I head off, heart lodged in my throat. My eyes snap to every face I pass, certain Loch will be here, and the whole thing will happen in the foyer—or the hall—or I'll run into Finn and she'll get into some argument with me and Loch will overhear and *that's* romantic, his sister screaming at me—

But I get to the door of the ballroom, across from the dining room. Its doors were always shut before; they're thrown open now, showing a wide space with rich mahogany wood in every corner, a roaring fireplace at the long end, a band on the opposite side. People spin through the room in varying shades of green, so at least I don't stand out.

And there.

Near the fireplace.

Talking with a group, a glass in one hand, looking so goddamn good in a dark hunter green suit that I come to a shaking stop inside the room, drinking up the sight of him. His hair is back in that red wave, his face a little flushed from the warmth of the room, and he smiles at someone, a flash of white teeth that jerks the air out of my lungs.

What am I going to say to him?

"Kris!"

Siobhán's shout rips across the ballroom, barreling over the music, the chatter of conversation.

Loch's head whips towards her.

He clocks where she's looking.

And he sees me.

I intended to walk up to him. I intended to move, at all, but the moment his eyes hit me, any intention vanishes from my body and

I am helpless but to stand there, in the crowded room, the music wailing around us, people dancing and Iris slowly pulling back from me with a wide grin.

Loch's eyes stay on mine as he cuts away from the group around him. He doesn't even say anything to them in explanation, not that I can tell. He puts his glass on a server's tray in passing, looking at me, only at me, and I try to pull in a breath but get a single trembling gulp.

Then he's in front of me.

The music is so loud. People spin and dance and it's making me dizzy, all that motion passing by, and him, the fixed pole around which everything revolves.

My lips part. "I—"

He grabs the collar of my jacket and kisses me.

And it's so much better than anything I could have said.

I throw my arms around his waist and arch into it and this is a form of wooing too, this is a conversation in the way his nails stroke across my scalp and hold me to him—*I'm sorry, I'm sorry*—and the way my hands cut up under the hem of his coat and clamp to his spine—*I came back, I came back.*

His fingers clutch into a fist in my hair and he pulls me away an inch. "Kris," it comes out breathy and he's smiling so big, his eyes darting all over my face. I'm smiling too because his hands are on me again, and it's that simple. That necessary.

Heat crashes into me—from him.

And from the realization that we're in a room full of people.

And most are looking at us now.

There are photographers. Journalists. Cameras flash and, ah, well, this is probably no less headline grabbing than tinsel-bombing him. I almost apologize before I remember *he* initiated this.

Siobhán whoops. Iris claps. I cast my gaze around, then look at Loch in wincing embarrassment.

He takes my hand, his smile wicked, and drags me out of the ballroom.

My lips are kiss-swollen and that knot in my chest is gone, so I follow him, I'd follow him anywhere.

He leads me through the castle, passing groups who call out to him; he doesn't stop.

"Loch." I hurry to walk alongside him. "I didn't mean to take you away from your people. You can stay—we don't have to—"

"Shush now, boyo," he orders and yanks open the doors to the library.

It's empty. The lights are off, the far windows showing the starlit night sky.

The doors slam behind us and I'm immediately shoved up against one, Loch's fingers around my neck, pinning me there, and I melt, an elastic, pathetic mess in his hand.

"You came back," Loch says, the fervor in his eyes set to ravenous as he fixes the whole of his attention on me.

My fingers are twisted around his wrist where he's holding my throat.

My smile slips. "I'm sorry I—"

"I will na hear a single apology from you." He kisses me, bruising, demanding, back on me hard and fast, pushing me up the door with his hand and the force of his body until my legs spread and I'm practically taken off my feet.

He peels back, panting into our space, whiskey and woodsmoke and his spicy cologne. His heated gaze dims, seemingly muted by physical control. "You came back."

It's a question this time.

"Yeah," I gasp.

"There's more we need to talk about." Another roll up at the end, a question.

I pause, a hundred thoughts fighting for dominance.

"No more lies," I say, and I mean it to come out declarative, but it's probing.

Loch nods immediately. "No more lies. None."

The awareness of his eyes on me, the intention behind them, is as effectively restraining as his hand gently pressing on my neck. He's waiting, waiting for permission, and I realize he's never been in control of this. He's always been reading me.

"Loch." It's a husky plea.

His brows pinch in a relieved groan as his teeth go to my neck, that sharp pain alternating with the burn of his beard as he eats his way up the column of my throat, and I tilt my head into it with a hapless whimper.

"The bedroom—is up the—*fuck,* Loch." I only know half of what I'm saying. The other half of me is ripping at the buttons on his shirt, trying to drag his coat off his shoulders.

"I will na make it to the bedroom." Loch's voice is jagged and fumbling already, and hearing the scrape in it shoves me right up there next to him. "I nearly took you in that ballroom, Kris. I've missed you so much, and I need to make you come."

"Okay," is all I can get myself to say, high and a little squeaky. "That's—yeah, okay."

He sucks a mark on my collarbone, and I scramble to anchor on him, lips moving in a soundless *fuck fuck fuck.*

"And do na pretend," he growls into the skin there, "that getting screwed proper nice in a library does na turn you on."

I laugh, head arched back. "And they say romance is dead."

His hands are on my belt, pulling, freeing it.

But the energy dips. Doesn't extinguish, just slants.

He backs away, hands gripped in the open edges of my pants. My shirt is parted, chest heaving, hair falling in my face.

A hundred romantic, sweeping speeches rush through me. All the things I should have said in the ballroom. All the things I've written about for years, the fairy tale endings and romantic stories that circled my fantasies. They collide against every moment I've spent with him—how I'm terrified but it's a good terror; how I'm anxious but it's a good anxiety.

In some alternate version of me, I weave such a poetic sonnet that it brings us both to our knees.

But all I can say, in the dimness of this starlit reality, is "I love you."

Loch's hands still.

He leans in and kisses me again, and it's sweet and we're both smiling.

"You'd better," he says into my mouth, "interrupting my coronation like this."

I tug at the waistband of his pants. "I had an invitation, asshole. I didn't interrupt shit."

"Arriving *late* then." His lips drop to my earlobe and he bites down. "Dragging me away from a very important conversation."

"I didn't drag you away. I was standing there, minding my own goddamn business."

He leaves a trail of sloppy kisses across my jaw, to my mouth, and we're both hard when I work us free of our pants and boxers, breaths devolving into matching groans.

He holds my gaze, raises his hand, and spits into his palm.

Every nerve in my body throbs.

"You come in looking like *that*." He takes both our cocks in hand and thrusts into that tunnel, rubbing against me, and I croon. "Sex walking—what hope did I ever have, boyo? This was your plan all along. Distract me, *tease* me."

My mind goes to static blankness, all needy pounding, his hand tightening as he twists and thrusts at the same time and *oh fuck*.

I wail deep in my throat. "Oh, yeah, this was just to mess with you," I say through a wheeze, fingertips digging in where his neck meets his shoulder. "I'm not getting anything out of it at—*fucking hell,* Loch—"

He fits his lips over mine, not kissing, just connected. I can taste his smile, can feel the joy in him winding up as he tightens his grip and rolls his hips and we don't need poems to bring us to our knees— I'm only upright because of the door and my hands on him.

His thrusts quicken, our breathing intensifies. He wraps his free hand around the back of my neck and plants his temple against mine, bracing, building us to the edge at ravaging speed.

And when a growl pulsates in the back of his throat, when he turns that growl into "Kris, *Kris*," I rocket over that edge with him, sweat-slicked ecstasy, a fierce unwinding.

I collapse against the door and he's there with me, forehead to my shoulder, both of us trying to catch our breath as hands continue to touch and grope, rememorizing curves.

Gently, he uses the edge of his jacket to clean us off and tucks us both away before tossing it to the floor. He stays as close as he can the whole while.

"Kris," he says against my neck. "I have so much to make up to you."

"You don't have to make up anything to me."

"Like hell I don't." He kisses my cheeks, my eyelids, like he's trying to brand every inch of me. "I do na even deserve to have you here with me right now, but *you* deserve every second of me proving how amazing you are. I love you too, and I—"

I kiss him, and he lets me take charge until we pivot and he's the one flattened to the other door now.

"How long until you need to get back to your party?" I ask.

He smiles. "It's my party; I can be gone as long as I please. The real concern is the more time that passes before we stumble our way back in, the more guarantee that everyone will know what we've been doing."

"Well, if you put your coat back on, they'll definitely know." I knot my hands in the lapels of the shirt he's still somehow wearing. "But where does all this gossip fodder rank on the St. Patrick's Day King's list of concerns?"

Loch cradles my head in his hands, my whole being in his hands. "'Tis na even on the list."

God, his accent topples over itself, and that's the final shred of convincing I need to haul him over to the cluster of couches by the unlit fireplace. I push him down and he sits with a bounce, gazing up at me in the low light, already looking thoroughly disheveled, so what's more making out, then?

"Good. Because, as you once told me"—I straddle his lap—"I'm not ready to share you with anyone yet. So it looks like I'll be responsible for your first scandal as King."

His smile goes cataclysmic. "I'd expect nothing less, Coffee Shop."

A laugh cracks out of me and I arch down to kiss him, embracing a happiness so potent that it becomes an immediate counterweight to every dark cloud of anxiety or panic I've ever felt. Not erasing them, not numbing them; balancing, so I see myself in a full spectrum between the two extremes, darkness to light and everything in between.

Iris told me I deserve this sort of ending.

Right now, I finally believe I do.

Chapter Nineteen

"Loch, I've seen your studio before. I don't know why the blindfold is necessary for—"

"Would you hush?" He positions me in the center of the room. "Christ, you're the son of Santy, you should be better at taking gifts than—"

I snort.

He pauses in front of me, adjusting where I'm facing. "Eh?"

"I forgot that's what you call him here. And, technically, Coal is *not* my dad."

Loch's quiet a moment.

Then he rips my hands around to press them firmly against the small of my back and *oh*. Oh.

"I might've misread what was happening here." Despite how many times we've made each other fall apart since his coronation last night, I immediately rub against his body.

He chuckles. "Nah, boyo, this is nothing sexual, but if you keep tryna distract me, I *won't* use this blindfold for all the plans I had for it *later*."

I whine. "Later?"

He growls. "Keep it in your pants."

"Oh, yeah, who woke who up this morning under the blankets with a—"

"That's hardly my fault." A rush of heat topples down the side of my throat from his exhale. "You looked too goddamn tempting laid out naked in my bed."

I stumble, but he's holding me, arms restrained, the suit I wore yesterday stretching between us.

I don't even remember why we're down here.

He nips at my jaw. "We are na gonna be late for that treaty signing of yours. You're gonna be good and proper about accepting this gift I have for you, then—shite, ya pervert, behave."

I'd been rubbing my hard-on against him. I stop with an eye roll he can't see.

"Good boy." He pecks my mouth and I fight down another whine. "Now, I was saying—you'll accept this gift and then we'll go to Christmas all composed and respectful, because I will na have your brother hating me for much longer."

"We can be late for the treaty signing. Coal would appreciate us making a dramatic entrance."

"All your brother associates me with is dramatics. I'm aiming to be downright *dull* for the foreseeable future."

"Being dull is not how you'll get Coal to like you."

"If it means proving I can be a steady force for you, I'll take my chances. Now, hold on. Do na move."

He steps away and I sigh in feigned exasperation. But I'm grinning too much, I don't think I've stopped since the library.

"He'll see how happy you make me," I say to the air in front of me. "He'll only torture you a little bit. Most of it will likely be payback for how I—*oh my god.*"

"What?" Loch's over by the far wall, but I hear him take a worried step closer to me.

An evil smile curls across my face. "The way I've bonded with Coal's boyfriend is by torturing each other. Or, to be fair, *he* tortures *me,* and I figured out a way to get back at him that I spaced on until this moment."

Something drags across the floor. A tarp falls.

"I'm afraid I'm na following," Loch says.

"You want my brother to like you."

"Yeah?"

"Do you think you could paint realistic-looking gore?"

Loch lets out a small, "The fuck?"

"Coal's boyfriend is, apparently, squeamish. So if you could paint my neck to look like it's been slashed, he'd hopefully freak out. Help me torment Hex, and Coal will see that that's the way to get along with you too." Okay, I'm starting to see the holes in my plan. "This is foolproof, I assure you."

Loch walks closer, the drop cloth crinkling under the dress boots I know he's wearing, and he lays a kiss on my cheek. "Despite how enticing you're making this sound, I think I might pass on this plan. But I promise, boyo, the moment I've earned back you and your brother's trust, my painting skills are yours to torture whoever you'd like." He pauses. "Keep Hex first in line, though. All that rubbish he was going on about, giving credit for *Irish* Halloween to *England*. Fucking *England*. Bloody dope."

I squint. It's lost under the blindfold. "We met because you went to a university in England."

Loch is quiet for a beat again. "No one's perfect, boyo."

He moves behind me, but I grab his arm, tilting my head towards him.

"I do trust you," I whisper.

It's hard not seeing him, but easier in some ways too. With one sense dulled, I hear the warble in my voice like a clanging bell, and I wonder if Loch hears it, too.

I think I trust him about as much as I trust myself, both connections tentative and so newborn.

He kisses my cheek again, but leaves his lips there, holding, breathing me in until I lean against him. "It's all right, Kris," he murmurs. "You will. Word by word, eh?"

I smile, rubbing the side of my face against his beard. "You're going to throw my own words back at me a lot, aren't you?"

He laughs. It sounds . . . nervous? "You have no idea."

He pulls off the blindfold.

My eyes blink open, adjusting quickly to the light of his studio.

There's a canvas leaning against the wall. It's just over his height, an explosion of red and gold with touches of emerald and neon green.

I take a single step forward, guided to it in an unconscious draw, all the banter going loose in my chest.

It's us. In that style of his, abstract swaths of color that braid together into an optical illusion of cohesion. He's kissing my neck and my head is thrown back and it isn't anything overtly sexual, but it rips through me in a typhoon, sensuality hanging in each bent stroke, in every drip of gold.

Loch comes around me as I step again, hypnotized.

"I, uh—see the spaces around you, eh?"

His voice shakes. He *is* nervous.

I bend closer and the breath evaporates right out of my lungs.

He didn't just use paint strokes to create me. He used words, lines from—oh my god, lines from the books I gave him, and lines from that letter to my mom I showed him.

"It's what I started on the night you came down, after Belfast," he says. "And I kept on it. Hoping I'd get to show it to you."

I stand up straight, throat thickening.

"I used that letter you showed me"—he's stammering now—"and you left it in the guest room, and I—"

"Oh." Blood rushes to my face. I left *all* of my writing in that guest room. Including the flowery, indulgent stuff I wrote about him.

Loch holds up his hands. "I did na read any but the letter you showed me already. Not for lack of wanting, mind. But I only used that letter." He waves at the painting. "It's meant to be all of you, because that's what I want. *All* of you, even the messy bits. And if, one day, you want me to read the rest of what you wrote, or show me that story of yours"—I told him last night, one of the breaks between touching and kissing and devouring—"I'll add words from that, too. We can build on this. Together."

Every muscle in my body is gilded and heavy. I look back up at the painting, can't get myself to break out of this incandescent spell.

"Kris," Loch whispers. "Say something."

I smile at him.

The strain in his eyes alleviates and he breathes out a sigh, and I realize he was afraid I'd be upset. Or afraid I wouldn't like it. Or this painting is a piece of his soul now, and he's showing it to me, and *I'm* part of that soul.

Every reason is at once equally unbelievable. I'm stuck in a dream state, suspended between him and this painting and this is somehow real, that he would see me, in all these pieces, and find a way to make those broken pieces beautiful.

I kiss him, throwing my arms around his neck, his body immediately fitting to mine in a way that feels like locking in place.

"We're going to be late," I inform him. "Like, really late."

"No, we are *not*." Loch manages to push me off of him. "I'll win Coal over, you'll see. And it will na involve torturing him with gory paint."

"Of course it won't. Coal's not the squeamish one." I wriggle past his grip and kiss his jaw. "But you should've thought of that before you showed me this painting. You cannot expect me to go to some treaty signing now. To sit in a ballroom and pretend I'm not slowly dying with wanting your cock in me."

I'm not playing fair. He's an expert at dirty talk, but it turns out he likes it just as much, maybe even more, when I talk dirty too.

Proven by the way I can *feel* his body temperature increase, his hands clenching tighter on my hips.

I suck at a spot below his ear. "And *fuck,* Loch," I moan licentiously. "I want it so bad. Need to feel you plunging into me again. Owning me. Need you to make me scream."

Loch grunts, choked. "Kris—*shite*—no, no, we're leaving. *Now.*"

I whimper overdramatically, but he gets me to walk for the door.

"Devil man," he mutters, one hand wrapped around my forearm, steering me ahead of him while he adjusts himself.

I laugh. Bright and happy.

"The question is"—I glance back at that painting—"where are we going to hang that?"

Out in the hall, the chill air has me leaning into him.

Loch threads our hands together. "Oh, the foyer," he says matter-of-factly.

"Yeah, sure, us making out is a totally respectable thing for any visitor to see when they first enter your castle. No way. That painting's for *me*."

Loch's cheeks go red, highlighting his freckles. "You like it, then?"

I stop. He faces me, and I can see the residual tremors of him worrying what I'd think.

"I love it," I whisper. "Really, Loch. I—" My chest constricts. "You see me," is all I can think to put words to.

He grins, a deep, reverberant sort of pleased, and kisses my forehead. "I was na sure how you'd feel about the words I chose. I told you once—there is no greater measure of value than what you give to a piece of art. And I've come to mean that in a bit of a different way. There is no value greater than what you have for me."

I weigh the ramifications that'll come if I miss the signing of the winter Holidays treaty. Like yes, it would be a huge snub—but god, what am I supposed to do when he says and does stuff like this? How can I not want to shirk every other goddamn responsibility and lose myself in him?

For the first time in my life, I don't feel any guilt about wanting to give in to those thoughts. It wouldn't destroy my worth, or my purpose, or who I am. I'd still be all the parts of me that Loch painted in his studio, words and mess and color and chaos and, most important, loved.

It's a work in progress. But all the best things are.

He takes a step away from me, lips pursed in amusement.

"But," he starts, "I mostly was na sure what you would think of that line on the bottom."

"The line on the—" I look back at the studio. What was on the bottom?

"The first line of poetry you spoke to me. You do na remember?" He takes another step backwards, his smirk cunning.

"I don't—"

"It was about '*breaching the agreed upon social constructs of the Spacefinder app.*'" He puts air quotes around it. "Pure poetry. I fell in love with you on the spot."

My eyes slowly widen. "You did not put that shit on our painting!"

Loch shrugs, but he's smiling so wide I know he very well fucking did.

"You asshole!" I dive after him, and he races up the hall, laughing, but he shuts up once I catch him in the stairwell and kiss the hell right out of him.

But I'm laughing, too. I'm laughing and he presses me against the cold stone wall of his castle. It should be such a mundane thing now, kissing him, but I know, god do I know, that it'll never stop feeling new and thrilling and vital.

That's the real happy ending I always wrote about—no big, sweeping orchestral situations, no constant churn of drama and emotion.

Just this.

Lips and tongues and his hips against mine.

Just him, over and over, unfolding into a meandering, uncertain path that ripples far off into the distance.

A happy ever after that we make together.

Turn the page for a sneak peek
at Sara Raasch's next rom-com!

The Entanglement
of Rival Wizards

Ali Hazelwood meets Dungeons & Dragons in this enemies-to-lovers
fantasy academia rom-com where rival grad student wizards are forced
to work together without killing—or falling for—each other.

Available Fall 2025

I roll the dice on the banquet restroom, the rubber soles of my Converse squeaking on the tile floor as I slide into the hall. At the very end, people in suits and nice dresses mill in and out of the banquet room. The only noise is chatter from conversation and the ting of cutlery, no official announcements yet—okay, breathe, *breathe,* it's fine. I have time. *Fucking breathe.*

But I'm gasping and my over-caffeinated heart is doing its level best to sucker punch its way out of my rib cage, and part of me wonders why I never took Orok up on his offers to, quote-unquote, *whip my scrawny ass into shape.* I wheeze a pathetically shrill breath and heave into the bathroom off the hall—

—only for the gods to hatch their final plan at my expense.

Who the *fuck* did I piss off up there?

There are no committee members. That might've been preferable.

Elethior's at the sink, washing his hands.

He glances up when I none too gracefully plunge inside, garment bag and messenger tote clutched to my chest like lifelines.

He's not wearing sweatpants and a T-shirt.

He's looking like a walking advertisement for why suits should always be tailored. His long hair is slicked over the side of his head and he's in a double-breasted black suit with a black shirt and tie, his shoes gleaming—

Fuck me up a wall.

I forgot my shoes.

My focus pings to my ratty blue Converse before I force myself to meet Elethior's eyes, feeling every bit of the sweat drying on my skin, of my frizzed-out hair, of my pulse jackhammering in my wrists and throat.

I look around, desperately hoping someone else is in here to serve as a barrier, but nope. We're alone.

Elethior scans me in a quick head-to-toe analysis and arrives at the same conclusion I would've come to had our situations been reversed: I'm screwed.

A cold, satisfied smile unfurls across his face.

He calmly dries his hands, throws away the paper towel, and leans against the sink. "And here I thought you'd made the first smart decision of your academic career and decided to skip the brunch entirely. I must say, showing up having just rolled out of bed? *Much* better. For me. For you?" He clicks his tongue.

"I didn't just roll out of bed. Not all of us have chauffeurs who can cart us around the city."

"True. But all of us have at least alarm clocks, don't we?" His grin is caustic. "Some might see your tardiness as proof that you don't take this program seriously, Sebastian. Others, like the grant committee, know you've already proven that tenfold."

My jaw sets. Our interaction last night is raw, and everything I've toppled through this morning has fallen on it like slow drips of vinegar—so I have exactly no resolve to shrug off the attacks he fires with an archer's precision. Especially when he's looking like he popped off a fragrance billboard, making every word he spews feel so much weightier, casting judgment and finding me wanting in every possible way.

He's polished and pristine, composed and orderly. Why wouldn't he get the grant instead of me?

The knot in my stomach is rock-hard. Takes up every free space inside me.

He doesn't matter. None of this matters, remember? It's all noise. Just get to the brunch. Get the grant. Rub his smug face in it.

I shift my garment bag and eye the bathroom stalls, but I'm hit with an image of dropping my shirtsleeve into a toilet, which leaves changing out here.

Elethior must follow my train of thought, because his smile grows slyer, and he doesn't move from where he's reclined against the sink, ankles crossed so the leg of his pants rides up and a flash of pale skin shows above his low-cut sock.

"They're due to begin the presentation in"—he checks a watch that likely costs more than my year's rent—"seven minutes."

His eyes pop up to me, amused and daring.

I think one of my molars cracks. "You gonna leave?"

With overemphasized deliberateness, he turns back to the mirror and swipes a finger along his eyebrow. "I don't think so. It *is* a public restroom, isn't it?"

It's a game of chicken.

Fuck him. Fuck this morning. *Fuck all of this.*

I toss my garment bag over one of the stall doors and drop my messenger tote on the sink next to him.

His eyes flash to mine in the mirror. For a too-long second, we stare at each other, challenge as thick as humidity in July.

Wrong day to mess with me, buddy.

The part of me that Orok's always worried will take over bursts up out of my soul like a rabid dog, feral and snarling, and before I can think anything else through, I shrug off my coat, remove my glasses, grab the hem of my T-shirt, and whip it off.

Our eyes disconnect. The moment the T-shirt brushes across my face, I slide my glasses back on and I can see him again.

The silence arching between us stretches. The difference between *come at me, bruh* and something that takes that knot in my stomach and douses it with kerosene and scrapes a match against my nerve endings to light it.

That light flares, illuminates a singular fact:

I'm half-naked in front of him.

What the fuck.

Elethior blinks twice, in rapid succession.

Prickles of chill race across my skin, goosebumps that make me shiver even though the bathroom's pretty warm, heated for late November.

Elethior switches his gaze back to his own reflection. "Classy," he says, but it comes out rough.

"Never claimed to be," I bite back, and when I move to untie my sweatpants, he clears his throat, or maybe coughs, some jagged, garbled sound.

"For gods' sakes," Elethior mutters and hurries past me for the door.

I should feel a *little* vindicated for winning this game. But something's off-balance, thrown into tumult by *him* again, and I'm so fucking tired of him rocking me, and I'm tired of this rivalry, and I'm *done*.

"Why are you even here?" I bark as he reaches for the door handle. "Why do you give a shit about this grant? What are you going to do with it that your family can't fund anyway?"

"It's not just about funding," he says to the door. "Not everything is about money."

The flames take me. The rage, the months of strain, all of it scorches through me and my mouth moves independently of my brain. "Spoken like someone who *has* money. This is about prestige to you? Gods, that's worse. Even if you win this grant today, those of us out here in the real world will know you didn't deserve it; you just got it because of your last name. You're not capable of earning anything yourself, you pompous prick."

His shoulders go rigid under that suit jacket that fits him like it's made of liquid. Color stains the part of his neck not covered by his hair, a bright crimson that spreads up the sides of his face.

Slowly, he pivots to me again. My hackles rise, that hindbrain awareness of a predator nearby.

His glower flits down my body, and when I shiver this time, it's from feeling exposed.

"At least people will know me," he says, eyes returning to mine. There's no challenge in them anymore. Just excruciating hatred. "Meanwhile, you will remain an immature fuckup who will die in obscurity because you have nothing substantial to contribute to this world."

He says it with such certainty that it knocks the wind out of me.

The restroom echoes with the door banging shut in his wake.

Acknowledgments

Two books into my first adult series, and this one was somehow even more fun than the first. Which doesn't seem the least bit possible, considering *The Nightmare Before Kissmas* was pretty dang fun.

I have many lovely people who can take full credit for *Go Luck Yourself* being even more fun, and they are, in no particular order (because chaos reigns here):

Amy Stapp, agent of my heart and soul and what few functioning brain cells I have on hand at any given time.

Erika Tsang. I still cannot believe the serendipity of almost working with you over there and then getting to work with you over here; we were led to each other much the same way Loch's magic led him to Kris.

Tessa Villanueva, who keeps everything running and without whom chaos would reign in the bad way.

Jordan Hanley, Caro Perny, Lauren Abesames, Emily Mlynek, and Sarah Reidy. Thank you for spreading Christmas cheer far and wide, and for similarly spreading St. Patrick's Day cheer far and wide, and for being truly wonderful to work with.

Lilith Saur. I did not think I could love a cover more than *Kissmas,* then you went and gave us *this.* I am honored that my books get to wear your art!

As always, to all the behind-the-scenes darlings, without whom this book would be a lump of text in a Word doc and nothing more:

Erin Wilcox, Sara Thwaite, Kira Tregoning, Lesley Worrell, Rafal Gibek, Megan Kiddoo, Greg Collins, and Jacqueline Huber-Rodriguez.

Maggie, Jordan, Alyssa, Gretchen, Korrina, and the entire OwlCrate team, who are all beings of pure magic.

I wrote *The Nightmare Before Kissmas* because I was tired of being sad and wanted to lose myself in something deliriously joyful. I wrote the first draft of *Go Luck Yourself* (can we take a moment to appreciate that title) immediately after finishing *Kissmas,* because I wasn't the least bit ready to let go of the joy I had found. And while Kris did his darndest to keep that joy going, his story is also about perseverance. About finding yourself. About realizing that you're *allowed* to be happy.

I hope, no matter what you're persevering through, that you surmount it like Kris: with a little bit of luck and a whole lot of joy.

About the Author

SARA RAASCH grew up among the cornfields of Ohio and currently lives in the historical corridor of southeastern Virginia. She is the *New York Times* bestselling author of ten books for young adults. *The Nightmare Before Kissmas* was her debut adult novel, offering all the joy, irreverent wit, and crackling sexiness of your favorite sweet-as-a-candy-cane holiday romp.